HELL'S Belles

By Paul Magrs

Never the Bride
Something Borrowed
Conjugal Rites
Hell's Belles

HELL'S
Belles

PAUL MAGRS

headline
review

First published in 2009 by HEADLINE REVIEW
An imprint of HEADLINE PUBLISHING GROUP

1

Cataloguing in Publication Data is available from the British Library

ISBN 978 0 7553 4644 8 (Hardback)
ISBN 978 0 7553 4645 5 (Trade paperback)

Typeset in Garamond by Avon DataSet Ltd,
Bidford-on-Avon, Warwickshire

Printed in Great Britain by Clays Ltd, St Ives plc

Headline's policy is to use papers that are natural, renewable and recyclable
products and made from wood grown in sustainable forests.
The logging and manufacturing processes are expected to conform
to the environmental regulations of the country of origin.

HEADLINE PUBLISHING GROUP
An Hachette UK Company
338 Euston Road
London NW1 3BH

www.headline.co.uk
www.hachette.co.uk

For Stuart Douglas

Whitby

North Sea

West Pier

East Pier

East Cliffs

Western Cliffs

St Mary's Church & Graveyard

Whitby Abbey

1. Brenda's B & B
2. Effie's Antiques Emporium
3. Hotel Mirramar
4. The Christmas Hotel
5. Cod Almighty
6. The Walrus & The Carpenter
7. St Mary's Church & Graveyard
8. Whitby Abbey
9. Bridge over Harbour
10. Woolies

Prologue

The journey took longer than she was expecting.

The train trundled through miles of greenish-gold September woods, tiny villages and fields that seemed to go on for ever. As they approached the coast, however, the skies grew wider and paler. Penny imagined she could smell the sea through the open carriage window.

Her various bags and cases were occupying the seat beside her, the rack above and the small bay behind. She was escaping with everything that belonged to her. She should have left some of it behind, she knew. She should have made a cleaner break. Left more of her stuff for her fella to chuck out.

There was something appealing about just walking out and taking very, very little. In recent months, Penny had felt so encumbered by everything.

She wanted her life to be very simple and new. Somewhere different. Somewhere to explore. Her mother had suggested starting anew abroad, perhaps. But she didn't feel brave enough for that. It was as if Ken had sapped all the courage out of her, in just the short time they had been married.

No, just a hundred miles or so would do her. It was far enough away.

She set out the guides and leaflets on the table before her once again, looking at the pictures of her destination. The town looked perfect. Gothic splendour. Nineteenth-century ambience. Sleepy spookiness. Somewhere to soothe and heal her wounded soul . . .

She even had a little job lined up. Receptionist work. A nice hotel she'd read about online. One that was experiencing staffing shortages. A room came with the post. It was perfect for her. And, with the Hallowe'en Goth festival coming up too, everything looked propitious. Penny had always meant to go to a Goth weekend in Whitby. Ken had scowled every time she had mentioned it. This wasn't a place he ever wanted to visit. And so she felt confident he wouldn't come running after her.

Her fingernails were tingling. They always did when big things were about to happen to her. It was as if she had a sixth sense or something. Right now the tingling made her get out the black nail varnish she'd stowed in her handbag. She wanted to arrive in Whitby with jet-black fingernails. It seemed just the right thing. Something that would have made Ken roll his eyes and complain: 'You're nearly thirty, Pen. Not a teenager any more. You can't pretend you're a bloody Goth, woman! You look too weird. Go and put something sensible on!'

She concentrated on painting her nails as well as she could, as the train rocked gently towards her new home.

And then, all of a sudden, the train ran out of countryside.

They were pulling abruptly into an old stone station, at the end of the line.

Blinking in the sunshine, blowing quickly on her nails, and lugging her bags, she struggled on to the platform. Other passengers streamed past her and she was disoriented for a while.

Penny took a hold of herself and clapped on her shades. It would be all right. Everything would be okay. She could do this. She could make a new life for herself. She just had to be calm. And look! She had already started.

She stepped out of the station, into the middle of the harbour town.

The train terminated right beside the harbour mouth. From where Penny stood with her bags she could see both sides of the town. Now she really could smell the sea, and candy floss and fish and chips. Straight ahead was the vast grey sprawl of the North Sea, churning and glittering under the cool sun. On the right-hand side was the high mound of the East Cliffs, where the ancient ruined abbey rose in a stark silhouette against the clear skies. To her right climbed the western side of town, with its serried streets of Victorian guest houses and hotels. How intricate it all seemed. How noisy with human chatter and honking of boats and screeching of gulls.

Penny grasped up her bags and took a deep, heady breath of briny air. She made for the taxi rank.

Here was where it all began. Her new life.

She was intent on settling in as soon as possible. Into routine and work and healthy peace and quiet.

And that was how it all was, at first.

It was only about a month later that things started to go really weird.

New Manager

Crikey, thought Robert. Perhaps I've gone and done it. Perhaps I've done what they always said I would.

I've gone and found my vocation. I've found my place in the world.

At last!

That morning he went about his duties at the Hotel Miramar with what might even be described as a spring in his step. He rattled through the duty rosters and went to the kitchen to have a word with Chef about menus for the weekend. He checked the stocktaking for the main bar and then the smaller bar in the basement nightclub. He found that everything was running perfectly. Everything was going smoothly and efficiently.

He was managing a whole hotel. Him! With no training other than what he'd picked up on the job, he had taken up the reins of this place quite easily.

Admittedly, the Miramar wasn't the most elaborate hotel in Whitby. It was big enough, however, and required a lot of very focused attention. This was something Robert hadn't been used to giving to anything. A drifter, that was what he was. A daydreamer was what his school reports had always said. He'd never stick at anything for long. His mind was always elsewhere. On higher things, perhaps, his mum used to say, with a stifled snort of amusement.

But Robert hadn't been thinking about higher things. He was just elsewhere. Mulling stuff over. He'd drift around, vague and abstracted. He'd grown up with a feeling that he was waiting for something, and never quite being sure what it was. But he would know it when he saw it. And he had, hadn't he? He'd been in charge of this place for months now. Almost a year, in fact.

He took elevenses in his new office. Coffee and macaroons, brought to him by Penny from reception. He had adopted the sumptuous office of the previous manageress. As he sank his teeth into the softly yielding coconut confection – still slightly warm from Chef Hughie's oven – he spared a thought for poor Sheila. Such a warm-hearted soul. Though she had a bit of a bad reputation in the town, Robert had known her to be a soft, sensitive person. One who hadn't deserved her fate. One who didn't ought to be where she was right now. He shuddered at the memory. He tried hard not to picture where Sheila Manchu was languishing these days.

Well, here I am, he thought, gazing about at the office. He had started adding a few of his own little touches to the place. Sheila's taste had been at the chinoiserie end of things. He didn't want to change too much, just in case she returned one day.

That was the thing about Whitby. You never knew who was going to turn up. Or disappear. Or pop up out of the blue.

For all of the town's unpredictability, Robert was happy living here. For all of its strangeness and its sometimes macabre weirdness, he was sure that he wouldn't be leaving any time soon. Nowadays – at the ripe old age of thirty-two – he was convinced that he had found his place in the world.

This ancient, gothic, bijou seaside resort. Here he had a good job and responsibilities. He had friends – most of them old women, of course, but he found he preferred the company of older women. They had *lived*. They had seen a thing or two. Robert could identify with that.

And besides all of this, there were other things keeping him here in Whitby.

Adventures.

And not just adventures of the mysterious or even spooky kind. Though there were plenty of those to be had.

He was thinking about fellas, too. Those kind of adventures.

Or rather, one fella in particular.

Recently Robert had found himself a bloke.

Of course, it was all quite secret and hush-hush just now. He didn't want to put the kibosh on it by telling everyone straight away. Brenda would want to see this bloke. Brenda was Robert's best friend, full of good sense and cheer. Effie, who was Brenda's friend and neighbour, would want to inspect the bloke too. She would be altogether sniffier and more pessimistic than Brenda. 'You'll never get a fella in this town,' she'd once said to Robert, rather caustically. This was last autumn, during one of Sheila's mad barbecues at the Hotel Miramar. 'This town's full of us old women. You'll have to move on. Get yourself to the bright lights and the big city! Leeds or somewhere.'

But Robert didn't want to move to Leeds or somewhere. He was happy here. And he was sure that Effie just wanted him out of the way. She was envious of his friendship with Brenda. Effie was scared of having her pointy old nose pushed out.

So Robert – successful hotelier and part-time spook-hunter – was keeping mum about his exciting new fella just for now. He loved the juiciness of the secret. He was bursting with it. Dying to tell the world all about it.

But he managed to keep it all in. Just for now.

He finished off his macaroon and was happily brushing away crumbs and flicking through the morning's post when there was a light tap at his door. He called, 'Come in,' and peered at Penny the receptionist over his new glasses. 'Ye-es?'

Penny had been overenthusiastic with her black eyeliner this morning, he noticed. She looked like a vaguely Gothy panda, quivering with excitement in his doorway. 'The film people are arriving!' she cried.

For a second Robert didn't know what she was on about. And then it clicked. It was Monday, of course. They had their massive block booking, didn't they? The crew members were checking in this morning. Thirty-four of them. And even some lowlier members of the cast were staying here at the Miramar for the duration of the filming of . . .

'What was it called, Penny?' Robert said, flicking through papers. 'This film they're making?'

Penny blushed. '*Get Thee Inside Me, Satan.*'

That was right, Robert remembered. It was a remake of a schlocky sixties classic. They were due to shoot the film's climactic sequences on location all over Whitby. They would be taking over its winding Victorian streets and the ruined abbey, all this Hallowe'en and for the duration of the town's infamous Goth Weekend Festival.

It should prove very interesting, Robert mused. He had never really had a keen interest in the horror film genre. Nowadays he had even less of one, due to his involvement in a series of queer events that had overshadowed anything ever thrown up on the silver screen. But he could feel a buzz in the air over this impending remake. There was something about the very idea of it that raised the hairs on the back of his neatly barbered neck.

Not least was the fact that a block booking out of season was extremely good news for the hotel in which he had been placed in charge.

Also he was intrigued by the legendary reputation of the film's star. She was the female lead in the original version of *Get Thee Inside Me, Satan*, back in the sixties. She was Britain's favourite horror film starlet. The vampiest vamp the world of cinema had ever known.

Karla Sorenson. And – miraculously – she had hardly aged a day.

Or so they said.

'Come on, Penny.' Robert hustled the excited receptionist out of his office, 'We've got film people to look after. There's work to be done!'

As they hurried upstairs into the main hotel, he was reflecting that it was a shame that Ms Sorenson had elected not to stay in the same place as her crew and minor cast members. What a coup it would be, to have the care of the most famous horror film actress in the world!

Maybe she'd want somewhere swankier. Somewhere more secluded.

But where?

Goth with a Heart of Gold

It was her afternoon off, but really, she would have preferred to stick around in the Hotel Miramar. Penny had never seen film people before. Not in the actual flesh.

As she struggled down the hill into town with her clumpy heels and her heavy bags, she reflected that film people actually looked pretty much the same as anyone else. Some of them even looked scruffy. But they were film people. They made films! They made horror films! It was like they were coated in stardust and shimmering with glamour.

It felt like a late summer's day in Whitby. The skies over the hulking headland and the abbey were a brilliant blue. Town was chock-a-block with tourists and locals, bustling about their business. Penny was pleased to be among them. Now, after a month in this town, she was starting to feel like a local herself. She knew her way through the warren of complicated streets, and she knew where everything she needed was. She liked the atmosphere of the place, where people let you be and didn't ask too many questions, but nodded her a brisk welcome if they happened to see her out and about.

This was her new home.

She'd left behind her old life in the little town near Darlington.

She'd turned her back on that whole debacle. Now she'd stopped trying to fit in as the person they'd all expected her to be. Here she was allowed to be herself. And here, no one looked twice if Penny dyed her hair liquorice black or painted her eyes with kohl like Dusty Springfield or Nefertiti. No one bothered if she Gothed up in the daytime and wore her favourite black wedding dress even when popping down the supermarket.

People here seemed to accept such things with hardly a second glance. Penny felt that she had found her spiritual home.

She was lugging with her a bin bag of old clothes. Her last bin bag of clothes belonging to the old Penny, from her old life. The salty sea breeze whipped up her hair and made the going hard, even on the sharp downward slope to LeFanu Close, where all the charity shops sat together in a line. She picked her favourite, where the two old ladies seemed very grateful for her donation.

The two of them talked to Penny as if her new persona was hardly anything out of the usual, and this pleased her greatly. She checked out the shop's racks of paperbacks, happily biding her time as the ladies unpacked and refolded her old clothes, cooing over the odd item. Penny lingered lovingly over a stash of horror novels. She was an avid reader. That contributed fatally, her husband had claimed, to her tendency to foolishly indulge her imagination. Pretending she was someone else all the time. When what she really ought to be doing was knuckling down in the real world. And living with him; looking after him.

'These woollens look too good to give away,' said one of the gentle old women at the counter. 'Are you sure, dear?'

'Yep,' smiled Penny, straightening up. 'I want rid of all that old stuff. I don't know why I brought any of it with me to Whitby. That all belongs to my old life.' She caught a glimpse of summery pastels, of flowery fabrics. They were the remnants of a person she now regarded as dead. Here, she was reborn, with a face of China white and boots of black rubber.

'Well, it's very generous of you.' The lady turned to her quieter companion. 'Say what you like about Goths. Some of them have got hearts of gold.'

Penny didn't see the other old lady's expression, or hear what she muttered at this point, because she was digging through the video-tapes and DVDs. She often checked this hidden-away section but there was rarely anything that took her fancy. But today she found that she had laid her ebony-painted nails on something rather interesting.

What a weird coincidence, she thought. She realised her heart was thudding madly. Absurdly. The DVD case actually shook in her fingers. Why was she reacting like this? She tried to snap out of it. She took a deep breath. The strong whiff of detergent and must in the very air of the place revived her for a moment. The DVD case felt slick under her sweaty palms. She glared at the cover disbelievingly.

Two pounds ninety-nine! That was all the old dears at the counter had deemed it worth.

If only they knew!

This was a rarity, surely. It was a film that shouldn't be here, in this shop. Why, it shouldn't be anywhere. It hadn't even been released. Its makers had sworn it would never come out. Never again. Not after the kind of things that had happened on its previous releases into the world at large.

How weird. Penny turned the case this way and that, reading the back, reading the front again, examining the lurid illustrations and photographs.

'Everything all right, dear?' the more voluble old lady called from her counter. They had noticed that Penny was behaving oddly. She looked avid. She had made some kind of amazing find. Penny straightened up, tried to look nonchalant. What was happening to her? She was no kind of film geek. She liked horror and all that, but she wasn't some sort of fan girl, going weak at the knees at a discovery like . . . like . . .

'Have you found something interesting? I just put that lot out this morning, didn't I, Helen? I didn't really look at them. Are you sure you're all right? You look very peaky . . .'

'Yes, I'm . . . I'm okay . . .' Penny muttered distractedly.

Get Thee Inside Me, Satan. What a weird, weird coincidence.

It was a copy of the film they were just about to remake, here in Whitby. The original film that had never been released on DVD. The film that had appeared in cinemas in only very limited runs in the late sixties, then in specialist late-night double bills in the mid seventies. Then it had had a limited life on home video, back in the eighties. As a cult film it was renowned. It was infamous. It was the film that was too dangerous for anyone to watch alone, or so they said.

The film that had driven people potty.

The film that was cursed by the devil himself.

Which was one of the reasons why they were about to remake it. Supposedly they wanted to cash in on its spooky cache.

But what was it doing here? In this dusty, dowdy shop? This impossible disc.

It was as if it was waiting for her.

For her, Penny Danby.

She had to have it. The old ladies raised curious eyebrows as they examined her purchase and popped it neatly into a paper bag and she handed them the cash. What on earth was she buying? they seemed to wonder, glancing at the cover. To them, it looked like a horrible thing.

The two of them would never understand, Penny reflected. Quaint old souls like them. What would they know about Cult Horror? She said goodbye and hurried to the door. In her keenness to be away, she almost knocked over the thin, frail-looking woman who was just coming in.

'Oh! Sorry! Sorry!' Penny cried, feeling clumsier than ever.

'Hmmm.' The customer glared at the galumphing Goth girl and pursed her lips. 'Less haste, more speed, as my Aunt Maud used to say.'

Penny looked down at the bony, disapproving face and was startled by the fierce stare she received in return. 'I'm sorry?'

'Stop apologising girl!' the woman snapped. 'You're Robert's new helper, aren't you? Up at the Miramar?'

'I'm the receptionist,' Penny said, and almost added 'miss', as if she was talking to her teacher. This woman made her feel about nine years old.

'He speaks very well of you,' said the old woman.

'Oh!' Penny smiled. 'You must be . . .'

'Effie Jacobs,' she was told. 'I'm a friend of a friend of a friend. Whitby, you see, is a very small town. You're quite new here, aren't you?'

'Oh yes.' Penny nodded, eager to be away.

'Early for Goth weekend, isn't it?' Effie smiled.

'I'm like this all the time,' Penny gabbled. She grinned in a very un-Goth-like manner. 'And I'm here for good now!'

Effie Lonely

To be quite truthful, the past few months had been pretty dull for Effie Jacobs.

She would never admit it, though. If asked, she'd tell anyone that she was quite happy with her life. She sat quietly in her antiques emporium every afternoon, keeping her hawklike gaze trained on her few customers. She'd maybe sell an item or two. She was doing a very nice line in theatrical jewellery these days that seemed to go down well with tourists.

But there was no excitement. There was nothing to send her pulse racing.

And, if asked, Effie would say that was a good thing too. She couldn't put up with too much excitement at her age. No, she wanted things to be as dull and repetitive as this. She was very happy at home, thank you very much, where she hardly ever saw another soul and had very few people to talk to. This was the way she wanted it.

And this was how it had been since her best friend had gone and got herself married. To her own ex-fiancé, of all people!

Well, Brenda had made her bed and so she could just lie in it.

Ever since that so-called wedding, Effie had hardly seen Brenda. It was as if the two friends had gone their separate ways.

'What a shame,' murmured the old dear in the charity shop. She was busily folding up Penny's cast-offs, and Effie could see that she was already bored with her conversation. Perhaps she'd heard it all before.

'Well, it's always the same.' Effie scowled. 'When silly old women get themselves hooked up with these men. They get their heads turned. They run around like teenagers, and they forget about their real friends . . .'

The woman in the charity shop – what was her name? Teresa? – stopped her sorting and looked up at Effie. Her eyes were milky and swimmy, which startled the older woman. 'Ach, I've had friends like that, who've gone off and found themselves a new husband. You're left in the lurch, aren't you? Eh? You don't know what to do with yourself.'

Effie recoiled. What was she doing? Opening out her feelings to this awful, insinuating woman? She felt as if she were betraying Brenda in talking like this. I must be terribly lonely, she thought. To be reduced to this. 'That's very true,' she told the charity shop woman, lowering her voice.

'You should get out and about more,' Teresa said, goggling her bleary eyes at her. 'You don't want to sit at home, festering. Get out of a night. Get yourself a fella of your own!'

Effie pursed her lips. 'No thank you very much. I've had quite enough of that sort of nonsense.' She shuddered. Her last dalliance hadn't ended at all well. Her beau had fluttered off into the dark night after Brenda's wedding, as was his wont, with scant regard for her feelings. Well, she was best off without him. She was better off without them all. What had Aunt Maud told her, all those years ago? Never let yourself depend on anyone, Effryggia. Be completely self-reliant. Be your own woman.

This was how she had lived most her life. Alone, and quite separate from the common rut.

It was only when Brenda had moved here – three years ago, was it? – taking up the guest house next door to Effie, that she had started to learn what it meant to have friends. To have people she could trust, and laugh with, and spend her evenings with.

Foolishness. Silliness. That was the path to disappointment. And so now she was lonely again. She gritted her teeth and turned to go. She was ashamed of herself. Visiting smelly old shops like this, looking for people to talk to.

'Ooh, wait!' Teresa suddenly burst out. 'If you're at a loose end on Wednesday night, what about this? A gang of us oldies have started going to this . . .'

Effie peered suspiciously at the lurid flyer Teresa slid across the glass-topped counter. 'Hmmm . . .'

'You're guaranteed a lovely night.' Teresa smiled. 'Wonderful music. Novelty acts. Even a little dance as the evening goes on and inhibitions loosen. And if there aren't enough old men to go around, we women pal up for the dancing. Much nicer that way, anyway.'

Effie frowned. She wasn't sure that she was desperate enough for company to hurry along to the Cosmic Cabaret at the Christmas Hotel on a Wednesday evening. She didn't like the look of the stars of the show – Denise and Wheatley – going by their photograph on the leaflet. It all looked rather tacky to her. Not Effie's kind of scene at all.

'Wednesday at eight, hm?' she found herself saying.

Teresa nodded enthusiastically. 'It's Whitby's hottest night out,' she grinned. 'For oldies like ourselves.'

Effie narrowed her eyes at her. 'I'll see. I'm rather busy just now . . .'

The charity shop woman nodded happily, and watched her leave. Her own eyes narrowed as she stared after Effie, tottering down the sloping path of LeFanu Close. Oh, you'll come along to the Cosmic Cabaret, lady, she thought. Just you see if you don't.

Then her companion came mincing through from the back with a tray of tea and biscuits. 'Was that that Effie Jacobs again?' she asked, rolling her eyes. 'You want to watch her.'

'How come?'

'They say she's a witch.' Teresa's workmate, Helen, heaved herself up on the stool behind the counter and flipped to the correct page in her Barbara Taylor Bradford, leaving chocolate biscuit smears on every page she touched. 'I swear down. That's what they reckon. She's got all sorts of magical paraphernalia in that house of hers, above that dirty old shop.'

'Is that a fact?' Teresa said lightly.

'She's got powers, or so they say.'

'Fancy that . . .'

Effie Writes

FROM: Effie@antiqueeffie.com
SUBJECT: Catching Up

Dear Brenda,

It seems like you've been away so long, I hardly know where to begin.

How's your holiday, anyway? I hope everything's been as lovely as your postcard and its spartan message seemed to suggest. I'm not sure I'd have been keen on the Lake District in October, but there you go. You were never one for convention, were you?

I do hope everything's working out with you and Frank and that the two of you have managed to relax a little and – what is it the young people say nowadays? – chill out a little bit. You were at such a fever pitch of antagonism and irritability when I last saw you, I thought you were about to rip each other to pieces.

Well – you know that I've got my reservations about Frank, Brenda. I always did have – right from the moment I first clapped eyes on the big brute in the ballroom of the Christmas Hotel. I don't have to remind you of the shocking

18

events of last winter – all caused, I hardly need add, by the reappearance in your life of your one-time fiancé. Well, anyway, I made my feelings quite plain back then, at the end of that particular hair-raising palaver, and I think you should have sent Frank off with a flea in his ear, but what did you do? You took him back. You know best, of course, and all I can say is good luck to the pair of you.

I knew there would be ructions, though. I knew there'd be fights. Both of you sharing that tiny attic space of yours above the B&B. It was your own little oasis, Brenda. Your own cosy sanctuary, made just for you. No wonder things got a bit tense and cramped when that great brooding monster moved in with you. No wonder the two of you have had some awful set-to's these past few months! Rows so loud and nasty I've heard them clear next door, across the alley, in my own humble abode.

Why, some nights I even thought about calling out the police, or screaming for help on your account. I thought your Frank was going to kill you, Brenda! Many's the time I've talked it over with Leena and Raf in the shop below the B&B. (The various fracas were easily heard through their walls, too, by the way.) And I've mulled over your domestic predicament with your good friend Robert as well. But he's got his hands full, trying to run the Hotel Miramar single-handed these days, in the absence of its flaky owner Sheila Manchu (and we all remember where she ended up, don't we? There's another silly woman whose head was turned by an awful man. She went to the bad as well, didn't she?).

Anyway, Brenda ducky, I hope everything is on a more even keel now and that you and your Frank have found a way to unwind and rejoice once more in each other's company. It's hard, I know, to sustain a relationship. I think that's why I've never really tried. I'm much happier on my own, without some boorish fella trying to tell me what and what not to do.

I imagine the pair of you taking tea on that terrace in the hotel gardens on Lake Grasmere. (Very swanky it all looks too, going by the postcard.)

Oh, help, look – I've not even begun to tell you what's going on here in Whitby, and all the news from home. There's been quite a lot of fuss, what with Goth weekend approaching. They're making a film up at the abbey. A horror film, of course. And there's some glamorous movie queen arriving in town. They're making such a big fuss about it. You'd think nothing interesting ever went on around these parts of ours . . .

And I'm thinking about going to this Cosmic Cabaret thing on Wednesday night at the Christmas Hotel. It looks a very glamorous, amusing affair. It's a reason to put on my glad rags, anyway. I wouldn't go if it were just me. But the girls are very insistent. By 'the girls' I mean the small circle of new friends I've been making recently. Oh, they are a good laugh. We have such lovely times, out and about in the evenings. You don't know what you're missing, Brenda!

Anyway, must go now. I seem to have a rush on customers this afternoon. All eager to snap up my humble vintage wares.

Yours ever,

Effie

Chopper

Penny's favourite haunt on her afternoons off was a stylish coffee lounge on the long sloping road of cobbles in the old town. Spector was an ultra-trendy joint that hadn't been open long, and didn't have a regular clientele as yet, but she found it suited her tastes perfectly, with its smoked glass tables and cowhide chairs. Unlike the run-of-the-mill chintzy pensioners' cafés that Whitby usually went in for, Spector provided a dizzying selection of gourmet coffees, teas and spirits. As well as fiddly lunches consisting of exotic ingredients and the tiniest portions. Alone in the middle of the room, Penny thrilled at having this whole fashionable venue to herself.

Soon enough Michael materialised at her side, flapping an oversized laminated menu.

Materialised? Did he really? Or did he just move around swiftly and silently like a great big . . . Celtic panther or something? She wasn't sure. She liked the idea of him simply fading mysteriously into existence.

He arched his dark eyebrows at her quizzically and she gazed up at those eyes of his, those delectably firm, expressive lips.

'Oh Michael,' she smiled. Simpered, she thought to herself. I'm bloody simpering over him now. Or under him. Oh, do get a grip, Penny. She looked him up and down. He was in a faded denim shirt and jeans. He didn't look at all scruffy, but it wasn't his usual neutrally immaculate black poloneck and tailored slacks. His jet-black hair was awry, too. All in all, he seemed *rumpled*. Which looked well on him, Penny thought appraisingly. 'What's up, Michael?' She smiled at him. There was something distracted in his manner as he gave her smoked glass table a hasty wipedown.

'I've been over the other side of the harbour,' he told her, dropping his tone and leaning in, even though there was no one else in Spector to hear his tale. 'I've just dashed back. I had to close the whole place, just to go there. To see *her*.'

Penny frowned. He could be a bit oblique, could Michael. 'See who?'

'Penny!' he laughed. 'You mean you don't know about the film? The great film that they'll be making here this month? The great gory horror movie they're gonna make here in our town?'

'Oh, of course, yes.' She nodded hastily, not wanting to appear slow. 'We've had the crew checking into the Miramar all day . . .' Suddenly her eyes widened. 'When you say "her", do you mean . . . ?'

He nodded at her, grinning broadly. He was wringing his tea towel unconsciously in both hands, and Penny couldn't help taking in the way his forearms rippled with muscles. 'I saw her, Penny. I saw her in the flesh!'

'Karla!' Penny gasped. 'Karla herself?'

'I am surprised you never heard the rumours,' Michael said. 'I hear all sorts working here, you know. And word had it, this morning, that the great star was arriving this afternoon by specially laid-on chopper.'

Penny tried to picture how anyone could manage to land a helicopter anywhere near the narrow, intricate lanes of Whitby. It was a Victorian town, and not really made to cope with new-fangled vehicles that could suddenly descend from the skies.

'They deposited her on the clifftop,' Michael explained. 'Near the crescent of all the big hotels. She drew quite a large crowd, who'd heard the whispers. Others, like me, had gone dashing over there, just to catch the tiniest glimpse of her.'

Penny was avid. She thought about the second-hand and mysterious DVD in her shopping bag. Karla Sorenson in the actual flesh. Less than a mile and a half from this very spot. And this lovely Irishman had even clapped eyes on her! 'So she's staying at one of the big hotels?'

'The very biggest, and the very grandest.' He nodded. 'The Christmas Hotel.' He pronounced the name with a flourish. 'Mrs Claus, the owner herself, was outside in her motorised scooter with all her staff, and they were lined up outside the frontage of the hotel, waiting to welcome Karla like she was the Queen.'

'She is!' Penny said. 'The queen of screen vampires!'

'Quite,' Michael chuckled. 'And she holds this amazing fascination for men, you know. The crowd assembled around her chopper as it landed, they were all men. Drawn there by her sex appeal. Her aura, or something. We were all blown about by the wind as her chopper came down. Someone nearly went right over the cliff edge; he wasn't looking where he was. But then the chopper was down and the blades stopped whirring. And out stepped Ms Sorenson's private staff. Her bodyguard, her dresser, her personal hair stylist . . .'

'Wow,' Penny murmured. 'What did she look like? Did she look like herself?'

'To be honest,' Michael frowned, 'it was quite hard to tell. With this crowd of crazy men bustling and pushing forward on the grass.

The police were even out, to make sure no one got too close to the star.'

Penny sighed, wishing she'd been there to see all this. But . . . Karla Sorenson was at the Christmas Hotel! Less than a mile from her own place of work. How amazing was that? It was like a creature had stepped out of myth, out of fairy tale . . . to come and dwell in the same realm as Penny.

'She was all wrapped up in furs and had these huge sunglasses on,' Michael said. 'But you could see it was her, all right. Something in the atmosphere . . . *tingled* when she paused to wave to all her fans assembled there. We all drew in an excited breath, and didn't let it out until she had turned and gone across the road to meet Mrs Claus and her waiting staff of elves. Then she was taken into the hotel, to be given their best suite, I'm sure. The helicopter took off and whirled away, back over the sea, and it was finished. All done. So we all split. I came back here.' His face was glowing. 'But I saw her. I actually saw her!'

'I never knew you were such a big fan of horror films,' Penny said. She toyed with the idea of telling him of her rare discovery in the charity shop.

He frowned. 'No, I didn't think I was either. Not particularly. But when I heard that Karla was coming here . . . when I heard that she was going to be here in this very town . . . I had to go to see her arrive. I remember watching her as a kid, in those late-night shows. Just hearing her name again reminded me of my childhood and watching films too late. Anyway, she's a glamorous lady. She's worth crossing town to take a look at. I was doing the sums. Did you know that she's got to be over seventy?'

'I did,' said Penny, who had borrowed a slim biography of the woman from the town library a little while before. 'She's been going for donkey's years.' She was disappointed by Michael's evident coolness towards the horror genre. 'So you should get some business this Hallowe'en, eh?' she asked. 'With all these metropolitan film-making types in town. Just up the hill, shooting at the abbey.'

Michael drew himself up proudly. 'Mine is the only trendy coffee lounge in town. The rest are all for old ladies. Of course I hope to see the film people here. I will treat them to my very best of everything.'

Penny raised an eyebrow. 'You might get Karla herself coming in, to sample your gourmet specialities.'

She watched Michael gulp. She stared at the firm but somehow beautifully vulnerable bob that his Adam's apple made. Oh, he'd be easy meat for Karla, she fretted.

'Would you like your usual macchiatto frappe with whipped cream and syrup?' He flashed her a grin.

'Oh yes,' she said, and fought off a simper. She could do with something sickly and sweet. She would sit by herself in Spector and look trendy. She could sugar-rush all by herself, and be shiveringly glamorous, at the end of her afternoon off.

Christmas Greetings

Tonight it was Seventies Night in the nightclub beneath the Miramar, which was always very popular. It would be standing room only at the Yellow Peril when Donna Summer came on. The hotel was bursting at the rafters with its usual freight of guests, plus the horde of crew members involved with the filming. They seemed to have brought a lot of their equipment with them, and were intent on getting it all into their rooms. All in all, this Monday was an extraordinarily busy one, and by early evening, Robert was frazzled.

He was at the main reception desk when the phone rang.

'Yes?' he snapped.

'Ohhh!' came an insinuating chuckle. 'Is that any way to speak to a prospective guest? I thought you might have learned a thing or two, Robert dear, being left in charge of that gaudy fleapit.'

Robert shivered at the sound of the old woman's fruity tones. It was Mrs Claus at the end of the line, no doubt calling from her grotto-like boudoir at the heart of her eternally festive establishment. There was no love lost between Robert and that decrepit old bat.

Once, not so long ago, Robert had been a member of her staff at the Christmas Hotel, and like most of her young, male staff members, had been expected to wear a horrible skin-tight elf's uniform. He had become aware of certain untoward practices at the

26

grandest hotel on the West Cliff – culminating in murder and cannibalism. This had been during the first of his involvements with Brenda and Effie, and though the events of that autumn had been terrifying, he looked back on them now with a kind of fondness, because they had introduced him to the company of Brenda and Effie.

Mrs Claus, though, was someone whose clutches he was glad to be out of.

'What do you want?' he said brusquely, turning away from the front desk.

'Well, dear,' she said, becoming businesslike, 'you may not know something about this film company lately arrived in Whitby—'

Robert cut in. 'Ah, but I do. I've got just about all of them staying here at the Miramar with me.' Was that a touch of boastfulness in his voice? He couldn't help it. He could just imagine Mrs Claus crowing about it, had *she* bagged the whole lot.

'I see,' she warbled. 'So that's where they got to. Karla *did* wonder. She was telling me, not half an hour ago, that she imagined her crew would be staying somewhere a bit more . . . shall we say, basic and insalubrious, and a lot less glamorous.'

Robert gritted his teeth. He'd walked right into that one. 'Karla Sorenson is staying with you?'

'Of course, my dear. Where else? Why, she is a big, big star. A huge star. Where else in this town is grand enough to cater to her every whim?'

'We could have looked after her properly, here at the Miramar.' Robert scowled. 'And with us, she wouldn't have had to pretend it was Christmas every day, either.'

'But you don't have a suite like we have,' Mrs Claus said lightly. 'I have given her the turret to stay in for as long as she needs it.'

Robert blinked. 'The turret . . . ?'

Instantly his mind was back to Brenda, and how she had been given the turret suite at the Christmas Hotel for her honeymoon. Except . . . it hadn't been the romantic occasion implied by that statement. Brenda had been forced – in return for her friends' lives – to go ahead with her farcical marriage to that brute Frank. And it had been Mrs Claus behind the whole twisted saga . . .

Or had it? That had been in a different world, hadn't it? A weird world that had looked like this one, and contained a number of the same people. An underworld, a parallel world. Mrs Claus was there, but she was beautiful and young in that reality. And even wickeder than the old trout on the other end of this phone. But now that whole infernal fandango seemed like some kind of flashback dream montage to Robert. One he had managed to push to the back of his mind. We went to *hell*, he thought wonderingly, listening to the buzz of the telephone wires. We went to hell in order to rescue Brenda. But on the way we lost my Auntie Jessie and we lost Sheila Manchu. And we brought back a terrible man-monster who is now Brenda's husband.

And again, it was all, really, the fault of Mrs Claus . . .

'You're off having a reverie of some sort,' she cackled down the line. 'Stop it! I've got something to ask you. Karla has made a request.'

Robert shook his head and brought his attention back to the present moment. A request! 'For me?' he gasped. A request from the great film star herself. How did she even know who he was?

'Listen up, dearie,' Mrs Claus said. 'Karla is very glad to be in Whitby. She wants to meet all the important people here. That's how she put it herself. She knows more about this place, and the people here, than I would have expected.'

Robert's heart was thumping now. He put it down to excitement, but if he'd thought about it, he would have realised it was a warning. There was danger in this. What did Karla know? How did she know it? What was she intending to do? But to Robert, at this stage, Karla was just a famous name. Nothing ominous. Nothing hazardous. And he was just flattered to be asked anything at all. He would have done anything just to get a look at the infamous vamp. 'Yes . . . and?' he said impatiently.

'She wants to meet some local characters,' Mrs Claus said. 'So to that end, I am organising a little drinks do. And—'

'When?' He reached for his desk diary.

Mrs Claus laughed. 'This Wednesday night. Late on. Before the midnight cabaret begins.'

Robert shuddered. This would be her much-touted Cosmic Cabaret. It sounded tacky to him, but because of its success he'd been feeling his own takings drop on recent Wednesdays. 'I can be there,' he said.

'Oh no,' she said. 'I'm afraid I didn't mean you, dear.' She laughed heartily at his presumption.

Robert could have bitten off his own tongue in embarrassment.

Smoothly Mrs Claus continued. 'You see, the person that Ms Sorenson is so keen to meet is a very great friend of yours. And someone we thought you might be able to contact, since she appears to be out of town at the moment.'

Robert knew what the old harridan was going to say next.

'It's Brenda. That's who she wants to meet. Could you fix it up, Robert dear? I know you two are very close. And Ms Sorenson was so insistent. She seems quite fascinated by our mutual friend.'

Foreboding

Dark clouds have been gathering all day above the coastal town.

But this town is used to being tossed around in storms, or drenched by bitter waves, or gripped by wicked frosts. Whitby is used to all kinds of inclemency.

Earlier this evening, as winds started to lash the black rocks of the harbour and rain stung the darkened windows of the hotels, guest houses, and public houses, all the residents peered up warily at the skies and wondered. Something was going on.

Bad things are coming to town.

It has to be said, this is something Whitby is also used to.

For almost thirteen hundred years the citizens of this town have been unconsciously aware that their place in this world hosts a most unusual natural feature. Or, rather, a supernatural feature.

A kind of nexus point for evil forces. A gateway to another world. To a dizzying vista of ever-darker worlds that lie beneath this one.

Or so the legends say.

Or so Effie Jacobs says. And she should know, because she's had her fair share of encounters with the darker side of Whitby's strange nature.

Tonight her beaky old nose quivers and goes cold. Her limbs twitch and tremble as she tries to lie straight in her bed at the top of the tall house bequeathed to her by her old aunties. Many generations of Effie's female forebears have lived in this house of hers, close to the harbour. And each of those doughty women, those witchy daughters of Whitby, represented the town's first line of defence against the dark powers that would occasionally come creeping out of that hellmouth in the grounds of the abbey.

Effie stirs and snores and gives in to terrible nightmares.

All over Whitby, nightmares are being had. Even Mrs Claus jerks upright in her sumptuous bed. When she rings her servant's bell for attention, it plays a tinkly Yuletide tune, but even this can't pacify her. Dark dreams are clinging to her and she sits there, helpless. Trying to imagine what's going to come.

The gateway to hell – or the Bitch's Maw, as it has been so misogynistically called for centuries – doesn't only spew out infernal beasts and nasties and demons.

It also *attracts* them.

Something in its wicked heart calls out a beating tattoo, raising sympathetic echoes in certain loveless chests. Over the years, many evil men, women and monsters have been drawn to this place to investigate. To plunge themselves into the heart of the fishy mysteries of this town.

And also the good, the brave and the curious – intent on mystery. They have traipsed here to see what all the occult fuss is about. To do battle with dreadful monsters. They have been here too. And still they come.

But now - and the locals can feel this awful idea stealing upon them intuitively - a terrible presence has come among them. One that is intent on causing misery and mayhem.

She has only just arrived, but now she is here, she will take some shifting.

Even she doesn't know how much chaos she will cause. She is, in many ways, an unwitting vehicle for the badness that always, always surrounds her.

Death and dismay dog her every step. They have done so for many years.

She is like a goddess, descending from the heavens. Bestowing her marvellous presence on this cold, windswept place. Only today she was whirled out of the sky, out of that empyrean blue. And she brought the darkness with her.

Tonight Karla Sorenson sleeps ever so peacefully in the turret high above the Christmas Hotel. High above the West Cliff. High above the endlessly heaving North Sea.

She dreams of nothing. Unusual for her. Something in the sea air has calmed her mind. Pacified her restless soul. It will do her good. Prepare her for the rigours ahead. Karla Sorenson sleeps deeply.

But all around her, Whitby is aware that she is here. And there is a dreadful sense of foreboding creeping about the place, subtle as the sea mist, and just as insidious.

Up All Night

Once again it had been a fantastic night at the Yellow Peril.

Robert watched his guests streaming out of the basement club. They went peacefully and woozily, their ears ringing to the gentle strains of the final smoochy number. It was gone three in the morning and he was mad keen for his bed.

The hotel staff went about their business efficiently, ushering out the guests in their rumpled glad rags, and starting to clear up the mess. As the house lights came on, Robert shuddered. Place looked like a bomb had dropped. This could wait until the morning. His staff were glad to hear it. With the extra work of seeing the film crew settled, it had been a very long day.

Upstairs he found Penny tidying round the reception desk. With all her black and white make-up, he couldn't tell if she was looking pale and drawn or what. All the same, he told her that she'd better get to bed.

'I was going to watch my film,' she told him. 'But I think I'd fall asleep.'

He was only half listening, locking up. 'Oh yes?'

'Did I tell you?' She rummaged in her bag. 'Look what I found in town today!' She held the DVD case under his nose. 'Isn't it amazing?'

He frowned. It looked like the same lurid horror stuff that Penny always seemed to go on about. It wasn't really his thing. If Penny had seen some of the things he had seen in real life, maybe she wouldn't be so keen on this kind of—

'Hey,' he said, realising. 'But isn't that the name of the film they're about to start making?'

She nodded, giving him a look as if he was slow to catch on. 'Exactly.'

'But how can you have a copy now, before they've even started shooting?' His mind whirled tiredly. Was it some kind of time thing?

'It's the old version,' said Penny. 'From 1967. They're making a remake.'

'Oh.' Robert shrugged. Bit less exciting than a time anomaly, then.

'But this shouldn't exist!' Penny gabbled breathlessly, waving the box around. 'They never released it on disc. They put it out on video once, but after terrible things started happening, they withdrew all copies and deleted it from the catalogues, and swore that it would never come out again, so people could never watch the thing in their homes again.'

Robert's interest was piqued as he came back to the reception desk and slid along beside her to read the box. 'What kind of terrible things?'

Penny was pleased to have his attention. 'Awful things. People going crackers. People wreaking havoc on crazy rampages. People making suicide pacts.'

'All because of some film?'

'That's what they say.' She lowered her voice spookily. 'The film company reckon they've destroyed all the copies of the original print.

They burned the negatives. All the footage that was shot. Even the film stills. Everything! And they buried the ashes under a motorway flyover, as it was being built.'

'Sounds a bit extreme.'

'Maybe. But there have been more accidents and pile-ups on that flyover in recent years than on any other stretch of road in the country. It's cursed, they say.'

'By some film?' Robert shook his head. He'd had enough of the conversation now. Penny was just revelling in this rubbish. She liked anything a bit gory and horrible. It was the last thing he wanted to hear about at three in the morning.

'The film is cursed,' Penny said. 'That's what they say. They reckon that when they filmed the thing, back in 1967, the devil somehow got summoned up on location in North Wales in the slate mine where it was shot. They called him up and captured his . . . like, essence, on the film itself.'

'Rubbish,' Robert said, but felt himself shiver involuntarily. 'That's just hype. That's the kind of thing film companies say to drum up some kind of mystique.'

'But there's got to be something in it, hasn't there?' Penny said. 'I mean, I've got a book with the statistics in. About who was killed at the location and the accidents that dogged the cast and crew in later years. And about the people who watched it on home video, and what happened to them.'

'So where did this disc come from then?' he asked her bluntly.

'I don't know. Maybe it's a pirate copy. I found it in Save the Kiddies.'

Robert rolled his eyes. 'It won't be real. Someone's having a laugh.'

'I'm still going to watch it,' Penny said, firming up her resolve.

'You do that,' he said. 'But don't you start going on a rampage or wreaking havoc in here. We've enough tidying up to do.'

'I'm going to watch it tonight,' Penny said. 'In my room. On my laptop.' Gulp, she thought. Now I've scared myself. Trying to convince Robert, I've given myself the creeps. Damn. Never mind. Be brave. She tried to look braver for his benefit.

'Well,' said Robert lightly, 'I'm for my bed. I'm dead on my feet. G'night, pet.' He turned fleetingly to watch after her as she hurried towards her ground-floor bedroom. She turned and gave him a smile, and for a second he was worried. What if the film really did have something wrong with it? Suppose she really did unleash something weird, simply by watching it tonight?

Penny paused to ask him, 'I wondered if . . . you'd like to watch it with me?'

'Me?' Robert laughed. 'Not on your nelly, lady!' He felt a rush of cold anxiety go through him, and shrugged it off. 'Listen, if you're too scared to watch it by yourself, I suggest you leave it alone. I don't want my best new receptionist getting the screaming abdabs in the night.'

Penny flushed at the compliment. 'I'll be okay,' she told him stubbornly, and hurried into the dark ground-floor corridor.

It was only as Robert stepped into the lift, heading for his own third-floor room, that he realised that this might have been a come-on of sorts from Penny. It might not just have been a scared thing. She might have been asking for his company in a different way. Oh, surely not. That he could do without. A receptionist with a crush. Maybe he'd have to have a word with her.

Up in his room he moved about stealthily, without putting on the lights. He undressed hurriedly and tugged on a robe and moved to the tall windows. From here he had a wonderful view of the bay and the abbey and the higgledy-piggledly rooftops of town. The moon was shining out as if through layers of gauze. There was something theatrical and fake about the whole vista tonight. It looked like a pop-up book; a perfect feat of paper engineering, opening out darkly for his delectation.

He wondered briefly about Penny. Was she watching her haunted movie alone? He imagined her under her duvet, propping her laptop on her knees. Scaring herself silly, probably. Daft kid.

Robert shook his head to clear it. Then he gazed down at the wide gardens at the back of the Miramar. There, the box trees and hedges had been replanted, and work was under way to restore what had once been a rather chichi beer garden. He dwelt for a moment on the hellishly awful events that had razed the gardens (and very nearly the entire hotel) to the ground a little while back. But at least soon it would be back to normal.

Tonight he wasn't inspecting the work in progress, though. He was watching for something quite different.

Ah. There.

By the tall blackened hedges. Sitting there so quietly you could hardly notice.

Robert was surprised to see him. It was only on the off-chance that he'd peeped out through his curtains. This late, as well! How long had his fella been sitting there? Waiting so patiently? Robert's chest flared with pity, and with pride, and excitement. This was something he was getting used to now, and he could hardly believe it. This . . . steadfastness. This patience. This amazing always-being-there-for-him.

His fella – lit so handsomely in the meagre silver light of the early hours – was waiting for him. Knowing he would come. Perched elegantly and incongruously on a green velvet settee in the former beer garden of Sheila Manchu. A green velvet settee! In the open air? How bizarre was that? But Robert wasn't complaining about his new fella's quirks.

He tapped on his window to draw the man's attention.

Those eyes! That hungry look!

Robert turned to hurry out of his room, out of his hotel, to meet him.

Belongings

The only valuable thing Penny owned in the whole world was her laptop. She had never been any good with electronic things. She was even mildly superstitious about not getting too close in case she broke them. But she was happy with her laptop. To her it represented her new life. It stood for escape.

As for expensive clothes and jewellery, and all that stuff, she couldn't be doing with them. For most of her life she had watched her mother glam herself up in dear designer gear. All that conspicuous expense just made Penny nervous. She liked cheap stuff. Things she couldn't spoil.

That was why she was given to the Goth look, perhaps. It was all home-made, recycled stuff. Henna and old tea leaves for her hair, Oxfam jewellery and tie-dyed shirts. Her own look was kind of latter-day punk in its defiant makeshiftness.

What she liked was having few enough belongings to fill her backpack and her bag-on-wheels. She liked to think that she could be up and out of here at a moment's notice. Just say this new life of hers didn't work out, she could just get up and leave. No problem.

Her bedroom in the Hotel Miramar was so tidy it was as if no one was occupying it. There were only a few telltale paperbacks stacked on the bedside table; smudges of hair dye on the floral pillows.

It was as if she was determined not to make herself at home, or to feel like she had found a home. She recalled behaving in a similar way when she had gone away to college – when? Ten years ago now. And guess what? She had felt out of place there too, had never quite felt she was fitting in. Funny that. Penny quickly got ready for bed, cleaning her teeth crossly, cold-creaming kohl and black lipstick away. She wondered why she never let herself settle properly. What was that about?

Oh, come on, she thought. Don't be so hard on yourself. What's all the rubbish psychology about? You've just walked out on a marriage. You've just left Ken, after four years together. Of course you're going to be jittery and weird for a while. You're not going to know if you're coming or going. It's only natural.

Perhaps. Or maybe this was her natural state. Maybe she was destined to be always a little bit alienated. Holding herself away protectively from the rest of the world. Maybe that self-centredness was what had ruined things for her and Ken, as well?

Between the hours of three and four in the morning really wasn't the best time to go churning over all this stuff.

She pulled the laptop over the bed and on to her knees. She flipped the lid, watching the machine come swiftly to life, basking in its friendly glow.

Her mother, Liz, had bought her this computer. Right at the end of that last, terrible year with Ken. When he was out all the time and Penny found herself at home. Wondering what she was doing there, in that new house full of his stuff. All that horrible masculine furniture he had chosen to suit his own taste, during one madcap dash through IKEA.

Her mother visited and was appalled at the lethargy and the hopelessness Penny had fallen into. Typical of her vivacious mother.

Flying into high dudgeon over the state Penny was in.

'You were going to do so many things. What was your degree for? Where's it all gone? You were going to write. See the world. You were going to make a name for yourself.'

Penny had just pulled a face at this. 'I should never have gone away and done a degree. All that studying. What's it done for me?'

Her mother was horrified. 'What's it done? I wish I could have done that, back in my day. You're just throwing it all away.'

'Degrees just make you think. Thinking just makes you unhappy. Dissatisfied. It's no good for you.'

Then her mother found out she was on antidepressants and went crazy about it.

Penny wished her mother would just go away.

But really, she found herself thinking, what *was* she doing with her time at home?

She wasn't being a housewife, that much was obvious. Ken would come back from work and go on about how mucky the place was. The dust and the heaped washing-up. The laundry half-done and thrown about just anywhere. He worked so hard. She was letting him down. What about her side of the bargain? What about their plan?

She was staying at home because they had planned on having kids.

They should be here by now, those kids, shouldn't they?

That was what Penny couldn't tell Liz. She stopped up the words inside herself when her mother bombarded her with questions. This past year – the worst year in her life – was the time she and Ken had fondly imagined that she would be beatific and huge, about to pop. Or maybe breast-feeding already and swanking about with a top-of-the-range buggy.

They'd had no reason to suspect that things might not go like that. They were both normal. All systems go. Everything functioning correctly. Or so they'd been told.

They had a brand-new house, just built on an estate where you could still smell the plaster and putty and the clayey earth. It was all fresh and waiting for new life.

And nothing had happened.

Probably just as well, Penny thought. If I'd succeeded in having kids I'd be stuck there now, with Ken, on that horrible bloody estate near Darlington. Stuck for ever being his missus. I'd never be able to run away, to come here. To become someone else . . .

Her mother had given her the idea of running away. Liz had always been very good at being able to change her own life and making herself brave enough to turn everything around. Penny – though she had spent much of her life exasperated by her single parent – also lived in awe of her mother's courage. She had watched Liz reinvent her life again and again, in the restless search for happiness.

Her own happiness was something Liz firmly believed she had a right to. And she wished her daughter felt the same about hers.

'Leave him today. Just go. You can go somewhere and think. And write. Like you said you were going to. Write your novel! I'll even buy you a laptop, so you can write on the run!'

Penny had laughed. 'What? Mam, I'm not you . . .'

Liz gave her a hard stare.

That day she had found her daughter watching DVDs at home. The blinds were pulled on the bright day. Penny was smoking and wearing pyjamas, working her way through a triple bill. *The Exorcist, The Omen, Rosemary's Baby*. She was nursing an emptied tube of Pringles.

'You've got to get out of this home and this marriage, Mrs Danby,' Liz told her firmly. 'Where is it you really want to go? In all the world? I'll help you. Just tell me. Where would you most want to be?'

Penny smiled, remembering her mam's earnestness. Her busyness, opening the living room windows and chucking Penny's fags into the bare front garden.

Mam. She would have to write to her. She hadn't come visiting yet. Penny wondered what she would make of this new place. Not as exotic as somewhere Liz might have chosen to run to, but still.

She shook her head, clearing it of all the personal stuff. Too late to stew over this.

Get that film on. Let's watch some lovely, terrifying nonsense in the wee small hours. If you're gonna be an insomniac, at least be a happily scared one. Let's escape, she thought. Let's escape into deliriously weird fantasy.

She clicked PLAY.

From Brenda with Love

FROM: <u>Brenda@Brendasbandb.com</u>
SUBJECT: HERE I COME!

Dear Effie,

Look at us two, on email! Who would have thought it!

I've found myself a little cafe fully equipped with computers and what-have-you, so here I am. I'm in Manchester. And we are on our way home.

Effie, thank you for your email, lovey. What a great surprise to find it in my inbox last night.

I was up tossing and turning last night, thinking all about it.

We were on our way back to Whitby anyway.

Mind, Frank's not so keen. He'd be happy wandering for ages yet, but I've told him – Frank, I've got a business. I've got to be back in Whitby toot-suite. It's Goth weekend coming up and I've got bookings right through from then, from Hallowe'en all the way up to Christmas. Now, I said, if you're with me, then you're a part of this business. My B&B is all I've got in this world.

Anyway, the upshot is that he's happy to come back.

We've fetched up in his old stomping grounds in Manchester. Maybe that's why he seems so ambivalent, these past couple of days. (Actually, where is he? Time's getting on. This cafe's by the bus station and I can see the coaches coming and going. Soon we'll have to clamber aboard ours. We've got to change about twenty times before we get home. It's not my favourite way to travel, but we're saving our pennies.)

This past week I've been meeting some of Frank's ... well, I hesitate to call them friends. Do you know, Effie, I think he was knocking around with a right rum bunch when he was here. They looked like proper rough diamonds to me. I dread to think what they're mixed up in. This week they've had us out to glitzy casinos and opulent eateries. We had a lovely banquet for twelve in Chinatown the other evening. Frank was splashing his money about, the show-off fool. (Hence our return by coach rather than by rail.)

All these blokes in dark suits and grim faces, with their dolly-bird girlfriends. Well, how out of place did I feel? I was in my best frock – the aquamarine – but I did feel old and dowdy, I have to say, next to these gangsters and their molls. But Frank said he was proud to be seen with me. My old heart glowed with that. Between courses, as we sat there sticky-fingered from our duck and plum sauce pancakes, he leaned right over and told me, all sotto voce, 'You know I fancy you rotten, Mrs Brenda.' Not the most elegant of compliments, but never mind...

That was last night. The culmination of our month (a full month!) on the road, in hotels, and away from home.

And Whitby – the idea of Whitby – really feels like home to me now. This is the first time I have been away since moving there and opening up my establishment, and I've got to tell you, Effie – I've been hankering to get back. When I've woken up in unfamiliar, lumpy, too hard, too soft beds in rooms that don't belong to me, that I'm not responsible for – I've been yearning with every fibre of my being. To be home. Working again. Looking after folk.

I don't think Frank minds really.

But he's got a bad case of wanderlust. It's written through him like 'Whitby' through a stick of pink rock.

Ooh, listen – I've gone on too long. It's so easy just to rattle away on these keys, tapping away on an ergo-nomic keyboard and saying just anything that comes into my head . . . (I'm sitting here on a high stool, swinging one leg. With a frothy mocha and a muffin of some description.)

So – Frank should be back soon – I had better draw to a close. It's Tuesday – and I'll see you Weds. We arrive back (I believe) in the early hours of tomorrow morning. It's like a right odyssey. But I'll be so glad to be back beside the seaside.

And Effie – this is what I meant to say, right at the start of this email – you were on about a film, a horror-type thing, that they're going to make in our town, weren't you? And I have to say, when I read your mention of this exciting prospect, a shiver went right through me. I really had the oddest feeling. Like something horrible had landed on my grave. With an awful thump.

Here's Frank now. I'm off! I'm setting off now. We're coming home!

I'll be with you v. soon!!!
XXX
B

PS The star of this horror film. I need to know. It isn't Karla Sorenson by any chance, is it? Oh, God help us all if it is.

Electronic Messages

Robert managed to grab an hour's sleep before he had to be back at work. It was all his own fault, he knew. If he hadn't gone flying around the town with his new fella and so on, he'd never be in this state.

Seven a.m. saw him brewing coffee in his office. The strongest coffee he had ever tasted. Above him, the Hotel Miramar was waking up and coming to life. I'll give myself till ten, Robert thought, when the worst of the morning is done, and then I'm going straight to bed for a couple of hours.

When he'd taken over the hotel, in Sheila's stead, he had pledged to be well behaved. No more running about and no more nights on the tiles. But that pledge had been before the advent of his fella. Now Robert knew he had no choice. When that strapping, quixotic presence announced itself to him – and it was always in the middle of the night – he had no choice whatsoever but to go to him.

If he thought about it, it was quite annoying. He was sapped of all volition. That was exactly how he felt right now. Sapped. But it was worth it, he thought, as the bitter coffee scalded his raw throat.

Up in reception, he was pleased to see his staff happily going about their business. Breakfast was in full swing and the air was pungent with fried bacon and kippers. He was puzzled. Why was Tony on the reception desk? Had he misremembered the rota?

Tony shook his head. 'No, you're right. It's Penny who's meant to be on again.'

Robert pursed his lips. 'I thought it was.'

'We've all tried knocking at her door,' Tony told him. 'But no one can shift her. I hear she had a very late night. No one wants her to get into any trouble. So I just stood in for her.'

Hmm, Robert thought. Touch of insincerity there. Tony was only too keen to dob Penny into trouble. He was smarmy, shrugging helplessly like that. So what was Penny playing at? Had she really sat up all night watching daft films? Surely she wouldn't let him down like this if she could help it. He knew she liked working here, living here. From what he had gathered, she was happier here than she had been for years. So why the no-show?

Then the automatic doors swished open and Effie came in. She was puffing and panting, with a wild look of triumph in her eyes. He noted that she hadn't done her hair up in its usual immaculate bun, and that was very unlike her. She never let herself be seen outdoors like this, with silver locks flying witchlike about her.

'Robert!' she gasped. Stooping over the reception desk, she fought to get her breath back. 'That hill! It's getting steeper!'

Robert smiled. No, it was Effie getting older. All of a sudden he was aware that she had indeed aged a fair bit in the past couple of years. Were these adventures taking it out of her that much? The Effie of old would have thought nothing of sprinting up the hill to the Miramar.

'I've heard from her, Robert,' she hissed, suddenly thrusting her face into his.

'Not . . .'

49

'Brenda. Of course! She emailed me!'

Robert felt himself relax into a delighted grin. It was absurd, that the mention of one email could have this effect. But the past month, bereft of Brenda, had been harder than he would have imagined. It was starting to feel as if the time she had spent here, among them, was nothing but a dream. It was becoming easy, even, to imagine that she had never existed at all. It was almost like that time last year when she had vanished over the cliff edge and was, for a nasty wee while, missing and assumed dead.

'I'm on broadband now, you know,' Effie was saying, showing off. 'Oh, I may be an antiques expert, but I'm very up to the minute. And I've become rather attached to email as a form of communication, it's—'

'What does she say?' Robert burst in. 'Brenda! What does she say?'

'She's coming back!' Effie let out a slight squeal, which she tried to suppress. 'Right this morning, crack of dawn, she emailed me from Manchester. She's on the coach now. With that husband of hers. They'll be here by the early hours of tomorrow morning.'

Robert wondered vaguely why they weren't taking the much faster train, but his feelings of relief and excitement soon swept every niggle aside. 'She's coming home!' he said.

'And not before time.' Effie lowered her voice. She narrowed her eyes and leaned even closer. 'Dark things are afoot.'

'Afoot?'

'Haven't you felt it?' She frowned. 'Surely you have. The very air is stiff with menace.'

'Perhaps you're right . . .'

'I've been feeling it for days. I think that bad things are about to start happening here.'

'In the Miramar?' Robert gasped.

'In Whitby generally,' Effie said. Then she took out a print-off of Brenda's email and pointed to the hasty postscript.

'What does she mean?' said Robert. 'She seems to know something about Karla Sorenson that we don't.'

'Exactly,' said Effie. 'I think we've got to be prepared. Now, I'm intending to be at the coach station tonight when she arrives. What about you, young man?'

A welcoming reception! He thought it was a brilliant idea, no matter how late. 'I'm in.' Instantly he was thinking to himself, but what if your fella comes calling tonight? Would you blow him out for your reunion with Brenda? Or would you let Brenda down for his sake? Robert was surprised at himself for even wondering. He was behaving like some kind of addict.

Just then they were interrupted by smarmy Tony, who had slipped away from the reception desk to knock on Penny's door again. 'I think you'd better come with me,' he told Robert.

'What?' Straight away Robert knew something was dreadfully wrong. Effie saw his face fall. She saw him turn white. She followed along after him as he dashed to Penny's ground-floor bedroom.

'You opened her door?' Robert said to Tony.

'I was worried,' Tony admitted. 'I got the spare key. She was completely silent in there. Everyone's been knocking here for hours this morning. She must have heard us . . .'

'And?' Robert said impatiently. 'Is she okay?'

Tony shook his head. 'I don't think so.'

'Well then see to her, man!' Effie cried out, surprising them both. 'Get an ambulance, if there's something wrong with the girl!'

Tony opened the door. 'It's not like that. I don't think there's anything physically wrong with her.'

In the small, spartan bedroom they found Penny sitting very still and quietly upright in her bed, under her black duvet. Her eyes were big as saucers and her mouth was hanging open, slack-jawed.

'Penny!' Robert gasped, and hurried to her side.

'No, don't touch her,' Effie shouted. 'She's under some kind of influence, by the looks of it. A spell, perhaps. If you touch her now you could shatter her mind into smithereens.'

'But what's happened to her?' Robert said.

Then they both looked at the laptop, which had slipped out of Penny's grasp, and lay still open upon the bed. Its dark screen hissed and fizzed with static.

'She was going to watch that film,' Robert whispered.

'What film?' demanded Effie.

He just pointed to the small silver disc that had ejected itself from the machine. It stuck half out of the aperture and glinted at them. It looked so innocuous there on the duvet. A second-hand DVD from Save the Kiddies.

But right now, it looked to Robert and Effie that whatever was on it had given Penny the fright of her life.

Taking the Back Seat

Being slightly larger than the average passenger, Frank always wanted to sit right at the back of the coach. He liked to be able to spread out a little and watch the road spooling out behind them in widescreen.

'I like to see where we've been,' he said to Brenda, some time that day as they trundled over the Pennines and into the muggy, misty receding miasma of the Yorkshire Dales.

Brenda nodded. That was her Frank all over – looking backwards, dwelling on the past. And her? She hoped she was always looking to the future. And hoping for the best.

She cast a surreptitious sideways glance at her husband. They had been married almost a year, but still she wasn't used to the idea. Look at him, with his great rugged profile. His head was tilted back on the worn velveteen of the seat. He was dozing contentedly.

He had hardly aged a day. How was that? More black magic in his genesis, perhaps. A bit more necromancy had gone into his beginnings. Maybe the lightning was flashier that night. Whatever it was, he wasn't looking or feeling the centuries like Brenda was. Nowadays he looked rather like her toyboy, which was galling, as Brenda was a good bit younger than him, as it happened.

The rollneck of his fisherman's jersey had slipped down a bit, snagging on one of the very obtrusions it was meant to conceal.

Instinctively Brenda reached out and gently tugged it higher, hiding the offending bolt. What would anyone think if they saw those weird protrusions?

Maybe nothing. They would just think it was some odd kind of up-to-the-minute jewellery. Some body piercing kind of thing. Trendy. Almost anything went, it seemed, these days.

This was mildly disturbing to Brenda, who had spent her whole long life feeling an oddity. A freak. All her life she had taken such great care to avoid drawing attention to herself. She had been so wary of ever revealing those features of her physical being that were outlandishly out of the ordinary.

Her scars, for example, were extensive. They were all over her body – little runnels and puckers – including in the bits of herself she couldn't cover with clothes. Her face and hands showed pale evidence of heavy scarring. Crude butchery. She looked like someone who had been involved in some sort of unspeakable accident. A good long while ago, perhaps, but the evidence was still there.

For years she had donned layers and layers of caked make-up. It was second nature to her, this business of slapping on her liquid disguise. Puffing on the mercifully concealing powder. She smarmed on her mask before she even left her bedroom each morning.

Except these days there seemed to be less time for putting on that protective shield. These days she was running around with this great gormless galoot of a man. He was impulsive, energetic. Especially on holiday, he wanted to be up and about, all at once. There was no time to go preening yourself. No time to mess about with all that filthy expensive muck. Forget about it for once, Brenda!

She had been scandalised at the very thought. Face the world? The open air? The populace at large? Look them all in the eye – naked – in all her deformed glory?

Frank had taken her face in both his massive hands. He shocked her by saying, 'You're not deformed. You're exquisitely made.'

Her heart banged in her chest. It clattered with amazement. She coloured and batted him away. 'Oh, rubbish. Stop it.'

But that day she had listened to him. She had gone out, as instructed, unadorned. Her face uncovered. Pale, flinching, exposed to sunlight for the first time in . . . she couldn't remember how long. All day walking in the Lake District. Yomping up and down through long grass and sucking in all the clean air. She had even picked up a tinge of sun. A blush that lasted as darkness dropped over Ullswater and they came down from the heights of Kirkstone Pass on trembling, exhausted legs. Brenda's pins were paining her somewhat, as she tried to keep up with Frank's colossal, confident strides. But when they sat on the shingle shore and watched the smooth, bronze-coloured waters and the shadows of the hills lengthening and stretching across, she was feeling serenely courageous.

True, they had hardly seen anyone all day. Just chattering sheep, skittish and resentful-looking. They had encountered a few fellow walkers, togged up in cagoules, flapping maps. They had stared at Brenda's Arran cardy and unsuitable shoes more than they had her un-made-up face.

'You've made me feel normal, Frank,' she told him, and he stopped skimming stones across the lake and looked at her.

'Frank thinks you'll never be that,' he said.

She found his expression unreadable. He was a dark silhouette on the lake's edge and she had to shield her eyes, looking up at him. Her great big fella. She hoped he meant something nice by what he'd said. She was always hoping that. Wanting him to be good. Wanting him to love her like he always said he did.

How had he made her need him like this?

As they thrummed and bounced over the moors in the bus she was still looking at him. His face was like an Easter Island statue.

I was all self-sufficient, she thought. I could take care of myself. I had done so for so long. So, so long. I never needed him. I never did.

But now she had got used to having a bloke about. This bloke. The bloke she had least wanted to bump into again in all the world. Face it, Brenda, she thought ruefully. He comes in handy at times.

Frank even helped out at the B&B. He lacked polish and finesse, and his manners with the guests could be a little gruff. She got him serving breakfasts and was charmed to find him nervous in dealing with the public. She encouraged him and he was keen to help. He didn't want to be seen as some kind of hanger-on. A fancy fella or a kept bloke. Brenda had laughed at that.

Soon they would be back home with new guests in situ. She loved the thought of getting back to work. Scouring and polishing and hoovering round. And making up beds and getting that washing machine swirling and thundering.

Maybe she'd let Frank dress up in honour of the looming Goth weekend. Give those guests of hers a pleasurable thrill as he brought them their eggs and bacon. He could even let his bolts show, and pretend, laughingly, that they were fake. Or he could come clanking in with tea and toast, dragging chains behind him.

Waking Penny

For a while, Robert was really scared.

He had seen some strange things here in Whitby, and some terrible things.

When he first saw Penny perched up in bed, catatonic, he had thought the worst. A dozen things flashed through his mind at once. Uppermost was the idea that they should fetch the local vicar. Did the Reverend Mr Small actually do exorcisms? Probably not. He never seemed to do anything much at all. Apart from play bingo.

Penny seemed to be lost to them. She was rock solid and staring straight ahead with unseeing eyes. Effie told him he'd better pick up the offending DVD and hide it in the safe in his office downstairs. If it really was the root cause of this situation, then it had better be put somewhere secure. He nodded and took the disc, trying to touch it as little as possible as he popped it into its case.

But could it really be haunted or cursed? Really? All that stuff Penny had been gabbling about last night. About how, when they made the film in the first place, they had summoned up Old Nick himself. Could all the old rumours be true? Or had Penny just scared herself silly?

When he slipped out of the room, Effie was waving her hand in front of the girl's blank eyes. 'It's all right,' she told Robert, in a commanding tone. 'I've seen this kind of thing before. It's a spell.'

'Can you sort it out?'

'I think so. Now – put that disc thing somewhere safe!'

Robert did as he was told. As he passed through reception he saw some of the film crew people wandering towards the dining room, looking unkempt and unwary. What were they thinking of? Remaking this film? Wasn't that just tempting fate?

Oh, he was being ridiculous. It was only a movie. And this remake wasn't even made yet.

He hurried to his office, and the wall safe that had once contained Sheila Manchu's shrine to her deceased husband. This was the first time anything untoward had happened while Robert was in charge of the Miramar. This morning's discovery had thrown him somewhat. He realised that he felt responsible for his employees. If they were hurt or frightened out of their wits, then it was his responsibility. He had to do something about it. And he liked Penny, too. There was something about her – an unguardedness and an openness that he found himself responding to.

He really hoped her state wasn't permanent. He should have told her. Warned her. Don't watch that disc. She had suspected it was something weird, hadn't she? She'd tried to tell him all about it, but he hadn't really been interested. She'd said that it shouldn't even really exist, this copy that had fallen into her hands. Shouldn't that have set alarm bells ringing in Robert's head?

He sighed, slamming the safe door shut on the disastrous film and locking it up again. No, he'd been too bound up in himself, hadn't he? All he'd been thinking about was his new fella, sitting there in the beer garden on his velvet settee. His thoughts had been caught up in the possibilities of seeing that man again, and he hadn't concentrated enough on Penny, to whom, as her employer, he had a duty of care.

And she was vulnerable, too, wasn't she? She was young for her age. A bit innocent in the harsh ways of the world. He knew that she had only recently run away from a marriage that wasn't working. He should have kept a better eye on her.

Back in her room, Penny was waking up with a violent jolt. She sneezed and blinked and grinned. Then she looked up at the triumphant Effie with huge, startled eyes.

Robert arrived back in the room and could hardly believe what he was seeing.

'How did you . . . ?'

Effie waved a plateful of hot bacon sandwiches about loftily. 'It's an old trick.' She smiled. 'I told you I knew a thing or two, didn't I? Much better than smelling salts. I got that Tony fella on reception to bring bacon sandwiches from the kitchen.'

Penny hefted a sandwich and took a huge bite. 'What's been happening? Why am I getting breakfast in bed?'

Robert was delighted that she seemed exactly like her old self. 'Don't you remember? You were in a kind of coma. We couldn't wake you.'

Her eyes boggled. 'A coma?' She looked at Effie, perched beside her on the duvet. 'It's that woman again!'

'Ah,' Robert said proudly. 'You've heard me talk about her. This is Effryggia Jacobs, spinster of this parish.'

Penny stared at the old woman. 'I know! You're the witch!'

Effie made a moue of satisfaction at this. She liked it when she lived up to the role allotted to her by all her female forebears. Town witch. Local wise woman. It made a change from being seen as just a snarky busybody.

'You're Brenda's friend?' Penny asked.

'That's right.' Effie flashed Robert a look. 'How much have you been telling this young woman about us?'

'Not much,' he said shiftily. 'I think maybe you and Brenda should look into this business with the DVD. I don't like it.'

'Me neither,' Effie murmured.

'Where did you put it?' Penny gasped. 'I hadn't finished watching it. I believe I fell asleep before it was over.'

'And a good job too,' Effie sniffed. 'We think there's something weird about it. Something that needs looking into.'

'Oh!' Penny felt strangely glad. 'You mean you're going to investigate? Robert's told me a little about what you get up to. I think he's been pulling my leg. I mean, if only half of it were true! Well . . .'

'Well what?' snapped Effie.

'I mean, Whitby can't really be a focus or a nexus point for all the dark forces in the world, can it?'

'Why not?'

'Because – well . . . it's just in North Yorkshire, isn't it? I mean, it's quaint and old-fashioned and everything. But, really. Actual witches and ghouls? Monsters? It can't be true.'

Effie turned to Robert. 'I think the shock of the catatonic state has turned her mind. This young woman is talking gibberish.'

'It's all true, Penny,' Robert said gently. 'Maybe we should get her to a doctor.'

'I'm fine, really,' Penny said, jumping out of bed. 'But I'm still not sure that I believe in the things you've told me, Robert.'

'You shouldn't have told her anything.' Effie glowered at him. 'What were you doing? Showing off?'

'And Brenda?' Penny asked suddenly. 'Is she really what you say she is?'

Robert nodded. 'She's coming back tonight. You'll get to find out for yourself.'

Effie left them then, looking rather cross. She hated people spreading tittle-tattle. What did they used to say in the war? About loose tongues? Walls having ears? Well, Effie still behaved according to those rules. Keep shtum when you can. This, as far as she was concerned, was still life under wartime conditions. But it was a war with demons, monsters and the undead, and it was, by its nature, never-ending.

As she marched down the hill into town, she mentally corrected that mission statement. She wasn't at war with *all* of the demonic undead. No, indeed. Some of her best friends were both. That is, dug up *and* possessed by demons.

And that didn't always prevent them from being nice people.

Date

Things were perking up at the Christmas Hotel and Mrs Claus was cock-a-hoop.

Summer had been something of a let-down. Takings had dropped. She had even started to suspect that her hotel's allure was fading. Perhaps its day was over. It was very unlike Mrs Claus to confront even the idea of defeat like this.

But now things were picking up. There had been an upswing in their fortunes. The place was heaving. Was it all down to Karla Sorenson?

It seemed that just the plain fact that a world-famous film star was staying at the hotel was enough to draw extra custom. People were booking in their droves for lunch and dinner and afternoon tea. Swarms of them were popping into the bar, just on the off-chance of catching a glimpse of the divine Ms Sorenson.

Making one of her regular perambulations about the downstairs rooms on her motorised scooter, Mrs Claus couldn't help but notice the increased number of men of a certain age in the bar. Each of them was sitting or standing by himself, sipping lager and glancing around the room with wolfish eyes. Some of them she recognised as locals. Others she'd never seen before. They'd come from out of town to be here, all at the same time . . .

'It's a generational thing, I think. The way I'm drawn to Karla,' one man told Mrs Claus. He was in his mid thirties by the looks of him and, once he got talking, rather friendly. There was a gorgeous Irish look to him. All swarthy, with that dark, tangled hair. Those smooth forearms. Mrs Claus gave an involuntary shiver as she looked him up and down. She had paused her scooter by his bar table to ask if he was all right, sitting there alone.

He went on, 'Men of my age all saw Karla Sorenson's movie appearances at a very formative point in their growing up. I was ten. It was one of those late-night double bills of horror flicks that the BBC used to put on. Well, I used to love those films and I'd stay up so late, fighting against sleep. Just to watch the monster movies. Except one week there was a double bill starring the vampish Karla. *Carnival of Flesh* and *Blood in the House of Love*. "Oh, you'll love this, son," my dad said, chuckling. "What a woman!" And, to be honest, after that I was never the same again. Karla became my ideal.'

Mrs Claus asked him, 'What is it you like about her?'

He looked at her like she was crazy. 'Everything. She's perfect. She's always been perfect!'

The poor man was just about drooling. Mrs Claus tutted and shook her head. Men were so weak. She smiled at him and glanced around at the other punters at the bar. 'I can see that Karla has attracted quite a few long-term fans like yourself to my establishment.' The fans were easy to pick out. They were quite different to the jocular, elderly guests that the Christmas Hotel usually catered for. They stood out plainly in the festive throng. They didn't look pleased or happy or excited. They looked rather fevered. That was the exact word for it, Mrs Claus mused.

She was discomfited by the thought. Yes, these men were hollow-eyed and fervent. Like sleepwalkers intent on some obscure mission.

Cultists, she thought. They all look like they belong to the Cult of Karla. Mrs Claus was somewhat irked by this. She was all in favour of the increased business and the glitz and glamour and a bit of free publicity. But she didn't want La Sorenson taking over the whole shop. She didn't want the starlet inculcating and seducing all the men in the town. That wouldn't look very good at all, would it? There'd be no end of trouble.

Karla Sorenson came with a bad reputation for that kind of thing. Some said she was demonised. Well, Mrs Claus wasn't sure about that. But she knew a man-eater when she saw one, and that lady in the turret suite had 'voracious' written all over her.

'Do you think,' said Mrs Claus's new gentleman friend, 'there's any chance that we'll actually see her down here? If we hang around long enough?'

Mrs Claus smiled. 'I'm sure you will, dearie. But she hasn't been down from her turret yet. She's luxuriating in my most splendid suite at the moment. Probably pampering herself rotten. But I am sure she will make her appearance soon. Very soon. In fact – and maybe I shouldn't say this, because she hasn't yet agreed . . .' Mrs Claus manoeuvred her scooter closer to him and leaned in. She breathed in his scent of – what was it? Something delicious. Pepper, nutmeg? Cloves? It was a long time since she had been this close to a man. She could feel the warmth of his skin, and see the pulse in his throat, gently throbbing. 'You see, I've asked her to sing at our cabaret tomorrow night. In the Grand Ballroom at midnight.'

His eyes widened. 'Sing!'

They both knew that Karla hardly ever sang in public. She had only ever released one album of songs, to cash in on her horror movie fame. Back in 1978 she had recorded a selection of disco anthems with a supernatural flavour: *Boogie with Beelzebub*.

His face shone at the thought of her performing live at the Christmas Hotel. A light sweat broke out on his forehead. Mrs Claus could hardly stop herself dabbing at him with her scarlet hanky.

'Can I come along? Can I get a ticket?'

'Alas,' she batted her dark green eyelashes, 'they're all gone by now, Mr . . . ?' She raised an eyebrow.

'Michael. My name is Michael.'

'What a lovely name. Well,' she faked a faraway look, 'perhaps there *is* a way you could attend tomorrow night's festivities.'

He looked eager. She pounced.

'I don't have a date yet.' She grinned at him. 'How do you feel about becoming my young gentleman for the evening?'

Michael swallowed hard and stared at her florid, crazed complexion and her wild lilac hair. She held out one dimpled, beringed hand for him to shake as if to seal their deal.

Anything! he thought recklessly. He kissed Mrs Claus's podgy hand, which was very warm. 'I'd be delighted to accompany you,' he intoned, and that glassy look was back in his eyes. Suddenly he felt queasy and very tired. Like he hadn't slept at all last night. As if the very thought of Karla Sorenson was keeping him awake in the wee small hours.

Mrs Claus gazed at her prize happily. His rumpled, tired style looked well on him, she thought. And then she started wondering what everyone would say when they saw her with this strapping specimen on her arm.

Reunited

Brenda asked Effie: 'Guess how many strange adventures I've had since I've been away?'

Effie pursed her lips. 'Go on. How many?' She felt a surge of – was it envy? – at the idea of Brenda and Frank having their own investigations away from her.

Brenda grinned. 'None! Nothing happened! It was all really dull! Ordinary as anything. We just toured around the north country, walking, eating meals, looking at shops and places of historical interest. And nothing mysterious or untoward happened whatsoever!'

'Oh,' said Effie, mollified by this.

'What about here?' Brenda asked her.

'Oh, you know. Business as usual.'

'You mean, there's been things happening?'

'Not quite. Not yet.'

Brenda frowned. 'What do you mean?'

Effie lowered her voice. 'It rather looks as if things might be stirring.'

'I see,' Brenda said. Then she brightly changed the subject. 'I must say, it's very nice of you and Robert and what's his young friend's name? Penny? To come and meet us like this.'

It was almost one a.m at the bus station. Frank was fetching their cases from the back of the coach; Robert and Penny were standing to one side, Robert grinning all over his face, and Penny seeming rather shocked by the appearance of these new arrivals. She smiled politely, Effie noticed, but kept a wary distance.

What are we doing here, this time of night? Effie wondered. She had had to see Brenda at the first possible opportunity. She didn't care if that made her look soft or ridiculous. 'We haven't half missed you,' she said now, staring up at her friend. Brenda looked the same as ever, thank goodness. Effie watched as her friend took a deep breath, sucking in the chill night air.

Brenda turned to stare at the black water of the harbour twinkling, and the mist hanging down over the abbey and the cliffs. 'Ooh, I'm glad to be back,' she said. 'But do you think we could all get out of the cold? Spicy tea at mine, everyone? That'll warm us through.'

In the Turret Suite at the Christmas Hotel

The woman looked out over the town.

As she argued over the phone she cut an elegant silhouette in the window of the turret suite. Tapping her fag ash and sighing deeply as she took in the vista of Whitby before her.

Anyone sitting across the harbour, beside the abbey, say, training a high-powered pair of binoculars at the Christmas Hotel would have seen a woman of indeterminate age. Not just because her hair and make-up were perfect, or because she was backlit against the bright room. There was also something spookily ageless about Karla. Even up close she looked a good thirty years too young.

Just then, however, she was giving hardly any thought to how she looked. This was very unusual for her. She was thinking instead — furiously — about work. And about what she had got herself embroiled in. She was in the middle of a phone call that was driving her crazy. She tossed her ciggie out of the window and sighed heavily over the stream of words coming out of the receiver.

She stared at the abbey and the darkening clouds. She caught her frowning reflection and turned away with a cry.

How could they? she wanted to know.

The original script had been as perfect as it could be. How could they mess it up now? What were they playing at? Fiddling and diddling and screwing things up.

At the other end of the phone, the producer's ears were ringing as she let him have it with both barrels.

It was a remake! The script was already there! It was perfect. In every single detail. Why, it had been written in the first place by that towering genius Fox Soames, and it was adapted from his own novel. Of course it was perfect. It was unbeatable!

What was it about these young people that made them think they could improve on perfection?

Karla groaned and flung herself back on the sateen coverlet as the producer whined and maundered on in her ear.

Blah, blah, something about updating and relevance to today's culture. What did that mean? It was a timeless classic. The deathless tale of one woman's possession by dark forces. What needed updating about that?

Now the producer was rabbiting on about contemporary sensibilities in a multicultural world and something about belief systems and tolerance and so on. Karla really had no idea what he was blethering on about. He was just getting into his stride when she cut him dead.

'Look. There is simply no way you're going to make *Get Thee Inside Me, Satan* more politically correct.'

The producer quailed. She could hear him. She knew she had him in her power now. 'That's not what we're trying to do, Ms Sorenson. We are simply attempting to—'

'You can't tamper with brilliance like this,' she hissed. 'That script, back in 1967 was sheer, ineffable genius. And what I've just read is bullshit. Plain and simple. You've ripped the heart out of this project, Adrian. You and that committee of simpering idiots you call script writers.' She took a deep breath, listening hard to the offended silence on the line. 'Now, I suggest you get straight back to work, sorting this thing out. Or just use the original. I'm sure it'll only take a few tweaks, to move the setting from Wales to Whitby.'

'Karla,' he said, brokenly. 'You don't understand . . .'

'Yes, I do. And I've more to lose from this film going tits-up than you have, buster. More than any of you. This is my big chance. My big comeback. And I'm not having it ruined by some corporate eunuch intent on a sanitised rehash!'

She slammed down the phone, and lay back on the sumptuous four-poster, breathing deeply. Pages of script were scattered all over the room. Okay, so she'd laid it on a bit thick for her producer, but she really was upset. Foolishly she hadn't read the script in advance of signing the deal. But then, she never did. That was her agent's job. And she trusted Flissy well enough, after all these years in the biz together, to know what was good for her and what wasn't.

At this point, though, after four years without landing a decent role in anything whatsoever, she suspected that Flissy would have agreed to let her client appear in anything. Even this. This travesty of a remake.

Sanitised. The very opposite of Satanised.

Karla rolled about on the bed, moaning furiously and scattering the many tassled cushions. I'm in my seventies. What am I doing here? In some frozen, godforsaken harbour. With people I don't even know. Young people who wouldn't know a decent movie if it bit them on the arse. I'm going to be doing my same old vampire lady schtick yet again. Haring about at midnight in a lacy batwing backless number, flashing my knockers to all and sundry, and trying to keep my false pointed teeth in my head. Looking fabulous, obviously.

But it was hardly dignified.

It was pitiful, really.

Karla hated turning up to start a new job. She always got like this. Feeling abandoned, lonely, nervous and worried. Feeling at the mercy of her new production team. Feeling lumbered with a bum script, a horrible wardrobe. And this time she was being put up in a hotel swarming with – as far as she could tell – elderly lunatics who seemed to think it was already Christmas, here in October.

She just wanted to go home to Cricklewood. To her cats and her old movies and her life in retirement. She was too old for all this nonsense now.

But it was like Flissy said. She had to keep working. The royalties weren't coming in like they used to. Her residuals were drying up. Even though she had appeared in twenty-seven of the UK's most famous schlocky horror movies, back in the genre's bloody heyday, Karla was close to penniless now.

She wasn't sure how that could have happened. She knew that she had been ripped off somewhere along the line, but she just couldn't see who by. All she knew was that she had to do what Flissy said. And she had to carry on working.

And so here she was. At the bleak, unwelcoming seaside. On a four-poster with a bad head and heaving bosoms.

Karla got up heavily, and schlepped over to the tall windows to stare at the harbour, where the waves were high and lashing at the piers and the craggy headland. She turned her gaze on the church at the top of those 199 steps, and the abbey, all magnificently broken down, beside it.

Ghastly bloody place. How long did she have to be here?

The whole film was resting on her shoulders. As usual. If it all went to the bad, it would be her to blame. She was the star. She had to make it work. But did she even have the energy any more? It wasn't 1967 any more. It wasn't even the same century.

She was too old for this. She didn't even want to be a star any more. She quite liked going into Tesco or Primark and everyone *not* recognising her. There was something to be said for sitting on the bus or the Tube and people *not* squinting at her and then crying out in pleasurable surprise: 'It's the vampire lady! It's Karla Sorenson! Look, everyone! Ooh, bite my neck! Go on! Bite me! Take over my mind!'

Such attention could get on your nerves in the end.

She wouldn't miss any of it if she was never famous again. She'd be quite happy to retire, and to fade away into obscurity and old age. She'd be happy to let go the effort of making herself look fabulous every day before leaving her house. It would be a relief, wouldn't it? To turn herself into a little old lady. And never have anyone turn to look at her again.

She could be happy like that.

Well. Maybe that wasn't true.

One thing, though. She could do without the Brethren breathing down her neck.

And as if on cue – BEEP BEEP BEEP BEEP. Her mobile phone was going bonkers, all of a sudden, vibrating on the marble-topped nightstand. She just knew it was them. It was as if, by thinking of them, even for a split second, she had drawn their attention.

There was a text. In gothic script.

Daughter! We r very proud of u. We the Brethren rejoice in news of ur new film role. Remember what u must do for us. Remember our plans.

She deleted it at once.

Agghh. What was she in for this time?

She looked at her own reflection in the tall dressing mirror. She took a long look at herself and sighed. Silly old woman.

Then there came a timid knock on the door. It was a little elf. A young fella. One of Mrs Claus's pimply lackeys. Not too ugly, actually. Overawed by her, clearly. Shaking in his pointy shoes. Karla considered him. Quite a pretty boy, in fact. He gulped as she leaned in for a closer look.

Maybe she would have to take him under her wing. She needed allies. 'What's your name?' she asked, in that trademark seductive purr.

'Kevin, ma'am,' said the elf.

'And why have you come to my turret?' She frowned.

He took a deep breath and stammered: 'Mrs Christmas would like to know whether you have been able to give any thought . . .'

'What to?'

'Her request . . . her suggestion . . .'

Karla rolled her eyes. 'Oh, this cabaret thing. No. No, I don't think so. My singing days are over. I've enough work to concentrate on at the moment, thanks.' She moved as if to slam the heavy door on him. But she didn't. Not yet. Now she knew she had him. Right in her palm. She raised an eyebrow at him.

The elf boy looked sick with dread. He wanted to flee, but he was held there, braving out Karla's crossness, determined to wheedle and plead. Karla realised what kind of a grip Mrs Claus must have on her staff. Interesting.

She called him to her. 'Dear Kevin.' She smiled.

He looked wary. He took a step towards her. He swallowed hard. 'Y-yes, Ms Sorenson?'

'Do come into my suite,' she said.

'Is th-there something the matter?'

She shut the door gently behind him and led him into her boudoir. Her base of operations. He tiptoed carefully between the scattered pages of script. 'Oh, there's nothing wrong that you could do anything about, my dear,' she sighed winsomely. 'Except, perhaps . . .'

'Yes?' he said, overeagerly, advancing on her like a puppy.

She paused and then gave him the full, devastating benefit of her beauty. 'Perhaps you'd like to obey me, yes? Instead of that old monster Mrs Claus. How would you feel about falling under my thrall, Kevin? And obeying me in all things, for ever? How would that be, my dear?'

Penny Writes to her Mother

Dear Mam,

You told me to get out into the world, and to see a bit of life. I wonder if that's what I'm doing now.

Sorry I haven't written much, Mam. It's been really busy here. At the hotel we're run off our feet every day. Especially now, when we've got this film crew in. Quite a rowdy lot, but harmless and quite good fun. They look like they have a whale of a time, actually. It must be a wonderful world to be in. They're all on a shared project, they all know what they're doing and they've all got their roles and their areas of expertise, even the extras and the runners, whatever *they* are. They're all up here, getting ready to make this horror film at the abbey, and there's a real buzz in the air.

Anyway, I am well and truly settled in here now. I don't even mind the work. It's easy enough and the boss at the Hotel Miramar is like a friend now. He's called Robert, and before you say it, there's no chance of romance there. I know, I know what you're going to say, about me always knocking about with gay men. I don't know what it is about me. I think probably straight men can't deal with me or something, I'm too special, hahaha. Anyway, so he's my new pal here now and he's all right.

But I think he's involved in weird stuff here in Whitby.

Now, don't go getting ariated. I don't mean weird bad stuff. Well, maybe I do.

I don't know. I get the feeling that I only know half the story here. People aren't telling me everything.

It's to do with his friends.

You're not to worry, Mam. I'm not getting mixed up in anything dangerous. I don't think. I mean, most of Robert's friends are old women. Or women of a certain age, anyway.

Last night we were at the bus station, waiting for a coach to turn up, bringing back his best friend from the holiday she's been on. Anyway, I was there to meet her, part of the welcoming committee kind of thing. And this great big woman comes clambering off the coach. Really, you've seen nothing like her. She had all this hair in a big beehive, jet black with a great blonde streak up the middle. She towered over me and Robert. She looked kind, though, and friendly enough. When she shook my hand I thought she would crush it, her paws were so huge. Under the streetlights it was hard to see her face. I was squinting up at her, trying to get a look. She was the oddest woman I've ever seen.

And her husband! This huge hulk of a man. He never said much. He carried all their luggage without seeming effort and followed along behind us. We went up the winding streets into the leafy part of town, where all the bed and breakfasts are. Every other house is a B&B and it's here that Brenda has her own guest house, and Effie has her junk shop.

Oh, Effie is Robert's other friend. This proper starchy-knickers old woman. I'm not sure I like her much. They reckon she's a witch, but I've not seen much evidence of special powers in her. Anyway, she was gabbling away at twenty to the dozen, telling Brenda everything that's been going on in the month she's been away. Robert was joining in and they all seemed so pleased to be together again. Brenda didn't say much, just beamed in pleasure at the way they were going on. And her hubby said even less. I turned, looking back down the steep pavement, to see if he was okay carrying all the bags and I caught this nasty, twisted look on his face. Like he was furious about being the porter. There was something really frightening about that look in his eyes. I wondered what such a warm-hearted soul like Brenda was doing with a man like that.

I'd heard Robert say that he didn't think they were suited. I'd heard him imply that none of Brenda's friends got on with her fella. It was a recent thing, by all accounts, but the two of them had been childhood sweethearts way back in the mists of time. Or something.

There was something about him, though. Something I couldn't put my finger on. He was wearing that very old-fashioned men's fragrance, Brut. Maybe that was it. (I remember you saying, years ago: never trust a man who splashes on Brut.)

Anyway, Brenda was insistent that we all come in and have something she called spicy tea. So we yomped up her side passage and up about twenty flights of stairs, with everyone exclaiming at the blown light bulbs and the general dustiness and mustiness of the place. Brenda seemed quite undeterred by it all, telling everyone how she was looking forward to getting to work and giving the whole place a good bottoming, which, it turns out, means scrubbing.

Her attic is gorgeous. Paisley and velvet, with knick-knacks and pictures. You can tell that every little oddment has its own story and reason for being there. There was something so relaxing about the place. We all sank into the comfy chairs as Brenda swept into action to make this wonderful tea – it was cinnamon, nutmeg and cloves and peppery. She didn't seem in the least bit tired now, unlike her rude hubby, who merely grunted at us from the doorway and announced that he was off to his bed.

We heard him shifting about in the room next door, banging the cases around and bumping exhaustedly into things. Robert and I exchanged a glance.

'Don't mind him,' Brenda laughed. 'He's been having so many late nights recently. We were out last night till who knows what time. Now, who's for a bacon sandwich?'

Robert says it's quite regular, that the three of them will sit up in the wee small hours, having bacon sandwiches together. No wonder Brenda's the size she is. Effie's a skinny little thing, but then she was just nibbling at the giant doorstops of bread that Brenda brought us. Fried bread! Who fries their bread in bacon fat these days? Well, Brenda does.

I was quite happily chomping away and slurping my tea and listening to the three friends gossiping. There was a lovely old jazz record playing on the turntable. Then I detected a shift in the conversation. A note of seriousness in the air. Now they were talking about something important, I could tell.

'No one has clapped eyes on her yet,' Robert was saying.

Brenda nodded solemnly, giving her tea a pensive sip. 'She'll make her presence known sooner or later.'

'What's this Robert was saying, though?' Effie spoke up. 'Mrs Claus inviting you to a drinks do, Brenda. About Karla wanting to meet you.'

Brenda frowned deeply. 'Now, that I do find quite disturbing. I'm surprised Karla would even remember me. It was all so long ago. Decades. And I was just in the background. I was nothing to her. Less than a servant.'

'But you were *there*, weren't you?' Robert said. 'You were *there* on the set of the movie.'

'Oh yes,' Brenda said, nodding grimly. 'I was there when they made the first version.'

Suddenly I realised what they meant. I choked down a sharp crust. 'You mean, the first version of *Get Thee Inside Me, Satan*?'

Brenda looked at me with these deep, deep, soulful eyes. They were violet. No, greenish. I think they were both different colours. At least they looked that way in the cosy lamplight. She said, 'Yes, I was there. When all hell broke loose.'

She clammed up after that. I was itching to know. But tiredness was getting to me. My bones ached to lie down in my bed at the Miramar. I was bursting with questions, but my thinking was too muzzy to put them right.

Brenda picked up our crockery, taking it to the kitchen corner of her attic space. The record finished. The others were looking at me strangely. Was I drifting off? I think I must have been.

I remember Effie said, 'She watched the whole thing. On her laptop. When we found her she had gone into a kind of trance.'

'Oh dear,' Brenda said. She was peering into my face. I smiled back at her. They were talking about me! About me watching that film.

It was true, Mam. I watched a copy of that film on my laptop. The computer you bought me. There must have been something strange about the copy because, well, it shouldn't exist. I got it in Save the Kiddies and thought I'd found a bargain. A rarity.

'No one should watch that film,' Brenda was saying. 'It's pure wickedness.'

Funny, she didn't look like a prude. Not like Effie did.

'What about the remake?' Robert said.

'They shouldn't be doing that, either,' Brenda said. 'They don't know what they're messing around with.'

Effie stared aghast at her friend. 'I was worried you'd say something like that.'

'Up at the Bitch's Maw, as well,' Brenda said. 'They're tapping into forces that they don't understand.'

Now I was drifting off, slumped there on a bobbly green armchair. My fingers were tingling oddly, like they sometimes do when trouble's at hand.

I closed my eyes. I heard Brenda say, 'It's a good job I've come back. Right in the nick of time, I'd say.'

And then, the next thing I knew, I was being shaken awake. Robert had called us a taxi, just to get us up the hill to the Miramar. It was gone four o'clock.

Anyway, we got back here and Wednesday was starting before we knew it. Bringing with it the promise of the Cosmic Cabaret at the Christmas Hotel that very night.

Tonight. It wouldn't normally be my kind of thing. It's like

80

an old people's kind of thing. But I think tonight should prove interesting.

Don't worry, Mam. I don't think it'll be dangerous. But there's something weird here, don't you think? The way these people carry on?

I'll write more soon,

Lots of love,

Penny

Ten Fateful Days in the Summer of Love

Brenda couldn't tell Effie and the others all she knew about Karla Sorenson. She couldn't remember everything just yet.

She lay in bed that night, grabbing a couple of hours before dawn. Her mind whirred and whirled around as she tried to force herself to remember. Frank, murmuring as he slumbered beside her, wasn't helping. Every now and then he would move one of his massive limbs and the bed would tremble and tip to one side. Being in bed with him was sometimes like clinging to a life raft.

There'd be no sleep tonight, Brenda thought.

She knew that the others trusted her intuition. If she said that Karla was dangerous – even if she couldn't remember exactly why – then they would believe her. Effie especially had learned to trust her.

On the other hand, Brenda wasn't quite so sure about trusting Effie's funny feelings. They seemed to be triggered by the slightest thing. These days Effie found menace in every single shadow. She had been completely wrong, this past spring, about suspected strange goings-on at the kipper smoking shop. And she had been quite mistaken about the curious artefacts found in the excavated lot where they were building a new supermarket. Effie could be a bit previous in anticipating weird shenanigans.

But Brenda never was. If her alarm bells started ringing – ringing as they were doing now – then chances were, something terrible was afoot.

Karla Sorenson was cursed. Wherever she went, awful things would happen. That much Brenda remembered.

Best not to force the memories, Brenda. Try not to cudgel your brains, she told herself. Lie still. Ignore Frank's snuffling and snorting. Try to forget that this old noggin of yours has been addled and raddled by a stupendously long and complicated life. No wonder whole chunks and vital portions of your mind have frittered and fallen away like old lace.

But the memories are still there, you are sure. You must be able to put yourself back there, in the past.

Let yourself drift back.

To 1967. That was when it was. The so-called Summer of Love.

Suddenly she could see it all.

She was in a dreadful, freezing slate quarry in North Wales. As far away from Carnaby Street and the Swinging Sixties as it was possible to get.

Caravans, mobile homes, heavy equipment, lights, cameras and electric cables were heaped about on the valley floor, tripping the unwary. The crew were mostly young, wearing trendy London clothes. Pulling their military greatcoats and shaggy Afghan coats tight about themselves in the icy wind and the lashing hail. Hail! Hail in June! They started saying that the film was cursed at first, simply because of the rotten weather. Here came the storms and the freezing rain that plagued the stark valley and heralded the arrival of the film's svelte and slinky star.

She was notorious even then. Karla specialised in this kind of movie. Hers was the sinisterly perfect face and the frankly astonishing body that had come to stand as an icon of those tales dealing with the occult, the dark arts, with what Fox Soames had always described rather pompously as the Ways of the Left-Hand Path.

Now that Brenda had conjured up the name of that ghastly old man, he came swimming into view. How could she have forgotten his shuffling gait? His insinuating smile? His lipless grimace? He was a nasty homunculus with liver-spotted hands and a somehow eery shine on his bald pate.

Brenda had been wary of him at first sight. He reminded her of the many villains, magicians and charlatans she had encountered through the years. She could see straight away that Fox Soames was no good. He looked malign – the way he rubbed his gnarled hands together, especially when he was in the presence of Karla herself.

Karla was his starlet. She was, in a sense, his creation – at least as far as this film was concerned. Fox Soames had written the screenplay based upon his original sadistic occult blockbuster, published the previous summer by New English Library. He was there in that benighted Welsh valley to observe the progress of these talented children as they brought his vision to life before his shifty agate eyes.

And me? Brenda thought. What was I doing there?

Nothing glamorous, of course. I never do, do I?

Ah. Now she could see.

She broke through the tenebrous webs of memory and could see her younger self quite clearly, back there in 1967. She had her very own caravan, and it was one that reeked of baked beans and curry sauce and chip fat. She was there to help cast and crew to keep body and soul together. She was there to slop up tasty, savoury, steaming-hot stodge all through the day and often late into the night. She was the dinner lady and she knew everyone at work in that valley.

She got to know everything that happened during that fateful – and fatal – ten days' shoot. All those years ago.

But the details? What exactly *did* go on? What did Karla actually *do*?

Brenda heaved herself out of bed, just as the dawn light was piercing through the heavy curtains of her attic bedroom. She almost drew them open, to bathe in that brilliant, clarifying North Sea light. But she didn't want to wake Frank, and to break his temper. She tiptoed out to put on the kettle and start her day. She had a house to clean, top to bottom. She had new guests to prepare for. She had stuff to do.

It was Wednesday, and tonight would bring a reunion with the woman whose story she was only starting to recall.

Why would Karla remember her? Brenda wondered. Why was Karla so keen on seeing the dinner lady from the set of that schlocky sixties movie? Did she even know Brenda had been there, a witness to events?

Or does she want to see me for some other reason? Brenda mused. Something even more sinister than the fact that we both once camped out and about for ten nights in Wales?

Video Nasties

This was a little bit awkward for Effie. It shouldn't be really, she knew. But she also knew that old women could be catty and jealous. She had to be on her guard.

'Oh, hello,' she said, entering the charity shop.

Teresa at the counter glanced up. 'Effie.' She smiled. 'Are we still on for tonight? Are you still coming along to the Cosmic Cabaret?'

This was the awkward bit. 'Indeed I am,' Effie told her. 'Though I'm afraid, if you don't mind, I won't be accompanying your party this evening.'

'Pardon?'

Effie noted that Teresa's tone had hardened. 'I'm going along with other friends of mine,' she went on. 'It was very nice of you to ask me to—'

'Had a better offer, have you?'

'No, it's not that . . .'

'It sounds like that to me, lady. Well, I knew you were looking down your snooty old nose at us. I told my colleague Helen, I said, I bet she doesn't come out with us in the end. We're much too common and vulgar for the likes of her. Her with her antiques emporium and her lah-di-dah ways.'

'That's not it at all,' Effie said, feeling both cross and ashamed because, really, there was some truth in what Teresa was saying. 'You see, Brenda's come back, my friend, and I'm going with her and her husband and we've got a special invite to a drinks do afterwards.'

Teresa reared up. 'I see,' she said in a leaden tone, her expression heavy with disapproval. 'Your best pal has fetched up back in town, has she?'

Hearing that something was going on, Helen came scuttling out of the back room with a heap of Mills and Boon's Temptation Series.

'Have you heard this, Hel? Effie here, she's dropped us. She's going with her real friends. That Brenda woman.'

'The big-boned woman? With the beehive?'

'Aye, that's her.' Teresa tutted. 'She's not even from around here, either. Just some interloper.' Now she glared at Effie, and it was as if she was dismissing her from the shop. 'Well, you've made your choice, lady. We know who our real friends are as well.'

'Look here,' Effie said hotly. 'I'm sure there's no need for any unpleasantness.'

Teresa shrugged and went back to folding loose garments. 'I don't know why you want to go hanging around with that Brenda anyway. I've heard some awful rumours about her.'

'Don't you go spreading vile stories about Brenda,' Effie snapped. 'And if I hear any nasty talk about her, I'll . . .'

'You'll do what?' Teresa raised an eyebrow. 'You'll set a spell on us? A hex?'

'I don't have time for this,' Effie said. The air was filled with animosity now. She had other business to attend to and one more important question to ask these two charity shop harpies, and then she could be on her way. She resisted the urge to argue with them further, making herself sound brisk and businesslike. 'Let's leave our personal feelings aside. There's something I need to ask you both. When I was in here the other day, I bumped into a young woman at the door.'

'Did you?' Teresa said unhelpfully.

'She was one of those Goth types. Penny, she's called. She bought a DVD here.'

Teresa shrugged. 'She might have. I can't remember.'

Effie gritted her teeth. 'It was a horror film. A very particular horror film.'

'So?'

'I wanted to know if you had any idea who might have donated the disc in the first place. And who might have brought it here.'

'This is a charity shop,' Teresa said. 'We don't keep records like that. What would be the point? This isn't some posh establishment like your place.'

Effie scowled at her. 'It would be really useful if you could have a think. Both of you.'

Teresa pulled a face. Her friend and co-worker Helen was more helpful, however. She pointed out the DVD shelf that Penny had been scouring the other day. There were two more horror movies there. New arrivals. Effie was surprised to see that they both also featured Karla Sorenson. *Prehysteria!* and *Carnival of Flesh*. She peered disapprovingly at the lurid objects, front and back. Either Penny had missed these on her shopping trip, or they had been donated, and appeared on the shelves at some point in the past few days. Interesting. 'May I take these?' she asked.

'Five pounds each,' Teresa snapped.

Effie fished around in her purse for the cash, and handed it over resentfully. Teresa put her purchases in a bag, even more resentfully.

She said, 'Mind, I wouldn't have thought these video nasties were your kind of thing at all.'

Effie didn't even bother replying to that.

Cabaret Night

It seemed like a very long time since they had all been out together. Especially to the Christmas Hotel, which, when all was said and done, was a place that Brenda, Effie and Robert tried to avoid these days. They had had some awful do's there in the past.

Robert had worked there, of course. He had slaved away as one of Mrs Claus's elves, tending to her mad whims and wearing a figure-hugging felt outfit. Brenda and Effie had once visited the place almost weekly, for its pie-and-peas suppers and bingo nights, or occasionally a dance. But in recent years they had encountered a few unsavoury experiences at the biggest hotel in Whitby, including human flesh in the home-made pies, vampirism, murder – and, of course, the return of Frank into Brenda's life, a reunion engineered by a troublemaking Mrs Claus. (To be fair, Effie thought, Brenda probably didn't think of this latter event as unsavoury. She went on as if she was quite pleased about Frank's return now, but at the time she had been just appalled.)

Anyway, they had witnessed some funny things at the Christmas Hotel, and they were supremely wary of going back there. But tonight was different.

They had been summoned by Karla Sorenson herself, though no one knew why.

'Same old place. It doesn't change much, does it?' Brenda grinned, as they marched up the prom, and came within view of the hotel's lit-up frontage. She was in black velvet, with a purple satin wrap, and Penny had to admit she looked very nice, even for such an imposing figure. She stared at Brenda and realised that she was starting to like this curious woman. There was something about her enthusiasm for everything that was infectious. Something warming about the way she wasn't daunted by anything at all. Even now, looking up at the tinselly glow of the Christmas Hotel and knowing that they were probably stepping into some weird adventure, she didn't look at all worried.

Penny's only problem was that she didn't have a ticket for the Cosmic Cabaret. The others had managed to get hold of them earlier in the day, just in time. Penny had equivocated and decided to make a late addition to their party. Robert had promised that they would be able to sneak her into the ballroom somehow.

'Have mine,' Frank grunted, ambling along behind them. 'Frank's not bothered about seeing some daft cabaret.'

Brenda linked arms with him. 'You're not standing at the bar by yourself! You're going to sit with us, at a proper table, and enjoy the show. And when the music comes on, you're going to twirl me around on the dance floor.'

Effie rolled her eyes. Having a man seemed like such an encumbrance. Still, a turn round the dance floor was a lovely idea.

As they crossed the road it started to rain – big, cold drops – and so they scurried hastily into the foyer, where the ringing chimes of Christmas muzak met them, and elves were waiting to take their outdoor clothes. Eyebrows were raised at Penny's Goth ensemble. 'It's isn't Goth weekend for another week yet,' Effie said, 'but you're like this all the year round, aren't you?'

'An evergreen Goth.' Brenda smiled. 'Or ever-black!' She chuckled at her own joke.

Around them, the reception area seemed even more Christmassy than ever. The tall tree was bedecked almost to the point of collapse with tinsel and presents. There were more twinkling fairy lights strewn everywhere. The pensioners gadding about between Mrs Claus's dining room, Rudolf's Bar and the Grand Ballroom seemed even more feverish with Yuletide cheer than ever. There was a definite febrile air of excitement to the place.

'Shall we go straight to our table in the ballroom?' Brenda asked them. 'We don't want to miss anything, do we?'

Robert – handsome in a green velvet blazer – was examining the events board in the centre of the foyer. 'Look!' he said. 'Here's the billing for tonight. The main act is Denise and Wheatley, with their knife-throwing and stage-exorcism combination novelty act. But then the star of the show, look! By special arrangement – Karla Sorenson making her debut at the Christmas Hotel. Singing a number or two from her classic album, *Boogie with Beelzebub*.'

Effie peered over her glasses. 'How common.' She sniffed disparagingly. 'She sounds like the kind of person who'll do anything to draw attention to herself.'

'Who is she anyhow?' Frank groaned. 'Another old woman? Is that why we're here? Just to gawp at another old bag?'

Brenda smiled ruefully. 'You'll see, lovey. Come on, let's go through.'

They passed through jostling rooms: Rudolf's Cocktail Bar, Frosty's Billiards Room and the Three Wise Men's All-You-Can-Eat Buffet Lounge. Then they came to the entrance to the Grand Ballroom, where the floorboards were shaking with the vibrations from the sound system. A harassed-looking elf was taking tickets on the door, and somehow the party managed to squash themselves around the petite Penny and get her in for nothing. Frank glaring down menacingly probably helped their undisturbed passage into the room, too.

'Isn't it lovely?' Brenda exclaimed.

The ballroom had been decorated quite splendidly, they all had to admit. The last time they had been here – when Frank had manifested himself on the dance floor, scaring the bejaysus out of Effie – the place had been looking slightly tatty and run-down. But now it was restored to its former glories. A wonderful chandelier glittered down from the central ceiling rose. It was as big as a family car, flinging dazzling shards of white light off the seven mirror balls it shared the ceiling with. The mirror balls lowered the tone, Effie pointed out, but the others didn't mind. In the shifting spots and splinters of light, it was like being in a gigantic jewellery box. It bestowed glamour on the guests as soon as they stepped on to the sprung floor. They felt they were gliding elegantly into the place, borne on the music and the flattering light.

As the others took up seats at their table (quite a good position, with a nice clear view of the stage), the show was just starting. Robert hastened to the bar, where he found that the only drinks being served this evening were, in Ms Sorenson's honour, Bloody Marys.

'Eeh, what do they look like?' Effie hissed, as the elderly novelty double act came on stage, waving and mugging at the audience and drinking up the applause. 'Silly old devils.'

'Welcome to our thrill-packed programme of knife-throwing and exorcisms!" breathed Denise huskily down her microphone as her husband set about strapping her to an upright frame.

Cheers. Effie clapped derisively; Penny and Brenda

93

enthusiastically. Robert arrived with the tray of gloopy crimson refreshments, prompting Frank to grump: 'What the hell's that? Where's my pint?'

And then the cabaret began, noisily, but with great verve. They drank, laughed and clapped along with the musical accompaniment (Denise playing the accordion as Wheatley chucked steak knives at her). Brenda kept catching Frank's eye and passing on an unspoken warning: You and me, buster. You watch out for when the dancing starts. We're going to be up on that sprung floor before the evening's out.

But underneath that thought, Brenda's mind was buzzing and churning over the adventure to come.

Agog

'Ms Sorenson, what an honour. Welcome to my boudoir.'

Karla glanced around at the sumptuous grotto of Mrs Claus. 'It looks to me like the best suite in the whole hotel.'

'This is simply my humble abode. Aren't you satisfied with your turret?'

'Yes, of course I am, Mrs Claus. It is wonderful.'

'Ah. I am glad to hear that. And my elf. Kevin. He's looking after you, isn't he?'

'Kevin's services are quite adequate, Mrs Claus.'

'Well, Ms Sorenson. My staff and I only aim to please. We know that you have got an arduous job ahead of you when you begin work here in Whitby. We know that starring in that film will take it right out of you. The least we can do is cater to your every physical, spiritual and mental need while you are in our care.'

'Very kind of you, I'm sure.' There was an awkward pause between them, as Mrs Claus poured her guest a tot of sherry. The hotel's owner wasn't used to entertaining virtual strangers in her sitting room. And something about this movie person made her feel uncomfortable. She was an unknown quantity. She seemed powerful to Mrs Claus. But how powerful exactly, she didn't know.

Karla wore a wry, inscrutable smile. And a silver sheath dress that made her look very like something that, if you pulled it, would go off with a bang and disgorge a party hat, plastic novelty and duff joke.

'And may I say how stunning you look this evening?' Mrs Claus purred.

'Oh, this old thing. Well. I thought I would make an effort. For your guests.'

'Does that mean . . . ? Do I dare to infer . . .'

'I'll do the bloody cabaret, yes. No rehearsal, nothing. But who cares? I was never much of a singer. I suppose they just want a look at me. That's all they want. They're not expecting Maria Callas, are they?'

'That is wonderful news. I'll tell my technical people straight away. This will be a wonderful night, an historical night at the Christmas Hotel!'

'I couldn't disappoint you, my dear. You have been so kind to me already. Making me so comfortable. Providing me with a personal helper, Kevin, and so forth. I just had to do something in return for you.'

'That's marvellous! I can't tell you how chuffed I am. Oh, by the way. This is my young man. For this evening, at any rate. My date for tonight. Michael. Michael? Say hullo to the nice lady.'

Michael stood there. He continued to stare at Karla. He hadn't moved from the spot or said a word since she had entered the room. He was agog.

'Is there something wrong with him?' Karla frowned.

'Oh dear. He's gone very quiet. He's not usually rude. Michael? Michael, you don't want to offend Ms Sorenson. Say good evening nicely, will you?'

'G-good evening, M-ms Sorenson.'

'Nice-looking bloke. I congratulate you on your taste in fellas, Mrs Claus.'

'Yes, he's quite a catch, isn't he? You appear to have sent him into a nigh-on catatonic state, though.'

'Sometimes I have this effect. It's an occupational hazard with me, I do apologise. Once I've left the room, I'm sure he'll return to normal.'

'I hope so. I don't want to be squired around all night by some flippin' zombie, do I?'

'Naturally. Ah. There's something else I came to tell you, Mrs Claus.'

'Yes?'

'A request, rather.'

'Go on.'

'This cocktail do at midnight.'

'I've told you. It will be my pleasure. We shall hold it in my rooms here, and I will be glad to introduce you to the great and the good of our town.'

'That's very kind. But I put in a request for you to rustle up some very special guests for me . . .'

'Oh, them.' There was a fleeting scowl on Mrs Claus's face.

'One in particular. I must ask, did you succeed? In rustling her up?'

'Of course I did. I'm Mrs Claus. Everyone in this town does as I say. They dance to my every whim, don't they, Michael?'

'Yes, Mrs Claus.'

'Isn't he a doll? Anyway, yes. I put the feelers out. Brenda was out of town, but she's back now. Snared and yanked home, and as keen to see you, by all accounts, as you are to see her.'

'Excellent. And . . . has she arrived yet in the hotel?'

'Apparently. And she's brought the whole posse with her.'

'The whole . . . ? You mean . . . ?'

'That husband of hers too, yes. He's there with them. With Effie and that ex-elf of mine, and some girl he's knocking about with.'

'Frank's here as well! How delightful! Oh, I can't wait to see him.'

'Aye, well. Frank's worth a look, I'll say that for him. He's all man.'

'So I've heard. Well, Mrs Claus, I must congratulate you on your skill in pulling these things together.'

'Anything, anything, Ms Sorenson.'

'Brenda and Frank in the audience, as I sing! How wonderful.'

'Do you know them, then? Because I must tell you, Brenda is no particular friend of mine . . .'

'Oh, I know them mainly by repute, you know. Just whispers and rumours and strange tales. That's really all I know.'

'I see.'

'I must return to my turret suite and prepare for my performance.'

'You go. I'll see you later. I'm sure you'll put on a marvellous show.'

'I will indeed! Au revoir, Ms Claus.'

'Aye, see you later, dearie. Eeh, come on, Michael. Snap out of it. Say goodbye and see you later to the nice lady.'

'G-g-g-g . . . S-s-s-s . . .'

'Bless him! Never mind. I'm sure he'll come to his senses eventually.'

'I bloody well hope so! You've got him all agog!'

Dirty Looks

Throughout the cabaret, Effie was all too aware of receiving filthy looks from the women at the table directly across the dance floor. As Denise and Wheatley carried out their famous high-speed exorcism act, the women from the charity shop were glaring at Effie's party and Effie just knew that she was being pulled apart. This print frock was too bold on her, she realised now. These orange and purple zig-zags – what was I thinking of? It was a vintage gown, hidden away in a wardrobe in her emporium. A wonderful find. But I should wear drab things, Effie thought. Things that don't draw attention to themselves. That's what suits me.

Even Brenda and Robert had stared silently when Effie eventually shucked her outdoor clothes as they took their table. 'What?' she demanded.

'N-nothing,' Robert had said. 'That's an amazing dress, Effie. Very striking.'

Brenda had beamed at her. Frank just looked her up and down and gave this horrible smirk. Now Effie felt foolish.

They slurped at their peppery Bloody Marys and enjoyed the cabaret, which was becoming wilder as it progressed. 'Oh, it is nice to be back in town,' Brenda sighed. 'Home again! Isn't it nice, Frank?'

They all looked at Frank, and his smile was sickly.

'And a new friend in our little party, eh?' Brenda grinned at Penny. 'Not so long ago it was just Effie and me on our nights out, wasn't it, Effie? Two lonely old spinsters out at the bingo. Effie? What's the matter?'

Effie's attention was riveted on the table across the dance floor, where Teresa and Helen – the harpies from Save the Kiddies – were deep in conversation with Mrs Claus. The corpulent proprietress had parked up in her motorised scooter and her self-satisfied guffawing could be heard even above the noise coming from the stage.

So Teresa and Helen are thick with Mrs Claus, are they? Effie thought, narrowing her eyes. In that case I was right to distrust them. They've got to be horrible if they're pals with that blowsy hag.

Tonight Mrs Claus was in a gold and crimson kaftan, shimmering with sequins. Her bouffant hair was apple red, as were her painted lips and cheeks. She seemed to take a huge relish in making herself as grotesque as possible, Effie thought.

She had a young man with her – and he wasn't one of her usual tame elves. It was the sight of this gorgeously swarthy young man that made Penny gasp, when she turned to follow Effie's gaze.

'It's Michael!' she burst out. They all stared at the young man in the brand-new, sharply cut suit. He'd had his tumbling dark locks trimmed a little, Penny observed with a pang of dismay. What was he doing with those old women?

'Who is he?' Robert asked, looking amused. He squinted, but couldn't get a good look at the fella. The old women were clustered about him like tiddly hyenas round a hapless zebra.

Quickly Penny explained her – well, it was only a fleeting acquaintanceship, really, with Michael from Spector in the old part of town. He had brought her caramel macchiattos and plates of crunchy bruschetta and they had passed the time of day during a couple of Penny's afternoons off with some idle, mildly flirty badinage. But the way she had burst out with his name like that told all the others how much she fancied him.

Brenda said, 'I do hope Mrs Claus hasn't got her, erm, claws into him, lovey.'

'Surely not!' Penny laughed.

Robert looked serious. 'Never underestimate that woman. I used to be an elf here, remember. I know the kind of thing she's capable of.'

'Mrs Claus has all of Whitby in her pocket,' Effie said. 'The media, the police, the local council – everything. She can do exactly what she wants – and frequently does.' She glanced at Brenda, and caught her eye meaningfully. 'We were going to figure out a way of dealing with her, weren't we? Of bringing an end once and for all to her reign of terror?'

Brenda nodded solemnly. They were indeed. Ever since that strange episode when, for unexplained reasons of her own – Mrs Claus had gone to elaborate lengths in order to reunite Brenda with her one-time beau, Frank. Brenda wondered if the Yuletide hag simply revelled in the chaos she had unleashed. Perhaps she had never expected things to end up as happily as they had. Certainly, she wasn't usually a benevolent matchmaker.

Brenda thought: Effie's right. We've let things slide a little, me and her. And I've been distracted by Frank. Maybe that was it. Mrs Claus had anticipated that a rapprochement with her man might make Brenda take her eye off the ball. It might lure her away from her true purpose and *raison d'etre* in this town.

For Brenda – along with her stalwart companion Effie – was the guardian of Whitby. The long-dead wizened abbess had appeared on a number of occasions to apprise them of this fact. This was a town in constant supernatural danger due to its proximity to the underworld and multiple chaotic dimensions just a whisper away. Brenda and Effie couldn't afford to let up in their fight against darkness and chaos and general unpleasantness. Who knew what might come crawling or slouching out of the ruined abbey? Or who might attempt to harness the eldritch forces swirling about this small fishing town?

Really, thought Brenda, I should never even have gone away for that break, should I? And definitely not for a full month. How selfish of me! Anything could have happened while my back was turned.

Then she thought of how the film crew was settling in and preparing to start work, and of the film they were intending to shoot, and of the cursed individual her little gang had come here to see this evening.

Brenda realised that things were already under way. Her absence had allowed the story to begin to unfold. She had returned home just in time.

Now the cabaret came to a splendid finish. Denise and Wheatley had excelled themselves with their flashing blades and lifelike ectoplasm. The crowded ballroom's occupants applauded enthusiastically and the chandelier glowed more brightly as gentle music started up, beckoning them all to move on to the gleaming floor. To fill up the few minutes before the star of the show made her ineffable appearance.

Karla Sings

Actually, she loved every minute of it.

She hadn't expected to. Not at all. Karla was a film actress. She wasn't used to getting up on a stage, or confronting a crowd. Tonight she expected to totter out in front of that lot at the Christmas Hotel and to lose her nerve. But she loved it.

A few shop openings, a few benefit gigs, a couple of nightclub appearances back when her album had been released, more than thirty years ago. They were the only live public shows she had ever given. They were all long enough ago for her to forget that buzz; the glow that came from the audience.

Karla stepped up to the microphone and waved her arms in the air like she'd just scored a goal. She threw back her glorious golden-streaked tresses and shouted her thanks and appreciation to the crowd. They were on their feet! A standing ovation – and she hadn't sung a note yet. This was all for her. Her stunning silver sheath of a dress and her divine figure. When she shook her arms triumphantly in the air, there was nothing slack about them. She was beautifully honed and toned.

Best thing was, she wouldn't have to sing a single note. The technical elf had explained it to her backstage, ten minutes ago. The only backing track they had of her material had her vocals on it. She would simply have to mime, and concentrate on looking marvellous.

Karla had been mightily relieved. She asked them to click her microphone on between songs, so she could address her adoring public. Silence fell whenever she did this.

'My friends! I must thank you so, so warmly for the welcome you have given me here tonight! Hello, Whitby! My new home-from-home!'

They were lapping her up. Then the disco music began, and she started hopping up and down and gyrating generous portions of herself, to the further delight of the occupants of the ballroom. Even Brenda and Effie were impressed by her performance. Robert's eyes were alight. 'She's fantastic!' he laughed, as Karla hit the chorus of the disco version of the theme to *Get Thee Inside Me, Satan*. 'I had no idea she'd be as good as this!'

Penny simply rolled her eyes. This wasn't her kind of thing at all. Music from the disco era was what her mother, Liz, loved, and Penny had been dragged out to many mother-and-daughter disco nights over the years. She herself preferred something a little heavier and more nihilistic. When she explained this – shouting down Robert's ear – he laughed. 'What could be more nihilistic than a disco song called "Get Thee Inside Me, Satan"?'

She couldn't explain it to him, but she was depressed by the whole experience. The way the old people around her were tapping their feet in a jaunty manner – even that witch Effie. They were carried along. They were dragged up on their feet by the music. Soon the dance floor was filling up and Karla thanked them heartily in the gap before her next song, the famous title track, 'Boogie with Beelzebub.'

Penny sat alone at her table and sipped her Bloody Mary, and watched the others twirl about the room. I should join in more, maybe, she thought.

That thought got her up on her feet and sent her quietly around the edge of the room, to where Michael was sitting with Mrs Claus. She was keen to have a word with him. Ask him what he was doing with that old bag. Maybe he'd even ask her up on the floor, and she might not be as disparaging about dancing then. Oh, what am I thinking of? she cursed. The vodka was obviously hitting the mark. And then she saw that she was too late. Michael was holding Mrs Claus's hand, and guiding her streamlined chair on to the floor. He was dancing with her! Swaying and thrusting provocatively at the old woman, as she sat in her bath chair, lapping it all up and clapping in time with the horrible tune.

Where have I come to? Penny asked herself furiously. She surveyed the whole room. It was filled with freaks and weirdos, hardly any of them under seventy. What's going on here? It's like some weird bacchanal. She shivered suddenly. Her fingers were tingling. Penny trusted her psychic insights. They always told her when something was up. And right now, she thought, something was definitely up.

She looked up to the ceiling, where the mirror balls were spinning and the vast chandelier in the centre of the room spilled out glorious cascades of golden light. There was something strange about the chandelier, she thought. Something was wrong. It was swaying, shivering, tinkling. The music was pounding. Surely its millions of crystals were vibrating and humming to the disco beat. Surely . . .

It was going to fall. The whole huge chandelier was going to snap off its guy rope and crash to the ballroom floor.

And who was directly beneath the chandelier? Who was dancing gently in the middle of the room, quite out of synch with all the others? Which couple held each other tightly and simply swayed, oh-so-romantically, directly in the firing line?

It was Brenda and Frank.

Penny screamed at the top of her voice: 'WATCH OUT!'

At first no one heard her. Then, as she moved towards the dance floor, still yelling, people jerked around, and backed away in alarm. Penny never took her eyes away from the chandelier. No doubt about it. It was twisting violently now, as if it were possessed and trying to wrench itself out of its fixings.

'The chandelier!' Penny screamed.

But it was no good. Karla's ghastly ululations seemed to become even louder. The thudding bass rhythm made the whole room shudder. Penny's bones felt as if they were pulsing in harmony with the horrible racket. It was too late!

She stared up at the chandelier and . . .

Now it seemed to go still.

Everything was on hold. Everything seemed to freeze.

But then one tiny crystal droplet – perhaps the tiniest on the whole chandelier – detached itself from its hook.

Penny held her breath as the minute crystal fell, scattering splinters of prismatic light all about the vast room. Could no one else see it?

Turning end over end on the hot disco air.

Slicing through the steamy darkness like a crystal sword.

'FRANK!' Penny screamed, and this time she was heard. 'LOOK UP!'

Frank reacted quickly. He had a great sense of self-preservation. He always had. And now, responding to the terror in Penny's voice, he knew he was in danger. Brenda was in danger. He gave his beloved a flat-handed shove, knocking her brusquely away from him. Brenda cried out in shock and windmilled her arms, crashing into the other dancers. Heads whipped around. Screams rang out. Karla carried on singing.

And the crystal tear continued to fall.

Frank whipped his head around. He looked up.

Penny gave a strangled shout.

The crystal dropped directly into Frank's eye. That was what she saw. Others must have seen it too, surely? They watched him standing there, stock still and silent.

Then he swayed and crashed to the floor.

The sprung floor quaked at the impact, alerting everyone that something untoward had gone on during 'Boogie with Beelzebub'. When the music stopped, they all came gathering round to inspect the twisted body of Frank.

Brenda scrambled to her feet and ran to him. The first thing she noticed was his eyes, screwed up so tightly, as if he'd hurt them, or something was in one of them.

'What is it? What's wrong with him?' Brenda howled, rocking his body and cradling his head on her lap.

Penny hurried towards her, fighting through the press of bodies. She knew what it was that had happened. She had seen the whole thing.

Felled

They were all full of concern, but Robert didn't trust any of them. He had been through too much at the Christmas Hotel to place trust in any of its staff. It did seem, though, as they came hurrying through the clouds of dry ice, that Mrs Claus and all her elves were very worried about the state of Frank.

He wasn't budging. He lay in the centre of the sprung floor, his limbs in a tangle, his breathing very shallow. His eyes were squeezed shut in a terrible frozen wince.

'Is he in a coma?' Effie hissed. She felt very knowledgeable about comas, having slipped into one for several fraught days only last year.

The music had stopped. The house lights were on – glaringly, brutally. The other revellers had drawn back and were watching from the ballroom's sidelines. Many of them had already obeyed Mrs Claus's exhortations to go home at once: the party was well and truly over.

Someone – perhaps it was Penny, Robert thought – had dragged a chair over for Brenda to perch on. She sat right beside Frank, looking mystified and lost. Her face had gone an awful fish-belly white. Robert had never seen Brenda looking so distraught. The steadfast Effie was hovering, rubbing her friend's broad back. 'It'll be all right, ducky. You'll see. The ambulance is on its way.'

'Ambulance,' said Brenda hollowly. Then she jolted and burst out, 'Ambulance? Are you mad? Effie, we can't put him into the hands of ordinary medics.'

'They'll look after him properly,' Effie said gently. 'That's what they're trained to do.'

'But you don't understand!'

'I do! I do!'

'He's not the same as other men.'

'I know!' Effie gazed down at the prostrate man-mountain.

'We can't let the medical establishment get a hold of him,' Brenda said, her words dissolving into jagged sobs.

Effie was distracted then, catching the eye of the women from the charity shop on LeFanu Close. They were finishing up their bloody drinks at their table, as if – come hell or high water – they would get the full value of this abandoned cabaret and the rather miserable drama being enacted before them. Effie scowled back at them, and kept on scowling as the women got up and went.

Penny whispered to Robert: 'What does Brenda mean about her Frank not being the same as other men?'

'Just look at him!' Robert said simply.

Penny still looked puzzled.

'I'll explain it all later,' he said. 'But suffice to say, Brenda doesn't want doctors poking around, finding out all of Frank's secrets.'

Penny's eyes widened. 'You mean – what you were saying before – you think it's all true, don't you? You weren't just kidding me along, were you?'

'What?' he frowned. 'What do you mean, kidding you?'

'About Frank. About what he really is.'

'Of course not!' Robert snapped. 'Why would I joke about a thing like that?'

'You said he was a monster . . .' Penny gasped.

'And?' Robert said.

'But don't you see? That's impossible! It's just a delusion. A game that you and your friends have been playing along with. Like a kind of in joke . . .'

Robert gritted his teeth. He felt a cold rush of anger go through him. Who was Penny to talk to him like he was daft? 'Like I say. We'll discuss this later.'

'Eeeh, my dears,' came the stentorian tones of Mrs Claus, advancing on them in her Bath chair. 'Oh my poor darlings. Whatever has happened to your Frank, Brenda? Was it a heart episode?'

Effie's head whipped round to glare at her wheelbound nemesis. 'I wouldn't put it past you to be behind all of this.'

'What?' cried Mrs Claus. 'But how could I be? I was way over on the other side of the room. And how could I do anything, such as cause a heart attack, or give a big man like him a stroke? I'm just a poor old woman in a wheelchair. I couldn't do any harm to a great strapping brute like Frank.'

'I don't know,' growled Effie. 'But I just know there was foul play involved in this.'

Penny was watching and listening to this exchange very closely. So, she realised – no one else had seen that tiny crystal shard dropping away from the swaying, glittering hull of the chandelier. No one else had noticed it tumbling down through the air to find its place, lodged in a corner of the big man's eye. Was it only Penny who had witnessed that strange event? Such a tiny thing, to fell such a huge bloke. She felt like she should say something. Tell them what she had seen. Where was Michael? He would listen to her. But he was gone. He wasn't with Mrs Claus any more. Penny shook her head. Now she was even starting to doubt herself. Had she really seen that little crystal tear falling?

They could hear the ambulance now, mee-mawing busily outside on the prom.

Midnight at the Christmas Hotel, Robert sighed to himself. And yet another disaster for us.

Brenda started crying: 'It was her! It's all because of Karla!'

'She's going hysterical,' Effie said. 'There, ducky, there. You must calm down if you're getting in the ambulance. They don't want you having hysterics in the back.'

Brenda was on her feet, shrugging off the earnest solicitations of her best friend. An idea had occurred to her at just that moment, and she couldn't calm herself until she had told everyone and convinced them of its truth. Her eyes were wild with fright as she wailed: 'It's all down to that cursed woman. That so-called star. It's her who's done this to Frank. It's Karla Sorenson behind this!'

Silence followed her words, and they all stared at her. Before anyone could respond, the paramedics came dashing into the ballroom, lugging their paraphernalia.

The odd thing was, reflected Robert – there was no sign of Karla. She had quitted the stage at the very instant Frank had had his funny turn and crashed to the polished floor. As if she knew that something calamitous had happened, she had flung down her mike and vanished into the swirls of fake fog. Could she really have been responsible, as Brenda claimed? But how could she accomplish a thing like that, at the same time as she was giving her all onstage to an ear-splitting backing track?

But that was the legend, wasn't it? Men always fell hard for Karla Sorenson. That was what they always said about her. She was a *femme fatale*. Even a glimpse of her could turn men's heads and make them her slave for ever.

The paramedics fussed expertly over Frank, and the rest of them could do nothing but stand there impotently as they lashed his massive form on to a stretcher.

'I'm his next of kin,' Brenda announced, calming herself down and getting up to follow them out of the gilded ballroom. 'I'm his only kin. In the whole world.'

Settee

'It's been quite a night. I haven't had a mad night like this since . . . Well, since the last time Brenda and Effie and I were out on the town. And up to our eyes in adventure and mystery and so on. Poor Brenda. She gets home from her lovely relaxing holiday and within twenty-four hours she's stuck in the middle of some awful disaster. She was pretty distressed about them carting Frank off to hospital. Well, she would be, wouldn't she?'

Robert stared out at the satin darkness of the sea, and the creamy frills of the waves dashing in. He sighed and sat back on the velvet plush.

'Maybe I should have gone with them up to the hospital. Not that they'd let me in the ambulance, of course, it being a crush already with Brenda and Effie and the paramedics and everyone stowed away in there with Frank. But I could have taken a cab, I suppose. Lent them my moral support. But Brenda wouldn't hear of it. She's so good-hearted. "You've got a hotel to run. You can't be up all night at the hospital. We'll keep you up to date with Frank." Secretly I was relieved, I have to say. Is that awful? I do feel a bit guilty. It can't be any fun for them, sitting waiting and dreading what the doctors and nurses have to say about Frank. I mean, how will they explain him? He isn't even really human, is he? Not really.'

They were sitting on a two-seater settee on the beach. Robert hadn't really thought about the oddness of their sitting here, so late at night. For the moment his sense of logic and propriety had fled and he was happy sitting here on the sand and watching the lemon-bright moon illuminate the harbour. And his new fella sitting here beside him, listening to all of his bizarre news.

'I'm glad Penny went off home,' Robert said. 'I wasn't really in the mood to answer any more questions from her tonight. And then she was saying that funny stuff about the chandelier. I don't know. Can it be right? Could she really have seen a piece of it fall into Frank's eye? Sounds pretty far-fetched to me. It looked to me like he had a sudden brainstorm or a heart attack or something, the way he went down like that. Felled like an ancient rotting tree. I don't know what Penny was on about. I mean, she's not been right, I don't think, since she fell asleep watching that film . . . I think it's had a funny effect on her.'

Robert was suddenly aware that his fella hadn't said a single word for quite some time. He turned to look at him. He was a lanky figure, elegant and poised. He raised an eyebrow at Robert – mildly ironic, amused – and quirked his mouth into a delicious smile. He was slightly older than Robert. It was hard to tell how old he was, exactly. Robert, in fact, didn't know very much about him at all. Only that he turned up on certain nights, and he was always on his settee. Waiting for Robert. He was Robert's knight in a black linen lounge suit and for a galloping steed he had a velvet settee.

'What?' Robert asked him, wanting to hear what he had to say. His fella rarely said very much at all. 'What is it?'

'Stop talking about those old women.' His fella smiled at him. 'And kiss me.'

After the Show

She was feeling all wrung out.

Luckily she had Kevin to help her back to her suite. They took the private lift and Karla leaned back against the burnished mirrors, smiling to herself.

Kevin beamed at her. 'You were magnificent.'

'Like I was in my heyday,' she said. 'That's how I felt. All that power coursing through my veins. All of that attention on me. I just drank it up, all their energy and excitement. It was like putting old roses in a fresh vase of water . . .'

She looked at Kevin and suddenly she wanted him. She suppressed a momentary doubting sensation – I'm old enough to be his granny – and focused instead on the compact, wiry strength of the man. His button-like nose and those tender green eyes. Yes, maybe that was just what she needed now. To work off some of her anxiety and pent-up tension with a little action in the sack with this elf.

She must have been staring at him rather hard, for he jumped, startled, when the lift pinged and the doors slid open, revealing the rumpled chaos of Karla's luxury suite.

'Let's have a drink,' she told him, switching her tone so it was less like that of an employer, and watching him as he crossed to the

115

cocktail cabinet and did precisely as he was bid. His hands shook slightly.

'What was all that fuss about, anyway?' she asked. 'All that kerfuffle in the middle of the floor? It was right at the end of my final song. It almost ruined my climax. Cheers, darling.' She took the gin and tonic he'd quickly knocked together and clinked it with his own. 'Come and sit here, next to me, dearest.'

'I-I don't know what was going on,' Kevin said, looking terrified to be sitting this close to Karla. 'But this is a hotel for pensioners. They're always having the paramedics in. There's always someone who goes too far during the ladies' excuse me. Or the hokey cokey. We've had some nasty demises on that dance floor.'

'I bet,' Karla purred. 'What time is it, by the way, sweetheart?'

'Twenty-five to midnight,' he told her. 'Well, you won't be having your drinks do now, will you? Your reception?'

Karla blinked. 'Why ever not?'

'Oh,' he said. 'Didn't you realise? Mind, I don't wonder why not. Not with all that dry ice and stuff swirling about and the funny lights shooting everywhere.'

Her voice hardened with impatience. 'What are you talking about, Kevin?'

'Him who had a funny turn. It was Frank. Husband of that Brenda. Them who you're meant to have a drink with at this midnight reception. Well, that'll be off tonight's social agenda now, won't it? What with disaster having struck.'

Karla reeled for a second. 'Really? That was Frank? Well I never. I see. I . . .'

'I don't suppose you can see much from up on that stage, when all the strobes are flashing and that.'

'What a pity,' Karla said sadly. 'And I was so looking forward to meeting them tonight.'

'How come?' Kevin frowned. He knew Brenda and Frank from other nights at the Christmas Hotel, and he didn't think very much of either of them. Or that skinny-minnie friend of theirs, Effie. Or Robert, who had once been an elf here. 'Why are you so bothered about seeing that lot?'

'You do ask a lot of questions, Kevin.' She eyed him indulgently. 'Why don't we forget about words and gossip and everyone else? Let's concentrate on each other, hmm? Why don't we relax, eh, Kevin?'

'All right,' he nodded, slurping his drink.

'We could fill up that nice deep bath with bubbles, couldn't we? And slip into its gorgeous, clinging heat.'

'T-together?' he whispered.

'Why not?' Karla grinned. 'Come on, Kevin. Let's get you out of that elf outfit . . .'

At that precise instant they were interrupted by Karla's phone. BEEP-BEEP BEDEEEP-BEEP! She groaned and reached for it. The gothic text leapt out at her and she sighed. It was like the Brethren knew her every move.

Well done, daughter! We the Brethren are so proud that u have performed again this evening for yr adoring public! A very special parcel will arrive for u 2moro at the Xmas Hotel from Parcelforce. Before lunchtime they said. With all our luv.

Karla shook her head. Oh, why do I have to be involved with them? Will I never be able to escape their malign influence? Am I doomed forever to do the bidding of the Brethren?

And she knew, even as she asked these terrible questions in the echoing, friendless caverns of her own mind, what the answer was. She would never be free. Because of choices she had made a long, long time ago.

She deleted the text and put all the further questions it raised on hold. Right now she had better things to fret about.

She lay back on the continental quilt and watched Kevin return from preparing the sumptuous bathroom. Nervously he began to strip off his elfin disguise.

B&E in A&E

'They've been in there for ages. What time is it, Effie?'

'Hush now, Brenda.'

'I want to go in and see him. I want to know what's going on.'

Effie was almost overwhelmed by tiredness. She felt sorry for Brenda, but she wished she would stop mithering. 'You can't make it any easier for him. You can't help.'

Brenda had been pacing up and down the bleak waiting room for what seemed like hours. Weirdly, they were the only people waiting in A&E that night. This only added to their feeling of being abandoned and forgotten about.

Effie stopped herself reading all the posters about smoking and exercise yet again, and picked up a silly gossip magazine in order to distract herself. Her eyes were stinging with fatigue by now.

'I doubt that the doctors can do anything to help him.' Brenda sat down heavily beside her on one of the nasty plastic chairs. 'Oh, what do you think happened, Effie?'

'I don't know. He's old, isn't he? He's getting on.'

'We all are. He's only a little older than I am.'

Effie felt absurd suddenly. The two of them were sitting there in the strip-lit room in their finest evening wear. She spoke more gently to her friend. 'Men always go first. They wear themselves out.

They're not built like us women. Maybe he's just exerted himself too much in recent weeks.'

Brenda was in a strange mood, though. Shaking her head. Looking grim and resolved. 'I doubt it,' she said. 'There's more to this.'

Effie turned back to her magazine. A thought struck her. 'You were shouting out Karla's name, back at the hotel.'

'I was upset.'

'But you said you thought she was behind this.'

Brenda nodded slowly, trying to recall exactly what she was thinking during that moment of crisis. 'It seems absurd now . . . but, yes, I did. I do.'

Effie pursed her lips. 'What was Karla doing? She was just up on the stage, singing that terrible song.'

'But we've seen things, haven't we, Effie? We've seen some terrible things done in the most underhand of ways.'

'That's true. But why would Karla want to hurt Frank?'

Brenda was back up on her feet, pacing. 'She's staying at the Christmas Hotel. She must be in league with Mrs Claus.'

'Well, that does seem logical, I must say . . .'

'Oh, Effie, what are we going to do? What if the doctors open him up? And see what he looks like inside? What will they think?' Brenda looked stricken. Her friend's flinty heart went out to her. But Effie tried to stay sensible and pragmatic.

'He'll look like just anyone else inside, won't he?'

'More or less. But what about all the stitching and scars and—'

'There's nothing you can do about that. Sit still.'

There was a touch of panic about Brenda now. 'And what if they can't do anything for him at all? What if they can't revive him?'

'Now don't talk like that.'

'What if he's dead? After all this time? What if he's gone and left me?'

Effie put down her silly magazine and folded her hands neatly, thoughtfully on her lap. She said, 'I suppose this is how it happens. On what seems a day like any other. You begin the day together, very normally. You even squabble. You carry on as normal. But by the end of the day one of you is alone. And there's no going back. One of you has opted out of the game for ever and now they can never answer back. They've abandoned you . . .'

She stopped speaking. Brenda was sitting on her other side now, sobbing into her great big hands.

'He can't be dead. We were . . . we were just getting to know each other.'

Effie patted her ineffectually. 'Ah, Brenda. There, there, lovey.'

'It's true, you know,' Brenda said. 'All those years of moving from town to town. Decades of it. I wasn't just doing it on a whim. I wasn't just keeping a low profile from everyone else, from the human world. I was hiding from him, too. I was hiding from Frank. I knew he was after me. I knew he wanted to have me, for his bride.'

Effie tried to laugh. 'The human world! Really, Brenda. I don't know anyone who's more human than you are.'

'That's very nice of you to say so. But you know what I mean. For years, for decades, before I ever came to Whitby . . . I was so separate from the world. I had to hide my nature away. I didn't know what people would do if they knew my true story. My horrible origin.'

'I'm glad you came here. Where things are easier for you. You found your place in the world.'

'I certainly did. And so did Frank.'

Effie chuckled. 'You were right mithered when you first had an inkling that he was here, hot on your trail.'

'I was furious. I was terrified.'

'You thought it was all some plot to drive you out of your mind, to drive you out of town.' Effie shook her head, remembering events of just a year ago.

'And so it was, wasn't it? In a way. It was all down to that Mrs Claus. She cooked up the whole horrible reunion. Just mixing it. Causing chaos. That's what she likes to do, the old witch.'

Effie squawked. 'There's nothing wrong with witches, I'll have you know!'

'You know what I mean. Anyway, it rebounded on her, didn't it? She never expected Frank and me to get on.'

'He *did* try to kill you first, ducky. Remember?'

'No he didn't. That was my fault.' Brenda blew her nose explosively. 'When we had our reunion out on the sea front, on top of the cliff. He was trying to talk to me, but I was all upset. I kept hitting him. Then we both went over the edge of the cliff and into the sea.'

'Your fault!' Effie gasped. She'd been blaming Frank all these months for what befell Brenda on that awful night.

'I can have quite a temper on me, Effie.'

'I know! But I do think you might have said that you were the guilty party. I've been calling Frank worse than muck for dragging you to your demise that night.' Then another thought struck Effie. 'And so it was all down to you that the rest of us had to go down . . . to the whatsit, the underworld, through the Bitch's Maw, looking for you.'

'I reckon it was.' Brenda looked uncomfortable now. 'I thanked you at the time, though, didn't I? Anyway, then there was the wedding and everything and, even though I was being coerced into getting wed in order to save your life, and Robert's, I managed to see Frank for the decent man he is.'

Effie's eyebrows went up. 'Decent?'

'He is, Effie. He's a good man, really.'

Hmmm, Effie thought. Good, indeed. To her eyes he was a primitive. A rudimentary man. The vague approximation of a human being, thrown together by a lunatic. She looked at Brenda, thinking she would never understand her friend's feelings. 'You fell in love with him. Right there and then, on your wedding night?'

'I suppose I did.'

'While the rest of us were trying to rescue you! Before the whatsits, the nuptials went off.'

Brenda patted her friend's bony hand. 'I was still glad to be rescued and taken home.'

Effie whistled a low note of astonishment as she thought over their lives in recent years. 'We've seen some times, haven't we?'

'You can say that again. To hell and back.'

'We brought your fella out of hell. But we left mine down there still . . .'

Brenda glanced at Effie warily. The subject of Effie's man friend was usually taboo. 'You've seen or heard nothing more from him since then?'

'Of course not. Not since his fight with Frank.'

'Oh dear. I'm sorry about that. Who'd have thought our fellas would have fought like that?'

'They're sworn enemies, Brenda!' Effie rolled her eyes. 'They've always fought, every time they've met. They've fought for two hundred years or more.'

'I suppose you're right.'

Neither of them had noticed the white-coated young man who was standing beside them suddenly. 'Is it . . . Brenda?'

'That's right.' Brenda jumped out of her plastic chair.

'What is it, Doctor?' asked Effie.

The medic gazed at Brenda, his eyes full of concern. 'Your husband, Frank.'

'Is he out of danger?'

'Astonishingly, yes. He was catatonic when he arrived. He remained impervious to all our tests. The nurse broke several needles on him, hooking him up to the drip. To be honest, we haven't seen anything quite like your husband before.'

Brenda nodded. 'He's a one-off.'

'He's awake,' the young doctor said. 'He came to, only moments ago. He sat up on the bed like someone coming back from the dead. He pushed us all away. He hit one of my nurses. I think she might report him . . .'

'Where is he now?' asked Brenda urgently.

'He was asking for you. In a rather confused way. He's roaming about belligerently, looking for an exit. I must say, Mrs Brenda, this isn't what we're used to at Whitby General. Giving him the benefit of the doubt, he may be concussed. We need to get him calmed down and back to bed.'

Brenda and Effie looked at each other. He was roaming around? What kind of a state was he in? Brenda shook her head confusedly. 'Oh, Frank won't be told what to do . . .'

There came a series of terrible noises from behind the swing doors. Brenda recognised Frank's furious voice, roaring incoherently. Doors smashed and clattered. Female voices – nurses? – wailed in protest as he rampaged. There came the crash and tinkling of glass.

Effie jumped up, clasping her bag. 'If I'm not mistaken, here he comes now.' She still remembered what it was like, last time he'd had a turn like this. She had been manhandled by him. He had almost throttled her.

At that moment the swing doors flew open and Frank swayed into the waiting room. His face was snarled up in a rigid mask of fury. He growled like a beast at the sight of the women.

'Frank!' the young doctor shouted. 'Frank, stop that.'

Frank had picked up a waiting room chair and used it to smash the wall-mounted antiseptic gel dispenser. Green jelly went everywhere and Frank snarled in satisfaction.

Brenda stepped forward hesitantly. 'Frank, love. Come on. Calm down . . . it's me! Brenda!'

'Come out of the way, ducky,' Effie hissed, pulling at her arm. 'He's uncontrollable!'

But Brenda wasn't to be swayed. This was her man. He was suffering somehow. He simply must be, to revert to this terrible, primeval state. She stepped towards him and he gave a warning growl. Brenda cried out. 'What's the matter with him, Effie?' she hissed. 'It's like he's turned back into the savage brute he used to be.'

The medic courageously stepped between the women and the patient. 'Mr Frank! You must stop this at once!' He was rewarded for his efforts by a slap from the monster's pan-shovel hands.

'Get off him, Frank!' screeched Effie as Frank took hold of the doctor. He looked ready to rip him in two.

'Stop this!' shrieked Brenda. 'Oh, Frank – you'll have us all arrested!'

By now, other medical staff were arriving in the waiting room. But there was little they could do to stop him. They managed to bundle the young doctor away. They surrounded Frank. He swayed on the spot and threw back his head, crying out incoherently.

Then he formed the words: 'Where is she?'

Brenda stood before him. He was talking about her. He couldn't even see her in the midst of his terrible rage. 'Frank,' she said, walking towards him warily, keeping her voice soft, her movements slow.

Frank howled out again. 'Where is Frank's woman?'

Brenda spoke up. 'I'm here! I'm here, Frank!' Why couldn't he see her? 'Calm yourself down.'

'Frank wants his woman! Where is she?'

Was he blind? Had he really had something horrible in his eye, as Brenda had at first thought?

But no. His jade eyes were open. They were staring and glaring straight at her.

'Frank, it's me! Brenda! Stop this! I'm here!'

His face twisted with scorn, and took on an expression of utter disdain. An expression she had never seen him wear before. It cut her to the quick, even before he intoned his next terrible words: 'You are not woman. Frank doesn't want you.'

Brenda almost fell over in shock. 'What?'

He lurched towards her, preparing to push her aside. 'Out of Frank's way. You are monster. Frank wants woman.'

'Nooo!' Brenda crumbled. Effie watched her friend sink to the floor. She hurried to help her as Frank strode past them, through the waiting room.

'Leave him . . . come away, Brenda.' She guided her friend to a chair. 'He's gone berserk.'

Before he slammed out of the waiting room and the reception area, Frank roared again. It was a terrible, animalistic cry of desire. His words rang out under the bleak strip-lighting: 'Frank wants . . . *Karla*!'

Brenda lifted her head. Her face was wet with hot tears. 'What did he say, Effie? Did I hear right?'

There was another crash as Frank stormed through the automatic doors of A & E. Now he was out in the night and the staff were glad to see him go.

Brenda looked at Effie. 'Did he say what I thought he said?'

Effie's expression was very dark. 'I'm afraid he did, Brenda.'

Brenda broke down into hopeless sobs.

Parcel of Doom

Most mornings the Christmas Hotel required a separate visit from the post van. Stood to reason, really, with so many long-term residents of the elderly kind, with relatives scattered all over the country and wanting to stay in touch. Also, Mrs Claus tended to order in her supplies of festive decorations through the mail.

The post van would pull up at the back of the hotel on the Royal Crescent not long before eight most mornings. Bobby was their usual postman, a hirsute man in his forties who had been postie here almost all of his working life. He knew the staff at Mrs Claus's establishment and took it for granted now, when he heaved the sacks of mail into the building, that there'd be carols and tinsel and a general air of festivity. It gave him a boost, most mornings, all through the year, to get a little bit of Christmas at about ten to eight.

What he enjoyed most, though, was sitting in the main kitchen for five minutes, to have a cup of hot, strong coffee and a nibble on a fried egg sandwich. This was his routine, mostly unbroken, for years. The women in charge of the kitchens seemed to enjoy his company. Even the hard-working elves did. Certainly, Mrs Brick, the stooped and rather leathery head cook, liked to see him each morning. It was as if Bobby was bringing a little taste of the outside world into their existence. To him, it was as if the staff of the

Christmas Hotel existed inside a bubble, quite apart from the real world. A glass bauble – that was what it was. Shiny and glittering.

Today he was frozen when he came into the kitchen. Mrs Brick urged him to get his coffee down first, then come and sit by the range, before he told her all the gossip. First of all he told her how he'd had to make a big detour from his usual route around the eastern part of town. A whole street – Silver Street – had been roped off. At first he had assumed there'd been a ghastly accident. Or maybe a homicide or something. But then he saw the vans and the lights. They weren't the kind of thing police would use.

'What were it, then, Bobby?' Mrs Brick brought him his plate of egg sandwiches and he inhaled their heavenly scent with a grin.

'Film people!' he said. 'They've started work. They must have been up since the crack of dawn. I couldn't see many people about, or what they were doing, but they look ready to roll.'

Mrs Brick pulled a nasty face. 'I don't agree with it. Films like that. They're mucky films, aren't they? The ones that that floozy stars in.'

'Oh yes.' Bobby smiled happily. 'I've seen them all. Mucky as owt. She gets her whatsits out at every opportunity.'

Mrs Brick tutted. 'And to think – she's up there in our very best suite!' She lowered her voice. 'And word has it she's got her hands on one of our elves. He went up to give her something, and he's never been seen since.'

Bobby raised his eyebrows as he sank his teeth into the thick doorstop bread and the hot slippery egg. 'She's seduced an elf?'

'I'll say.' Mrs Brick tapped her nose. 'Awful business. Kevin it were. I'd have thought better of him.'

'I wonder if she'll be out on location today, then,' Bobby mused. 'She'll gather quite a crowd, I reckon, when Whitby wakes up and sees that they've starting shooting.'

'I don't like films much,' Mrs Brick sighed. 'Especially not that sort. All I need is my Bible to read at night. I don't need any other form of entertainment.'

Bobby nodded. Sometimes the old woman could be so boring. But it was worth keeping in with her, just for the breakfast baps. 'Speaking of Karla Sorenson,' he said, through a delicious mouthful, 'there's a parcel come for her. It's in my sack with the rest of the stuff. Here, pass it over . . .'

Mrs Brick did as he asked, a fastidious look on her face. The box was quite large, done up in old-fashioned brown paper and string. A label on its top said simply:

Ms Karla Sorenson
The Christmas Hotel
Whitby

'Heavy.' Mrs Brick frowned, looking at the parcel as if she could barely imagine what kind of obscene object it might contain. Bobby took it and shook it close to his ear, careful not to smear the paper with greasy finger marks.

'It rattles,' he said. 'It makes a strange kind of noise, if you put it up to your ear.' He held it up for Mrs Brick to listen to, which she did, briefly.

'I don't like it,' she said. 'Whatever's in it, it's . . . horrible.' She took an involuntary step backwards.

Bobby nodded. 'That was my feeling exactly. When I picked up the sacks this morning at the depot. They'd just come from the station. They were sitting there as usual. This was on the top, waiting for me, with the rest of the stuff. And it just seemed to be . . . emanating.'

'Emanating?' Mrs Brick rolled the word around in her mouth, as if she had never heard it before.

'Evil,' said Bobby. 'That's what it is. There's something evil inside of it.'

Mrs Brick jumped, realising that he had put the thing down on her scrubbed table. 'Get it off there. I don't want it in my kitchen. Take it to her. That devil woman in her turret! I don't want to know anything more about it.'

'Should I?' Bobby said wonderingly. Usually the hand delivery of individual letters and parcels within the hotel would be left to the elvish staff. But . . . this was a unique opportunity, wasn't it? This would never happen again. Not to Bobby.

Mrs Brick watched his eyes light up. 'I wouldn't go anywhere near that woman,' she warned. 'Look what happened when she lip-synched last night in the ballroom.'

Bobby blinked at her. He hadn't heard the tale yet. 'What?'

'Bloke had a funny turn. Big bloke. That Brenda's bloke. Had a seizure right there on the dance floor.'

'How could that be Karla's fault?' Bobby tried to laugh it off. But that was exactly the kind of thing that happened in the films Karla starred in. The vampire lady could cause all sorts of chaos with just one bat of her eyelashes. He picked up the parcel. 'Would anyone mind if I went up there? Gave it to her in person?'

Mrs Brick glared at him as he dabbed his napkin to his greasy lips. 'I'm warning you,' she whispered. 'Nothing good will come of this.'

Bobby shrugged and hurried out of the kitchen and into the interior of the hotel, keeping away from the public areas. For some reason he didn't want anyone to see him. What was he doing? Nothing illicit. If challenged, he could just say that he had instructions to deliver a precious cargo to Ms Sorenson herself.

Nothing dodgy about that. He paused by the back stairs and the staff lift, examining a diagram that would show him how to get to the suite in the turret. The fanciest set of rooms in the whole Christmas Hotel.

Bobby clutched the parcel nervously all the way up in the private lift. Checking himself out in the gilded mirrors. He was really going to see her. In the actual flesh.

When the doors opened, there was a young man standing there in a white bathrobe, looking rumpled and cross. Presumably Kevin. The postman calmed his nerves. Why was he so nervous? 'I-I've got a parcel I have to deliver to Ms Sorenson herself,' he stammered.

'You can give it to me,' Kevin said. 'I'll sign for it.'

'It has to be into her own hands.'

Kevin frowned. 'She's still in bed.'

Was it Bobby's imagination? The parcel seemed to . . . crackle under his palms. Maybe it was a static charge from the plush carpets. Or the string was twisting under his fingers. The box seemed to tingle urgently. Like a phone set to vibrate.

A voice – smoky, alluring – drifted into the hall from the next room. 'Oh, I'll sign it for him, Kevin, whatever it is. Is he sexy?'

Kevin looked him up and down. 'He's got a pretty big package with him, put it that way.'

Karla hooted with laughter. 'Then show him through!'

Bobby couldn't say a single thing in reply. His throat was jammed tight with fear. He took shambling footsteps down the opulent hallway, to the boudoir of . . .

Of *doom*, he thought. The Boudoir of Doom!

Now, why am I thinking that? They don't mean me any harm, do they? Surely not . . .

Penny's Qualms

Dear Mam,

You're going to think I've got myself involved with a right bunch here. I don't know if I dare tell you the kind of things that have been happening. Will you even believe me?

It's early morning at the Hotel Miramar. I'm due on duty in about an hour, and I've hardly slept at all. It's been a rough night and my head's spinning around with all this stuff. I've come for a sit outside, where it's bright and quiet and the sea air is fresh . . . I'm hoping it'll blow away some of the cobwebs. My head feels thick with them.

I feel like I'm in a fairy tale. It wouldn't be so bad, all the weird stuff that's been going on, if I hadn't seen the flying settee as well.

Oh, you'll think I'm rambling and making daft stuff up. But it's true, Mam! When I couldn't sleep in the middle of the night, I went to my bedroom window to look at the moon – full and huge over the headland. And I saw a settee floating about, rising above the rooftops of the town. Two figures were sitting on it, like it was the most normal thing in the world. It felt like a dream. It disappeared behind a bank of woolly purple cloud and for a moment I was wondering whether I had imagined it. I mean, a floating sofa?

Weirder things happen, I suppose. Especially here. Robert tells me things, a bit at a time, in small snippets, letting me into the secrets of him and his friends and their various adventures. It's like he's scared that if he tells me the whole lot at once, he'll lose my indulgence or attention.

I don't know if any of it is real or true, or what.

One thing's for certain, though. I saw it with my own eyes. That crystal droplet falling from the chandelier, and into Frank's eye. In the very second before his collapse. Funny, when I tried to tell them, they weren't listening. Too busy panicking. How come no one would listen and believe in me?

They expect me to believe in them. Going round saying the oddest things. Claiming that Brenda is over two hundred years old, and that Frank is even older. That Brenda has, in her attic above her B&B, a whole supply of spare limbs and organs for herself. Really! And she rotates them, when her old ones wear out. But how does she replace them? I mean, how? I asked Robert and he didn't know. He'd never thought about it, he said, he preferred not to. I mean, does she perform surgery on herself, or what?

It's true, though, that she's got these awful scars. When you get up close to her, you can see, just under her hairline, and under her chin. Her hands and wrists are criss-crossed by these crude zig-zags. I've not had a good look at Frank – I wouldn't want to get too close – but it looks as if he's the same. The pair of them – maybe they had some terrible car accident, once. Maybe they had horrible injuries. That would be the reasonable explanation.

But what Robert's been hinting . . . I just don't know. In a way, I want to believe it. I want to believe the supernatural stuff can be true. I mean, you know that, Mam, don't you? All my life, I've wanted to believe in magic. I want to know that impossible things can happen. The everyday world was never enough for me. All my childhood I read books where incredible things happened to ordinary people. Fantastic adventures and revelations.

And all the while, I was waiting for those things to happen to me. I kept on looking for Hyspero and Oz and Wonderland. I was looking in wardrobes and cupboards and holes in the ground, and even in the bins.

Nothing ever happened, though. I got to eighteen and school was over and I was just, like, ordinary and it was time to join what they laughingly call the adult world.

It was all such a disappointment.

You were always a pragmatist, Mam. I know you fretted about my unrealistic expectations of the world. But . . . it was because of you in the first place! You, Liz. You told me that I could do anything I wanted. There were no limits to what I should expect from the world. I could do magic, I really could, if I chose to. Was I daft for taking that at face value?

I really, really wanted magic to exist. For it to be alive in the world.

And if I'm honest with myself . . . I still think it is. It's why I'm here. I believed that from the first moment I got off the train that brought me here, over a month ago. I could smell it on the breezy air. I could taste it on the north wind. There was magic infusing the wet rocks of the harbour, the gnarled stone of the ancient buildings. A nonchalance about impossible events seems to run through the place, as if this town has borne witness to incredible things for a long, long time, and now no one hardly notices when they come to pass . . .

I knew it. I knew it from the first instant. And I wanted *in*. I wanted to *belong*.

Maybe now I'm not so sure. I've got qualms. Creepy qualms. With the strangeness, I can feel danger in the air, too. A sense that anything could happen here. I don't feel at all safe.

Sorry, I don't want to worry you. I really don't. I'm okay. I've just got a friend of a friend who reckons she's a zombie or something with spare body parts in her loft.

But I'd better get to work. The film crew are setting up on Silver Street this morning. Full English breakfasts all round to insulate them against the freezing cold. I've hardly noticed it, sitting out here.

Do you think I'm crazy? For believing it could all be true? The weirdo stuff that happens here? Maybe it was that funny film I watched the other night. Maybe I've been possessed by some eldritch spirit that was trapped on the disc . . .

Anyway – must sign off now!

Lots of love,

Penny

XX

Frank Adrift

He was homeless again. He knew this feeling well. Skulking about in the night. Moping about from one doorway to another. Hoping no one would see him as he snatched a few minutes resting here and there. He tried to go over what had happened that night. He tried to figure it out in his mind for himself. What was he doing out here, in the cold and the dark? He was supposed to live here now, in this town, wasn't he? Didn't he have a home here?

He couldn't think, though. For some reason, he couldn't think straight.

He went to look at the sea, as if its restless incoming tides would calm his mind. Down on the prom he slipped past the amusement arcades, all shuttered up for the night, and watched dawn breaking over the headland and the abbey.

He rubbed sleep out of his eyes. There was a deep, jagged pain in his left eye that made him gasp. There was something in it. He poked a blunt finger into his eye, rubbing and making it smart even more. He forced himself to stop.

He knew he was supposed to be going somewhere. Surely the idea hadn't been to stay out all night, freezing like this?

True, he had lived out of doors before. His fingers and toes had turned black with frostbite before. He had lost sensation in whole portions of his massive body, as he slept in bus shelters, doorways, anywhere he could find. He was used to living the hard life. Now he was worse off because a few months of comfortable living had spoiled him. He had grown used to a soft and pampered life, hadn't he? He was used to living with . . . with . . . that woman.

Why couldn't he remember that woman's name? What was happening to him?

He had had this before with his memory. Bits of it falling away, melting like a layer of ice into the deeper swirl of murky river beneath. Now, it seemed, his faulty mind was taking his most recent past away from him.

Brenda.

That was her name, wasn't it? Brenda, forgive me . . .

He wished he was there with her now. There, wherever she lived, and in the place she had made him feel so safe. This town was a small one, but as he looked back at the slate-blue rooftops, he knew he'd never be able to find which one was hers.

Frank was out in the wilderness again. He was drawn elsewhere.

But how? And by what? What had happened to him last night?

He walked some more, enjoying the exertion of hiking up the steep winding paths to the West Cliff. The cold winds buffeted him. The endless noise of the sea stirred his damaged senses. He felt like he was moving somewhere, in the right direction. He was moving towards where he needed to go.

And then he was faced by the immaculate prospect of the Christmas Hotel. Its vanilla and cream painted frontage looked welcoming. It was just starting to come to life for the day ahead, its grand chimneys smoking gently and the dull golden lights in the lower windows beckoning him onwards.

He was here, wasn't he? Last night? He remembered being here.

This was where he had fallen under a spell. A spell that still held him. Something still needed to be played out to its conclusion.

He stared up at the highest turret of the grand building. Up there. Waiting for him. She was up there, he knew.

Brenda? Was it?

Once, in a hotel very like this one, he and Brenda had had their brief honeymoon. He remembered. Last year. They had been in a suite in a turret just like this . . . but not here . . . He frowned deeply.

He didn't understand his own memories. Was it Brenda he was heading towards right now, as he strode across the grass and the wet tarmac of the road and stood before the grand entrance?

No. It wasn't Brenda.

Another woman was up there. And she was calling him on.

Ready for Work

That morning Karla had woken determined to work. She had reminded herself that this wasn't some holiday. If she was going to make a go of this movie, and actually produce something on screen she could be proud of, then she had better start getting her act together.

Even as her personal stylist Lisa fussed about her with the straighteners, Karla had her lap and dressing table full of photocopied pages. This was the shooting schedule, laying out in great detail everything to do with the crew's plans for the next few days. Karla squinted and gulped down scalding coffee, trying to work out when she was needed.

Her hairstylist wouldn't shut up. 'I was here once before,' she said, yanking away with the sizzling tongs. 'It's a very pleasant place to have a weekend break, is Whitby.'

Karla was also aware of her other members of staff – Kevin the elf and the newly recruited postie – hanging about in her suite. For a second she almost felt claustrophobic. Mrs Claustrophobic in the Christmas Hotel. But she batted the feeling away and gave her stylist a bright, showbizzy smile.

'There's no chance of me having a break,' she said, rattling the schedule and script pages. 'They don't want me on set until this evening, but after that it's pretty much constant until the end of the month.'

'Oh,' said Lisa, tugging on Karla's dry hair. 'Lovely. It's nice to keep busy, isn't it?'

Karla went back to studying her pages. Now she was looking at the plans for the final, climactic sequences. These would surely be the most arduous hours she would spend on this shoot, when they were filming up at the abbey. According to this, they were going ahead with their original promise and filming the finale on Hallowe'en itself. Hmm. She had to admit, it was a pretty good gimmick. Especially with that Gothic weekend thing that they held here each year. It was a way of grabbing a bit of publicity attention. That was something they could hardly do without. In the old days a new horror flick with Karla Sorenson never failed to draw the blood-hungry punters. Not any more. They would have to fight to get all the attention this film and its star deserved. Times had moved on, and they must prove themselves in a modern world and a market glutted by schlock. I have to prove, Karla smiled to herself, that I'm still the shlockiest of the lot.

But where's the director? she wondered crossly. He hadn't been to see her yet. She had seen him in London, of course, when they had signed and first talked about the project. She had hoped she would see a lot more of him, however. Right now he should be smarming and charming her and making sure she was as happy as can be.

But he wasn't.

Karla decided: her director needed to get over here and butter her up a bit more. 'Kevin,' she snapped at her day-dreaming elf. 'Get on to the reception desk. Ask them to contact my director. Tell him I'm not happy.'

As Kevin reached for the phone, Karla smiled at her stylist. 'So, you've been here before, have you, Lisa?'

The blonde, rather vapid girl nodded brightly. 'Couple of years ago. Work, mind you. I was doing the hair on a cable TV show. It was a kind of spook-hunting outfit.'

'Oh?' Karla was studying her own reflection critically. She had to admit, the girl was pretty good with her hair.

Lisa shuddered, going on. 'We were camped out all night in some old biddy's attic. Scared us half to death, the whole experience. Never again. I went to work in children's TV after that. And then ended up in films, and now here I am again.'

Karla nodded thoughtfully. 'Funny how these careers of ours go round in big circles. Look at me! Remaking the film that I made over forty years ago.'

They fell quiet for a while. It seemed that Kevin was having a struggle trying to get put through to the director. Perhaps I'm being subtly punished, Karla mused. Left to languish in my luxury suite while my director ignores me. Getting me seething mad and hanging on his every word. She had worked with a lot of directors in the past and she knew their conniving ways.

Now she was wishing that she had behaved herself a bit better. For example, why had she had a go at the producer over the script? That would have got back to the director by now, that Karla wasn't happy. She bit her lip. Why did I kick up a stink about it? Why didn't I just do what Flissy always says I should? The agent always knows best, Karla. Learn my lines, shut my gob until it's time to say them. Let the experts do their jobs. Maybe I was wrong to go kicking up a fuss soon as I got here.

Kevin broke into her reverie and she jumped.

'Ms Sorenson? Reception says there's . . . someone wanting to see you. Demanding to see you.'

Her heart rate sped. This was it! Her director had come running to see her. Running to check that she was doing all right. She blinked. 'What? Who is it, Kevin?'

'A . . . gentleman, they say.'

Another one! She looked round at her already quite busy boudoir. She glanced at the latest addition, Bobby the postie. She hadn't even opened that parcel yet. She knew who it was from, given the spiky handwriting on the label, and couldn't face opening it. What kind of horrible thing would they have sent her? Some nasty bouquet for her first day on set, no doubt. Good luck *fleurs du mal*.

Focus on the present, she commanded herself. Who is that battering at your door? Demanding access to your suite? Who's the new knight asking the princess if he can come into her tower?

'The gentleman's quite insistent. He says he knows you. He says you sent for him.'

'Really?' Karla frowned. 'Well, I sent for no one apart from my hair and make-up lady here. Is it my director, do you think?'

Kevin held the receiver away from his ear. 'Sounds like a kerfuffle going on down there.' He listened for a moment and added, 'He's on his way. I don't like the sound of him.'

Karla was intrigued. Someone was barging their way in. Who could it be? She found the idea rather provoking. This place was filling up. She smiled, waving her stylist and her tools away. It's like a party up here. Mrs Claus won't be pleased . . .

Mrs Claus Has a Funny Turn

Mrs Claus was well aware of the comings and goings around Karla's suite. Who does that woman think she is? she snarled to herself.

She sweetened her tone and called Michael, over in the old part of the town. He had a tiny flat above the Spector café, she had learned, not far from the abbey itself.

'Darling Michael. I wanted to thank you for being a wonderful dance partner and companion last night.'

'Oh, well, er . . . thank you, Mrs Claus.' He still sounded half asleep to her.

'Angela, please.'

She knew that Michael had only really been there last night in order to get a glimpse of Karla. His idol. Angela Claus was no fool. Of course he'd have gone nowhere near *her* had he the choice.

If only he could have seen me as I once was, she thought. Before I was trapped in this ungainly body. This horrible person I've become.

Before I got myself ensnared.

Before I became the person I had to be.

Mrs Claus felt herself sinking into a weird day-dream as she held the phone. Michael was still there at the other end, mouthing

144

pleasantries (yawning them, really) as he went about his early morning duties. But Mrs Claus was having a twinge of vertigo.

She was tumbling, stumbling into her own past. A rush of images flitted past her mind's eye. She saw herself being carried off on horseback. She was a young girl. Criminally young. Strapped to an ebony steed. She was in the clutches of . . . of the most devastating man she had ever seen. She was being driven off into the wilds of the night.

Why am I thinking of this now? When I've thought about none of it for so many years?

She made boring small talk with her new friend Michael, but inside she was churning with all the fear and pleasure of being seventy years younger. She could taste the bloody terror again, and the reeling bliss of falling under that enchantment.

What had brought this on?

She shook her head till her earrings tinkled. She seized control of her galloping thoughts and brought herself back to the present moment.

'Perhaps, darling,' she said, hearing herself sounding a lot less sure of herself than usual, 'you would consent to be my special friend some other time. I did so enjoy your conversation last night.'

On the end of the line Michael answered vaguely, 'Oh, oh, yes, sure . . .'

She finished the call.

Truth was, Michael hadn't said very much at all. In this call, or last night at the hotel. She felt that he had been cowed by her. Maybe he was scared of her, as so many people seemed to be. It wasn't easy, having the kind of powers that Angela Claus had at her disposal. People could be very wary of you. Powers like hers meant that no one would ever trust her. She could never really be close to anyone.

That was how it had been for so long. For decades. Ever since she had been a young girl.

Ever since she had run off with . . . *him.*

She could smell him now. His scent of sugar and cloves and patchouli. Nutmeg, cinnamon. Wild and spicy. Now she was back to that night again, when he was whisking her off on his huge black steed.

She shook her head. She shook it again.

This was madness.

This was her crazy past rising up to claim her once again.

Or was it because she was daring to hope? She was thinking about desire again. Like an old fool. Like an old monster. A slumbering troll. A dragon. Waking filled with hunger. With ravenous need. Desiring again – a man, a sprightly little man, all creamy flesh and dark-eyed. She fancied being fancied again. At her age! In her state! How ridiculous!

And as soon as she set her mind to fancying again, the past came up to grab her. This is where desire leads. It leads a merry dance and a winding path. It leads you to places you've never imagined. Is that where you want to be? Come along, come along . . .

No. Not any more.

There was work to be done. There was a hotel to run. It was Christmas morning. Again! Yet again! Bells to ring, guests to greet, elvish ears to box. Pull yourself together, Mrs Claus, she grumped at herself quite sternly.

It was then that one of the elves came by to tell her about Frank. He was back at the Christmas Hotel, and kicking up an unholy stink in reception.

Mrs Claus growled. 'Is it about his mysterious accident last night? He can't pin that on us! What's he after? Compensation?'

Her servant shook his head. 'He's demanding to see Karla.'

Mrs Claus shrugged dismissively. Karla could deal with Frank. She was so keen on having this procession of men at her door.

Mrs Claus's thoughts were elsewhere this morning.

Shooting on Silver Street

That morning, Brenda was far more cheery than Effie had expected to see her.

'Open up! Come on, Effie! We've got work to do!'

Perhaps it was a false, brittle kind of cheeriness. Perhaps Brenda was flinging herself at life in order to prevent herself from dwelling on the events of the previous night. Either way, Effie was pleased to hear her rattling at the front door of the antiques emporium and demanding to be let in.

'We've got to get to work. It's no good me moping about. Mooning about after Frank.'

'Where's he gone, then? Did he go to . . . her?'

They were sitting on high stools in Effie's galley kitchen at the back of the shop. Effie poured tea into cracked and dusty china, but Brenda didn't care. She was buzzing with plans and ideas.

'You said you went to the charity shop and bought more Karla Sorenson DVDs, didn't you?'

'Why, yes. But what's that got to do with anything?'

'We need to get that one from Penny, too. Robert put it away in his safe. We need to watch these dreadful films, Effie. I suggest we put aside some time this evening to do so.'

'I'm not watching them! I don't like things like that.'

'It's research. We need to know what we're up against.'

'Hold on. What are you saying?'

Brenda looked very serious all of a sudden, perched on one of Effie's kitchen stools. 'Karla is our enemy. She's taken Frank from me. She's up to something wicked here in Whitby. I just know it.'

Effie frowned. 'But she's just some old film actress! What can she do?'

'She's far more than that, Effie.' Brenda took a deep breath. 'You see, Karla is exactly what she appears to be in the movies.'

'A vamp?' squawked Effie. 'A vampire?'

'She has powers. Satanic influence over all and sundry. I've seen it before. Years ago. I was sent . . . to keep an eye on her. Back in the sixties. I watched her powers come to fruition . . . and people died, Effie. Karla is a conduit for the forces of evil. As soon as she appears and starts to act . . . that's when bad things start to happen.'

Effie tutted. 'She *would* have to come here, wouldn't she?'

'Exactly. She's been drawn here, to the Bitch's Maw. Isn't it true that they're going to film up at the abbey? On Hallowe'en? During Goth weekend?'

'You're right.'

'It's our job to stop anyone messing about with those powers, Effie.'

At that point Brenda explained that the film crew were working on Silver Street that morning, working with some of the minor characters. Karla herself wasn't yet on set.

'You've been up there already?' Effie asked.

'Checking it out. They've started work. I can't believe they'd even attempt to remake that film . . . after what happened last time. The deaths. The curse. But people's memories are short. They don't take things seriously enough. They don't listen to the warnings of those of us who managed to get away safely from that valley in Wales during the Summer of Love . . .'

Brenda trailed off, and it was as if her attention was subsumed by some horrible parade of memories.

'What happened, Brenda? You keep alluding to it, but . . .'

Brenda stirred herself out of her thoughts. 'They really did summon up dark forces. They really did capture them on film. Evil walked among us.'

'And that was in Wales!' Effie exclaimed. She helped herself to a Viscount biscuit and yanked off the green foil. 'Imagine what they can do here! At the very mouth of hell.'

'Exactly.' Brenda snatched up a minty biscuit for herself.

Effie looked rueful as she munched. 'Frank might have been useful to us. His strength and power.'

'We'll just have to set about this on our own. Rely on just ourselves. Brenda and Effie, together again!'

As they finished up their tea and Effie bustled around the tiny kitchen, Brenda found herself surmising that her Frank must somehow be vital to Karla's plans. If she really had gone to the trouble of drawing him away from Brenda, there must surely be some reason for it. Not just simple lust for a monster.

Her thoughts continued along these perplexing lines as she and Effie headed into the chilly morning. They toiled up the hill and through the winding lanes and soon found themselves at the corner of Silver Street. It was roped off, as if some ghastly crime had been perpetrated there. A gaggle of stragglers, tourists and shop people had gathered to watch the film crew going about their work. It seemed rather noisy, with a generator chugging away and someone shouting at the others, demanding silence – which suddenly fell.

Brenda and Effie pushed through the small crowd of onlookers and shimmied under the plastic tape.

At the centre of attention, further down the road, two young people in Goth dress were talking earnestly, as the rest of the crew gathered and hung on their every word. Microphone booms and cameras surrounded them as they exchanged a few terse words. It was a boy and a girl in their twenties being filmed and it seemed that they were two of the stars of the show. Should we recognise them? Brenda wondered, but she never recognised famous actors. These two were heavily disguised in their Goth get-ups anyway.

The crew were going for another take as Brenda and Effie quietly approached. A man they took to be the director – stocky and fair-haired – was berating everyone for their lack of concentration. 'I know it's early! I know it's cold! Can we get a little bit of focus here, people?'

'But Alex,' the Goth boy said, breaking out of character for a whinge, 'isn't this supposed to be a night-time scene?'

'Filters!' shouted the director furiously. 'Day-for-night! We can't do all the night stuff actually *at* night! Are you *crazy*?' He tossed his shaggy head. Someone waved a clapperboard and shouted out, 'Take Three!'

At that moment Brenda noticed the director's name chalked on the slate, and she gave a sharp intake of breath. Effie glanced at her, 'What is it?'

'His name,' Brenda said in a strangulated tone. 'Alex Soames. The director is Alex Soames!'

The man in question gave a cry of exasperation. He whirled to see the two women standing a yard or two away from him. He shouted at the sound man, 'Did you get them? Those two old bags?'

'Yep!'

The director bellowed at Brenda and Effie: 'Get back! Get behind the barrier! You can watch but don't get any closer! Go away!'

Brenda and Effie ignored him. Effie was asking her friend, 'So? Who's he when he's at home?'

Brenda lowered her voice, narrowing her eyes at the furious man. 'It's not who *he* is, so much as who *his father* was.'

Effie tossed her head. 'Yes, I've heard that showbusiness is like that. It's not what you know, it's *who* you know . . .'

Brenda's expression was very grim. 'His father was Fox Soames. His mother was Magda Soames. Fox was the author of the novel and the screenplay of *Get Thee Inside Me, Satan*. He was there on location in the quarry in Wales. They were both there. This fella's parents.'

'It's a family affair, then,' said Effie.

'Magda died tragically during the filming,' Brenda said. 'She was the first of the people connected with the movie to die.'

'And Fox?'

'He survived. For a while. But he was never the same again. He was a horrible man. Evil.'

'And now the son is following in Daddy's footsteps,' Effie mused. 'And even remaking the same film. I wonder why. Eeh up. He's coming over. He looks wild, doesn't he!'

'Absolutely livid!' Brenda gave a jolt of surprise. 'He was there too! He was a toddler. I remember thinking at the time, how awful that his parents brought him to the film set of a horror movie. It could have scarred him for life.'

'Perhaps it did . . .'

Now Alex Soames was before them, confronting them, his face contorted with barely repressed anger. 'You can't come this close. You're ruining our shoot.'

'It's a free country,' Effie said with asperity. 'We can go where we like. My friend and I stroll here almost every morning together. The bakery's up this way.'

'Today you'll have to go round,' the director snapped. 'We're making a very important film.'

'Pah,' said Effie.

'Alex?' Brenda said. 'Little Alex? Do you remember me, hm?'

He stared at her. 'What?' Clearly he thought she was mad.

'Auntie Brenda? That's me! You remember, surely, Alex?'

Brenda saw at once that he did.

Open the Box

By now Karla had so many fellas she hardly knew what to do with them.

It put her in a good mood. It was like the old days. Back then, when she turned up on location, or anywhere, she would always accrue this kind of doe-eyed entourage, seemingly from nowhere. Blokes would fall under her spell. This morning she was delighted to find that nothing much had changed in that regard. They sat around her, waiting for instructions.

But this one was different. Here was Frank. Standing before her, swaying with fatigue. His eyes were dark and confused. He was crazy-looking. She stared at him as he stood, submitting to her inspection.

Karla had never seen anything like him before.

'Can it really be true?' she whispered. 'Are you really what they say you are, Frank?'

She was aware of the others watching her as she went over her new prize. They were envious, Kevin and Bobby. Karla's attentions were so fleeting, and so easily pulled elsewhere.

But this was different. She had never seen anyone like Frank before. She had heard rumours over the years. She had heard the stories. But here he was now, in the unhealthy-looking flesh.

Standing to attention. Giving his whole self to her.

'Frank wants to serve you, Karla,' he said. 'Frank has come here just for you.'

'But . . . what will your Brenda say?'

A flicker of dismay crossed his face. 'W-who?' he said.

Karla was thrilled. 'Just wait till Mrs Claus hears about this! Won't she be amazed?'

Where was she going to put them all, though?

Kevin brought her the phone just then.

'It's the director's PA. Making a dinner appointment for tonight. Eight p.m. at Casa Diodati. Is that all right for you?'

'Why's he put his PA on?' Karla huffed. 'Shouldn't he be calling in person?'

'They've got a situation on location in Silver Street apparently,' Kevin explained. 'They've got some of the local ratbags protesting.'

Karla chortled with glee. 'It'll be religious nuts, objecting to the subject-matter again. Well, wait till I start doing *my* scenes! I'll give them what for! And yes, that's fine for dinner this evening.'

That sorted, Karla turned to more immediate matters.

'Kevin, Bobby . . . I need some time alone with Frank. You understand, don't you, boys?'

From the looks on their faces, it was clear that they didn't.

Karla brushed aside their hurt expressions and opened a door that stood to one side of the opulent en suite. She flung it open unceremoniously and waved them through.

'You're sending us away, Ms Sorenson?' Bobby the postie looked bereft already.

'Only for an hour or two. While Frank and I get better acquainted.' She smiled, but her voice gave a telltale tremble. There was something about that gigantic man that made her feel curiously weak.

'It's a beautiful attic up there,' she said. 'Under the very highest eaves of the Christmas Hotel. It's sumptuously done out. I had a look earlier. It's just another part of this fabulous suite.'

Bobby and Kevin looked at her with misery in their eyes. She marvelled at herself. What power she had over these men.

'Go on, boys. It's just too crowded in here right now. And Mama's got a lot of work on, as you know. They're sending over the new script pages today. I have to start learning, and you boys can't help with that. So why don't you be good and go up to your attic room and just wait for me to need you?'

They would obey her in the end. She knew that. They were completely subsumed by her arcane powers. Even if she didn't know how it worked, Karla was confident in her ability to twist men round to do exactly what she wanted. She watched the elf and the postman troop through the attic door and up the stairs, where they would wait until she had need of them.

She clicked the door shut and turned the key in the lock as quietly as she could.

I've got fellas in the attic, she thought giddily.

Then she turned to see that Frank had moved.

He was over by the dressing table, which was in messy disarray from the protracted business of Karla's toilette. She watched him as he picked up the brown paper package that Bobby had delivered to her in person early this morning. All of his attention was on the parcel. His expression was very troubled as he lifted the box up to his ear and shook it, and listened.

He saw that Karla was watching him. 'What is in this thing?'

She shrugged. 'I've no idea. Why?'

'Frank wants to know. Frank can . . . smell something.'

156

Karla frowned. 'Smell something? In my suite?' All she could smell was her perfume, specially mixed for her, and something that Frank oughtn't to be turning his nose up at.

He still looked perplexed as he turned the box over. More than perplexed. Disturbed. And he had lost all interest in Karla, it seemed, in favour of the parcel.

'If it means that much to you, then open it,' she sighed, fluffing up her new coiffure, and catching sight of herself in the dressing table mirror. That girl Lisa had done an excellent job.

Frank grinned at her. A ghoulish grin, revealing the worn stumps of his teeth. He wrestled with the hairy string and ripped at the brown paper, revealing a cardboard box inside. He yanked roughly and tore into it.

'Careful!' Karla said. 'You'll have it all over—'

Which was exactly what happened.

The contents of the well-protected box flew across the room. In his over-keenness, Frank scattered it through the air.

A fine powder landed on the carpet, the bed, the dressing table, and Karla herself. She felt granules spattering on to her hairspray-sticky hair and she screamed. Bigger bits were strewn across the room as well, landing with a series of muffled thumps.

Frank looked stunned at the result of his foolish mistake, his dreadful clumsiness. He stood there clutching the empty, ripped-up box. He didn't know his own strength, the fool. Karla almost laughed at his stupid expression as he peered into the empty wrappings. But she didn't laugh. She was much too appalled.

'What have you done?' she cried. 'It's everywhere! My hair's ruined . . .'

He looked like he was going to cry. He visibly cringed under her tongue-lashing. Then he found a small square of card at the bottom of the box. Exquisite handwriting. He passed it to Karla, who snatched it crossly.

Our dear daughter . . .

Please find preserved within this parcel some very precious remains. The Brethren have had the special care of these priceless revenants for many years. These are among our holiest of unholies and we send them to U for a very special reason. These ashes and charred bones must B given new life. The mortal man they once belonged 2 must walk again. U will bring flesh and blood back 2 his old bones. We have faith in U Karla. U will make the Creator live once more!!

With all our love,

The Brethren

XXXXX

Karla looked up from the note and back at Frank. Then she stared at the suite all around her. Every single surface was coated in the horrible grey powder. Bigger, knobbly chunks of bonelike matter were scattered willy-nilly.

She swallowed hard. Her throat was rather dry.

Karla wasn't one to mope. She wouldn't sink in despair. She had a task to get on with. She had to think of a solution. She could bollock Frank later. But for now . . .

'We need a Dyson,' she told him. 'Quickly!'

Alex Soames Grown Up

Little Alex had grown up. Brenda looked at this red-faced middle-aged man before them, and could hardly credit it. She remembered him as a toddler, sitting quietly in the back of her mushy-peas-and-deep-fried-chips-scented caravan in North Wales. The poor mite had stared up into her massive face. He had clutched her fingers, completely unaware of the maelstrom of disaster and upset that was swirling around that deep slate valley.

His mother had perished that evening, and the child had been shoved into Brenda's arms for safe-keeping. Brenda remembered that his face had been as red and harried as it was now. She had never looked after a child before. In almost two centuries of life, no one had ever trusted her to babysit their offspring. Then, as the valley rang with crying, shouting, the panicky revving of engines, she had felt a powerful maternal rush of adrenalin going through her. She felt like running away at once. Stashing him safely under the counter, jamming the doors and windows closed, gunning the engine of her dinner-lady's van, and dashing away with him for ever.

His parents didn't deserve him, did they? Fancy bringing a child as young as he was to an environment like this. It wasn't just the inhospitality of the valley, it was the rest of it. The location's atmosphere was stiff with occult menace. The child's father was clearly carrying on an affair with the leading lady. The child's mother was going off her head on a cocktail of booze and pills and stinky French fags. She had been wandering around the site at God knows what time in the early hours when she had come a cropper. The crew was quite used to seeing the superfluous Magda Soames in her ratty fur coat and her jet-black hair, clutching a tumbler of vodka and screaming curses at her wayward husband. She had interrupted filming a number of times with her drunken antics. Once she had even slapped Karla in the face as the actress emerged from her meditation caravan to start the day's filming. But now Magda was dead. She had taken a tumble from the highest rocks above, having missed her footing on a late-night ramble. She interrupted filming yet again, with her mortal remains making a mess of the valley floor.

Brenda hid away in the back of her van with the child. She hoped fiercely that he would remain unaware of what had gone on that day. If she thought about it too much, she couldn't bear it. Magda had been a strange woman. Rather shrewish and nasty-tempered. She had treated Brenda and the other members of the crew as servants. But she hadn't deserved to slip and plummet to her death on those damp blue rocks. No one deserved that. What would become of her young son? The father, Fox, was no good. He was too busy running after that trollop Karla. What would become of the poor mite? Nannies, public school. He'd never know that once he'd had a mother who'd loved him. Brenda clutched the kid to her and wept for him, and for the love that he'd been robbed of. What kind of a person would he turn out to be without it?

Well, now she knew. Now she was seeing it for herself. Here he stood.

Alex Soames in middle age, piqued and confused by Brenda and

Effie's presence as he tried to work, to create cinema magic, all these years later, in a back street in Whitby.

'Maybe you won't remember me?' she found herself saying, though she knew that wasn't true. She could see it in his face, the way he looked at her, as if he was peering through fog. He knew who she was.

'Auntie Brenda!'

Effie was looking from one to the other, amazed.

'You were just a toddler,' Brenda laughed.

'But I wasn't later on,' Alex said. His voice was gentle now. He lowered it and turned his back on his impatient cast members and crew. He was earnest, beseeching, staring up into Brenda's face. 'Later. When I was at school. You came to see me, didn't you? Checking on me.'

Her expression brightened. 'You remember?'

'You sent me birthday cards. Presents!'

'Did I?' Her memory was so patchy. She was glad to hear that she had tried to keep up with him, this child who had been flung into her care, if only for a couple of hours.

'You came to see me at school. For a while you lived nearby. You were a cleaner . . .'

Brenda couldn't remember this. Some of the seventies was a closed book to her, for a variety of reasons.

'You've grown up,' she said, switching her attention back to him. 'You're a . . . movie director.'

He pulled a face. 'If you can call it that. Low-budget straight-to-DVD tacky horror films.'

'But you're a success. A brilliant success.'

He shrugged, looking embarrassed.

'Oh, this is my friend Effie. She lives in Whitby too.'

'Good morning, young man.'

Alex shook Effie's hand, very politely. Nicely brought up. Brenda smiled approvingly. He seemed to be undamaged from having grown up without a mum, and with a father who surrounded himself with flighty actresses and black magic lore.

'I'm afraid I have to go back to work, Auntie Brenda,' he said, wincing. 'The crew is waiting for me. We have to get a few shots in the can before—'

'Shots in the can!' Brenda grinned. 'He knows all the lingo, doesn't he?'

Effie nodded stiffly. She put in, 'So you are responsible, are you, Mr Soames, for the remaking of this film?'

'It's a job, isn't it?' He shrugged. 'It wasn't my idea, no. But I just take whatever comes up.' He cast a worried glance at his impatient crew. 'I can meet you later, Auntie Brenda. Just now I need to . . .'

Brenda was frowning. 'But Alex, don't you worry about the bad luck attached to the original film? Don't you think you might be,' she dropped her tone, 'tempting fate?'

He laughed. 'What . . . *the curse?*'

Brenda couldn't believe he was scoffing at her. 'Your father! The original film . . . and Karla! Your mother! Everything! Just look – hardly anyone from the film is still alive. They all died in grisly ways . . . and bad things even happen to people who simply *watch* the damned thing.'

Alex suddenly looked furious. He drew closer to Brenda and hissed: 'Don't go spreading stuff like that, okay? If my crew start getting cold feet and jumpy, then we're knackered.'

'If there *is* a curse,' said Effie drily, 'then you're *knackered* – as you so quaintly put it – anyway.'

'There's no curse,' Alex snapped. 'That's just publicity rubbish.

What better way to get attention for a rubbishy horror flick? Don't you worry about it, Auntie Brenda. There's no such thing as real magic or any of that gubbins. We'll be all right.'

With that, he kissed Brenda swiftly on the cheek and hurried away, to carry on with his work.

'Oh dear,' Brenda said quietly. 'He doesn't know what he's getting into, does he?'

'Hmpf,' said Effie. 'Youth.'

Fellas in the Attic

So far Frank wasn't doing that well.

Within two minutes of arriving at the suite of Karla Sorenson, having pledged his undying devotion to her, he had disgraced himself. Right now, several hours later, she was still furious with him. There was a taut silence in the luxurious turret as Karla applied herself to learning her lines.

Frank had offered to help with brushing and scooping up that strange dust from the parcel he had burst and strewn everywhere, but Karla had waved him crossly away. 'Oh, you'll just make it worse, you clumsy oaf.' Instead she had called on Mrs Claus's willing staff of elves to bring a powerful hoover and to set about gathering up every scrap of alien matter from the carpet, the bed sheets and her own person.

'But what is it? Why is this powdery stuff so important?' Frank beseeched her.

She looked furious with him. 'I don't know. But the Brethren say that it's very precious indeed. And now I've got it all in my fricking hair.'

She had stomped off to the bathroom to wash it out, ruining her new style, of course. She sieved out the dust and chunks of grit using a pair of tights.

'I think we've got most of the bits,' she said worriedly, watching the helpful elves empty the Dyson cylinder into the crystal fruit bowl, where she was gathering all the vital granules. 'We must have lost some. There seems to be less, somehow. What do you think, Frank?'

'Frank doesn't know,' he said huffily. He was more concerned about the weird feeling that the powdery substance was giving him. Like it was poisonous somehow. Noxious. Could it be radioactive? Was that what made him shiver inside his oversized clothes and boots? His very scalp tingled. The bolts in his neck seemed to bristle and click with static electricity.

And all because of the contents of the parcel that Karla had been so keen to salvage.

Now the precious dust was heaped in the bowl, pride of place on the coffee table in Karla's suite. Karla was curled on the sofa, flicking through her script and frowning as she strove to commit her lines to memory. Frank was at a loose end, and in disgrace. Karla hadn't said anything to him for hours. Was this what slavish devotion was meant to feel like?

Glumly he stared out of the turret window, studying the swelling sea and the few brave souls walking on the stormy prom.

Brenda. That was who he was missing. His brain had jolted back into action suddenly. It was like sobering up. Suddenly he remembered his wife and his home. He remembered that he shouldn't be here, with this bad-tempered woman. He didn't belong to her. What would Brenda think?

He had spent so long trying to get back to Brenda, and now he had flung it all away. In just one night and one day it was all gone. The future he had imagined. He had been lured by the charms of Karla. Just like those two men she had sent up to the attic.

'Oh, Frank,' she said, making him jump. An elf had arrived with a large covered tray of food. 'I've had some sandwiches brought for the fellas in my attic, Kevin and Bobby. Would you mind carrying the tray up to them?'

He was glad of something to do, even if she had started to treat him like the home help. He sighed. 'Club sandwiches. Very good. Is there a sandwich for Frank too?' His stomach growled savagely as he spoke, and he realised that he had eaten nothing all day.

'Of course.' Karla nodded. 'Now, I'd like you to eat up in the attic with the other two, if you don't mind. I'll lock the three of you in there, for the rest of the day and the evening and overnight, while I go out for dinner with my director.'

Frank baulked. 'What?'

Karla held up her hands to placate him. 'Just a precautionary measure, Frank. You three are my boys. My special boys. I am here to protect you. I don't want anything bad to happen to you, so I am putting you up in the attic, where you will have everything you need.'

'Frank doesn't need protecting.'

Her expression darkened. 'Strange things are coming, Frank. You don't understand. You are very vulnerable.'

'Frank? Vulnerable?' he boomed.

Karla's eyes narrowed. 'Indeed. You think you are invincible. But all you have is brute strength. That's not enough for the powers massing about Whitby. Oh no. You came here seeking my protection. And this is how I extend it. You will join the others in the attic, Frank. And sit there and wait until I have need of you.'

Frank glowered at her. What was he doing? He didn't have to listen to her. He didn't have to obey. And yet . . . he couldn't help himself. He was grateful to her. She knew what she was talking about. She knew how to keep him safe. And she was only doing it out of love. He could see that.

He took the tray and hefted it in his arms, turning to the doorway and the ladder up to the attic.

'You'll see it makes sense, Frank.' She smiled at him.

To Frank, as he heaved himself up the wooden steps, it made very little sense at all. He just had to listen to her voice and do everything she said, and everything would be all right. He just had to trust that she knew the right thing to do. He jumped as the door behind him slammed and she hurriedly turned the chunky key in the lock.

Downstairs, Karla was glad to have him out of her sight for a while. The way he looked at her! Like a giant puppy.

As she returned to her script, her mobile trembled and bleeped. She sighed. Them again. Another message.

Darling daughter. We assume the parcel arrived with u safely. The precious contents must b treated in the correct manner. U need the blood of the man-monster. Only that will work. Do u understand? We cannot say 2 much by text. Just a pint of his blood will do, stirred in2 the remains, then leave it in the moonlight and u will c.

Oh, great. Karla deleted the message crossly. Now they were wanting her to do some fricking voodoo thing. Well, she'd done this kind of thing before at their request, and it always went to the bad. Why couldn't someone else do their will?

She looked at the grey mess in the crystal fruit bowl and shuddered. So what exactly *was* this stuff?

And more to the point, *who* was it?

It's Only a Movie

Back in her attic rooms that evening, Brenda was holding up a certain shiny disc, saying: 'I didn't think Robert was going to give us this, did you?'

'You never saw the state that poor girl Penny got herself into after she watched that bally thing.' Effie's expression was unfathomable. 'I did. I saw her face. I was the one who brought her back to life.'

'Well, we're hardier than that, aren't we? We don't scare easily.' Brenda bit her lower lip as she squinted at the controls of her DVD player.

'That's true enough. But I don't like anything vulgar.'

Brenda had put on a light buffet-style supper for them both, so they could nibble as they examined the evidence.

Despite the nature of the viewing material they had selected for that evening, Effie was glad to spend some time with her best friend alone. For ages now, it seemed that whenever they got together, a gaggle of other people were orbiting too. Tonight it would be just like it used to be.

'That was a turn-up for the books, wasn't it?' She smiled, sinking into the paisley two-seater. She had loaded up her plate with chicken legs and coleslaw and mixed bean salad, and they were settling to watch *Prehysteria!*.

'Hmm, lovey?' Brenda was reading the box. It was some kind of dinosaur movie, it seemed, starring Karla Sorenson and a tribe of primitive females dressed in skins.

'Your friend Alex turning out to be the director.'

'There are no coincidences, Effie,' Brenda said darkly. 'Not in an affair like this.'

'How do you mean?'

'We are being drawn into this together. Nothing is happening by accident. Someone, somewhere is moving us about like chess pieces on a board.'

'Who, though, ducky?' Effie sounded alarmed. 'That Karla woman?'

Brenda pulled a face.

They watched the first film, crunching and munching their way through the salads Brenda had so lovingly tossed together. (Eating healthily! Effie thought. If we keep this up, we'll be all slim and lovely for the winter holiday period. We should go on a cruise!)

The film was awful. It all took place on what was obviously a studio set. The caves that the women inhabited looked plasticky and terrible. The dinosaurs – when they eventually made an appearance – seemed to be made out of old socks and papier-mâché. Brenda laughed ('That cave woman is the *spit* of Jessie!'), but Effie merely rolled her eyes. 'Do we have to watch this rubbish?'

'We're learning about Karla,' Brenda said, becoming particularly alert when Karla's character – the rebellious cavewoman Urtaka – made her appearances.

'But the film's got no dialogue,' Effie moaned. 'It's all grunting.'

'Robert would have enjoyed this.' Brenda smiled. 'He likes a nice tacky B movie.'

Effie bristled. 'Well then maybe you should have asked him instead of me.'

Brenda didn't say anything. Robert had merely acquiesced – eventually – to their request to borrow Penny's DVD of the original *Get Thee Inside Me, Satan*. He had been worried about them viewing it – but only in a distracted way. His mind was on other things, Brenda realised, as he led them into his office and fetched the disc out of his safe. She even asked him, 'Are you worried about work, Robert?' He shook his head briskly. 'No, that's all fine.' But there was still clearly something that had him foxed.

They didn't get very much out of *Prehysteria!*. As Effie changed the discs, Brenda went to fetch the cheesecake out of the fridge. She cut it into dainty slices and dolloped it with double cream.

'It was an impulse, buying these silly things from Save the Kiddies,' said Effie.

'Know your enemy.' Brenda nodded approvingly. 'You were right to.'

Carnival of Flesh was a little more illuminating. In this early seventies picture, Karla was playing her more usual lady vampire character, and arriving in a backwoods town at the head of a bizarre freak-show-cum-circus. Entertaining the lowly superstitious villagers and striding about in a succession of alluring outfits, she was on top form in this particular show.

'It's got more of a story, this one.' Brenda nodded, forking up her cheesecake. 'Says on the back of the box it's a classic of its type.'

Effie was pursing her lips. 'I think it's bally awful. And the woman can't act for toffee.'

There Brenda had to disagree. She thought Karla was pretty good at what she did. It was a kind of stylised performance. Sheer camp, she supposed. Karla was larger in gesture and vocalisation than every other character on the screen

Both ladies were a bit surprised when the sexy scenes started up. 'Goodness!' Brenda said.

'Brenda!' Effie cried out. 'I had no idea it was as rude as this!' (What were Save the Kiddies doing, offering this kind of nasty smut for sale?)

Karla's character was a woman bent on wholesale corruption of every man and woman in this backwoods village. One by one she seduced them, ripped out their throats and – as a nice extra touch – ate an eyeball or two as if they were pimento olives.

'Why would they even *make* films like this?' Effie said, hiding behind a tassled cushion. 'It's not very true to life, is it?'

Brenda did a kind of facial shrug. Some of the places she'd been in her long life, this was social realism.

They discovered the DVD extras. ('Oh no! There's more? Haven't we seen enough?' The very concept of DVD extras was a new one on Effie.) Besides some rubbishy out-takes and extra scenes, there was an interview with Karla, from the time of the making of the movie, summer 1970. She was wearing chunky curlers and a bathrobe and was sitting in her trailer looking worn out and sounding stiffly polite. To Karla's bored bemusement, the interviewer was trying to get her to articulate why exactly she thought her movies were popular.

'People enjoy the thrill of being scared and seduced, don't they?' she said. 'And I suppose I embody both things. I am one of the few stars of these kind of fantasy movies who could thrill you both ways. In terms of fear and in terms of sex appeal.' The 1970s interviewer – comb-over and leather sports coat – nodded energetically at this.

Effie snorted. 'She thinks a lot of herself, doesn't she? When was this? Nineteen seventy? Why, she looks about the same age then as she does now, doesn't she, ducky?'

Brenda shushed her. She had a feeling that Karla was on the verge of laying herself bare – even more than she already had in the movie itself – and Brenda was going to learn something vital, she just knew it.

The questioner had mumbled something else; Brenda had missed it. Something about a then relatively recent movie. There had been scandal and controversy.

'There is always scandal for my pictures,' Karla said. 'They thrive on it.'

'Yes, but this was a different kind of scandal. Some say that *Get Thee Inside Me, Satan* was doomed from the outset. Even before the tragic death of Magda Soames, or Fox Soames, or the director or the producer or anyone else.'

Karla's eyes widened slightly. The pulse in her delectable throat quickened. Even through the poor quality of the ancient film, it was possible to see that the actress was fighting her true feelings down. 'It is true. Quite true. We were lucky to get out of that valley in Wales alive, the majority of us. But I feel that the . . . evil tendrils of that movie . . . the wickedness that swirled about us the whole time . . . it will never let us go. Does that sound melodramatic?'

'It sounds like you're building up the hype,' chuckled the interviewer.

'No,' Karla snapped. 'I am not. That film has been banned, has it not? After people died at late-night showings. After further deaths. I tell you, that film is cursed. It is pure evil, distilled on to celluloid. It should never have been made. And now, luckily, three years on, it is no more, I hope. The company is trying to recall all copies, so they can be buried safely, away from the viewing public.'

'An overreaction, surely,' the interviewer said. 'Are you certain this isn't about garnering yet more publicity?'

Karla looked very pale. 'You weren't there in that valley. No one who was there will ever forget it.'

The interview segment cut off abruptly, sending them back to the lurid animated menu. Brenda was quite still when Effie turned to look at her.

'Hecate!' Effie exclaimed. 'I believed her. She certainly looked like she meant what she was saying. She isn't *that* good an actress!'

Brenda looked bleak. 'I wish I could remember more. I was there . . . I remember things happening. Looking after Alex. Hiding in my dinner-lady caravan. I remember that night with the lightning and the noise . . . like the valley floor itself was cracking open and . . . I don't know! I can't recall the rest!'

'Knowing you,' Effie smirked, 'I can't believe that you would have just hidden away in your caravan. You'd have been out there in the thick of it.'

'I wish my memory worked better,' Brenda sighed. She went over to the DVD player. 'Well, that was a bit more interesting.'

'Hmmmm . . . The way she talked about the curse and all,' Effie mused. 'She looked genuinely fearful, didn't she?'

'That was just a few years after making it,' Brenda pointed out. 'It was still fresh in her mind. What is it now, forty years? The fear must have faded. Or she must be more desperate. More hard-up, perhaps. Maybe she's forgotten, too, just how bad it was that night in North Wales. Or maybe . . .' She tailed off, picking up the disc that they had borrowed from Robert's safe.

'Yes?' prompted Effie.

'Maybe she's being coerced into taking part in this remake,' said Brenda. 'Maybe she's being moved about the chessboard like the rest of us, and is in charge of her own destiny about as much as we are.'

Effie was eyeing the disc of *Get Thee Inside Me, Satan* as Brenda shunted it into the machine. 'Are you sure you're wanting to watch this now?'

'I think we have to. If we are to understand . . .'

'Maybe we should wait until daytime,' Effie said. 'We'd be less tired. We could concentrate better.'

Brenda shook her head. 'I want to know what it's all about. Tonight. This film that shouldn't even exist on disc. We have to find out, Effie. We must be brave.'

Effie smiled wanly. 'Shall I make some tea first, before you start it up?'

Brenda nodded. 'Spicy tea, please, Effie.'

To Effie's eyes, Brenda looked haggard and drawn. She was fretting over Frank, of course. Neither of them had mentioned Brenda's wandering husband all night. Effie had tactfully avoided the subject. But he was never far from Brenda's mind, she could tell. She mulled it all over as she dug around in Brenda's cupboards for the aromatic tea she favoured. One thing Effie was sure of. That brute didn't deserve a woman like Brenda.

Casa Diodati

Karla's dinner with her director was at an upmarket hotel across the harbour on the eastern side of town. Casa Diodati's discreet entrance was hidden in an alleyway. Very exclusive. Karla was delighted to have a car sent for her, and to be delivered to the upper restaurant, which was tasteful in dove-grey and magenta plush.

Now she was gazing out at the whole of the town. From here she could see the West Cliff and her turret at the Christmas Hotel. There she could make out a chink of light that she knew was her attic.

Alex handed her the menu.

The two of them were hardly aware of the waiting staff. There didn't seem to be any other punters. This was a private dining room for the star.

She surveyed her director. His wavy, slightly fluffed fair hair. The incipient corpulence. The edge of nervousness about him as he fussed. She found it all pretty pleasing. Oh yes. This was the kind of life she could get used to again.

He was treating her with such decorum and tact. It was all so refined. Terrines and soufflés and sorbets. That kind of thing on the menu. It put Karla back in mind of her lovely glory years. Such a long time ago. When she was passed around among the movers and shakers as if she was made out of crystal.

She could have wept, just thinking about that. How she had fallen. How she was almost always on her own nowadays; how rare it was that anyone took any responsibility for her.

But now wasn't the time to dwell on her tragically humdrum everyday life.

Alex coughed and they toasted each other. 'This film,' Alex began, and he started to talk about how he saw their joint venture. Gradually it dawned on her that he loved the film. He loved the story, the script, the character. Everything about it was important to him.

She had been worried that she was going to be appearing in some kind of spoof. There was a current vogue for remaking the old classic horrors and slyly sending them up. Making them look deliberately stupid. Karla, of course, had never taken herself very seriously, and was as good at making fun of herself as the next bisexual vampire lady. But . . . but she didn't want to be part of something that set out to trash her life's work. Those sixties and seventies movies had been her lifeline for donkey's years. She respected them and the professionals who had made them, and their loyal audiences. Naturally, she couldn't have afforded to turn down this starring part in the remake, but she'd really rather not – if possible – make a mockery of the whole *Get Thee Inside Me, Satan* legend.

She needn't have worried. Now Alex was talking about the earlier film, and indeed all of Karla's past successes, with a breathless enthusiasm. With the glint in his eye that she recognised. Aha! she thought. She had his number now. Of course! He was a *fan*. High-powered, successful, brilliant he may be – but he was a fan none-theless. Suddenly she saw that he was determined to make the picture that would do justice to Karla's talents at last.

'Those movies you made, they're wonderful,' he was telling

her. 'But they could be even better, you know. If they were remade with proper care and love and attention. And using today's expertise and knowledge and special effects. A little touch of contemporary sophistication and magic: that's what those great stories need. Back then, in the sixties, they were turned out so quickly, so carelessly . . .'

'It's true,' she said. 'We did *Carnival of Flesh* in two weeks flat out. I was a shadow of my former self by the end of that fortnight.'

'So,' Alex smiled winningly, 'I think we could make something really special here . . .'

Karla suddenly saw the little boy he must have been. A needy child, perhaps. Keen to say the things that would win the attention of the grown-ups. Over-eager, almost, to say just the right thing.

But there was something else in his expression.

Something in the way he was looking at her. She'd been looked at like that before. Fox Soames had looked at her like that. And now his son was echoing his expression, all these years later.

Oh, she could always put men into her thrall. She could enslave them, all right. But which of them came willingly into her arms? Truth was, hardly anyone.

Don't kid yourself, Karla, she thought. This young fella-me-lad Alex is only buttering you up. Making charming small talk as you rummage through your moules marinière and tweeze their firm jaws apart. Dripping garlic juices and cream. This is just his job. He has to appear dedicated and keen.

No. She knew that there was more to it. He really meant what he said about her movies. He really did want to put her back on top.

She squeezed a lemon wedge, studying his expression as he focused on his own food. He caught her sceptical glance and winced. Then he smiled warmly at her.

'I mean it, Karla. I think you are a genius on screen. I want the world to know how good you are.'

Her heart thrilled at that.

The rain was rattling at the windows now. A storm was coming in across the headland and high winds were bowling down Church Street below. It wasn't until now that she noticed it.

People had laughed at her. A camp classic: that was what she was. A bit rude, a bit saucy. Flashing her knockers in every film she was in. Past it now, of course. Sometimes people marvelled that she was still alive. Guest star spots on *The Little and Large Show*, *Crackerjack*, *Celebrity Squares*.

If I was French, she'd often thought, I'd be in arty movies. They'd see my brilliance. I would be a cult of a different stripe. I'd be celebrated properly. This was an old refrain. One that had kept her awake many nights in Cricklewood, poring over elderly scrapbooks.

Did she feel like she was seducing Alex? Enslaving him? No. Not tonight. Not this time. It was the other way around tonight. Karla felt like *she* was the one who was being reeled in. It was so unusual for her. It was very nearly exciting, to be the one not in charge.

Suddenly she burst out, 'Drunk! You've made me drunk! I never get tipsy!'

But she was now. Two bottles of Prosecco they'd gone through. In what seemed like a flash. And here came dessert wine.

Under his fascinated stare and his helpful pauses she attacked her sticky toffee pudding with gusto and found that she was telling him too much. All her bloody awful secrets. Making an exhibition of herself. But did she care? Not tonight. Not in the slightest. She found herself opening up to her director's gaze.

She talked about her childhood. Her young womanhood. About being taken to live in Kendal during the war. A child evacuated out of the back-street slums of Salford. And how she had been placed with practising witches who had drawn her into their strange cult. Dancing and making merry in the wintry woods at night. How she had been *inculcated*. The foul blessing put upon her. Or the curse. The spell that had brought her fame and attention. Had made her looks last seemingly for ever, or at least well past their sell-by. That spell had kept her flesh supple, fresh, keen.

She talked about the genuinely dark powers she had pledged her soul to such a long time ago. When she was still a girl.

She even spoke about her fears. Her feeling that she would never escape the men who controlled her destiny.

'Who?' Alex frowned, and cracked the caramel topping of his crème brûlée.

'The Brethren,' she said. Their eyes locked. She shivered. She never said their name aloud. Never to outsiders. She went on, in a lower tone, even though they were alone in the private dining room. 'Your father knew all about them. He always said that he wrote his books about satanists and witchcraft and black magic cults in order to warn the world. He used to say that there were shadowy organisations in the background in every country, working ceaselessly to make the devil master of the whole world.'

'And this all started for you in the Lake District?'

'There are dark powers everywhere,' Karla said. 'And their followers are everywhere too. Even a cosy place like Kendal. Or Whitby. Your father knew all about where the true dangers lurked.' She scraped up the last of her sticky pudding regretfully.

'Yes, he used to tell everyone who would listen,' Alex said. 'It was his mission in life. I think . . . I think he had been part of one of these cults, back when he was young and silly. It scared him. He saw it as his duty to protect the world.'

'And the message is still carried on. By you, his son, remaking this movie. Warning the world about dabbling with dark powers.'

He was studying her. 'And you? You really believe in these forces? That you are at their beck and call? You really sold your soul?

'Oh yes,' she said. 'I know I did.'

He blinked. He looked shocked. Karla necked her hot, bitter espresso and wondered if she had indeed said too much. She would scare him off. He might get some young, nubile actress to replace her. Someone without baggage. Someone who hadn't actually sold her soul to the devil.

After dinner they took a little walk.

When was that decided? It was his idea. Had he even asked her? Or had she just taken his arm as her evening wrap was placed over her shoulders by invisible hands. She had merely acquiesced to his more forceful will. They took a gentle walk up the hill, even though it was raining. Karla felt she was under some kind of spell. She was heavy with dinner, gravid with sparkling booze. Her head swam with the thought of future glories. She could be a star again. The star she was always meant to be.

Alex led her along. Alex wanted to see the abbey.

Quite honestly, Karla could have done without hauling herself up the 199 steps at that time of night, but she didn't want to sound old and complaining. She wanted to seem fit and willing, and eager to do exactly what her talented young director told her.

He was going to make a star of her again. And this time she would get her dues. The world at large would see how marvellous she really was.

Up at the abbey, he explained a little about how the film would climax. She listened to roughly half his words as the wind turned wilder, ripping them away. Something about sacrifice. Chanting hordes. Blazing torches. The gateway into hell.

Oh, the usual stuff. Wasn't it the climax of everything she got involved with? Didn't every party end with her stripped bare on a cold, hard altar, waiting for the knife to fall? Didn't she always get sacrificed sooner or later?

And yet somehow Karla felt different this time. What was the matter with her? She even felt a bit . . . *scared* somehow. But she couldn't back out. Not now. She had never backed out of anything. Nothing ever scared her. Nothing ever fazed her. She was a pro! She was the original vampire lady! And she could do anything!

That fannish, fervent expression was back on Alex's pale, unlined face. He was obsessed with this project. He had been subsumed by the story and by the ideas behind it. *Get Thee Inside Me, Satan* had taken over his life. A novel his father had written while his mother was pregnant. A novel his father laboriously typed in one room, drinking champagne through the night, smoking fat cigars, while Magda lay in another room, heavy with the child that would become Alex. It was as if the story had tapped its way into his infant's soft skull. Semi-formed bones had echoed with the tip-tapping of the typewriter keys, drumming the tale into the very core of his being.

Karla stood in the long wet grass, surrounded by the crumbling stones, and listened to Alex bang on and on about how it was all going to be.

The Story of Mrs C

Penny was sitting at the glass-topped bar at Spector.

Michael was pleased because the bar was busy, Whitby's trendier crowd being supplemented by a number of technical people from the film. Penny recognised them at once.

Here I am, having a drink in a bar filled with film people, she thought. She was on nodding acquaintance with all of them, and kept hoping that someone might invite her over to join their table.

Principal photography – as they called it – had begun today, and everyone seemed in a pretty good mood about it.

She watched Michael work, strutting about behind the long bar in his immaculately pressed white shirt.

During a rare lull, he came over to slouch across the bar and chat with her.

'So you never saw Karla after all?' she asked teasingly.

He gave a mock scowl. 'There was so much going on. What with all the upheaval and that man being taken off to hospital . . .'

Penny nodded. She was considering having another cocktail. She liked watching Michael whisk them up, fussing on with all the ingredients.

'And to think you went around with that old woman all night – for nothing!'

He shrugged. 'Mrs Claus is a very interesting woman, once you get talking to her.'

Penny was surprised. She said, 'Robert and all his friends can't stand her. They say—'

Michael interrupted. 'Yes, she says she finds that rather upsetting. She isn't sure what she's done to make them hate her so much. All she wants is for people to be friends.'

'The others were saying how wicked she is . . .'

'I never saw her being wicked,' he said. 'I saw a very lonely, rich old woman, who has had a hard life.'

'I see.' Penny pulled a face. He was sounding far too attached to the sinister Mrs Claus for her liking.

'All that Christmas stuff,' he went on, 'Don't you think it's a bit sad? A bit desperate?'

'It's a gimmick. That's all it is. The hotel where Christmas never stops. It would drive me mad, but it seems to work for some people.'

He shook his head, his dark locks tumbling about. 'No, no, no. I think it *is* sad. A desperately unhappy woman trying to bring some cheer and goodwill into the world. Fiercely hoping and wishing it was a happy Christmas all the time. It is upsetting, really.'

Penny gawped at him. 'You'll be telling me next that everyone misunderstands her. That no one sees the real Mrs Claus.'

He shrugged, smiling embarrassedly, as if those really had been the next words on his tongue.

'Well, she's certainly done a number on you, all right.' Penny was struck by a horrible thought. 'Er, she didn't make a pass at you, did she? At the end of the night?'

He stared at her. For a second he looked furious. Penny knew at once she had gone too far with her mockery. 'Of course not,' he snapped. 'We took a nightcap in her private sitting room, to calm down after all that noise and confusion at the end of the cabaret. And she told me a little more about herself.' He frowned at Penny. 'So you can get your mind out of the gutter.'

Penny stared down at the bar top, ashamed of herself. 'What did she tell you about herself, then?' she asked at last.

He shrugged. 'I was just interested in how she came to own and run such a big hotel, all by herself. I asked about her past. And she was quite open. I think she was pleased that someone was taking an interest . . .'

'You have put your finger right on it, my dear,' Mrs Claus said, with a huge sigh. 'How sensitive of you. How very thoughtful. You are a rare man, Michael. There can't be many like you.'

For their nightcap they were having snowballs in tall glasses, decorated with paper umbrellas and flowers. Michael didn't particularly like them, but felt he couldn't turn down her kindness.

So here he was again. His second night running, in the sitting room of Mrs Claus, ready to hear more of her story.

'Penny was in my bar tonight, asking about you.'

'Penny?'

'The girl who was with Brenda's party last night. She seemed surprised that you and I got on so well.'

'Did she?' Mrs Claus smirked. Tonight Mrs Claus's evening attire was even more elaborate. She was keen to scrub up well for this handsome near-stranger. She was in a tinselly kaftan of silver and green, and her make-up was at its most stunningly garish. Her thinking was, I may not look much these days, but I always stand out. You can see me from a long way off. And that was how she liked it.

'So where was I?' she said, settling to her tale. 'I never tell stories in the correct order, of course. My mind's always all of a muddle.'

'You told me that your family disowned you. And how you ran away . . .'

She scrunched up her doughlike face. 'Oh, are you bothered about hearing all my tales of woe?'

'I find it very interesting,' he said stiffly.

'And it's true, I've never talked about any of this for years.' She smiled. 'All right, then. I'll go on. Just for you, dear.'

They both settled for the telling. Mrs Claus paused reflectively before going on.

'This part of my story concerns a Christmas a long time ago. I was a slip of a thing. It was before the war. And I met my fancy man. That's what I called him. Straight away. I knew that's what he was. My fancy man. I was walking one Sunday with my sisters – Beryl, Eliza, Natasha and Maud. We were taking this long walk round to Robin Hood's Bay. Have you been there, dear? Have you taken the walk? Oh, we used to love it. All along the clifftops. Spectacular.

'My sisters and I used to gather grasses and herbs all the way there and back. Not in winter, of course. Not on those crisp, snowbound mornings. In winter it was bitter berries and black bark that we collected for our potions.

'He came galloping along on horseback. On this towering, magnificent steed. We saw him coming from miles away. Heading right towards us. Who was he? Some rich noble? Some highwayman or bandit? He was sending up massive flurries of snow all around him, ruining the smooth tranquillity of the land. My sisters were intrigued, even a little bit scared. My oldest sister wasn't, though. It took a lot to scare her. Old Maud was imperturbable. She always was. She set down her shopping basket and folded her arms and watched him approach. And she was scandalised when she saw how I reacted to him. She could sense it.

'He came trotting up, yanking off his scarf to show his pale, beautiful face. He shook out his tangled mane of hair, black as his steed. Maud knew I was breathing harder, my eyes had widened. I was used to her scrutiny. I was used to all of my sisters studying me like that. I was used to knowing that I did the wrong things, that I wasn't the same as them at all.

'And when my fancy man turned up that Christmas Eve, glittering with snow, grinning at us mockingly – the five solemn virgins trudging along the cliff edge – I knew my future had arrived. Everything had turned a corner that day.

'I knew that soon I'd leave my sisters for ever. I would go with this man. I'd leave Whitby behind and go wherever he told me.

'What did he say? You know, I can't even remember. Some flattering, flirtatious nonsense. Flim-flam. Daftness. My sisters tried to cover my ears, but I was too far gone. Already. I was fifteen and my head had been turned. Earl, he said his name was. Was that an American name? He certainly seemed foreign, exotic. Not from round here. Earl. It was romantic, aristocratic. I wondered if he really was an earl, or something noble. We didn't get a lot of those round our way.

'I was distracted all that Christmas. In our tall house on the harbour, my four sisters and I made merry in our usual ways. I was the youngest, and the petted, spoiled child. I helped with the steaming of puddings, the roasting of fowl. I helped brew up the potions and sift the powders that my sisters required for their everyday work.

'The shop at the bottom of our house was a kind of apothecary. We dispensed lotions and potions, tinctures and tonics, all made by our own fair hands. We had learned the skills from our aunts, who had all but passed away by then. There was a lot to learn. Sometimes I would despair. I would never be like Maud or the others. I was deficient somehow. I was made for some other kind of life.

'My mind was filled with superficial things. Silly things. Dancing and dresses and Christmas and silliness. They called me a flibbertigibbet. That was their name for me. They made fun of me all the time, though I knew they loved me really. My sisters were not beautiful. Some of them were downright ugly. Poor Eliza. But they were kind. And they saw in me all the beauty and hope and lightness and grace. Everything they weren't, I was.

'And I was their best hope for the future. One day I would bear a child and she would carry on our work. My sisters were past all that. None of them would be having children. It would have to be me.

'Throughout that final Christmas at home, all I could think about was my fancy man on his horse. Smiling down at us. Looking through the others. Staring at me. I knew he was staring at only me.

'On Christmas morning a card came through the front door of our shop.

'"It's from him," Maud said tersely. Her hair was in curlers, her dressing gown wrapped tight about her. An awful silence fell over our gift-giving and unwrapping. There was tense silence in our sitting room.

'"Who?" asked Natasha, never the brightest of our bunch.

'"The fella on the horse," Maud growled. She nodded at me. "It's for her."

'"Me?" I stopped unwrapping the nettle-green jersey Beryl had knitted for me. It smelled pungent and weird, but that's not why my head swam for a second. "He's sent me a Christmas card?"

'Maud made a moue of displeasure. "Here you are."

' "But you've opened it! You've opened my Christmas card!"

'It was a lace-edged thing, more doily than card. Beautiful, exquisite thing, purple and black. I held my breath, opened it, and read his spiderlike writing inside: *Will you come away with me?*'

'And?' Michael was leaning forward on his chair. His snowball was finished; just a yellow foam was left in the bottom of his glass.

'Well.' Mrs Claus chuckled, breaking the mood. 'I went to him, didn't I? That Christmas night. Just for a walk along the front, as he requested. And oh, but my sisters weren't pleased. There was war on at our house. They thought they had to protect me at all costs from this terrible, beautiful man.'

'And did they?'

Mrs Claus smiled at him, and reached out with one of her chapped red hands to tap him lightly, affectionately on the knee. 'Oh no,' she said. 'I was fifteen. I was a fool to myself. And I wasn't the same as them. I wasn't destined to turn out the same as my sisters.

'And so I went with him. I fled. And I never looked back, once.'

The Film's Release

Before they passed out, Brenda and Effie managed to get the gist of the plot.

Were they just tired? It was possible. It had been an exhausting couple of days. And this was, of course, the third movie they had watched on the trot that evening. The attic had grown warmer and cosier, and they had worked their way through all the snacks they had assembled. And usually, watching any film, Effie would start dozing at about the twentieth minute, if her friend wasn't there to nudge her awake. She'd shout out, 'What? Whassat? I was awake! What's happening? Who's he?'

Before they started on the film at the top of the evening's bill, Brenda read aloud the review she had found in a second-hand copy of *Nelliwell's Guide to World Film*.

'Here we are,' she said, finding the place. 'Erm . . . "Nineteen sixty-seven's infamous *Get Thee Inside Me, Satan*. Satanic trash. Cast and crew reputed to be cursed. Deservedly so, we say."'

So they put the disc in the machine and started to watch. But by then it was very late. It was the early hours, and this time, twenty minutes into the movie, both of them were starting to drift off.

They were fighting sleep during the psychedelic dream sequence into which Karla's character sinks ineluctably. When the devil comes to her in the form of an evil beautician and promises mastery over all mankind, the two ladies were struggling to keep their critical faculties engaged and their attention from sagging. The music and pulsating lights were hypnotic, and Brenda and Effie found that they were quickly mesmerised.

They snored gently in time with the soft prog rock of the soundtrack.

The film's bizarre narrative ran on without them, luridly, violently.

Though neither enjoyed horror films of this type per se, both had been intrigued by the storyline. It was more believable than either had expected, and focused on the fate of a woman who worked on the make-up counter of a swanky London department store. Plagued by dreams and desires and the blandishments of sinister beauticians, Karla's character's plight touched them both. She was possessed by Satan and there was nothing she could do about it. She wasn't one of those who willingly chose her fate, who flirted with evil and danger. She was plucked out of the heady world of Swinging Sixties London and sucked into a life of wickedness and cruelty.

Brenda and Effie sat up in their chairs, Effie on the paisley two-seater, Brenda on the bobbly green. Both slept deeper than they had in years, eyes wide open, faces slack. Swirls of light licked and tickled at them as the film rolled towards its end and the final showdown between the devil and the shop girl, somewhere in a quarry in Wales.

The light from the TV screen was the only illumination in the attic room. It played delicately and teasingly over the ladies' forms. The pale colours drew together into wraithlike beings. They seemed to twist in mid air, transparently. The light coiled itself and went hunting snakelike about the corners of the sleeping room. Then it found the cooling fireplace and explored the sooty recesses, rushing towards the salty night air outside.

The lights danced and trickled over the rooftops of Whitby.

Ribbons of transparent blueness transmitted themselves, freed of the disc by the DVD's laser. Sometimes faces could be seen, rising and grimacing. There was the steady throb of an unfolding tale. The movie swirled and eddied about the town, thrilling to its own liberation.

Released at last!

Then it found the Christmas Hotel. It knew it had found its quarry.

The phantom movie swept about the rooftops, prying and sniffing at windows. Peering down gutters and overflow pipes. Then it was wreathing ecstatically about the turret that contained the suite of Karla Sorenson. In here, up in the attic. This was what it had come for.

Inside, two men were slumbering and a third was keeping awake, watching the others. Three prisoners in the attic. It prised itself through the tiny cracks in the dusty window pane, high up above the Christmas Hotel. As it issued into the confined space, it felt the crash and boom of the surf buffeting around the room. The phantom blew in with the sea winds, crackling and flickering with intent.

Kevin was awake in the turret, feeling betrayed, if he was honest with himself. He felt a fool. What had got into him, going with Karla in the first place? He had hardly left her suite ever since she got here. In fact, had he left it at all? He had been like some lapdog.

But it was as if, now that she had been away for a few hours, her control had faded. The link between them had stretched and snapped. And he found himself lucid again. Up here. Locked in. Full of misgivings. Still dressed as an elf in the middle of the night.

She had used him. He had done her bidding. He had slept with her. Suddenly it came back to him. Being squashed in her still lithe arms. Her insatiable demands. That was all real, wasn't it? It wasn't just some terrible dream. He had gone willingly to her bed and had stayed there.

Now he was here. Shoved to one side. Hidden away in the attic, with the rest of her toys.

There the others were, too. Bobby the postie, who Kevin knew well. He'd been drawn in too. Sucked of his own volition. At first Kevin had been resentful. Who was this new plaything of Karla's? Who was this to rival him? But that was part of the strange spell. He knew the woman enjoyed that kind of vying and posturing. She loved the idea of men fighting over her.

The third man, too. The monster. He lay in half-shadow, breathing heavily, horribly. His expression was tortured as he lay there, as if he was having dreadful dreams.

What kind of dreams would a monster have?

The three of them should be finding some way to free themselves. Surely if they put their joint strength behind it, they could smash down the locked and bolted door? But it was thick, reinforced. Kevin had already examined it. The door to this attic had been specially prepared for this eventuality, it seemed. Mrs Claus had created this space as some kind of hideaway prison, and Karla had adapted it to her own uses.

Then Kevin was aware of the light at the small window growing brighter. Quivering at the corner of his vision. He thought at first it was a lighthouse, sweeping its beam over the town and spilling into the turret. But it wasn't. It slunk into the dark space. Emerging from the shadows and presenting itself to Kevin's view. He blinked. He could see phantoms inside that weird shaft of light. Faces and forms. He could hear voices and . . .

He could even see the credits rolling. 'I'm sorry about this,' the credits said. 'I don't want to do this. But I have to. *He* is making me do this. *He* is in control of my actions now. *He* is directing me to do this. I'm so, so sorry . . .'

Kevin blinked and shook his head. The credits were communicating with him as they swirled about his head in lurid shades of blue.

'I cannot resist his awful powers! His terrible will!' the credits scrolled. 'What am I? I'm only a movie . . .'

The film took him over.

Get Thee Inside Me, Satan had got inside Kevin.

He blinked again. It was subsuming him. It had slipped down a treat. Now it was looking out through his eyes and he knew what to do. He knew exactly what he had to do.

Kevin stood up stiffly in the confined space and set about shaking Bobby awake. The hairy postman glared at him. 'What? What?' He looked confused about where they were. Then he grew belligerent, until Kevin fixed him with a steady gaze, allowing the shimmering light to flood into Bobby's eyes as well. Then Bobby could see the point. He too could see what needed to be accomplished that night.

It was a difficult task. A gruesome one, but someone had to do it. They were the men for the job.

They found ropes and chains lying ready for the purpose. They stole closer and closer to the man-monster, Frank. They tried not to let the chains clank or the floorboards creak. Frank stirred and moaned in his sleep, but his eyes never opened. He never saw them or paid any heed as they looped ropes about his wrists and ankles and tethered him to the rafters. They chained his waist and throat, and that was the worst moment. They thought he would rip suddenly awake, suddenly alert. He would seize them by the necks and dash their heads together.

They could sense the strength in the slumbering giant. If he caught them, they wouldn't stand a chance. But they were driven by the strength of someone else's convictions. They plugged on with the task of tethering the monster. At the very last moment they tightened the knots and secured him completely. Only then did he jerk awake.

'What are you doing?' he growled. Then he saw them. The fluctuating outlines of the two men confronting him. The blue light played like cool flames around them. He twisted and roared and shouted at them. But he couldn't break free. 'What are you doing?' What are you trying to do?'

But the two men now had the next part of the task to fulfil. It was the hardest part. Now that the monster was secure and pinned to the dusty wooden floor, they had to get on with the next bit. It was vital.

What could they use to accomplish their task?

This attic space was a prison. There was nothing here. Nothing they could use.

Ah. Bobby smashed the tiny window. Cold air and noise came rushing in. The panes cracked apart into jagged segments. He shared them with Kevin. Their tools. These would do. The glass shards had cruel edges. They were sufficient to the job, which, let's face it, didn't have to be carried out very neatly or carefully.

'What are you doing?' Frank said uneasily, shrinking back instinctively, as far as his bonds would let him.

The two men were intent. Moving towards him, sloppy grins on their faces, glass daggers held aloft . . .

Frank howled and tried to kick out at them.

But he couldn't move.

He gave one last despairing screech as they descended upon him.

The Flying Settee

Robert saw the miasma of blue light that spilled from rooftop to rooftop. He saw it spread across the old town and creep around the attic eaves and turrets of the Christmas Hotel.

He saw it all, because as it was happening, he was sitting on the green velour settee belonging to the man he had been seeing for a number of weeks now. It being a very special settee, it was hovering several hundred feet above the seething palaver of the dark sea. For all the heavy rain of the hours before midnight, it was a fine night right now. Perfect for flying about the place with his daring young man on the flying settee.

Robert didn't even question it now, the fact that they went floating and zooming about the place in the night. He had a pretty good head for heights, as it happened, so that didn't bother him. Neither did the magical aspect of the whole business. He supposed it meant that his new fella had some peculiar abilities and, most probably, some dark secrets. He wasn't particularly forthcoming about these, and since Robert was just pleased to have a boyfriend again, he didn't push too hard with the questions. Still, it was a new one on him. The flying horsehair sofa. It was pretty comfortable though, and it did add a certain frisson to their fooling around in the night air, the fact that they were swooping about under the baleful glare of the moon. The moon, which, as ever, behaved as if it had seen it all before.

Tonight was different.

The atmosphere between them was a little more tense than usual, as Robert had insisted on talking about some of the recent mysterious goings-on. His fella had looked impatient and uninterested. This in turn had piqued Robert, who felt that his fella should be more concerned. 'This is important to me, what happens to my friends,' he said. 'And it should be to you too.' He looked earnestly at that sharp profile. That gently mocking expression. Those perfect full lips.

'Why? Why should it be interesting to me? The silly things a bunch of old women get up to.' His fella shrugged and laughed.

'That's not very caring.'

'I'm not a very caring person. You should know that about me.'

Yes, thought Robert miserably. And here I am, stuck several hundred feet up in the air with you. At your mercy. With no visible means of support. Oh God. I know how to pick them, don't I?

He had never really picked this bloke, though. The bloke had swept down out of the sky one evening on his strange steed and picked Robert up without a by-your-leave.

'Look, Robert,' the fella said. 'This is just what it's like. I don't care at all about your everyday life. Your daytime life. I just care about you when you're here with me. Whenever that is, and however long we keep it going. The rest of it is irrelevant. Boring to me. Don't bring all your mundane stuff up here with you.'

'It's not mundane! It's my life! And there's lots of interesting stuff in it. There's loads going on lately, actually!' He couldn't keep the gall out of his tone.

The man laughed. 'Oh dear. I expect you want to hear all about my everyday life as well, don't you? All the boring details. And then you want me to meet your family and friends. And you can meet mine . . .' He broke up in laughter, as if he couldn't imagine anything more ridiculous or banal.

Robert burst out, 'Yes! That would be nice! Normal!'

'This isn't normal,' he was told stiffly. 'This is outside all of that.' It was a cold voice, as fathomless as the North Sea below them.

Robert felt tears of frustration starting up. 'I don't know what you mean!'

'This is enchantment. This is you under a spell. When you come with me, when we fly together around the town, we are beyond the normal human world. We've stepped beyond the veil. You can't share that with anyone else. You haven't told anyone else about me, have you?'

Robert pulled a face. 'No.'

'Good. This is just for you and me.'

'I wish it was less dysfunctional. I wish I could introduce you to Brenda and Effie – well, maybe not Effie, since she's so disapproving of just about everything, but certainly Penny and—'

'It isn't going to happen. You have half sold your soul into the world of faerie now.'

Robert blinked. 'What?'

'Your soul is half submerged in the eldritch world of the dark faerie.'

There was an awkward pause between them.

'Yes, I thought that's what you said,' Robert said. 'And that isn't very good, is it?'

'Depends how you look at it.' His fella crossed his slim legs as he mused, looking for all the world like a young professor considering a knotty philosophical proposition. 'From my point of view, it's a very good thing. Since I'm the one setting out to ensnare mortal souls.'

'For the world of faerie. Yes, um, I see now.' Robert's head was in turmoil. At this point he even felt a twinge of vertigo. 'Let me get this straight. You don't really fancy me. You just popped down to steal my soul and now I'm half enslaved by the, um, faeries?'

'That's more or less it,' said his fella. 'Though you do me a disservice. And yourself. You are rather cute, as they say, in a rough-hewn, unfinished, exasperating kind of way.'

'Exasperating!' Robert burst out. 'I'll give you exasperating . . .'

And then he focused on that liquid blue fire hopping around the rooftops of the old town. He watched it dance around the main turret of the Christmas Hotel, and for the first time in his idle observation of its weird properties, he saw where it seemed to be emanating from. A particular sharply pointed rooftop, which, if he wasn't mistaken, belonged to . . .

'Brenda!' he cried. 'Look! It's coming from her house!'

'Careful, man,' his fella said crossly. 'You nearly dropped off the settee. If you do, I can't be held responsible.'

Robert turned to him. 'Take me over there. Over the harbour. To Brenda's. Do it now.'

A smile curled on those perfect lips. 'You want to leave me? Is our night together over so soon?'

Robert said, very deliberately, 'That's right.' He almost added that after the way their conversation had gone, it was the end of *all* their nights together. But he didn't want to go burning his boats just yet.

Was that shallow of him? Would he really put up with any amount of spooky nonsense and weird suggestions, just for the sake of a snog and a bit of sex on a floating settee? With a man who had never even told him his name?

Yep. If that was shallow, then yep. That was fine with him.

His fella dropped him off on the sharply descending street where Brenda had her guest house and Effie her junk shop. The elm trees rustled and swished as the settee sifted gently down and touched soundlessly on the cobbles.

Robert jumped up. 'I'll see you soon.'

'Kiss me,' said his fella.

Robert leaned close. 'You've never even told me your name.'

'What do names mean?'

'Is that some faerie thing?' Robert said mockingly. 'If you give me your name, then I've got some kind of power over you?'

'No,' said his fella, looking up at him and grinning. 'Okay. It's Michael. Call me Michael.'

'Right. Michael.' It felt weird, after four weeks. Putting a name to the face at last. Robert kissed him goodbye. He tasted of spices. Christmassy spices.

Then he looked up at Brenda's rooftop, where the blue light was still pulsing and flickering and transmitting itself across the old town. Something was going on. As per usual. Something was up, and Robert wanted to be part of it.

Time to rescue Brenda and Effie again, from whatever bizarre state of affairs they were embroiled in this time.

He turned back, to say goodbye to Michael. But the settee had already whizzed off again into the night.

Stumped

It was very late by the time Karla returned to the Christmas Hotel. Anyone still sitting up in the lounge in the conservatory would have been surprised to see the famous film star trolling home on foot. She looked rather the worse for wear too, having been dragged around the abbey by her director. She had snapped a heel, lost an earring and worn herself to a frazzle. By the time she got back to her hotel, she was in a vexed mood.

There was no one to see her, however, apart from the ancient concierge, who came to attention and saluted.

'Good evening.' Karla nodded, and swished past him, towards the lifts.

From the old man's point of view it was a pretty impressive entrance. It was just past two o'clock, and the glass doors opened and Karla Sorenson glided in on waves of chilling sea mist. She was all togged up in vampire finery and looking haughty and piqued. It gave the old man a thrill of pleasure to see her issuing past his front desk.

All Karla could think about was her discomfort from roaming about in the long grass all night. Her aching legs and feet. Her frozen, goose-pimpled flesh. She really hadn't been dressed for a night out in the October cold. In her opinion, Alex Soames was a singularly selfish, inconsiderate young man.

Once she was ensconced in her suite, Karla poured herself a generous brandy and felt the warmth seeping back into her body. What about all the things Alex had said about her career, hm? About putting her back on top. Making the world see what a genius she was. The queen of horror. He had really meant all of that, she was sure of it. She could tell by his eyes. He was so earnest, so determined. This film was all for her. She had no right getting in a huff about a bit of physical discomfort. Or the weird sense of foreboding that was tugging at her raddled flesh and her aching bones.

Where were her helpers? The elf boy and the kidnapped postman? What was the point of having fellas in servitude if they weren't there to tend to you when you came in at night?

Ah yes. She'd locked them both away for safe-keeping, hadn't she?

She unlocked the attic and creaked open the door. 'Boys?'

There was a stiff draught from above.

The attic was dark, striated with shafts of soft lilac moonlight. They spilled down the wooden staircase. She wrinkled her nose. Beside the scent of old wood and mould and dust, there was a heavy smell on the air. A rancid, bloody smell she didn't like at all.

'B-boys? Are you up there?'

There was a shifting, a stirring above. The boys were waking. There was a shout. An awful cry of dismay. Oh, what now? Karla thought crossly. She hauled herself up the stairs in her stockinged feet.

'Hello?'

What she found at the top of the stairs ranked among the most horrible things she had ever seen.

'What have you done?' She stared at Kevin and Bobby, who were dragging themselves to their feet and looking in terror at the prone figure with whom they shared the attic.

'I d-don't know!' Kevin protested. 'What's happened to him?'

'Did we do this?' asked Bobby, tugging at his beard. 'Did we? I don't know . . . How . . . ?'

His voice trailed away and the three of them stared at the prone body of Frank in appalled awe.

'Is he dead?' Kevin asked.

'I don't know. How should I know?' Karla went to Frank, steeling herself for the sight of all that blood and carnage. Who'd have thought he'd have so much blood in him? she wondered. There was a bucket beside him, and his crazy assailants had filled it with his turgid liquids. This was the source of that heavy, metallic, slightly off smell.

The worst thing about the unconscious Frank wasn't the bucket of his drained blood, or the fact that they had chained him to the wall by his arms and he hung there like a broken puppet. The very worst thing was that they had sawn both his legs off.

One at the knee, the other at the thigh. The two broad, hefty limbs were lying straightened up a little distance from their owner. They were pale and smirched with darkness.

'You've pulled his legs off.'

'It wasn't us!'

'It had to be you, you idiot! Why did you do this?'

The two men gawped mindlessly at the vile tableau.

'What's the blood for?' Karla asked. 'Why did you take his blood?'

Their dumb silence aggravated her. The smell of blood was making her sick to her stomach. This was like appearing in one of her own fricking movies.

Then she thought: a bucket of his blood. Didn't the Brethren say something about that in their last message? To do with the ashes and fragments of charred bone they had sent her? Didn't they tell her that blood was necessary?

In which case, was that why her boys had turned on Frank? Did they know what she needed? Had they taken the messiest job off her hands?

Poor Frank. Look at the state of him. How much blood did he still have chugging through him? Was it enough?

The ragged stumps of legs were no longer bleeding. She examined them quickly and they were strange things. Like something off the delicatessen counter at Waitrose. Pressed meat or something. She had to remind herself. Frank wasn't the same as other human beings. He was a makeshift being. He was already dead. Taking his legs off in this grotesque fashion might not be fatal to him. It might not affect him at all, apart from preventing him from running about the place too much.

Which might come in handy, actually, she thought grimly. Perhaps her fellas had done her a service.

Frank was dead to the world. What would his reaction be when he eventually woke up?

She shuddered and picked up the pail of blood, with a sigh.

All Karla wanted was a decent night's sleep.

Kevin and Bobby watched her warily. Would they be punished for the terrible thing they had done in their sleep?

'Come with me,' she told them, and led them downstairs. She was careful not to spill a single drop of Frank's bloody essence as they descended back into the luxury suite.

Brenda and Effie Transfixed

Oh *no*.

He should never have given them that DVD. They had all sensed that it was dangerous. Effie had seen what it had done to Penny.

But they always had to go investigating, didn't they? You couldn't hold them back.

Robert still had his key from looking after Brenda's guest house in her absence. Now, in the early hours, he let himself in, dreading what he would find when he got to the top and her attic rooms.

He was careful not to make too much noise. He wasn't sure if she had any guests staying with her this week. The whole house was frozen and silent, so it didn't seem that she had. The heating was off. The lights were off. It was as if Brenda's B&B had died in the night. As if those pale lights he had seen issuing from its chimneys were its life force, somehow.

Stop being fanciful, Robert, he told himself sternly, and thundered matter-of-factly up the side stairs.

Silence coming from her sitting room. He took a deep breath and flung open the door.

'Brenda!' he couldn't help yelling out when he clapped eyes on her. 'Effie!' he squawked, when he saw her friend sitting in exactly the same way. They both looked as if rigor mortis had set in. They were rigid on their respective armchairs, faces slack and hands shaped like talons, gripping the armrests. The antimacassars had slipped off. It struck him crazily that they looked like one of those photos people have taken on roller coasters, their faces forever twisted in wild fright.

They were both staring at the television, but nothing was playing. Just a monochrome field of dancing snowflakes. Its restless shadows played across the faces of his two friends.

Oh my God. They've been possessed by whatever horrible thing is on that disc.

Robert tried to remember what Effie did to bring Penny round, the other morning. What was it? Some kind of witchy spell thing. No way Robert could replicate it. Should he shake them? Shout in their faces? Make them a mug of hot, sweet, spicy tea? Or brandy?

He crept over and touched Brenda's shoulder. She was rock hard with tension. He wouldn't be able to get her to drink anything at all. She was completely unresponsive. It was as if her mind was elsewhere.

He tried yelling at them both, right in their faces.

Not a flicker.

They disturbed him, the way they sat there, staring straight ahead, unblinking. Their knuckles showing white.

Maybe he could find something in Effie's house, among her old magic books. He could find the spell she had used to bring Penny back from her own horror-induced coma.

Where had the disc come from in the first place? Why, it couldn't be a coincidence, could it? It had turned up just as Karla Sorenson herself arrived in town. All roads led back to her, it appeared. If – as seemed likely – these investigations were left solely to Robert now, then he'd better look into Save the Kiddies, and Karla herself. That was what Brenda would have done.

Having said that, the logical thing was never usually what Brenda did next. Her investigations never followed a rational line of development. She'd wind up doing something like this, sending herself into a horrible trance. Robert had to admit that no matter how fond he was of them, he couldn't lie about their success rate. Brenda and Effie were never the most subtle of investigators. More often than not, when they were supposed to be sneaking about and gathering evidence and clues, they would end up being discovered and having a wild fist fight with their enemies.

God, he missed them already! Those two obtuse and maddening old bags.

But he couldn't let himself wallow in this. He had to get to work.

He rang the Miramar and was pleased to hear Penny at the front desk.

'Oh, crikey!' she burst out, when he'd explained what had gone on.

'I know,' he said, grimly. 'They're exactly like you were the other morning.'

'You should never have let them watch that thing,' Penny told him tactlessly.

Robert grimaced, but Penny was right. Sometimes he forgot that Brenda and Effie were two old ladies. He behaved as if they were indestructible. He quickly blinked away tears of guilt. 'Listen, I was out of the room when Effie brought you round from your trance, but can you remember what she did or said to you?'

'Bacon sandwiches!' Penny burst out. 'She had some bacon sandwiches brought up, to use as smelling salts, do you remember?'

'Yes, but she must have said something, too. Some kind of spell.'

'I'm sorry, Robert, but I wasn't conscious. I don't remember.'

He sighed. 'I'll try the bacon thing anyway. It's worth a go.' He was starving anyway, he realised. He asked Penny a few desultory questions about the running of the hotel. Things seemed to be fine up the hill at the Miramar. (Really, he marvelled at how Brenda managed to keep her own business going in the midst of her adventures.)

Penny started telling him about how rowdy the film crew were at night, drinking at all hours in the Yellow Peril, but he wasn't in the mood to hear that just now. He said his goodbyes and hurried over to have another look at his friends.

There was no change. Those blank, staring eyes discombobulated him. It was as if the two women were astonished by something that he would never be privy to.

He turned to the small attic window and drew open the curtains, just in time to see the light spreading across the harbour in fabulous banners of pink and baby blue. He craned his neck to see if those pale ribbons of magical lightning were still rippling over the rooftops, between Brenda's and the Christmas Hotel.

That was a point. What *was* that strange lightning? Was it connected with his friends' predicament? And what was it doing going to the Christmas Hotel?

He stiffened. Evidently this was some ploy of Mrs Claus's. She and Karla were obviously in league.

Perhaps they had stolen the minds and souls of Brenda and Effie and transformed them into rippling light and pulled them across the town, slithering like ghosts through the dawn skies.

Brenda didn't have a soul, though, did she? That was what she had always claimed.

But Robert couldn't see those strange Northern Lights any more, whatever they had been.

Could his fella help? The thought struck him forcibly. Michael could zoom about, airborne on a settee, couldn't he? He obviously had some pretty special magical powers. Even if Robert was unaware of their nature or their extent, they were still powers of some kind. Maybe Michael could help out here?

But how trustworthy was he? After this evening, Robert wasn't at all sure.

Oh, anything, anything. He was clutching at straws. He couldn't leave Brenda and Effie like this.

He turned back to look at them. An awful feeling of desolation swept over him. He was the one who'd have to sort this out. They were depending on him utterly.

What an absolute *bugger*.

You Can Do Magic

Karla had never been big on the magic rituals.

In recent years she had even stopped going to the Brethren's solstitial do's at their Cricklewood sanctum. She liked the dancing, but it was the chanting that got on her nerves. Really, all those arcane rites and so on, mostly it was an excuse for a bunch of quite unattractive people to get their kit off and flaunt themselves about the place, and maybe indulge in some of the orgiastic revels that satanists were so famous for.

Karla tended to find it all a bit embarrassing these days. Also, with magic, you never knew what was going to happen. Over the years she had seen people bite off more than they could easily chew. It was best not to go mucking about, was her view these days.

Though she'd had a whole life steeped in black magic and its practices, it was something that still gave her the willies.

As dawn broke over Whitby, here she was again, trying to do magic.

Her servants, Bobby and Kevin, were intoning strange verses for her in low, tremulous voices. She had asked them to recite the room service menu backwards for her. It didn't really matter what the words were about. It was the atmosphere that counted, and she had to admit, her boys were making the atmosphere pretty spooky with their chanting.

Aromatherapy candles had been lit, rather than the regulation black ones. They had turned all the mirrors to the wall, just in case Satan popped by. He didn't like to see his reflection, for some reason (though from what Karla remembered of her induction at the age of fifteen, he was quite a looker. That had been in Kendal, hadn't it? Such a long, long time ago. A frisson of occult nostalgia went through her).

And now she was swaying and undulating her supple limbs above the glass fruit bowl filled with ashes. She was chanting too, but she had no idea what she was saying. Some weird kind of language was coming out of her. She knew it was the Brethren speaking through her. They were using her, once more, as the vessel, the conduit through which their wills would be known.

Karla hefted up the bucket of oily blood and held it steadily above the bowl.

'As the Brethren will, so mote it be,' she moaned. Bobby and Kevin moaned too, and the candles sparked and flared in response.

She began to pour a thick stream of blood into the bowl. The smell was awful, and she almost gagged. She watched in fascination as the life blood mixed with the grey ash, making a kind of horrible satanic roux.

She wondered if she should perhaps give it a stir, but as she continued to pour, the sauce thickened and quickened, and lumpy shapes stirred beneath the crimson surface.

Kevin and Bobby drew nearer to see what was happening.

'What is it?'

'What's that?'

'There's something in there!'

'Sssh,' she calmed them, and emptied the bucket of blood.

But it was true. The two men drew back, disgusted at the sight of the thing that was forming in the glass.

Karla herself felt her gorge rise, but she couldn't take her eyes off it.

A tiny man was forming in the reeking broth. A pale homunculus, all curled up like a hairy foetus. And he was growing, slowly but surely.

Karla baulked and gagged as the realisation hit her.

I-I've made a man . . . she thought.

Ladies of the Canyon

'Effie? Effie lovey, are you all right?'

'What? What is it?'

'I think . . . I think we've arrived.'

Brenda was getting shakily to her feet. She swayed unsteadily as she cricked back her head and stared about at their new environment. They were in a canyon of dark blue stone. The jagged walls stretched high above them on either side. Every move they made dislodged shards of slate, and the sluthery noise echoed about them.

'Arrived where, ducky?' Effie said crossly, opening her eyes and struggling to stand. 'What are you talking about? We weren't *going* anywhere. We were sitting in your living room and . . .'

She couldn't deny the evidence of her own senses, though. Effie was a pragmatist above all else. Suddenly it was daytime and they were in the open air. Or at least, in the chilly confines of this—

'Quarry,' Brenda said. 'We're in a quarry.'

Effie drew nearer, as the realisation hit. 'Just like the one in that film!'

'I've been here before,' Brenda said. 'This chill in the air. The atmosphere of this place. It's all so familiar. We're in Wales . . .' Her voice trailed off, and they listened to the sibilant echoes rolling away.

213

'But how?' Effie said. 'By magic? Who would want to send us to Wales? What would be the point?'

A shower of dust and gravel pattered about them, and instantly Brenda was on the alert. 'Effie! Move, quickly!'

Someone high above them had dislodged a chunk of rock. The two ladies barely had time to scurry away before it came crashing to the valley floor. They got themselves under a convenient overhang in the nick of time.

'Someone's trying to kill us,' Brenda squawked. She tried to see, but the rock face was too high, and the fall had sent plumes of blue dust everywhere.

Effie was elsewhere. 'Look. We're wearing the same clothes that we were tonight, at home in Whitby.'

'So?'

'Well then, we really *have* been transported. This isn't a dream, or anything like that. We're really *here*.'

They wandered for a while along the valley floor.

Soon they could hear the not-too-distant sounds of others who had come to this desolate place.

They came within sight of a film crew, working busily at the end of the valley.

'You know what this means,' Brenda said, grabbing her friend's arm.

Frankly, Effie didn't. She was cold and confused and rather tired by now. She didn't even know what day it was. 'What does it mean?' she snapped crossly.

'We've come back in time,' Brenda told her. 'We've gone into the Making of the Movie. We've gone Behind the Scenes. We've ended up *inside* the DVD extras! I don't know how we got here. Or whether it's even possible. But somehow we're back in 1967.'

Effie was scandalised. 'But how can that be?'

'All I know is that over there, that's the cast and crew of the original version of *Get Thee Inside Me, Satan*. Those are their caravans and everything. I was here, remember. And now I've come back.' Brenda looked as perplexed as Effie had ever seen her. 'I wonder why.'

'But there's no such thing as time travel,' Effie burst out. 'There can't be. It's impossible!' What she meant was that if such things were possible, then people going willy-nilly into the past and future would mess everything up. It involved chaos theory and suchlike, which Effie had read about in the Sunday supplements. If one little thing was changed in the past, as it certainly would be, even by the mere presence of travellers, then that would put the tin hat on causality itself and the whole blithering cosmos would unravel.

But Brenda was looking at her as if she was being obtuse just for the sake of it, so Effie didn't go on and explain. She didn't want to cause a row.

'Why've we come into the past?' Brenda was wondering aloud. 'We must be meant to do something here. But what can it be?'

All Effie knew was that she had found the late sixties quite hard work the first time round. And Wales was somewhere she had never been keen on, though Llandudno was nice.

She really, really hoped they weren't stuck here.

Uncharitable

When Robert went to their charity shop that morning, Teresa and Helen were in the window, dressing up mannequins Goth-style with an assortment of ill-matching black garments and accessories. They liked to enter the spirit of the thing when it came to Goth weekend.

It had come round again so quickly. This time, its imminence made Robert shiver with foreboding. I'm getting as prescient as Brenda, he mused as he entered the shop. Inside smelled of air freshener and detergent, sort of starchy and preserved, and this in turn made him think of Brenda and Effie sitting frozen in their chairs. He had felt rotten leaving them like that, and locking Brenda's B&B behind him. But what more could he do? The scent of frying bacon hadn't roused them. There had been nothing he could do to bring them round. But they were safe enough, surely, locked securely in Brenda's house, until he could find some kind of solution to their plight.

But maybe that was it for them, he thought, as he gazed abstractedly at the shelves of knick-knacks and the rows of paperbacks. Maybe they were gone for good, their minds shattered by the experience of viewing that terrible movie.

But what was it he had seen crepitating out of Brenda's chimney and swooshing over to the Christmas Hotel? What was going on here? There were so many questions. Now he was determined to set about getting some answers.

Teresa and her helper, Helen, were facing him across the glass counter of the charity shop. Both were glaring at him with undisguised dislike. What had he ever done to them? he'd like to know.

'I'm here to make some enquiries,' he told them, drawing himself up, and trying to look determined.

'Enquiries, is it?' Teresa smirked, and nudged her friend. 'What would that be about?'

'Two of my friends have bought second-hand DVDs from your shop in the past week, and I'd like to know—'

Teresa interrupted him rudely, 'We've had that Effryggia Jacobs in here asking similar questions already.' She folded her arms under her hefty bosom. 'And there's nothing we can tell you. People donate these things. We price them up and put them on the shelves. That's all there is to it. We can't be responsible for the content, or what becomes of those people who buy our goods.'

'Don't you think it strange?' Robert persisted. 'Three Karla Sorenson movies turning up at the same time?'

'She's a very famous actress. Some people like that kind of thing.' Teresa pursed her lips. 'I can't say I think she's got much talent, but then I never liked those video nasties or horror films much, I have to say.'

Robert wondered fleetingly whether it could be Karla herself donating these films of hers to the shop. Knowing they would have the weird, entrancing effect that they seemed to, she was planting them in strategic charity shops in Whitby, hoping to cause maximum chaos and—

No. That would be ridiculous.

Now both women were glaring at him as if they wanted him to go. He could see that he was drawing a blank here. Teresa was tapping her nails on the glass counter.

'If there's nothing else you want,' she said, 'perhaps you could leave. We don't like your sort in here.'

He raised an eyebrow. 'What do you mean?'

Helen leaned across the counter and gave a long, deliberate sniff. She said, 'You're right, Teresa. I can smell it on him.'

'I beg your pardon?'

For a second he was sure that both shop volunteers' eyes shone red. He blinked, and then they were back to normal.

Helen, the meeker of the two, suddenly piped up, 'You know, it's the most incredible coincidence. But when I was sorting through some recently donated books in the storeroom upstairs yesterday, I am sure that I found an old hardback copy of Karla Sorenson's memoir, *The Sinister Sixties*. Or was it *The Spooky Seventies*? One of them, anyway.'

Robert clocked the vexed look that Teresa shot her. 'Oh, really?' he said. 'I'd like to have a look at that, if I may.'

Oh, Teresa looked furious. This Helen was a loose cannon. She had let something slip that she shouldn't have. Surely the memoirs of Karla would contain some kind of clue? Something that would prove useful?

Helen told him, 'You'll have to help me move some of the heavier boxes, young man. The book in question is buried under quite a monstrous stack.'

'Of course,' he said eagerly, turning to follow her to the stairs at the back, and completely missing the glance that passed between the volunteer ladies.

Later, he was furious with himself at falling for such an old trick. But Helen seemed kind of innocent and good-tempered, at least compared with her bullish workmate. He watched her flutter nervously about the storeroom's heaps of donated tat, peering into one crate and then another.

'I'm sure it was here somewhere, with all these Jackie Collinses,' she said.

'Helen, you must know. Where is all this Karla Sorenson-related memorabilia coming from? Is the source of it Karla herself?'

She looked helpless. In the murky air of the storeroom she seemed almost scared. He knew at once that she was fretting in case Teresa downstairs heard her tell him anything.

'We get things donated by all kinds of people,' she said. 'And of course we don't keep track of who gives what. However . . .' She turned to a work bench nearby, and hunted amongst papers, bills, a scattering of brown paper. 'I do remember that those DVDs came a long way. Very unusually, they were sent by post.'

'Really?' Robert was sure he was on to something.

'Aha,' she said with satisfaction, and passed him a sheet of crumpled brown paper. 'The writing is so beautiful, I kept it. Look at that gothic hand.'

Robert examined it. 'Indeed. London postmark, look. But why would people in London donate Karla Sorenson films to a shop in Whitby?'

Helen gave a cry of triumph. 'Here it is!' She delved into a deep cardboard box, almost toppling over in the process. 'Her autobiography! I knew I had seen it!'

As Robert reached out for it, he was distracted by a heavy tread on the staircase behind him. He turned to see the ungainly Teresa joining them in the storeroom.

219

'We'll have to hurry,' she puffed. 'I've left the till unattended.'

'What?' Robert scowled at her. He'd had enough of the belligerent woman.

'We can't let you out again,' Teresa said softly.

'Oh dear, can't we?' asked Helen. 'I'm sure he doesn't really mean any harm.' She hugged the brick-thick memoir to her skinny chest.

'We can't let him run around asking questions,' Teresa spat. 'We just can't. He and his friends have a bad reputation in this town. For getting in the way of things.'

'I see,' said Robert. 'You're in it up to your wattled old neck, aren't you?'

She ignored him. 'And he reeks, too. You know why.'

'Stop saying that!' Robert shouted. 'Why do you keep saying I smell?'

Helen put in, 'You have been touched in the night, haven't you? We can smell faerie on you.'

His stare moved from one charity volunteer to the other. 'You're both crackers. I'm getting out of here. Give me the book.'

'We can't let you just walk out,' Helen warned.

'You've let *him* touch you, haven't you? We can't let you go to *him*.' Teresa was crooning softly, and advancing on Robert.

His hackles were right up now. 'Look, I don't want to hurt either of you ladies.' What could they do to him? These two ancient ratbags? He was in his prime. All he'd have to do was push past and dash down the stairs. They'd never be able to keep up with him. (But what if one of them fell and broke a hip? He'd feel terrible. They might even press charges, and then it'd look awful, wouldn't it? A young bloke like him, assaulting charity volunteers in their own storeroom.)

WHOOMPPHH.

Helen swung Karla's heavy memoirs in a graceful arc. Robert didn't even see it coming. The hardback connected with the back of his skull and sent him crashing to the dusty carpet, out cold.

'Right,' said Teresa, admiring Helen's handiwork. 'We'd best get on to the Brethren. See what they want doing with this one.'

From *Fangs for the Memory:*

The Memoirs of Karla Sorenson

Volume Three: The Sinister Sixties

Chapter Nine

What do I remember about being in that valley in Wales? Such a long time ago now.

One thing you have to realise about this movie-making business. It isn't very glamorous when you're actually there. Doing it. Mucking in. And what I remember most about the shooting of the infamous *Get Thee Inside Me, Satan* is that it chucked it down most of the time.

If I was the same as some of the lily-livered others, I wouldn't really like to say the film's title, or even write it down. It is a film famous for all kinds of reasons now. Mostly as the source of a curse that is meant to have killed various cast and crew members down the years since 1967.

Let us see. Well, Magda Soames plunged off one of the slate

quarry cliffs during the night, just before filming wrapped. Nobody knows what she was doing up there, wandering about.

And the director, Kenny Wearmouth came to a nasty end in a motorboat disaster in the Caribbean the following year. Then the casting director hanged himself, haunted by the devil himself. His wife drank herself to death, giving interviews to anyone who would listen, ranting about the curse on this particular picture, and blaming me – me! – personally for the plague of bad luck that had followed certain people connected with me.

I say it's all horseshit. Really, I do.

I'm still here, aren't I?

Some people would say that's because I'm protected. By occult forces. Just like my character – the divine Jenny Sommers – in the film. Satan wants us to live. As his pawn. As his emissary on earth. But really! These stories are just fairy tales. Why are supposedly sensible adult human beings so intent on believing them?

Film crews number their members in the dozens. Of course, if you examine what happens to each and every individual over the ensuing decades, it's going to look like a litany of disasters. Such is life. None of us are in it to win it, are we? It all goes to the bad in the end. At least, that's what I've found.

Then, of course, there have been the late-night screenings of this, my most famous movie, at which people have apparently gone mad or screamed the house down, or fled on to the streets to do themselves in or murder someone, etc., etc. And I say that's all bullshit as well, frankly. Where was this? America. That's just some flashy executive type, drumming up publicity for these low-rent double bills. Curse of the B movie strikes again. It's all just made up!

And that's showbiz, folks.

Still, I've enjoyed the notoriety. I always do. Pretty early on in this ramshackle career of mine, I realised that it wouldn't be for my acting talent that I would become famous. I'd be famous for flashing my boobies in tacky horror flicks. For being the queen of cult.

But I can live with that.

What I do remember about being in North Wales during that dismal Summer of Love, besides all the rain and damp and hard work, and then the shock at the deaths on set and the accidents and so on - I do remember Fox Soames talking to me.

I thought he was a genius. He was nothing to look at. A hunched-up bald old creature. Yet he had this way with him. Olde-worlde charm, I called it. Swishing about the place in his velvet smoking jacket. He'd had crates of champagne brought to his caravan. Flown in from God knows where. France, probably. And these huge fricking cigars too. He tried to play it so elegantly cool. So debonair and sophisticated. Well, he'd seen something of life, hadn't he? He'd written a West End hit when he was just twenty-two. At the Berlin Olympics he'd come third in the long jump. He claimed to have explored every continent on earth and even been taken up the Limpopo by the natives. He'd been in Churchill's secret war cabinet. He'd flown missions as a spy all over Europe. He was a best-seller and a *bon vivant* and I thought he was just the most dandy little thing I'd ever seen.

Of course we were having an affair. I felt almost obliged to. I had become Jenny Sommers, hadn't I? I was his creation. So I hereby declare the truth: Fox and I were lovers. And no – to scotch the awful rumours – we didn't drive his wife Magda crazy with jealousy, so that she topped herself by jumping off the cliff. She had everything to live for. She had a beautiful son, Alex. Millions in the bank. A huge house in the Cotswolds and an apartment in Manhattan. She was so, so used to Fox's indiscretions. He'd never have left her for me, or anyone else. He just liked his little adventures, did Fox. And my goodness, so did I! We set his dinky little luxury trailer to rocking, we did, whenever we could!

But sex wasn't the main thing. Oh, it was nice, and he was surprisingly agile for a man of his years and stocky build. No, what I adored more than anything was his conversation. He was such a learned man. A genius. Now, you may laugh. You might tell me his books were potboilers. Silly spy stories and Satan-routing penny dreadfuls. But Fox knew that as well. His real genius wasn't in his books. It was in his conversation. It was in his eyes. I find it hard to explain.

He was clever enough to know that he needed to wrap up his ideas and his message in a popular form. Not for him some difficult, artsy book that no one would read. He wanted to communicate with the world at large.

And what did he want to tell them?

The old, old message: beware of the devil. He is out there. He's closer than you think. And he's listening to your every word.

You'd better watch out.

Fox was scandalised by the permissive society. By everything that I, in a sense, embodied. And he saw in it the devil's work. Beelzebub's era had come again. And Fox's way of combating that was with his novels, and with movies like *Get Thee Inside Me, Satan*.

I remember sitting late in his caravan one night. Before Magda died. We were drinking champagne and he was fixing me with those terrible eyes. Forget-me-not blue.

'You must be more careful than most,' he told me.

'Me? I'm all right. I can look after myself. Why do you say that?'

'Because you know that the dark forces I describe are real, don't you?'

'What?'

'You have felt them. You know their power.'

'I . . .'

'Don't pretend, Karla. You put on this amusing spectacle, this persona. You pretend to be just another whore actress. A callow, vulgar flibbertigibbet.'

'I am! That's me!'

'But you are so much more, aren't you? And you must beware, Karla. The people you are connected to always exact a high price in the end.'

'But—'

He cut me dead with a swipe of his hand. 'No. No more. What have they offered you? Eternal youth? Stardom? Riches?'

I gawped at him.

Well, as you my fans know, it has long been rumoured that I made a pact with the devil when I was fifteen years old. Another tale cranked out by the sordid publicity machine. I made a deal to keep my youth eternally, and to be famous and rich beyond my dreams.

Well, I ain't rich, am I, darlings? And I'm only famous amongst the culty film fraternity. A dwindling band of benign anorak-wearing young men. And as for my youth . . . oh dear. I'm getting slack and saggy and baggy. Sorry to disappoint you! Though I'm still fabulous, obviously. But I'm not some supernaturally nubile and unblemished creature of Satan.

So, I am very sorry, Mr Soames. But I am afraid you were quite, quite wrong. You were believing in your own kind of story. And I can't blame you for that. That's what we all do, isn't it? In the end?

We make the world around us into the story we want it to be. We make ourselves the star of it. And we tell ourselves we know how the world works, and that the stories we tell about it are true.

Location, Location

As they tracked through the desolate valley, Brenda paused thoughtfully. 'The thing I don't want to do is meet myself.'

'Why not?' asked Effie. She was feeling wretchedly uncomfortable in yesterday's clothes.

'I think it's probably a bad idea.'

'But why?' Effie asked. 'You could warn yourself about all sorts of things. Change the things that happened to you.'

Brenda frowned. 'That's what I'm worried about.'

Now they were very close to the film set and its shanty town of caravans and trailers. It was rather like happening upon Marco Polo's entourage as it rested up for the night on its long voyage.

Brenda nodded at one particular vehicle. 'Look, that caravan with the opening at the side.'

Effie squinted. 'The burger van?' There was a smoky, greasy smell that was making her stomach roil with hunger.

'That's my home from home. I'll be in there.'

'I can't see anything for the queue . . .'

It was true. A ramshackle queue of film people were waiting none too patiently for their breakfast. A ragged chorus of 'Why Are We Waiting?' broke out. Effie could see the ones who had been served taking their loaded trays off to a double-decker bus,

228

which had been customised, and turned into a two-tier dining room.

'Are you sure, Brenda? I mean, this business of going into the past and everything. Are you sure that if we got closer we'd see you over there, slopping out the breakfast beans and scrambled eggs?'

Brenda nodded grimly. 'Look.'

Now they had moved close enough to see the woman working in the hatch of the van. Brenda and Effie hung back where they thought they might not be seen, squinting in appalled fascination at the large woman in the hairnet. She was laughing and joking, clearly on first-name terms with the cast and crew.

'But,' Effie boggled, 'you look exactly the same!'

'Of course.'

'It's forty or more years ago! It's the nineteen sixties!'

'You know me, Effie. I never change.'

'I know. It's just a shock seeing it demonstrated like this, I must say. I mean, at this point in time I'm a young woman still. I'm about thirty-odd, I think . . .'

Brenda sat heavily on a handy rock. 'I've always been old. And a drudge, too. It depresses me a bit, to think that I'm still doing the same job. Slopping up cooked breakfasts.'

'At least these days you're not in a quarry any more.'

'I can't remember how I ended up working in the film industry. Curse this brain of mine. This rotten memory.'

'You could ask her,' Effie said.

'What?'

'You could wait for a quiet mo. When she goes on her break, say. And you could quiz her. About all the things you don't know. She'll know things that you have forgotten about. It stands to reason, doesn't it?'

Brenda looked troubled by this whole time-bending business and

Effie couldn't blame her. 'Maybe you're right. I don't want to tempt fate, though.'

Effie asked, 'What does that mean?'

'It feels like interfering in the past too much. I'm sure that whoever has brought us here, through the mists of time, doesn't want us to do that.'

Effie couldn't help herself. 'Hahahaha! Listen to you, Brenda! The mists of time indeed!'

'Sssh. You'll draw attention to us.'

A man's voice spoke up, quite near to them. Fruity and rich and amused. 'She already has.'

Effie let out a shriek of surprise at his approach, which she quickly stifled.

Brenda recognised him at once. He was a dapper, rotund figure, puffing on an expensive cigar and wearing a floor-length purple silk dressing gown. He had obviously been behind them for some time, earwigging with fascination on their hushed conflab.

Fox Soames said, 'I wonder if you two ladies would care to explain your presence here on my film set? What are you? Fanatics? Groupies?' He looked them up and down very carefully.

'What?' gasped Effie. 'How dare you? My friend and I are here to do some investigating.'

'Investigating, is it? I see. And what would you be investigating, hmm? As you see, this is a very ordinary, run-of-the-mill location shoot.'

Brenda shook her head slowly. 'It's hardly that, Mr Soames.'

He quirked his sandy, overgrown eyebrows. 'You know me, do you? How fascinating. You have done your research.'

He gave Brenda a long appraising look. She stared back at those brilliant eyes of his.

Effie didn't like this strutting, pompous ass one little bit. Carrying on as if he owned the whole set-up. And he wasn't even a star, or the director. He was just the writer, according to Brenda. She stared at his liver-spotted pate and was horrified to see it pulsing. It was like watching the soft skull of a young infant, beating slightly in time with his thoughts. But Fox was an old man and it was very strange to see. The pulse quickened and his face flushed as he gathered his thoughts and hissed at them both: 'Do you know what I think, ladies? I think you are here to sabotage this picture. Perhaps to prevent it from being made.'

'No, no. That isn't it at all,' said Brenda.

Fox went on excitedly, 'I believe you are cultists. Sent to put a spanner in the works. Your superiors – your brethren, shall we call them – they don't want the world to see this movie. Because it will give away too many of their secrets.'

Effie tutted. 'Balls.'

Brenda stared at her. 'Effie!'

'Silly old fool doesn't know what he's talking about. How can he think we're cultists?'

'Look at you. The pair of you. There is something very strange about you both.'

Brenda smiled in what she hoped was a reassuring manner. 'You've got that much right. But we aren't working for some terrible cult, you must believe us.'

'Oh no? Then what is it that I sense about the two of you? I am very sensitive, you know. I am alert to the effects of sorcery and necromancy. I quiver when I am in the presence of those steeped in magical lore.'

'Oh yes?' Effie smirked. She was hunting through her bag for a clean hanky. Her nose had turned cold and drippy, standing about in a quarry bottom like this. She glared at Fox. 'And are you quivering now?'

'My dear, I am rigid. I am tremulous and agog. Now, why would that be? Are you magical, you and your friend here, hmm?'

Brenda said, 'Yes, all right. If you like. We're very magical indeed. But we really don't mean anybody any harm. You must believe that, Mr Soames. We are here to help.'

Fox frowned at her earnest expression. 'You, my dear. I already know you, don't I?'

'No.'

'Aren't you the dinner lady here? You look very like her. I can't be sure. I don't queue up with the rest of the hoi polloi.'

'How very nice for you,' snapped Effie.

Fox ignored her scathing tone. 'You two intrigue me. Will you come to my caravan? Perhaps you would join me for coffee? It is mid morning to me. I began my work at five. Writing, writing, you know how it is. No rest for the wicked . . .'

Following the stocky man across the valley floor to his mobile home, Effie suddenly recalled where she knew his name from. Fox Soames. Her aunties used to read his novels. He had been going since the 1930s, back before Effie had been born. He wrote the most horrid, lurid, ghastly ghoulish stuff about black magic. Effie's aunts – especially the usually sensible Aunt Maud – lapped up these bodice-ripping, swashbuckling tales of satanists and adventurers. Aunt Maud would read them aloud to her sisters, Eliza, Beryl and Natasha – and her niece Effie, who would be hiding round the living room door. Maud would be doing all the voices, holding her family in her spell.

And so this was he. And he was the author of *Get Thee Inside Me, Satan*. Effie wondered if that had been one of the books she had heard as a young child, crooking her ear to the gap in the door.

Funny how things always seemed to link up.

As they reached Fox Soames's home from home, Brenda was studying their new surroundings with extreme interest.

Fox's mobile home was a very up-to-the-minute American job – at least it was back here in 1967. Even in the present day, it would be quite a marvel. Inside it was decorated like a stately home's drawing room, all velvet and ornate gilt. At the far end stood a wide desk, scattered with papers and ashtrays and a fierce-looking black typewriter. It looked as if Fox had been working studiously through the night.

'Magda, my dear!' he called. 'We have visitors.'

A door opened and a woman somewhat younger than Fox stepped out, rather hesitantly. She was in a filmy muumuu of swirling psychedelic patterns. She had straight black hair and a somewhat unfocused expression. Was the woman on drugs? It was no good if she was, for she was carrying in her arms a fair-haired toddler.

The child fixed the two new arrivals with an ice-blue stare that exactly matched his father's.

'And this is Alex,' Fox purred, snatching up a brandy goblet and swishing the contents around. 'My son, meet . . . oh dear. We haven't been introduced properly, have we, my dears?'

'I'm Brenda and this is Effie,' Brenda blurted out. 'And we have come all the way from the future to warn you. This film you've written and that they're shooting out there in that valley right now – it is *the pure quintessence of evil*!'

Penny Writes Another Letter Home

Dear Mam,

Now Robert's disappeared. Seriously. He's not been back to the hotel all day. He went out this morning on some secret kind of mission and we've seen neither hide nor hair of him since.

So it's yours truly left in charge of the hotel tonight.

Which is no biggie, really. Everyone knows their jobs. It's all working like clockwork actually, but we can't go on like that for too long. We need Robert back at the helm!

So, where is he?

This morning he looked very perturbed. I tried to talk to him during the breakfast rush, when everyone was dashing about looking after the film people. All he would say was that something terrible had happened to Brenda and Effie. After they watched that film I watched, the one I bought from Save the Kiddies. Apparently they have gone into a trance just like I did, only much worse. I think what Robert was saying was that he was going to find out where the film had come from in the first place, but I was so busy running things at this end that I didn't get all the details.

And now he's gone! It's evening again and we're about to

serve dinner and he's still not here. I try to jolly along the staff, but they know something is up.

But then, of course, there has been another development to take our minds off Robert's vanishing act. Guess what?

There's been an accident on the film set today.

The curse of the movie strikes back!

I mean, it wasn't a massive thing, like someone's head getting cut off or someone getting electrocuted. Nothing like that. But Mimsy Stark, one of the supporting artists, choked on a sausage-and-egg bap on location at the abbey this morning. She closed up one of her passages and there was a right panic on, because she couldn't breathe for about ten minutes or something. They had to get an ambulance out and everything, and she's still in hospital now, so the filming is held up and everyone's furious.

The crew and technical people came trogging back here at teatime, muttering and complaining about poor suffocated Mimsy. She wasn't very popular amongst them in the first place. She's proper stuck-up, apparently. Anyway, they're all saying it's the dreaded curse starting up again. In the form of sausage-and-egg baps.

I must finish up, Mam. I wonder what you make of these strange letters of mine.

Tonight I was going to go over to Spector, to have a drink with the divine Michael. But I don't think I can now. Not with Robert missing. I'll have to ring Michael, and explain. And before you ask, or rush to assumptions, I don't think there's much chance of anything blossoming between me and Michael. It seems really weird, but ever since the night of the cabaret, he's been fixated on that old woman from the

Christmas Hotel. She's the only woman he'll talk about. So I think he's probably some weirdo, actually. I'm best off out of it. Anyway, I'll write again soon!

Love,

Penny

Epiphanies and Pie and Peas

It was Pie and Peas Night at the Christmas Hotel, and Mrs Claus was sitting at her favourite table. High table, from which she could survey her festive kingdom, watching the pensioners slurp up their peas and gravy, and fork up mouthfuls of glistening mince.

'There's no elves in my pies!' she cried out, laughing, tapping Michael on the shoulder playfully. 'You cheeky thing! Where did you hear that? What makes you think we go in for cannibalism round these parts, eh?'

He grinned ruefully.

Oh, but he looked a sight for sore eyes tonight. He was in a green paisley shirt, the exact shade of his eyes. His hair looked blue-black in the fairy-lit ambience of the dining room. 'I don't know,' he laughed. 'Just general gossip. Penny, I think. That girl who hangs out with Robert and that lot.'

'Ooh, they do say awful things about me. But it's all in fun, you know. At least, I hope it is! They don't really hate and fear me. They just say silly things for a joke. I don't know why. They know I'm big enough and old enough and ugly enough to take a joke.' She sighed and waved a cracker at him, which he pulled energetically. She let him have the hat.

'You're not ugly!' he protested. 'I think it's plain for anyone to see that you have been a very beautiful young woman in your time. And that you're a beautiful person inside.'

He sounded so earnest. So ridiculous. Mrs Claus thrilled at his voice as he leaned over the table to tell her this. She flushed and turned back to her pie and peas, keen not to betray her own emotions.

Because she didn't know what he was playing at yet. Was this all real? The way he had latched on to her? She couldn't trust him. Just as she couldn't trust anyone. Her days of snaring men were long gone, she had accepted that. Faced with this puppy-dog attachment from Michael, she was starting to think he was mocking her somehow. Maybe it was all some horrible plan of that Effie and Brenda's. To draw her into a compromising situation. To expose her. To ridicule her.

Why would a young man like this think anything of her?

She spooned up suet and gravy and thought hard as carols crackled over the tannoy and the pensioners in her care mumbled along with the old, sentimental words. Maybe it was all for real. Stranger things had happened, surely? Maybe Michael really *was* starting to feel something for her.

After all, she had so much to offer.

She chuckled inwardly at herself.

He loved her story. She knew that much. That was what kept him coming back to sit by her. To make himself comfortable at her side in her Christmassy boudoir.

She had been telling him a little more about how her sisters had been scandalised when she met her fancy man. All those years back.

They forbade her to leave the house in case he came galloping by again. The twelve days of Christmas ticked by and she sat stewing indoors. Snow came down heavily over the harbour town, freezing the place solid. Jamming them into their homes. But she would lie in her bed at night and hear hooves clanging through the streets. No one else was about. It had to be him, braving the weather. Reminding her that she was his.

Every morning until Epiphany there was a new present left on the doorstep of the sisters' shop. A teddy bear. Hot peppermints. A bunch of blood-red roses.

Maud was furious. 'We will put a hex on him, sisters,' she announced over breakfast. 'We'll prepare a spell to make his eyes pop out and his tiddler drop off. And then where will he be, eh? This awful seducer. This mucky, disgusting, perverted man?'

All the sisters laughed at this. But Maud caught her youngest sister's eye. Maud knew it was serious. She could feel the power bristling about the place. She could sense this man's determination. Her sister's steely will. Angela stirred golden sugar into her hot, thick porridge and smiled enigmatically.

'I picked up the presents each morning from the doorstep. I stared at the hoofprints he had left in the snow. I'd hide the offerings in my room and stare at them when I was alone. A doll that could walk and speak and give marvellous advice. A mandrake root. A golden ball that bounced so high it took a full day to come back to earth. A bell that when you tinkled it thinking of a certain person, you could blight them with double incontinence.' Mrs Claus threw back her head and laughed at the memory of her Christmas gifts.

'No wonder you went to him,' Michael said. 'With temptations like these.'

'It was a poor time,' she said. 'This town is so spruced up and lovely now. But you have to understand that back in the thirties, I suppose this was, it was still filled with warrens of filthy back streets and tumbledown shacks. The place reeked of fish and unwashed human beings who never changed their clothes from one season to the next. They just put extra layers of filthy rags on themselves.

'Oh, it was a mucky old place. And here was this man, leaving me tiaras and necklaces. Dolls that could talk. I was a greedy child. And it was as if he was all made out of spices and sweets. His skin pale as fondant cream. His lips like cherry-red boiled sweets. His eyes were peppermint green.'

Mrs Claus darted a look at Michael. 'So I went with him. I defied my sisters and I clambered out of their house one night in a snowstorm. The walking, talking doll had told me where and when he would be waiting. On the way out of town. The road leading north. So I went. And he took me away for a year and a day.'

'Where did you go?'

'Hmm?'

'His home? His mansion? Where did you say it was?'

'Oh, dearie. We galloped so far that night. Through the blizzard. I don't know how far it was. I always understood it was somewhere north of Newcastle, but he once explained how geography was immaterial. In leaving with him, I had left this realm. I had entered the world of faerie.'

Michael raised both eyebrows.

'He was the faerie king, was what he told me on that long ride through the night. Epiphany night, in more ways than one. And his castle was in a different land.'

'Oh come on.' Michael smiled, suddenly sceptical.

'We dismounted somewhere near Hexham. On a high and windy hill. He fetched out of his saddle bag a pair of bright, shining pinking shears. I asked my talking doll, who I had kept clutched close to me, throughout the escape: "What's he doing, Mrs Claus?" And my doll said, "Why, those are his magic pinking shears. Now he's slicing through the very fabric of time and space. Into another land. His land. And that's where he's taking you." And then she started laughing at me. A not-very-nice laugh, I thought. She jumped out of my arms and – I swear – landed on the snowy ground and ran away, into the night.

'My husband turned to me. Beckoned me and the horse towards the gap he had cut in the air itself. It was a scintillating space of darkness. A glittering miasma lay beyond.

'All he said was "Come with me." They were his favourite words. So in I went, after him. To his kingdom of faerie, north of Newcastle.'

Michael was gawping at her.

Maybe I'm telling him too much, she mused. She snapped her fingers at the elf waiting on their table. Time for Christmas pud. Time for sherry. Time for the next hook in her tale.

'So there I was. In a new land. I'd seen nothing like it. I was his queen. I was untouchable. Until . . . until my downfall. Some would say it was inevitable. I'd stop finding favour in his eye. But it came as a shock to me, I can tell you.'

'What happened?'

'Well, nine months on I had a baby. And they wouldn't let me keep it. They stood me before the whole faerie court and he was up on his throne, looking aloof and like he'd lost all patience with me. Like giving birth to a human child, a daughter, was in such bad taste. Less than a year and he was out of love with me. You know how it is.'

'Yes . . .' Michael said.

'Help yourself to the brandy butter, dearie,' she told him. 'I was arguing back. Wanting to keep my daughter. Of course I did. She was beautiful. Perfect. But they said that if I was to remain in their wondrous land, I had to give her up. I had to send her back to my sisters to raise. Well. What could I do?'

'You gave her up?'

Mrs Claus smiled sadly. 'In his realm of faerie, north of Newcastle, it was Christmas every day. Like I say, I was a greedy child. It wasn't some sappy, religious-type Christmas. It was a Christmas where you got given presents all the time. Where you ate and drank to your heart's content. Until you popped. I was still only a child. I wouldn't leave it all behind.'

'You gave her up?'

She nodded. 'I was so ashamed of myself. But I hardened my heart. I was greedy, but only because I had been starved in the world I had come from. Starved of sweet things and affection. In the land of faerie, I had it all. One screaming baby seemed such a little thing to give up, really. I mean, it wasn't as if we had even bonded yet. She thought nothing of me, this twisting, crimson mite in my arms. She'd be better off with my sisters, with Maud, who knew so much more about bringing up kiddies than did I.'

'I can't believe you gave her up.' Michael frowned.

'There was silence in his throne room. Then the sound of hollow plastic legs marching into the room. I turned, and there was my mechanical doll striding across the flagstones towards me. Mrs Claus, in a bright red robe with ermine trim. The doll had come to take my baby from me, and all the faeries watched. My fancy man watched too. As I gave her up, they clapped and laughed. And I watched the doll bear her away, back to the dreadful, dingy world and the town by the sea where I had grown up.'

Mrs Claus pushed her unfinished pudding away, her appetite spoiled by the recounting of her bitter tale.

'But you came back here eventually. To this town.'

'That's another story,' she said primly. She was disappointed in his reaction tonight. He wasn't sympathetic enough. She thought he might understand better than this.

'And the baby? Did you see her again?'

She gave a huge sigh. 'Much later. A long time later, when I stole those pinking shears of his from under his pillow. I set off into the freezing night winds. I cut me my own hole in the fabric of time and space. I was homesick. But it was much too late for me and my baby. She hated me. She still does.'

Her voice was drowned out for a moment, as the other diners put down their cutlery and pushed away their bowls, all in one mass movement. An elf had announced the commencement of bingo-calling in the main lounge, to be followed by a dance. The hokey cokey, March of the Mods, all their silly favourites. Mrs Claus offered Michael her arm.

'I hope I haven't horrified you with my tale of Christmases past?' She smiled. Needily, she thought. I'm being too needy with him. What am I doing, offering all my secrets? I'll scare the young fella away.

He guided her around the table, wheeling her steadily towards the ramp and out of the dining room. 'Not at all,' he said stiffly. Too stiff, she thought. Too polite. Then he bent to kiss her softly on her cheek, which burned at his touch. 'I love hearing all about your life,' he said.

Bound

Dear Brenda,

I am writing this to you with no legs.

In fact, I am writing this to you with no paper and no pen. It is all in Frank's head, my love. I hope my words will get to you somehow.

Even in Frank's very darkest days he was never as lost as this. Here I am in the same town as you. I am only a few streets away from your guest house, from the home where we have lived together these past few months. But Frank feels so far, far away.

They have taken Frank's legs, Brenda. They have made him a prisoner. They have tied him with ropes and chains and put him in this attic. My spirit feels crushed. My soul's squashed small. I have been treated like this before. The fight has gone out of Frank. Something terrible has happened to me.

The bleeding has stopped.

The madwoman's servants have been checking on me. Staunching my wounds. They have the decency to look appalled at what they have done to me. They were under some kind of enchantment. That's how they try to excuse themselves. But Frank clams up. He won't forgive them. He won't engage in conversation with these two men, these lackeys of the Sorenson witch.

They sit across the attic from me now, staring at me. We're all prisoners together now.

Brenda, hear me, will you? Come to my aid?

You're sensitive. My beautiful bride. You will hear me, won't you?

Later . . .

Another prisoner for the attic.

Unbelievable.

I fear all is lost.

Robert. Your friend Robert is here.

He was pushed in about fifteen minutes ago. Shoved up the stairs to sit with us. Came in at a stumbling run. Woozy. They'd clobbered him round the head. Two old women from Save the Kiddies, evidently more servants of Karla Sorenson.

And now here he is. Looking sick with dread. His eyes just about popped out of his head when he saw me. And me with no legs.

'What are they doing, putting us up here, Frank? What's happening?'

Frank doesn't have any answers for him.

A terrible feeling of dread has swept over Frank. Frank has a sense that something even worse is to come. Worse than being locked up. Worse than no legs. Worse even than being separated from the beloved bride of Frank.

What is it?

I feel a presence.

Something in the hotel below. In the suite below belonging

to the evil Karla. She has someone there. Someone I haven't seen for a very long time.

Frank's hackles are up. The hairs are standing up all over his body. Frank's got gooseflesh bumping up everywhere. The tiny alarm bells ringing even overwhelm the steady, heavy throb of pain from his gory stumps and his ghostly limbs.

But who is it down there?

Who has Karla got with her now?

Fox in his Den

'I must say, my dear, I find you absolutely fascinating,' Fox purred. He sat down gracefully behind his gilt-edged desk and surveyed his guests. 'You, too, my dear,' he told Effie. 'But Brenda even more so. Absolutely fascinating.'

Brenda shifted uncomfortably. 'There's nothing so fascinating about me. The important thing, Mr Soames, is that you see the sense in what we're saying. We believe that we have been brought here, to this time and place, to prevent this film from ever being made.'

'So you say.' Fox steepled his stubby, typewriter-key-scarred fingers and propped his heavy chin on them. 'And you came through time. From the twenty-first century. Forgive me, dears, but you hardly look to me like twenty-first-century ladies. You're not exactly futuristic, are you, now?'

'What did you expect?' Effie snapped. 'Jane Fonda?'

There came a snort from Magda Soames, Fox's surly and slightly-stoned-looking wife. She was at the art deco minibar, mixing a row of martinis and dishing up bowls of olives, smoked oysters and nuts. It was as if they were here for a cocktail party. Effie found herself revolted by the imperturbable Soameses. She didn't like the look of the kid, either. He was propped on a priceless armchair, glaring at the visitors from under his fringe.

Fox said smoothly, 'I could almost believe that the dinner lady from the catering van was having a silly joke with me, for what purpose I know not. And that she had roped her elderly friend in to help. Well, I suppose there is one way of finding out, isn't there?' He snatched up a golden phone on his desk and spoke urgently to the person at the other end. When he was finished, he smiled at them both and carried on with his interrogation. 'My dears, this is only a movie, isn't it? What possible harm can a movie do? Indeed, surely it can do a lot of good, hmm? If it warns audiences around the world about the dangers inherent in flirting with the powers of darkness?'

Magda shuffled over to them, lurching a little in her filmy muu-muu, revealing a hitherto unsuspected hump on her back, which came as a surprise to Brenda and Effie as they took their drinks from her gleaming silver tray. Effie sipped and grimaced: it was sinfully strong, drowning in gin. She sipped again. Time travel, it seemed, could make you light-headed.

Brenda tackled Fox's question carefully, 'I know that is your mission, Mr Soames. That I understand. In the future, Effie and I have watched some of your films, and documentaries about you on the DVD extras. And we believe that you really thought you were doing good, in warning people not to meddle in the ways of the Left-Hand Path.'

Fox looked at her blankly. 'What are these DVD extras you speak of?' He puffed on his cigar.

'It doesn't matter now. The thing is, in setting about warning the world, I think you end up causing even greater chaos and danger. In allowing this film to be made, I think you succeed in doing the very opposite of what you *want* to do.'

'Balderdash.' He coughed.

'Listen to her,' Effie urged. She loved to hear Brenda explain things like this, right in the midst of a fraught and hectic scene. In the middle of one of their adventures, she loved the way Brenda was able to keep her head.

'I believe,' Brenda said steadily, 'that this film you're making now—'

'I'm not making it, though, am I?' Fox snapped. 'I'm here only to observe. I'm only the writer.'

'Let her speak!' Effie growled, sipping her drink, which she was starting to enjoy by now.

'Think about what films consist of,' Brenda said. 'Light and sound, trapped on celluloid. Trapped energy. Light jammed tight, for ever perhaps. And darkness, kept cool and preserved in tins, idling away the decades and waiting. Now, I think that this particular film opens up a hole into a different reality. Somehow something happens during this shoot in Wales, and a chink of light from hell gets into the workings. And this film absorbs that. A bit of the devil gets into the very frames of the picture . . .'

They were all staring at her. 'Very poetic, Brenda,' Fox said. 'Utter nonsense, of course. How does that devil get in? Where does he come from? There are no Satanists here. No followers of the dark path.'

'Are you sure?' Brenda frowned at him.

Fox paled slightly. 'You mean . . . ?'

Effie blurted out, 'Your leading lady! That Karla one! Her!'

Fox darted a quick glance at his wife and child. 'Magda, take Alex for his afternoon nap, would you?'

Magda looked at him dreamily through the bottom of her martini glass as she drained it. 'Yes, my dear?'

'Take Alex to his room. And go and lie down yourself, while

you're about it. These ladies from the future and I have important matters to discuss.'

Magda's face creased into a feral snarl, which unsettled the visitors somewhat. 'You. You're always wanting to be alone with the ladies. You liver-spotted lothario.'

'Yes, yes, my dear. Call me what you will. Now, take my son out of here.'

Magda went to pick up Alex, who squirmed and kicked, mussing his miniature black velvet suit and ruffled shirt. 'He doesn't want to go,' Magda sighed. 'He wants to stay here and hear all about the devil. And your fancy women. He likes a nice story like that.'

Effie raised her eyebrow. What a dysfunctional family! she thought, using a phrase that wouldn't have been current back here in 1967. Well, that was the sixties for you. She watched as Fox lost his temper and demanded that Magda leave at once, and take their son with her – by force, if necessary. Both Brenda and Effie winced at the kid's shrieks and howls as he was taken away. They could still hear his muffled cries through the thin walls of the mobile home.

There came a knock at the exterior door.

'Ah!' Fox cried, his scowling face lighting up in pleasure. 'Here comes your proof, my dears.'

He hopped across the priceless Arabian rug and flung open the door. He leaned out, obscuring their view, but they could hear an oddly familiar voice saying, 'It really isn't fair, Mr Soames, to drag me across here to serve you your elevenses. Of course I don't mind, trogging my way all across the valley floor, but you have to think about the rest of the crew. I've left a big queue over there, waiting for chips and so on.'

Effie suddenly clutched Brenda's arm. 'He's brought *you* over!'

'What?' At first Brenda didn't get it.

'In here, my dear,' Fox was saying, his voice filled with glee. 'Bring the tray into my sitting room.'

Brenda and Effie watched, appalled, as he led a tall, ungainly woman into the room. She was carrying a silver salver, which she placed on a free corner of his desk. She whipped off the lid to reveal a plateful of steaming fish and chips. 'Will that be all?' she asked crossly.

Fox clapped his hands. 'Look! Look at my guests! Are they at all familiar, hmm?'

The dinner lady frowned. 'Guests? You want more chips bringing over, do you?'

Fox swayed dreamily over the fish and chips. 'Food of the gods, my dear. No, I have quite sufficient. But look! Behold! Your future self.'

Effie took a step forward then, almost protectively, as the dinner lady swung round and the two Brendas were suspended there, on the carpet of purple arabesques, staring into each other's identical faces.

'It's true!' cried Fox. 'You were speaking the truth. You really have done something fiddly and clever with time.'

'Of course we have,' said Effie's Brenda. 'Why would we lie about a thing like that? You needn't have brought *me* in like this. I mean, *her*. You'll confuse the poor thing. Addle her brains with paradox.' Brenda stared pityingly at her younger self. She had so much still to come, this Brenda. So much she hardly suspected as yet.

The other, younger Brenda shrugged. 'Oh well. That's me, is it?'

'Yes!' Fox simpered. 'You from the future! Come back in time!'

'Very nice.' The younger Brenda nodded. 'Time travel. Lovely. I suppose this is all to do with some kind of spooky investigation you're caught up in?'

Older Brenda nodded enthusiastically. 'Isn't it always?'

'Then I'd better leave you to it,' said the careworn dinner lady. 'I'll try to keep out of your way. But I must say, I'm glad to see that we're still at it. When did you say you come from?'

'Forty years hence!' said Effie, in a very portentous manner, Brenda thought. Effie was really building up her part as the ominous emissary from the next century.

'Oh, this is Effie,' Brenda told her younger self. 'You don't know her yet. But she'll be a good friend to you.'

Fox glared at one Brenda and then the other. 'What's wrong with you both? Can't you scream? Can't you react? Can't you behave as if this is something even just a little bit out of the ordinary?'

The younger Brenda rolled her eyes at him. 'You can bring your own tray and crockery back to my caravan. I won't be dragging myself all the way over here again today. I've got a lot on, as it happens.' She looked back at Brenda and Effie and smiled politely. 'Well, it was nice to meet you. Best of luck with your investigation. What was it about again?'

'Satanism,' Brenda told her cheerily. 'Karla Sorenson, the star of this movie, is in a pact with the devil himself, which means that this film they're making, and everyone involved in it, is going to be cursed for ever.'

The younger Brenda tutted. 'I thought so. I thought there was something funny going on. Anyway, cheerio, lovey. See you all later.'

And then she was gone.

'Nice woman,' Effie said.

Volunteers

Teresa and Helen, the charity shop ladies, took the lift down from the turret where Karla was living, and slipped through the rest of the Christmas Hotel, hoping no one would notice them.

Helen was feeling bad. 'It can't be right. What we just did.'

'We were doing our duty. What we had been told to do.'

'Who by, though, Teresa? I don't understand!'

'You don't have to understand, Helen.'

'But that young man. What were we doing, dragging him halfway across town? Bundling him about like someone's luggage?'

Teresa snapped: 'What are you complaining for? You got to meet a film star, didn't you?'

'Oh yes, of course. That was very nice. She's every inch the star, and it was a real honour. But I still don't see, Teresa, what she wanted with the boy . . .'

Helen stopped and glared at her colleague. They were in a corridor somewhere in the middle of the vast hotel. The dark, avid look on Teresa's face made Helen step backwards.

'We work for the same people as Ms Sorenson. The same organisation.'

Helen gulped. 'Save the Kiddies?'

'No, something else. A shadowy organisation. A secret fellowship.'

253

'But ... I don't!' Helen's voice turned into a kind of rough squawk. Shadowy organisation? She wanted none of it.

'You're my friend,' said Teresa softly. 'You don't really mind helping me out, do you, Helen?'

'Why, no. Of course not, Teresa.' Helen fought to make her voice steady and brave-sounding. 'But when it comes to keeping people captive. And putting them in attics against their wills. I'm not so sure. Did you see? She had other men in there. Other prisoners.'

Teresa patted her on the arm. Teresa's hand felt like an old claw to Helen. 'Our job is to keep quiet, and to pretend that we haven't seen anything. Come on now, Helen. Our work here is done.'

Superstitious

Alex delivered the new shooting schedule in person.

'As you can see, the old one is in tatters. Everything has had to be switched around and reordered. It's given me an awful headache, this.'

Karla had her servant elf Kevin pour him a stiff whisky. 'Poor dear. I can imagine what a faff it's been.'

'You don't mind? Being shunted around, I mean? You haven't been able to get on with anything yet, because of all these minor mishaps. You haven't been able to really get your teeth into anything . . .'

She laughed, throwing back her head. There was a manic tinge to Karla's laugh. 'I'm an old pro. I can hold myself in check. I understand how these things work.'

'I wish I was as understanding as you.'

'I've been around film-making for almost fifty years, my dear. I know the kinds of things that can go wrong.'

'Silly young women half choking themselves on sausage baps? Oh, and there's Ralph, too, tonight. One of our best technicians. Slipped in the shower and broke his leg. He's got concussion too. He's out of the picture.'

'My goodness. You'd think there was a Jonah about, wouldn't you?'

'That's what the crew are starting to say. At least, those of them staying up drinking all night at the Hotel Miramar are. They've been talking about the famous curse on this project . . .'

'And on me?' Karla smiled.

'You know how they are. Film people. Apparently there's some young woman, works up at that hotel, going round telling everyone that whomsoever watches the original film goes into a trance, and comes to a bad end.'

Karla shook her head firmly. 'Every print of the original movie was recalled. No one can watch it.'

Alex sipped his drink. 'I've seen it. Someone from the company slipped me a copy just as I embarked on this project. They thought I should see it. It seemed imperative.'

'Who?' Karla felt herself go rigid. 'Who gave you it?'

'Strange executive type. I'd never met him before. Came knocking on my office door and said he'd brought me something special, and vital, in person. And it was the disc. *Get Thee Inside Me, Satan*. Very strange kind of executive. Black suit. Colourless face. Didn't even tell me his name.'

'You watched it? All the way through? And nothing happened to you?'

He smiled ruefully. 'Well, it was kind of late. Apparently I fell asleep in front of it. My girlfriend Janice found me still sat there the next morning, staring at the fuzzy screen like I'd lost my marbles. I hardly remember anything of what I saw.'

'Poor Alex. You shouldn't have watched it. I watched it once. It's not a good idea.'

'I see.'

'It's . . . a living thing, that film.'

'What?'

'I mean it, my dear. Sometimes I think the movie really is alive. It comes to me, speaks to me. Insinuates things in my ear. It can creep up on you. Snaking through the airwaves, playing itself again and again in your mind's eye. Once you have let it in, it stays there.'

'Yes, well, um . . .'

'Oh, sorry. I'm letting actressy superstition get the better of me.'

'There seems to be a lot of superstition around this film.'

Karla studied this out-of-shape, blustery man. He looked uncomfortable under her gaze. He was in her realm. Here, it wasn't so easy to avoid her enchantments. She asked him, 'Don't you remember, my dear? Don't you recall what happened on that particular night in 1967?'

'I was too young. I was little more than a toddler.' He chuckled at the very idea of remembering so far back.

'Oh, I suppose so. You wouldn't have understood any of it anyway.'

Alex stiffened. He even felt a bit cross at Karla, raking this up. 'Besides, my mother was killed that night. Tragically. I don't like to even think about it, to be quite honest.'

Karla wouldn't let it drop. She curled her legs under her and surveyed him from her recumbent position on her white leather chaise longue. 'And yet, in making this picture, I think you are facing your demons.'

'No!' he cried, too forcefully. 'As far as I am concerned, nothing out of the ordinary is happening now, and nor did it back in 1967. There was a thunderstorm. There were some accidents. There was no . . . devil walking amongst us.'

'Oh, Alex. You know that's not true.'

'All I know was that I was with my Auntie Brenda, in her chip van. And there was a storm, and she kept me safe.'

'Your Auntie Brenda, was it?'

'Yes! And that's another thing, Karla. The most curious thing. A weird coincidence. She is here! Brenda is here!'

Karla smirked, and lit herself a cigarette. 'Oh, really?'

'Perhaps you don't remember her. In fact there is no reason why you should. She was just the dinner lady on the set.'

'No, I'm not sure that I do remember her at all.' Karla inhaled the smoke deeply and luxuriantly. 'But she was kind to you, you say, this Brenda person?'

Alex nodded.

'What an amazing coincidence. Ah, now I think on, you know, I do remember Brenda. Very well indeed. She's a very special lady, you know. A unique woman.'

'Really?'

'I know her father, you know. Nice man.'

Alex blinked at her. He was trying to imagine a man old enough to be the father of Brenda.

Karla was amused as she watched him. They drank and she smoked and she thought about the old man having a lie-down in the very next room.

He was here. Right in this very suite!

Once reborn, he had been exhausted and disorientated. Karla had helped him lurch into her bedroom, where she tucked him in and watched him fall into a deep and healing sleep.

He was a skinny old thing. Stick-insecty. She'd urged him into a plush dressing gown, to hide his stringy old body. His face was fleshless, almost skull-like. Expressionless, too. He hadn't paid any heed to his surroundings, merely pulled the dressing gown tight about him, shivering violently, as if he had spent many years somewhere devoid of body heat. Which was probably true.

He lay down and closed his eyes and Karla had watched over him for some time. The old man she had made out of ashes and bones and the blood of a monster. Her very own creation. She had watched over him closely until Alex came round for his drink.

Victor. It was Victor she had recovering in the very next room. Recovering from his resurrection, which must be a very tiring process indeed.

Karla couldn't wait to see Brenda again, after all this time. And to spring this particular surprise upon the old dear.

Confronting Karla

'Fox! You really can't expect me to listen to this. It's ridiculous. Ludicrous!' Karla Sorenson threw up her hands and laughed out loud.

To Brenda and Effie's ears it was a very false-sounding laugh.

They knew that Karla knew that she had been caught out.

'I think this film of ours is going to your head, Fox. You've started to believe in your own stories.'

She laughed again and swivelled round fully on the low stool in front of her make-up mirror.

And there she was. Karla Sorenson forty years ago. In her absolute prime, and tip-top condition, as a horror movie starlet. Even in a chenille bathrobe and with a turban round her head she looked magnificent.

Effie couldn't help catching her breath.

'Really, Fox. Who are these women? Why have you brought them to my trailer? I've got a lot on, my darling. We're doing the big scene tonight. You know the one. I've got to prepare myself, mentally and physically.'

Fox studied her carefully. She was shifty, all right.

They were bearding her in her den.

Her trailer was almost as luxurious as Fox's, but not quite. It was dusky, with purple lampshades, crimson flock wallpaper, and black candles sending smudgy fumes everywhere.

Brenda spoke up. 'It has to stop, Karla. You're placing everyone in very great danger.'

Karla snarled, 'Who is this woman? What's she on about? Fox, get rid of her.'

Fox sighed deeply. 'She's come a very long way to give you a warning, Karla. A very serious warning. You wouldn't believe how far she has come.'

'I don't give a monkey's. Just get her and her gawping chum out of my fricking trailer.' She glared at Brenda with sudden recognition. 'I know who you are. You're the dinner lady.'

'Yes and no,' said Brenda gently, with a pleasant smile. 'Would you spare us a few moments of your precious time, Ms Sorenson? We've some rather important things to tell you. About the future, and so on.'

'No. Certainly not. Get out of my sight, you old bag.'

Fox frowned. 'They know, Karla. These two women know what fire you are playing with. The thing you confided to me only two nights ago. Your deepest, murkiest secrets. These women know all about you and . . . the Brethren.'

Karla's eyes widened. 'Don't be ridiculous.'

'We do,' Brenda said, though she wasn't at all entirely sure of the specifics.

'Get out of here at once,' Karla snapped. 'Otherwise I'll call security.'

'There is no security here,' Fox said. 'This is the middle of nowhere.'

Effie harrumphed and said decisively, 'We are getting nowhere with reasoned argument. We'll just have to scrag her.'

Karla blinked. 'What?'

Instantly, Brenda and Effie were upon her.

The two ladies had become quite used to a certain amount of hand-to-hand combat during their escapades of recent years, and were undaunted by the challenge of grabbing a woman of much younger years and securing her.

Fox stared helplessly at them, blocking the trailer door. Soon they had Karla pinned to the floor.

'You listen to us, lady,' Effie snapped. 'We have every respect for your talent and your stardom and all of that. But you really have to listen to us.'

Brenda was leaning in close, 'This film you're making. At its climax there's a scene where your character summons up the devil himself, isn't there? Here in this rocky valley?'

Karla clamped her mouth shut.

'There is,' said Fox. 'It's what they're shooting tonight. Except the devil won't be there, of course. He'll be played by Dan Konigsburg, who'll shoot his lines in the studio at Pinewood. They'll add him to the location footage using the magic of film trickery.'

'They're shooting it tonight?' Brenda said. 'Then we're here just in time, aren't we?' She turned back to the mutely scathing Karla. 'Look. The thing is, in calling up the fictional devil, you do something tonight that brings the real one running. And as a result, he gets into the film itself.'

Karla snarled contemptuously, 'What are you talking about? How do you know about such things?'

'Are you sure, Brenda?' Fox said worriedly. 'It seems so unlikely.'

'It's true,' said Brenda grimly. 'We come from the future, where for some reason others are trying to recreate the phenomenon. What you succeed in doing is unleashing unholy chaos and terror. But it can be stopped. Right here, today. Tonight. By you, Karla, deciding to change history. By refusing to shoot tonight's scenes.'

They all stared down at Karla.

'I'm under contract. I'm a professional. And I don't believe a word you're saying.'

'But we're from the future,' Effie said. 'We've seen the film you're shooting here. We know the deaths it has caused. Just the mere fact of watching it has sent Brenda and my future selves into a trance, and propelled us back here, through time . . .'

'Fox,' sighed Karla. 'Where did you pick these two up? They're clearly crackers.'

Brenda was gabbling away to herself. 'I think *the film itself* has brought us here. That's what it was doing, sending us into a trance. It wanted us to come here, to do what we're doing now. It was trying to prevent its own completion . . .'

Fox stared at her. 'Are you saying that *the film itself* doesn't want to be made? I can't believe that!'

'Just get out!' Karla bellowed, twisting and wriggling in her makeshift bonds.

'You must listen to us,' Brenda said. 'If the devil imprints himself on this film, then he's preserved on celluloid, in the world at large, for ever. There'll be no getting rid of him.'

'There never is,' Karla spat. 'He's always here. He's here right now, listening to you all rambling on. He's looking at you right now!'

Effie put in, 'The thing is, Karla, you should consider what we're telling you at a purely selfish, professional level, too. As an actress. After you star in *Get Thee Inside Me, Satan*, all the good parts dry up for you. You will be doomed to play the same satanic vampire ladies for the rest of your natural life. In our future you are seventy-odd, and you're still reprising the same tawdry role. You become a self-parody. Is that what you want?'

Karla looked uncomfortable at this. Then she said, 'What are you talking about? I'm already beyond self-parody. How many times do you think I've already gone through this same horror-flick shtick? I've been doing it fifteen years or more already.'

'It's true,' Fox said. 'She's well known for it.'

'Karla, we're begging you,' Brenda said. 'Don't shoot those scenes tonight. Change history. Don't let the devil come through . . .'

'I must admit, I wasn't relishing the idea of doing all those nude scenes tonight.' Karla frowned. 'I've got to lie on an altar in the middle of the valley, quite starkers, while all the satanists go dancing round, calling up the devil. Fireworks and all sorts going off all around me. It's not something I was mad keen on doing.'

She looked stricken then.

'But what will the Brethren say?' she asked them. 'I have to do their bidding. I have to. I must!' She turned her blazing eyes on Fox. 'If you love me, you must help me. You want this film to be made, just as much as I do! Untie me, Fox!'

Fox dithered. 'I-I . . .'

Brenda and Effie were glaring at him too.

'If you help her, we'll give you such a scragging,' warned Effie. She was rolling up her sleeves.

'I boxed in the navy,' said Fox. 'I'm pretty handy in a fight.'

'Help me, Fox!' Karla cried. 'Get me out of here!'

'Look,' said Brenda. 'Do we really have to have a fight about this?'

After the Punch-Up

'That went well,' said Brenda.

Next to her, Effie's face was empurpled with fury.

They were locked in Karla's trailer.

'How could we have let them overpower us?' Effie growled.

What Effie really meant was, how could Brenda have let them be overpowered? Brenda was extremely strong, as Effie knew. Surely strong enough to put up a decent fight against Karla and Fox.

'They're obsessed,' Brenda said. 'They are possessed by the strength of their convictions. We never stood a chance. They were like demons! Karla doesn't understand what's at stake. And Fox just wants to get his rotten movie made.'

Brenda examined her face for cuts and bruises. On the dressing table she discovered a sheaf of curling papers. Contracts, scribbled notes, letters in a distinctive gothic hand. 'Oh dear, Effie. Look at these. Letters to Karla.'

Effie was kicking at the caravan door. 'What time is it now? What time do they start shooting?'

'I don't know,' Brenda said distractedly. 'But look. These are from some kind of organisation. The Brethren, just like Fox said. Telling Karla that she's doing a good job. Addressing her as "daughter". Telling her that she'll live for ever as a legend and an icon and—'

'Pah, fan letters,' Effie sniffed. 'Something else puffing up her deranged ego. Can't you find something useful? Like a jemmy or a crowbar or something?'

'No, listen, lovey. This is important. From the looks of these curious missives, it seems that these Brethren people are some kind of satanic cult. Real devil-worshippers. And Karla is all caught up with them, for real.' Brenda looked solemn. 'These people have manoeuvred her into this role. Into being here, making this film. They want her to be shooting these scenes tonight. This is the crucial moment!'

'Can we stop it? You said that back here in the past, all hell broke loose. That you only just managed to escape alive, taking the Soames child with you. What makes you think we can do anything about it now?'

'We've got to try, Effie. We've come back here for a reason. Something has brought us back. There must be something we can do.'

Effie shook her head. She didn't have Brenda's faith in the benign organisational skills of fate or the universe. She believed that things were much more random than that. To her, they had come back in time simply in order to suffer, and to see disaster at close hand. There wasn't anything they could really do to make it better.

But now Brenda was looking resolute. 'Stand back, Effie.' She rolled her sleeves up. 'I'm going to break down the door.'

She managed – after flinging herself bodily at the reinforced steel door several times. It flew open and they held back from shrieking in triumph: they didn't want anyone knowing they had escaped from their makeshift cell. The two of them clambered down the high steps of the trailer, trying to be as quiet as possible.

They needn't have bothered.

On the film set in the valley's cleft, all attention was firmly fixed on the job in hand. The sun was setting, casting a brassy glow on the proceedings, as arc lamps were lit and generators throbbed, and the members of the crew busily set about their jobs.

Brenda and Effie paused in the shadows of the trailers for a hurried consultation.

'By the looks of things, we don't have long,' Brenda said. 'They shoot Karla's climactic scene at dusk, before the dark really takes hold.'

Effie pursed her lips. 'That's pretty soon, then,' she said, peering up at the azure sky, the stars just popping into view, one at a time, it seemed.

'I'll tackle Karla,' Brenda said determinedly. Effie had seen that look in her eyes before. It was when she knew there was a real struggle coming up. 'And you must return to the Soameses' caravan. Fox won't be there. He'll be at the set. They all will, for Karla's nudie scene. But Magda will be in the caravan, along with little Alex.'

Effie gasped. 'Isn't it tonight that Magda . . . ?'

Brenda nodded. 'That's how things went first time around. But we're going to change things. We're going to change how history happens.'

'Are you sure about this, Brenda?'

'Grab them both. Convince them that they have to get out of the valley immediately. Take them to me. To the other Brenda in the dinner van. She'll listen to you. I hope. Make her take them away early, before everything kicks off.'

'What if she won't listen?'

Brenda frowned. 'I should listen. I hope I will. If I look doubtful, give her – me – these . . .' She passed Effie the rolled-up letters that Karla had been sent by the Brethren. 'They might help convince her that something bad is about to happen. They'll prove to her that this valley on this night is a very bad place to be.'

'All right.' Effie nodded quickly, stowing the papers away in her bag.

'Let's do it, let's split up. Good luck, Effie.'

They looked at each other. Suddenly it seemed to Effie that they might be saying goodbye for ever. They were facing one of their most dangerous challenges, it seemed to her. Here they were – back in the past, somehow – with no idea how they would ever get home again. They were stuck in Wales, of all places. And they strongly suspected that a nude Karla Sorenson was about to film a scene in which the devil literally came to pay her a visit.

She clasped Brenda's hand, squeezed it hard, and turned to hurry away.

T'Other Brenda

Brenda was between shifts when there came all this knocking at her trailer door.

Soon they'd be shooting again and she'd have to be ready. Ready to be mobbed by the hungry crew. Somehow they were always hungrier during a night shoot.

She usually enjoyed these affairs: the easy camaraderie and the hard work. But there was something about this location that she didn't like at all.

BANG BANG BANG.

'All right!' she called. 'I'm not ready yet . . .'

There was an old woman's voice on the other side of the door. 'We don't want feeding! Quickly! Open up!'

Brenda was up to her eyes in clarts, peeling potatoes and doing what felt like a hundred things at once. She wiped her hands quickly and flung open the van door. 'What is it?'

There, framed in the darkness, was the old woman she had met earlier, and she had a kid with her. The Soameses' kid, looking bleary and half awake.

'I've brought the child. Alex – look. Here's your Auntie Brenda. Quick. Get inside, before anyone sees.'

Brenda's eyes widened. 'What's going on? That's the Soameses' child! What are you doing?'

'Listen, Brenda,' said Effie, all businesslike. 'I haven't got time to go into it all.' She was out of breath and, Brenda suddenly noticed, she was shaking. Something had rattled the old woman badly. No wonder! Breaking into other people's mobile homes and stealing their children!

'I think a few explanations are in order . . . erm . . .'

'Effie. My name is Effie. But you don't know me yet. You won't know me till about 2006.'

'Ooh, my goodness! The future! It's true, then?' Brenda ushered Effie and the child indoors and wedged the door closed.

'Indeed. Me and your future counterpart Brenda have come back to deal with a certain situation here. To stop something from happening.'

Brenda nodded and toyed with her potato peeler thoughtfully. 'Yes, I guessed there was a situation. I'm here undercover as well, you know. It's thought that there's, you know, black magic and things going on here.'

Effie frowned. 'Who sent you?'

'Oh,' said Brenda, a tad evasively. 'Just some people I work for these days.'

Effie waved these considerations aside. She would have to quiz her own Brenda about this later. That was if her Brenda could even properly remember the sixties. She said, 'There isn't time for that now. I've come here to pass the child into your care and to tell you to get yourselves away from this valley as quickly as possible.'

Brenda wasn't keen on being told what to do. Especially by some elderly and mysterious time-travelling operative from the twenty-first century. 'Hang on a moment.'

Now the child had picked up on the agitation and the tension passing back and forth between the squabbling women. He burst into jagged sobs. 'I want to go back! What am I doing here?'

'Sssh, child.' Effie rolled her eyes. So far it had been too simple. Breaking into the Soameses' mobile home had been a doddle. The child had been easy to find and to wake. He hadn't even asked who she was, as she led him away, into the night. He must be so used to having a succession of nannies and nurses looking after him. In a way Effie's heart went out to the child, with those terrible, preoccupied parents of his. Plonking him in this weird world of sorcery and devilment. She told herself he was best off out of it, and in the care of this younger – if more argumentative – version of Brenda. 'Don't make a fuss, Alex.'

'Where's my mum?' he sobbed.

'Alex, lovey. Look, I'm your Auntie Brenda. You know me. I give you chips, don't I?'

The child's eyes narrowed suspiciously. 'I know who you are. But who's she?' He jabbed a finger at Effie. 'Where's she taking me?'

Effie sighed. 'I've never been any good with children. Explain to him, will you, ducky?'

Brenda hugged the kid to her and stared at Effie. 'How did you get him away from them? And why? Why are you and the future me kidnapping children, Elsie?'

'It's Effie, not Elsie. And it's essential: that's why we're resorting to desperate measures like this. Tonight's the night Satan gets unleashed on this film set. Seriously. We *know* these things. You have to get the child away safely, Brenda. You have to do it now.' Effie's voice had gone very low and commanding.

'I see,' said Brenda, looking hopelessly at her half-prepared chips.

Alex started up again: 'What's she talking about? Where's my mum?'

Effie said, 'They left him alone in that luxurious caravan, poor mite. His mum and dad. Sneaking out. Well, we know where *he* was going . . .'

'To be with Karla?'

'In her meditation trailer. That's what she calls it, apparently. I can't imagine that much meditation goes on there. So you know, then, that they're carrying on an illicit affair?'

'Of course. The whole crew knows. Karla's famous for this kind of thing.'

Effie remembered something and started feeling around in her handbag. She produced a bundle of papers, which she thrust at Brenda. The Brethren letters. 'T'other Brenda wanted you to have these. Look after them. They're important. Evidence, they are.' She watched Brenda take the papers and stash them away safely in a drawer and nodded with satisfaction. 'Right. I must go. I've got to help your future self try to dissuade them, while there's still time. And you, Brenda, you must get ready to get your chip van out of here, taking this little one with you.'

Brenda put on her most determined expression. 'Are you sure there's nothing more productive I can do?'

'That will be helpful enough, ducky. Getting Alex away. You be good, young man. And when you grow up, don't even think about becoming a film director and doing a remake of this ghastly film.'

'I don't know what you're talking about,' said Alex.

'That doesn't matter.' Effie smiled grimly. 'I'm going. Take care of him, Brenda. And . . . look after yourself. I'll see you in about thirty-eight years, dear.'

Brenda nodded. To Effie, she really did look like the Brenda she knew. But how strange, not to be recognised by her. To have none of the history nor understanding between them that she was so used to, and relied upon, especially in adventures like this.

You're on your own now, Effie, she told herself. Be brave.

'I'm going to try and bring Alex's mum back,' she told Brenda. 'I want to save her. Or at least try. Will you wait here until midnight? It isn't long now. Forty minutes. If I'm not back then with Magda – then you must go. You've got to get this little one away. But we're going to try to change history – and rescue his mum . . .'

Effie turned then, without a backward glance. She threw open the chip van door and dashed out into the terrible night.

Brenda watched her go. What a strange woman, she thought.

In Flagrante

Magda Soames had an awful lot to put up with. Her life with Fox might have seemed, from the outside, rather glamorous and easy. She had everything she wanted. She had the perfect child. She had an array of famous and fascinating friends. She had seen the world.

She had decided that, on the whole, the world wasn't worth seeing. Not all of it. It was pretty much overrated in her eyes.

I never used to be cynical like this, she thought miserably, as she traipsed across the valley floor. It's Fox who has made me like this. Together we have seen too much, done too much. We've left the whole world standing still.

There's no magic in it any more.

And now here she was. Ready for another tawdry confrontation. Ready to have a catfight with yet another of Fox's mistresses. Why did she even bother? Why did she leap to the bait each time? It wasn't like she was even jealous. Not any more. Not for a long time. She'd had quite enough of his raspy blandishments. She'd seen quite enough of that dreary old todger of his.

Still, something in her found it galling that he kept popping over to Karla's meditation trailer to give her one. That frightful, blowsy hag. What did she have going for her?

Once more into the breach, thought Magda wearily, and threw

open the caravan door. It wasn't even locked. They didn't care, did they? They didn't even care who saw them up to their mucky, nasty business.

And there they were. Karla supine and splayed on her narrow truckle bed. Fox perched awkwardly on top of her with his best worsted trollies concertinaed about his trembling thighs. All goosefleshy and pink. Magda shuddered and gave a discreet cough. Then she spoke up.

'You are welcome to him, Karla. Look at the state of him! That sorry old arse waving about in the air. Ugh.'

Fox groaned and ceased his forlorn efforts. He glanced back at his wife, yanking at his trews. 'Magda. You're always so melodramatic.'

'I don't want to hear about it, Fox, you repulse me.'

Resting perilously on his side, he reached for his smoking materials. Beneath him he could feel Karla trembling copiously. As if she was about to erupt. And in quite the wrong way.

Fox lit his fag and told his wife, 'We got carried away, my dear. The excitement of the movie. Of everything we're making here.' The draught from the doorway was wicked on his nethers. He had another go at making himself decent.

'You're making a big mistake, buster. That's what you're making.'

Karla sat up. She almost dislodged her lover in the process. 'Cool it, Magda. It's the sixties. We're only having a bit of fun.'

Magda could have run over there and smacked her in the face. 'Fun, she says! You bloody demon woman! I could . . . I could . . .' But something was holding her back. There was a primal force about Karla. A savage beauty to her nakedness and her sexuality. It repelled as much as it attracted. It was like happening upon some ancient goddess, Magda thought wildly. As if, with one glance, Karla could destroy her rival.

Karla spat at her, 'Come and have a go. I could do with a good fight. I'd like to see you try, missus.'

They were interrupted by someone running up to the caravan and scattering loose bits of slate. The figure loomed up behind Magda and banged hard on the trailer's open door.

'It's me! Brenda! I head the shouting. What's . . . ?'

Karla was appalled to see yet another face gurning at her from the doorway. She pushed Fox away from her and seized the satin bedsheets. 'What are you doing here? Get out! This is a private caravan, expressly for the purposes of meditation!'

'Her again!' Fox growled.

Brenda gabbled breathlessly, 'Look, you have to listen to me.'

Magda snapped, 'Is this another one you've been knocking off, Fox?'

'Hardly.'

It was only then that Brenda got a good look at Fox and Karla. Immediately she wished she hadn't. 'Oh! Goodness! I'm sorry for bursting in like this.'

'Go away!' rasped the old man. 'We've got no clothes on!'

Magda tutted. 'I'm sure she can see that for herself. God, you disgust me, Fox. Well, I'm off. I'm taking Alex and I'm going.'

'You're drunk!' Fox roared. 'You're not going anywhere. Don't you dare try to drive anywhere with my son!'

Karla stared daggers at her lover. 'Fox, this is all very well. But I'm already due on set. I'm late.' She gave him a light shove and proceeded to hop off the makeshift bed. She seemed completely unabashed by her nakedness, stooping to fetch her dressing gown from where it had been chucked. 'Well, that's me ready,' she sighed, fluffing up her silvery mane of hair. 'Would the rest of you consider fucking off now?'

Magda was hunched over and twisted up with loathing. 'I'll get you, madam. You just see if I don't.'

Karla wasn't scared. 'I'd like to see you try, you old soak.'

'If I could, I would curse you,' hissed Magda. 'I'd like to curse this whole stupid film. But that's more your line, isn't it? Necromancy? Witchcraft?'

Karla laughed. There was a slightly mad tinge to her guffaws. 'It certainly *is* my line. It's right up my fricking street. And unless you leave me to prepare myself for my big scene, I'll set a spell on you that'll make you knockers drop off, you lousy old bitch.'

Magda turned on her expensive heel, pushing roughly past Brenda as she made her exit.

Fox gave an impotent bellow: 'Magda! Wait!'

Karla glared at him as he fumbled with his underpants. 'Run after her, Fox, if that's what you want. But if you go, that's the last you'll see of me. I need you here. Right now, with me, when I shoot this scene.'

Brenda told them: 'I'll go after her.'

They both ignored her.

Karla continued to berate the old rake as he dressed himself. 'I mean it, Fox. I need you there. When they put me on the sacrificial slab. When . . . whatever comes. When the devil is supposed to appear. It will help me . . . fake it. And give a genuine performance, if you are there just out of shot. Giving me your support.'

He tucked in his shirt and felt his dignity returning as he flicked his cuffs into place. 'My dear, of course . . .'

Brenda could see that she wouldn't get through to them. She could hear Magda's footsteps growing fainter as the spurned woman made her way back to the family trailer. She suddenly remembered what was meant to become of Magda this night.

She saw what she had to do. Fox and Karla would just have to get on with things themselves. They were in a kind of bubble of shared madness. An erotic, satanic haze. It was fascinatingly wicked. Brenda had to wrench herself away from watching them, and turned to stumble after Magda through the jagged shadows of the camp.

Evil Stirring

Meanwhile Effie was stumbling towards the brilliantly lit film set. She paused in mute disapproval at the sight of the near-naked Karla making her way to work. Fox led her daintily by the hand as she minced through the rubble. There was a huge round of applause from the crew.

This is where it all happens, Effie thought. She could feel the evil stirring in the air. She was trying to get it into her head that this was the film she had already watched. She had already seen the results of this night. And now she was here. Behind the Scenes. Inside the Extra Features.

Aha. Her attention was caught by other figures, out on the periphery. Other figures not inside the bright cascade of film lights.

Brenda. Her Brenda, from the present day. Chasing after Magda, away from the movie set. Now where were they going?

Precipiced

Brenda was out of breath already. 'Magda, you have to calm down . . .'

Magda wasn't having any of it. She swayed and lurched into the velvety darkness. Up a steep incline. The road out of the valley. She had walked this way before. These past few nights, when she needed to get away from the madness of this closed-in place. But now she was being disturbed. She was after some peace and a little sit and a swig of her special medicine, maybe. And here came this foolish woman, panting after her. She stopped to swipe at Brenda. 'Who are you? Go away!'

Brenda tried to be patient. 'I'm a friend. Look, you have to realise—'

'What? What do I have to realise? That I have to allow an artist like Fox to behave exactly as he wants? That I just do not understand the freedom that a genius needs?' She looked stricken in the eerie spill of light from the set.

'Er, no,' said Brenda. 'That's not what I was going to say at all.'

Magda staggered onwards, up the twisted slope, sending scree rattling in her wake. 'That's what he usually says. That I do not understand. I am just an ordinary woman. A drunken floozy. I cannot give a genius like him the stimulation he needs. Well, let that

280

succubus Karla stimulate him all he wants. I'm getting my son and me out of here.' Her voice was getting shriller as she went. Small stones flew up behind her, hitting Brenda's shins as she grimly kept up her pursuit.

'We've already sent your son away,' Brenda told her.

Magda was brought up short by this. 'What?'

'My friend Effie and I. We've – hopefully – managed to get Alex away to safety.'

Magda teetered right at the edge of the path. 'What are you talking about? Alex? Alex!' From here could be seen the whole gypsy-like encampment. From here it was obvious that all eyes were on the main set and the stone of sacrifice glowing molten gold in its centre. For a second Brenda thought Magda was going to run straight off the side of the path. She cast one hand out towards the Soames trailer, at the valley edge. Brenda was shocked to see how far away it seemed, and how high up they had come during their breathless conversation.

'Sssh, it's all right, Magda. We are on your side.'

Magda's voice was cold and savage. 'How can you be? Stealing my child . . . !'

'Not stealing. Helping. Oh dear.' Brenda found herself wrestling with the woman, who, it turned out, had a tenacious, wiry strength. She was trying to push past Brenda; to turn back on the narrow path, desperate now to return to her son.

'But . . . who has taken him?' she screeched in Brenda's ear. 'Where is he?'

'He's in my . . . the other Brenda's catering van. They're leaving here before everything kicks off.'

'Other Brenda?'

Brenda coughed embarrassedly. 'There are two of me here.'

Magda's hands flew up to her raddled temples. 'Oh, I can't cope with this.'

'I know. But we will keep him safe. It's just important for you to understand that your silly husband and Karla have been dabbling in things they shouldn't have.'

'I could see that for myself.'

'No. The occult.'

'But Fox is always so against it . . . he always says—'

'Nevertheless, Karla reeks of it. And she has reeled him in, the foolish man. And tonight . . . it's what you'd call their apotheosis. Everything going on over there. On that set. It's for real.'

Magda took in a shuddering breath. 'I don't believe it.' But Brenda could tell she was frightened. She knew it was all true.

Lighting Effects

Despite herself, Effie was quite fascinated by the behind-the-scenes action on the film set. All of that very focused, almost frenzied activity just before the director called out: 'Action!'

The extras were milling around the central stones in their hooded robes. Their torches flung long, wavering shadows up the valley walls. Cloying smoke streamed through the air and Effie found herself trying her hardest not to cough. She listened to the chanting and could almost have believed she was attending a quite genuine witches' sabbat.

There was Karla, with a gossamer-light negligee draped over her shoulders, and the rest of her shockingly, tantalisingly nude. She was being led along by this pack of sorcerers, towards the main altar. Effie stared at her and marvelled at the woman's ideal form. Perhaps, if you were perfect like that, then you would feel no shame, as other mortals did. Maybe you'd feel the need to flaunt yourself like Karla did. Would Effie feel like that? If she were like Karla? She drew back into the shadows, pursing her lips. Of course not. Nothing would make her behave like Karla. Nothing on this earth.

But there was definitely something very compelling about the scene as it unfolded before her. Not least the déjà vu that she felt tugging at her with every second that passed by.

The druidic figures helped Karla to lie in place on the stone. Her last wisp of clothing was whirled away effortlessly. She was bound hand and foot and lay uncomplaining as the rather catchy chanting reached a climax.

And there were lights, too, hovering all about her. Amazing, mesmerising lights. Psychedelic and very fitting, Effie supposed, for 1967. This had been the era for all of that, hadn't it? For lurid colours and acid trips. But surely . . . these lamps they had on set were far too primitive to create these kinds of effects? This was rather like watching the finished movie. These were some kind of special effect, dubbed on to the film cells afterwards . . . and yet here they were right now. Live.

Could it be, perhaps, that these vivid, technicoloured lights above the supine Karla were quite real?

Effie gasped. She jolted her attention away from the hallucinatory spectacle. As she did, she turned to look into the darkness from where she had come and realised with a sinking heart that Brenda's chip van was still there. Its shutter was down, but her friend hadn't made good her escape with the child. And things were surely reaching their climax here in the valley. The chanting was turning to discordant shrieking and the air itself was buffeting her as she turned back to look at the film set. Was she imagining it? A breeze had plucked up out of the still night. Pages of script went scudding across the shale-strewn ground. The pagan robes of the celebrants were swished along in the wind . . .

This was real, too.

Effie found that she was frozen to the spot, in the lee of a great rock. These weren't special effects. This was happening for real.

She watched Karla writhe on the stone as the lights clustered about her. She watched as Karla let out one almighty scream of triumph and dismay.

Feral

Up on the rocky path, Magda and Brenda were also watching the weird scene unfold.

'I can't take my eyes off it,' Magda said hoarsely.

Brenda tried to take hold of her. 'You must!' she cried, full of resolute good sense. Everything she had expected was coming to pass. Everything she had warned them of. Now time was getting too tight. They'd never get away from here unless she took Magda in hand. 'Come on, woman. We can still do it. We can get you away.'

But Magda was like a feral creature. 'I can't run away,' she spat. 'I can't. I have to stay here!' Brenda flinched from her nails as Magda slashed at her. 'Oh, Fox. You fool.'

'Magda, come with me,' Brenda insisted.

Magda tottered to the edge of the path and started to shriek: 'Fox! Fox, listen to me! Fox!'

Carry On Chanting

Only a couple of yards from where Effie was cowering, Fox had his own vantage point. He was alarmed by the chaotic scene, but determined not to show it. At precisely the most interesting moment he was horrified to hear the voice of his wife echoing off the valley walls. Her drunken soprano ululated back and forth from somewhere above.

'Oh God, she'll ruin it all, silly old cow,' he cursed.

Suddenly he was aware of Effie beside him, yanking at his smoking-jacket lapel. 'That's no way to talk about your poor wife.'

He boggled at her. 'What are you doing here?'

The director was crying out, 'Cut! Cut! Cut!' all of a sudden, perhaps in recognition of the fact, at last, that what was happening on the set was not of his making. The scene was progressing under its own diabolical momentum. Everyone was staring at Karla's heaving, bucking form on the glowing altar. The chanting was fading now, into awed murmurs.

'No!' Karla exhorted them. 'Carry on chanting! CARRY ON! Don't stop. This isn't a film. This isn't a scene. This is the real thing!'

At this point a sudden vortex of brilliant whirling light opened up before the stone altar. There were screams from the robed priests and extras and howls of fear from the crew.

Effie appalled herself by making a noise that sounded just like 'Glooopp!' They've done it, she thought wildly. They have opened up a gateway into hell. She had seen this awful kind of thing before.

Fox had seized Effie's hand. He was gibbering uncontrollably and his fingers were slick with cold sweat. 'It's really real. This is what I always said it would be. It's what I almost imagined . . .'

Effie couldn't tell whether he was pleased or what.

Her attention was now focused on a tall, slender dark shape growing larger in the eye of the vortex.

'A figure's forming,' she whispered. She blinked as the form clarified itself. Who was she expecting? What was she expecting him to be? 'Oh no . . .' she squawked.

Slippage

Up on the perilous stone ledge it was even harder to see what was going on in all that brilliant light. Magda swore at Brenda and yelled, 'What are they doing? Tell me, woman! You seem to know what's going on. Explain to me!'

But Brenda was more concerned then about Magda in her high boot heels, staggering towards the lip of the slate path. She lurched after her, reaching out with both hands. 'Magda, come back from there, please!'

'I have to see.' Magda knew her husband was to blame. She had seen this coming. His dabbling. His bullishness. At last he had brought down hellish disaster on them all. She shouted into the pulsating night: 'What has he done? I can't see . . .'

Brenda leapt forward. 'Magda – watch out!'

Magda took one step too many. Broken shale scattered under her feet as the lip of the track crumbled suddenly. She lost her footing and squawked as she tipped backwards. Brenda lunged out and grabbed her, but Magda threw her off. Brenda watched as the woman's momentum took her backwards over the ledge, her skinny arms windmilling in the air. Magda's shocked screams tore the darkness apart all around her.

Without even thinking about it, Brenda flung her arms out and managed to grab hold of one of Magda's wrists. The woman felt frail in her grasp.

'Magda! I've got you! Just keep hold of my hand! Don't let go!'

Magda kept screaming and thrashing. Brenda held on with all her strength.

'Don't panic! I'll pull you back to safety. Keep calm!'

Magda wouldn't keep calm and she wouldn't help herself. She kept flailing about as if she was eager to take off somewhere. She didn't make her rescue any easier as Brenda started painfully reeling her to safety, inch by inch . . .

Brenda was sweating. Her own purchase on the edge of the cliff felt precarious now. Magda's wrist squirmed in her grip, slick with sweat.

Brenda – she told herself firmly – you have to hold on. Just a few more moments . . . just a little bit more . . .

Manifesting Himself

As predicted, all hell had broken loose on the film set.

In all of the fiery tempest and panic, Fox had time to stand up and look quite pleased with himself. Effie clambered arthritically to her feet and joined him in staring at the figure that had come through the aperture and was now standing beside the naked Karla. 'You've really done it,' Effie sobbed. 'Oh, you foolish man.'

All about them, members of the film crew were running away. The arc lights toppling and smashing as the wind continued to blow a gale through the tight valley. But none of this registered on the appalled Fox Soames. He stood swaying on the spot as the revealed figure grew more substantial.

'The prince of darkness!' said Fox, with suitable awe.

Karla sat up on her altar, covering her breasts rather demurely. Too late, thought Effie.

'Master!' said Karla, with a slow smile at the new arrival.

Effie blinked.

She stared hard at the figure as it made itself fully manifest.

She couldn't help herself shouting out. 'That's not the devil, you flaming idiots. That's . . . that's . . .'

Perhaps her eyes were deceiving her. She set off at a gallop towards the sacrificial altar. 'Kristoff? Kristoff Alucard?'

He turned to her with a savage welcoming grin.

Effie screeched at them all: 'He isn't the devil! He's *my fella!*'

And then – as Alucard winked at her – everything went plunging into darkness.

Both Effie and Brenda were whisked away in an instant.

And found that they weren't in the sixties any more.

Meanwhile, Back in the Present

Dear Mam,

This week I've proved to myself that I can actually do this. I can hold the fort. I've stepped into Robert's shoes at the Miramar, easy as anything (almost). I think you'd be proud. It's just a case of being on the alert and thinking fast, and trusting that everyone in the hotel knows what they're doing. I mean, all the others members of staff have been here donkey's years – the waiting staff and the chambermaids, they know what they're doing. How could I possibly mess it all up?

I just have to be bright and breezy and pretend like nothing is wrong.

But how many days would you leave it, Mam, before phoning the police? Because really Robert's a missing person, isn't he? But he's a grown-up too, isn't he? And I guess he's got as much right as anyone to slope off . . . even without giving any warning. (Just like I did! Just like I left my marriage! Aaagghhh!) Oh, I don't know. Maybe tomorrow. Maybe I'll call the police then.

The days are just whizzing past. I've never been as busy or as involved in stuff in all my life.

The film crew are busy too, and before they come back to the Miramar and the late bar here, they drink in Spector. They've moved to locations over that side of the harbour, all around the abbey. They seem, after a couple of tricky hurdles last week (the sausage bap and the broken leg) to be cracking along at quite a pace.

I was over at Spector last night, seeing Michael. Hanging around the film people, giving myself an evening off, and they were in a celebratory mood. I got talking with one of them – the young stylist, Lisa Turmoil. She said they were all amazed that things were on schedule. Even with the famous curse (loud guffaws from some of the others at this) and the various mishaps along the way, things were actually going pretty well.

I said something about how it all seemed very quick. I mean, I don't know much about how filming works. Lisa told me that Alex the director was like a kind of genius. The crew all loved him. And Karla Sorenson was turning out to be a wonderful person. A real star and an old pro. Gracious and easy to work with. She got it down pat, first take, every time.

They'd soon be finished, I learned. Once the climax was got through, this coming Saturday night . . .

Finished! I was astounded. And then I had to be told – like a dumbo – that the bulk of the movie was going to be shot on sound stages down south. Pinewood or somewhere, I thought Lisa said. It all sounded very glamorous. I was like – d'oh! I know nothing, really, about how it all works. I was just asking nebby questions and trying to fit in. I'm just a fan, really.

Then Lisa was going on about the different films and TV

294

series she's done the hair and make-up on, and it was quite interesting for a while. But then I was distracted by Michael. He was looking so washed out and knackered, clunking about on his coffee machine. I sidled over – a bit sexily – just as he was doing the froth on somebody's macchiato.

He said, 'I'm okay. Late nights. I'm not sleeping. Or rather . . . I think I'm not. I fall asleep – but then, when I wake up, it's weird . . .'

I didn't know what he was on about. So I pushed him further, as you do.

He said, 'It's like I've been out somewhere. I'm aching tired . . . my shoes were all muddy and tossed into the corner of my room. There was sand in my pants.' And then he asked me a corker: 'Do you think I'm going mad?'

I told him I thought he was probably sleepwalking. What do you think, Mam? I used to sleepwalk, didn't I? When I was a kid?

But then I was thinking to myself – God, I bet this has all got to do with that nasty Mrs Claus he's been knocking about with!

Do you think that I've got myself involved with another weirdo bloke again? I bet you do, Mam.

And then he went on to say that he had tried to ring his old dad. I felt sorry for him when he said this bit. He had to look up the number in his little book, because he couldn't remember it for some reason. So he rang him and the automatic voice at the other end of the line told him no such number existed!

Michael looked like a little boy just then. Lost and alone in the world. He said he'd used the number loads of times before.

He'd talked to his dad, even quite recently. But now . . . He was so puzzled-looking. My heart flew out to him.

But I had to get home. I had work to do. Damn damn damn. There's a fella opening up to me and telling me all his woes. And I have to go, and all because of work and responsibilities! Just as he's looking all vulnerable and gorgeous. Robert really, really owes me.

So, here I am today. I've just spent my morning coffee break dashing down the hill to Brenda's B&B. I try to pop in twice a day. I've been in every day this week, using the keys to Brenda's place kept among Robert's stuff. I've been checking on the sleeping ladies. Except they're not really sleeping, are they?

These two, I'm even more worried about them than I am about Robert.

They're still just sitting there. Staring at the blank telly. They haven't eaten or drunk anything for days. I keep thinking – God, what if they die? Dehydration! Anything!

But this is magic, of course.

Isn't it?

All my life I've wanted to see something magic. Now here it is. In the flesh. Petrified old womanly flesh. And I don't know what to do.

I'm hoping they'll just snap out of their trance. Like I did.

This morning I've had a go feeding them natural yoghurt and some honey. Desperation, really. Made a hell of a mess of Brenda's cushion covers.

They just stared past me . . .

Oh, Mam. What a terrible week it's been. Worked off my feet, and all the new friends that I've made in Whitby have either gone missing, are frozen solid and catatonic, or they're having funny amnesiac do's in the night.

Do you think it really could be the curse of Karla's movie coming down on us all? Or is it just me?

I'll keep you posted,

Love,

Penny

Legless in the Garret

Time passed in the attic. Robert had no idea how long went by. Days and days and days, it seemed. Water was brought. And a few stale sandwiches. He had been given something to make him sleep, to stop him from getting too worked up and smashing himself against the walls, protesting against his imprisonment.

The others were quiet. The elf and the postman kept themselves quite separate and apart. They seemed weirdly quiet. Shocked into submission, perhaps. Still horrified at what they had done to Frank.

Frank himself slumped in chains, legless.

Robert managed to wriggle his way over to sit with him. He strained at his own bonds, but gave up, and passed the unfathomable time talking to Frank.

'Frank feels very weak . . .'

'Brenda will come, you'll see. She'll sort this out.'

'Frank's never felt like this, in all his long life.'

'They took a lot of your blood. That's why.'

'They have taken Frank to pieces again. Rest in pieces. Huh-huh.'

He seemed to be regressing. His speech was slow and slurred. He was referring to himself in the third person more than ever, and Robert knew from Brenda that this was a bad sign. When Frank called himself Frank it was when he was thinking most like a monster. Thinking of himself as just a *thing*. A creation. A compilation of body parts. In the half-lit attic gloom, Robert felt his heart go out in pity to the man next to him.

This past year he hadn't thought much of Frank. Like Effie, he had thought of Brenda's so-called husband as just some boorish lummox. Someone who had blundered into their lives willy-nilly, and who had ruined things for all of them. Their little gang wasn't as tight as a result. Whenever they tried to have fun, Frank would be there, unpredictable of mood and slow of wit. It could be quite trying, just having him there.

And Brenda hadn't even been noticeably happier with him in tow. Having a husband hadn't improved her life, in Robert and Effie's eyes. So how come she was even bothering?

Pity, was what they decided. She had taken him in because she had felt obliged to. He had put the emotional screws on her. All that 'I was made to be with you, and you with me' nonsense.

Now Robert looked at him and he was feeling pity too.

'Where is Brenda?' Frank asked him. 'Why hasn't she found us?'

He sounded more lucid. More time had passed. It was dark; the smashed window high up in the roof space was black again. The wind was chilling, bringing with it tendrils of sea mist. Robert couldn't have felt any colder.

'She'll come, Frank,' he said.

'She'll know we're at the Christmas Hotel, won't she?' Frank said. 'Everything that's bad happens here. She knows that. She'll realise.' His massive fist smashed against the floor. A futile gesture. Thump. 'Why can't Frank help himself? Why can't Frank save himself?'

But he couldn't, and neither could Robert.

The elf and the postman were watching from the shadows. Timidly. Guiltily. Where was Karla? She hadn't been anywhere near for ages. Her mind was elsewhere. She was up to some other terrible business and she had forgotten her prisoners upstairs. The novelty had worn off.

'*Brenda!*' Frank sobbed.

What can I tell him? Robert thought miserably. That Brenda and Effie are both in a catatonic state. There'll be no help from them. Not now. Perhaps not ever.

Things looked pretty bad.

There's nothing I can do, Robert thought.

Except . . .

And then he thought of his fella.

He's magic, isn't he? He can read my thoughts. He can fly around on an old settee.

Can he hear me now? Can he find us here?

Can he rescue us, maybe?

Robert closed his eyes to concentrate. His heart was beating harder with gladness now that he thought he had a plan.

A Permanent Solution

Neither Penny nor the film stylist Lisa would have described themselves as best buddies yet, but they liked each other. To Penny, Lisa seemed like she was up for a laugh. And what was more – weirdly – Lisa already happened to know Brenda and Effie. That night, as the film crew sat up late in the Miramar bar, carousing and telling funny, silly stories, Lisa explained to Penny how she had been working in Whitby a couple of years ago, when she found herself caught up in a mad seance in Effie's attic.

'So believe me, I know the kinds of things those two get themselves involved in.'

'Tell me again, why were you there . . . ?'

And Lisa explained how she had been the stylist on a cable TV show about the paranormal. But being round Effie's had spooked her for ever. Though she had liked the two old ladies a lot, she said.

Penny felt that she could confide in Lisa. So she told her what was going on. The peculiar situation at Brenda's house.

Lisa was horrified to hear that Brenda and Effie had been sitting immobile on armchairs for days on end.

'And you've just left them there?'

'What else can we do? I've been popping in and checking on them each day . . .'

'But what sent them into this trance thing?'

Penny took a deep breath and explained to her all about the DVD and what it had done to her when she had watched it in the middle of the night.

'It really is cursed, isn't it?' Lisa said, turning white. 'Both the old film and the new . . .'

The two of them thought about that for a bit, and then Penny had to serve some of the others. When she was done, she brought Lisa another gin and tonic and they came up with their plan.

'Let's go there now,' Lisa said impulsively. 'This minute.'

'To Brenda's?'

It was a relief to Penny that someone else was involved. It wasn't just her, left alone with this weird situation. She closed the bar and sent the film people to bed. They grumbled woozily, but no one caused too much of a fuss.

At last Lisa and Penny hurried out and tottered though the quiet streets. It was almost three a.m. The town was weirdly quiet.

They crept into the tall guest house. And up into the attic rooms.

There the two old ladies were sitting. Like waxworks. Like mummies in the British Museum. Pallid death masks squinched up in concentration. As if they were both finding something intensely interesting; something that was occurring only inside of their minds.

It was a very unnerving experience, standing there in Brenda's living room, staring back at them. It was like being in a funeral parlour.

Penny realised then that the bag Lisa had brought contained her hairstyling equipment.

She went all businesslike and no-nonsense. She flipped on the lights and told Penny to get some coffee going. She was laying out her curlers, hot tongs, scissors and other styling paraphernalia on the coffee table.

'Why haven't they starved? Or died of thirst?' Lisa peered into the old ladies' faces. 'Maybe they already have . . .'

Penny felt a leap of panic inside her as she went to put the kettle on.

What did Lisa think she was doing, giving them a makeover?

All she would say, as Penny watched her setting to work, was: 'They wouldn't want people seeing them sitting here with terrible hair.'

She was combing out Effie's silvery locks. Unwinding the bun she wore and untucking yards and yards of spun silver.

She worked intently for ages. Penny sipped her coffee and wandered around Brenda's place. She examined the books on the shelves (mostly crime, some old poetry) and the knick-knacks on the windowsill and the wall unit. You would never think there was anything at all unusual about the old woman. But there was, wasn't there?

Soon Effie was sitting there resplendent, hair shining as Lisa washed and combed it out.

Still, not a flicker from the old lady. Lisa mauled her about as she kneaded the conditioner into her scalp, but there was no reaction at all. Effie sat there all toffee-nosed, proud as an empress, as if these ministrations were beneath her.

'I'm going to give them both perms,' Lisa decided.

Penny wasn't sure that was such a good idea. How would I react, she wondered, waking from a coma, or whatever this was, to find that someone had been in and given me a perm? I'd be mortified.

'And a blue rinse,' Lisa added, rummaging in her stylist's bag for more bottles of stuff.

'Erm,' said Penny. 'We don't want to go too far.' She was starting to regret bringing her new friend round. There was a fervent glint in Lisa's eye. She was a born stylist, you could tell. She was behaving as if she had been given free rein on the heads of these old ladies, and now Penny was really worried.

'They'll be delighted. Old ladies always are. That's what they love. Perms and blue rinses. Just you see!'

Brenda's hair came away in her hands. A wig. Of course.

Lisa was appalled at herself – for just a second. 'Never mind. I can style her wig for her. It needs doing, doesn't it?' She held up the wig for Penny to examine. It was almost as big as a cat. Penny looked at it, trying not to study Brenda's bald skull. She couldn't help it. Brenda's head was criss-crossed with tramline scars. They were viciously deep around her ears, and at the back of her neck. Penny's insides went cold at the sight of them. How would Brenda feel, knowing that these girls were here, looking at her like this?

Now Lisa was back at work. She got Penny hefting mixing bowls and Tupperware out of kitchen cupboards. She carefully mixed up her potions and lotions. She was looking pretty witchy herself as she ground and pounded and whipped them up. Perming solution, rinses and dyes.

There was a horrible smell of ammonia. Nasty, astringent chemicals filled the air.

And then Penny saw it.

Brenda's nose twitched.

Effie's eyes flickered.

Brenda sneezed. Her eyes were watering.

Penny couldn't believe it. 'Lisa! The smell!'

'I know,' she said, still mixing away. 'I'm used to it. But some of these chemicals are pretty potent.'

'No, I mean . . . look!'

Lisa went round to where Penny was. They both stared at the old ladies.

'They're waking up! You're waking them up with your pong!'

Effie coughed and spluttered and her eyes flew open. She glared at the girls and then at Brenda.

'Oh dear,' said Brenda, in a worn-out-sounding voice. 'We seem to be back!'

Nocturnal Styling

They looked about wildly at the room and each other. They were shocked to find that someone had been giving them hairdo's in the night.

'How long have we been here? Sitting like this . . . ?'

'Oh no! Don't you see, Brenda? This is absolutely the worst moment to leave!'

'We've been dragged back to reality – to our own time . . . Effie! We've been pulled back out of the film! Out of Behind the Scenes of the film!'

'I do see that, Brenda.' Effie's voice was desolate. She was filled with a sense of failure. Suddenly she could remember what had been happening at the very moment they were yanked back into the present. Out of what now felt like a dream of the past.

And who has done it? they wondered. Who has woken us up?

Penny and Lisa were standing there, shocked. They felt like intruders in some sacred sepulchre, watching the dead return to life.

Lisa coughed nervously. 'I-it's me, Effie, Brenda. Remember? I'm Lisa Turmoil – the hairstylist. I was here a couple of years ago.'

'Oh yes! Of course. How lovely to see you, er, Lisa.'

'The question is, though, why are you here now? Messing about with our hair . . . waking us up like this?' Effie's hair was hanging loose, gleaming in the moonlight in a ghostly fashion. Brenda's wig was hanging askance and the two of them were surrounded by all of Lisa's tools of the trade.

Brenda said, 'We might have died. The shock might have carried us away – for ever ...' Then she shook herself, recalling her manners. 'Oh, but we're glad you girls tried to help us.' Lisa and Penny were looking so dismayed, so horrified. 'Thank you for waking us.'

Penny spoke up at last. 'You've both been asleep for nearly a week!'

'Really?' Brenda frowned heavily. 'But it was only a matter of hours for us. Oh dear. I suppose time moved differently where we were ... behind the scenes. We've frittered away days and days, Effie!'

'It was just at the wrong moment ... the crucial moment ...' Effie moaned.

Penny hurried off to make them some spicy tea, while Lisa dithered over putting away her hairdressing equipment.

'No, you can finish off our do's,' Brenda told her gently. She didn't want to hurt the stylist's feelings, though even she felt it was slightly unusual, the way the girls had chosen to wake them up.

Brenda and Effie took turns to explain where they had been.

They decided it was rather like being in a kind of weird trance.

They tried to describe what had been happening at the very moment they had been drawn bodily back into Brenda's attic.

They both had to nip into the bathroom. It was out on the landing that Brenda suddenly remembered the horrible feel of Magda's fingers slipping out of her grasp. That was the last thing she remembered, about being stuck inside the DVD extras. She remembered the hash she had made of saving Magda Soames's life.

At that very last second she had been dragged away. Back here. Back to real life. And Magda must have plunged to her certain death.

Effie came out of the loo just then and saw her face. She nodded at her friend. 'Rotten timing, eh?'

Back in the living room, Penny was stooping to open the DVD player. The little tray whizzed out, and there was the disc, looking innocuous. Now she held it she realised that it was, in fact, doing something odd. A faint blue mist was rising off it. Like steam pouring out of a kettle . . .

It caught her by surprise. She yelled and dropped it on to the sheepskin rug. The glowing mist continued to rise from the sliver of plastic, and now the others, alerted by her cry, were gathering to watch.

'The film,' Brenda gasped as she returned from the bathroom and saw what was going on. 'It's getting away!'

They stood and watched as the mist gathered itself together and went feeling its way to the window. It seeped through the cracks in the frame, as if it were seeking the night air.

'Where's it going?' Lisa asked, not for one moment questioning that such a thing was possible. The film itself was slipping through their fingers and escaping into the night.

They were so busy gawking out of the casement window that no one saw Penny turn to stare at the harmless-looking disc on the sheepskin rug. Well, I was the one who bought it, after all, she thought, as she bent swiftly to pick it up and pop it into her bag.

Bingone

It was bingo night with a twist.

As Mrs Claus knew, the pensioners who came to stay at the Christmas Hotel tended to expect something a bit different.

'You might not think it, just by looking at them,' said Mrs Claus, 'but this bunch are right thrill-seekers.'

Michael laughed at this, as he wheeled the old lady through the foyer of her hotel. She waved regally at the guests as they made their way to the Mistletoe Lounge.

'You won't believe this,' she told him. 'It's a new craze here.'

'Oh yes?'

'Ordinary run-of-the-mill bingo isn't any good for them any more. No, they want more danger and excitement than that.'

Michael watched the old people go by, all got up in their festive finery. It was true, there was a furtive edge to the atmosphere tonight. And the guests at the Christmas Hotel weren't wearing the usual Christmas clobber either (tissue-paper hats and tinsel leis). Tonight was the Thursday before Goth weekend got going, and a certain number had started dressing accordingly rather early. Elderly Goths! Something Michael had never seen before.

'Just you wait,' Mrs Claus said breathlessly, staring up at him. 'It's like Russian roulette, this. It was all my idea.'

'What happens?' He smiled. Really he should be back at his own establishment. At Spector. If it was the first night of Goth weekend, then it would be packed. How could he have let time creep up on him like this? He had spent so much time with Mrs Claus in recent days, he had been losing track; losing purchase on his own life. He felt as if he had hours missing from his life, just as he had told Penny. He woke up and wasn't sure where he had been. It was like living several lives at once . . .

'You see, what happens here,' Mrs Claus was saying, 'is the opposite of normal, boring bingo. Here, a full house is exactly what you *don't* want. There are small explosive devices placed under all the chairs, and when someone yells out "House!" the device is triggered and it goes off with a bang! Like spontaneous combustion! Oh, it's very dramatic.'

'What?'

She laughed at his earnest expression. 'Oh, it's all right. We've only had one death. Most people take it in good part. And they know what they're getting into. They're thrill-seekers, as I say.'

'But . . . you can't go blowing them up!'

'Why not? *Bingone*, we call it. It's much more popular now than the old-fashioned *bingo*.'

Michael shook his head. They watched guests streaming into the Mistletoe Lounge, eager to play this game. He didn't know whether to believe a word she was saying or not. His mind was very mixed up these days. He felt like she was laughing at him with every word she said.

'Are you all right, love?' she asked. 'You look a bit woozy . . .' She touched his elbow gently as he swayed on the spot.

'I'm all right, I think. Can we sit in the bar?'

'Of course.' She gunned the engine of her motorised scooter and cut a swathe to the bar. There she snapped at the bar elf to mix them a couple of strong snowballs.

Mrs Claus looked at Michael. He was rubbing his eyes blearily. 'I'm so tired,' he said.

'No wonder. Sitting up with me each night. Listening to my old stories.' She looked him up and down appreciatively. Male company! she thought. Who'd have thought I'd be so spoiled and revelling in it, so late in my life? He's a triumph for me. A feather in my Christmas cap. But all my tale-spinning and sneaky mesmerism is taking its toll on my little toy boy. I've worn the poor thing to a frazzle. He caught her eye and was about to say something when there came a muffled explosion from the direction of the Mistletoe Lounge, followed by a lot of shrieking.

Michael's eyes widened. 'It's true! You're blowing them up!'

'Sshh, never mind that,' she said. 'What's the matter, Michael? You look and sound terrible.'

'I don't know. I feel like I shouldn't be here. I should be at work . . .'

'You said that your staff at Spector can cope without you.'

'That's true enough. For a couple more nights maybe.'

'It's me, isn't it? Me and my stories. All the stories of my life. Do you wish I'd never told them to you?'

'No, it's not that . . .' He looked at her and the confusion was all over his face.

Mrs Claus reached out to him with her mind. She thought she'd have another go. It was very strange. He was resisting her. He had resisted her every night she had spent talking with him. He didn't know he was doing it, but his mind forged a barrier against her influence whenever she went out to him. He wouldn't and couldn't be controlled by her. He wasn't like one of her elves, so easy and

311

pliable. There was more to him. Something about him . . . something that even *he* didn't know . . .

It was all very delicious.

Maybe I'm getting in too deep, she wondered. I've not felt like this for a long time. If ever. I feel soft. I feel vulnerable. I feel like I could even tell him how I feel.

But what's he going to think about that? A young bloke like him. Beautiful, strong and in his prime. He's not falling for my charms. Not in a million years. And somehow he's even eluding my mind control.

And yet . . . something mysterious *is* happening to him. It's as if his real life isn't on the surface. It's underneath, somehow, and he doesn't even realise what it is . . . She watched him sip his snowball. He put it down gently.

'I have to go.'

She nodded. 'All right.'

'Thanks for your hospitality, Angela.'

'You know that's all right, love. I've loved talking with you these past few nights. I've no one to tell my secrets to usually.'

'I've loved hearing them.' He frowned. 'But what about your daughter? Will you ever . . . will she ever know you? Will you ever tell her who you are?'

She shook her head tersely.

Michael nodded, understanding. He made to say something else. Something on the tip of his tongue, but then it was gone. Suddenly he had a splitting headache. He just knew he had to get away.

Mrs Claus clasped his hand as he lingered and kissed it. It didn't matter to her who saw her make a fool of herself. That elf at the bar was having a good look at what was going on.

Michael strode out of the Christmas Hotel without a backward glance.

It felt good to be on the sea front, hurrying along by the cliffs, back into town. Clearing the potpourri scents of cloves and eggnog and artificial spray-on snow out of his head.

She was making him fall in love with her. Somehow. And when he looked at her, he was starting to see the young woman she had been when she first fled from this town. The one whose heart and mind were stolen away by the faerie king . . .

What disturbed him so much about that tale? Why did it get under his skin like this?

Michael raced through town. It was Thursday night, just before the start of Goth weekend, and already the streets were filling up with vamps and spooks. Ladies in bustles and basques and fangs. Fellas with white faces and high collars. The pubs were pumping out music and the sun was starting to set. Michael hurried on across to the eastern part of town, over the harbour.

Victor

Today was Friday, and in the past week, while Robert had been stowed away with the other fellas in the attic, and Brenda and Effie had been in and out of something very like twin comas, Karla had been hard at work shooting the scenes that would ultimately lead into the climax of the movie.

The elderly vamp had gone from being a mysterious – some even said ethereal – presence in the turret suite of the Christmas Hotel to being sighted all over the place, dressed to kill in a variety of Gothy but glamorous ensembles.

She was hard at work and it took even her by surprise how much she was enjoying it.

No one spoke of the curse in her hearing. In fact, so enthused for the project was Karla when she got herself in front of the cameras once more, it reignited the enthusiasm of the remaining cast and crew.

Alex and the others observed her closely and with dawning amazement and delight. They found themselves thinking: we might have something special here.

Karla slipped back into the role of an older, wiser Jenny Sommers with ease and aplomb. In this version of the story, the woman who was about to let Satan into her life was a travel agent in

Whitby, frantic for a bit of excitement and stimulation.

Karla is giving it her all, Alex thought. He watched the daily rushes and he saw a woman there who he could believe in. A portrait of disappointment. A crushed and bruised spirit. A woman who was apt for seduction by forces dark as chilli soy sauce. A woman ready to be tempted. With just a few scenes completed – a few deft, bold brushstrokes on the canvas of his movie – Karla had brought this woman to life already. Alex applauded her skill as he watched the small scenes fall into place, forming the bigger picture, knowing that she had the same vista building up in her own head.

The cast and crew loved her. Alex had been worried she'd be too aloof. Too much like a diva, as she had been rumoured to be, back in her heyday. This small, hard-working crew would have no truck with that. But from the first, Karla had rolled up her sleeves and mucked in with them all. She was a delight to be with, every day on the set. She ate happily with the others, wherever they stopped for lunch or tea. She mixed, she shared jokes, she was generous with the younger, less experienced actors. They found that they wanted to be good for her, to impress her. Everyone raised (though Alex hated these sporting metaphors people seemed to use nowadays) their game.

'I know what it is,' he said to her one morning, as they stood together during a break.

'Hmm?' Karla shook out her long silver tresses and hugged herself inside the large puffa jacket she wore between takes. It was pretty sharp and breezy up here by the abbey this morning. Six a.m.! Look at us, she thought, swigging coffee out of a flask and chomping down bacon sandwiches. This is the life! 'What was that, darling?' She was abstractedly staring at the jumble of Whitby rooftops, sending up their plumes of early morning smoke.

'I think I know why you seem so . . . happy,' he said.

'Do I seem happy, dear?' She laughed. 'Well, I'm happy working, aren't I?' She fixed him with one of those captivating smiles. Her eyes wouldn't let him go. 'And you've got to take a fair amount of credit for that, Alex. I mean it. You have created such a convivial atmosphere for your crew. I've never known such a good team. Of course I'm happy working with you all. I've never felt so looked after and respected.'

'This will be your best performance bar none,' he told her, very seriously. 'You realise that, don't you?'

'Ah-ah!' Karla laughed. 'You'll jinx me, telling me things like that. And remember, we've got the hardest bits still to do. All the Goth weekend stuff. Shooting the climax. That's always a right chew-on.'

Alex was cocky. 'It's in the bag. What we've . . . What *you've* created here is something extraordinary. This will be a horror film they'll just have to take seriously.'

Karla snorted. 'We'll see about that, dear. I'll believe that when I see it. At the end of the day, it'll still be a genre piece, for a niche audience. Maybe it'll get the respect it deserves in twenty, twenty-five years. Who knows. You must be patient, Alex.'

He shook his head almost crossly, and bit into his steaming bap. 'No. It's going to be great. People just have to see that.'

Karla looked at him anxiously. He was sounding a bit like his father had, back when he kept banging on about the importance of his blasted novel. About how his message had to reach the whole globe . . . Obsession, Karla mused. Funny how it made some fellas go odd.

'Anyway,' she said. 'I'm much more comfortable on this set than I was on the set of the original film.' She laughed lightly. 'You've made an old woman very happy.'

316

'But it's not just this, is it?' he said eagerly. 'It isn't just the film.'

'Hmm?'

'It's your gentleman friend. He's made you happy too. All the crew is talking about him. Some of them have met him and say he's wonderful.'

'Ah,' she said. 'Yes, well, he's a very special person.'

'But who is he? Someone you met here in Whitby? An old flame, maybe?'

She tutted at him, smiling. But she was discomfited by the interest he was taking in her private life. 'He's a new friend,' she told him. And she wouldn't be drawn.

Soon it was time to get back to work. They had shots to get in, making the most of the early morning light, as Karla's character went traipsing around entranced in the ruins of the abbey, searching for the reputed gateway into hell.

That lunchtime, Victor turned up to fetch her.

He was in his mid seventies, Alex judged. A slight, bony figure, beautifully dressed in three-quarter-length frock coat and cravat. His face was pleasant but pinched. The skin was thin and he had the sensitive look of a nineteenth-century artist, perhaps, or a musician. His fingers were long and pale. They ought to belong to a great violinist. Or a surgeon . . .

'My dear.' He greeted Karla with a courtly bow. He had brought her anemones, a tangle of indigo petals and hairy stems. Karla took them and turned to Alex. 'You were asking about him, Alex. Here he is. My new beau.'

Alex shook hands with the fine-featured gent. 'I'm Alex Soames, director of this piece.'

Victor regarded him keenly. His thin lips twitched and there was a gleam in his pale eyes. 'I have heard a great deal about you. And I am honoured to meet the son of the great writer, also.'

'Thank you, sir,' said Alex stiffly. He always felt awkward when people brought up his dad. If truth be told, Alex hardly remembered his renowned progenitor.

'My name is Victor Frankenstein,' the old man told him.

Fish Supper

Cod Almighty, the day after their return, and the two ladies were at their usual banquette.

'I can't stay out long, Effie. There's so much to do back home.'

Effie pursed her lips approvingly. It felt good that they were both back to their routines. 'You say you're packed out with guests for the weekend?'

'Really, it's no bother. And I can't afford to turn custom away, can I?' Brenda fiddled with the teapot and their cups and smiled as she thought of her B&B being filled with eager Goths, chattering excitedly about the coming weekend. They were particularly keen on the impending film-making at the abbey. Word had gone round on the Goth networks and websites that the film crew required willing and able extras for walk-on parts, and the Goths were all stirred up at the thought of that.

Effie sipped her tea gingerly, all the while studying her friend. 'But you're exhausted, aren't you? We're both worn out.'

Brenda nodded. 'It's not every week that you . . . you know, *travel into the past.*' She lowered her voice. It would be awful if anyone overheard her, she thought. They'd think she was mad.

'Time travel!' said Effie. 'I know! I can hardly believe it.'

'I'd think it was me hallucinating if it wasn't that we both remember being there.'

Effie lowered her eyes to the gingham tablecloth. 'And seeing what we saw. And who we saw.'

'Indeed.'

The waitress came bustling up and the ladies put in orders for their favourites: poached haddock for Effie, and a plate of crispy whitebait for Brenda. They began with very thinly cut slices of bread and butter, which they nibbled hungrily as they talked.

'Well, we were definitely there,' Brenda said. 'I can even prove it.'

'I don't need proof.'

Brenda told her. 'I looked in my wall safe. You know, where I keep mementos and useful keepsakes from all my adventures.'

Effie shuddered as a number of memories surfaced quite involuntarily. She recalled handling a rather nasty (though ultimately practical) monkey's paw found in Brenda's secret cubbyhole.

'I found Karla's papers,' said Brenda. 'The ones we took from her trailer and gave to the younger me to look after. I'd kept them in a special file for all these years, folded up inside a *Woman's Weekly* from 1967 that I'd saved for a poncho knitting pattern I had my eye on.'

'Any use?' Effie asked.

Brenda shrugged. 'I was never a very good knitter, to be honest. And I don't know what I ever saw in that poncho. Shapeless, horrible thing . . .'

Effie rolled her eyes. 'I meant Karla's letters from the Brethren . . .'

'Oh, yes. Sorry. They were spooky things indeed, in all this ornate handwriting. Giving her instructions and so on. They were behind her all right. Egging the woman on to have that affair with Fox Soames, and to dabble in the dark arts.'

'Foolish woman. And she's still doing it! That's what gets me.'

Effie stuffed a whole lot of buttered bread into her mouth, rather crossly.

Brenda admitted, 'I feel a bit sorry for her. What chance has she ever had? Those letters were going back years. She's been up to her eyes in satanic machinations since she was just a kid.'

'Pah.'

They quietened down then, as the waitress brought their dinner.

Effie said, 'I don't have much sympathy, to be honest. Look at me. I was brought up to be a witch. I bet my aunties were just as fierce as these Brethren people. I hated magic. I still do. I wanted nothing to do with any of it, and so I defied them. I stood up for myself.' She toyed with slivers of mouth-watering fish while she talked, eating very little as she dwelt on the past.

'Not everyone has the same strength of character as you, Effie. Not everyone can stick up for themselves.'

'Yes they can. If they put their minds to it. I'm nowt special. Everyone has a choice, Brenda, about how they're going to live their life.'

They ate in silence for a while, starting to enjoy their food and each other's calm company. It felt good to be back doing something as ordinary as this. Sixties music was playing through the speakers, and Brenda found herself bouncing along in time, very gently, to Cilla Black as she munched and crunched her way through the whitebait. She had rather enjoyed the sixties. It had been quite pleasant, in a way, to return there, albeit to Wales.

As they pushed away their plates, she said decisively, 'We need to get on with finding the men.'

'Where do we start?' said Effie.

'Penny says that Robert went looking into those DVDs and where they came from . . .'

'Then that's where we should go tomorrow. Those grisly old women in Save the Kiddies will know a thing or two, I imagine.'

'And Frank!' Brenda burst out. 'Where did he wander off to, in his confused state of mind? You know, I'd be very surprised if his disappearance wasn't mixed up in all of this.'

'Hmm,' said Effie. 'You're probably right.' But right at that moment Effie was thinking of her own man.

'You're miles away. What is it?'

Effie looked her friend dead in the eye. 'We haven't yet talked much about . . . events in Wales. In the past.'

'I can't bear it,' Brenda sighed. She looked very uncomfortable. 'I couldn't say anything when the two girls were about, Penny and Lisa. They're both so cock-a-hoop that they saved us. Dragged us back to . . . reality.'

Effie touched her hair. 'I'm not sure I'd choose such a livid blue rinse for myself, but I'm getting used to it. It was kind of them.'

Brenda nodded brusquely. 'But they aren't to know that they dragged us back at such a crucial moment.'

'No.'

Brenda's face twisted in anguish. 'I just wish . . . A few seconds more, and I might have been able to save Magda. I could have yanked her back to safety. I would have changed things . . .'

Effie poured them the last of the tea. 'It's the past, Brenda. Perhaps it's impossible to change.'

'No. We got . . . behind the scenes. We could have changed things. I just know we could have.'

'But we didn't.'

Brenda nodded dolefully. She looked close to tears. 'And things went on as normal. The climax of the film was shot, just as Karla and the Brethren planned. And in those last few seconds we were

322

there . . . the devil really did come through, didn't he? He manifested himself for all to see.'

'No,' said Effie.

'But we saw him, Effie! I mean, I was caught up with poor Magda and all, but I could see enough . . . that swirling vortex of light, just like the gateway to hell we've seen before, and that figure starting to step out . . .'

'It wasn't the devil, Brenda. And he didn't manage to get all the way out. He was furious. He was still trapped. He put on an impressive show, and scared the bejaysus out of everyone there, but he never escaped from hell. Not yet.'

'Then who was it?' Brenda blinked. She had no idea what Effie was talking about.

Effie leaned in. 'It was Kristoff.'

Brenda blinked. 'Your Kristoff? Alucard?'

'We left him in hell, remember? On two occasions now. And he wants out, doesn't he? Oh, it makes perfect sense. And he looked so incensed, Brenda. He caught a glimpse of me too, staring back at him, which gave him quite a turn.'

Brenda looked at her friend. Could she really trust what Effie thought she had seen? Clearly she wanted that figure to be Alucard more than anything, but really . . .

'I know how sceptical you are, Brenda, when it comes to anything about my Kristoff. I know you've got all kinds of grudges against him.'

Brenda repressed a shudder at the diabolical man's name. 'I suppose you . . . erm, love him and everything, Effie. But he's tried to kill me and suck out my blood on numerous occasions down through the years, as I've explained to you before. I knew him decades before you ever did and you just won't listen to me; he isn't to be trusted.'

'He was coming through . . . in order to help us,' Effie insisted, with a wild look in her eye. 'He wanted to save us all!'

Brenda snorted. 'Rubbish. Since when did that cadaverous dandy ever do anything to help anyone else? Never!'

Effie glowered and set her mind to dividing up the bill. Brenda tactfully dropped the subject of her man-friend. Though she did wonder for a bit how *time* worked in hell. Could Alucard really try to escape through portals elsewhere in time as well as space? In Brenda's own not inconsiderable experience of similar matters, she had found that time moved very oddly in the region popularly thought of as hell, so maybe a cameo appearance from Alucard in 1967 wasn't quite as unlikely as all that.

As they shrugged into their good winter coats, Brenda was examining a copy of the local rag, *The Willing Spirit*, which someone had left on a neighbouring banquette. The cover showed colour photographs of Goth visitors swanking about on the prom and in the streets. The banner headline read, 'Whitby Welcomes Back the Goths'. Brenda wondered whether she had the heart to wear the outfit she had planned for herself. This was the first Goth weekend she had felt like dressing up and joining in, and to her surprise, Effie had promised to do the same thing. But had recent events put them off donning their finery this coming weekend?

She flipped through the newspaper to find a double-page spread of pictures covering the filming of the remake of *Get Thee Inside Me, Satan*. There was an interview with the enthusiastic director, Alex Soames ('Bless him!' Brenda thought), and glossy glamour shots of the buxom Karla in a variety of famed Whitby locations. She looked every inch the vampish star.

'She really doesn't seem to have aged at all since we saw her back in 1967.' Brenda frowned.

' "Film Location Exclusive," ' Effie read, over her shoulder. ' "Hollywood comes to Whitby. Great Excitement about Saturday Night Climax: Celebrity Black Mass and Witches' Sabbat Planned as Culmination of Goth Weekend Extravaganza. See page six for exclusive competition." ' She tutted. How common.

A shiver went through Brenda. 'So . . . it's happening again,' she said. 'We're going to have to be there when they shoot the ending of the film for a second time.'

'Who is that old man?' Effie asked suddenly.

'Hmm?'

'There. By the looks of things, Karla's hooked herself a fella, soon as she's got here.'

'What?'

They pored over the photo that appeared under the sub-heading: 'Love at last for lonely vamp lady?' Karla was on the arm of a very pale, skinny old man. He was a smart-looking gentleman, Effie thought. His silver hair was swept back from a high, intelligent brow, and he wore a silk cravat, which was something Effie always liked to see. Karla had picked herself up a bit of class.

' "Who is the Elegant Mystery Man?" ' Effie read aloud.

Brenda fell silent as she studied the small article intently. Then she crumpled the paper and stuffed it into her bag. 'I want to examine this in greater detail at home,' she said gruffly, and led the way out of Cod Almighty.

Effie followed on, wondering why her friend's mood had changed so quickly. You never could tell with Brenda. Sometimes even the slightest thing could send her on the turn.

Turmoil on her Nerves

Lisa Turmoil was nice and everything, Penny was sure. But as they sat at the bar in Spector that night, the hairstylist was getting on her nerves.

The place was swirling with Goths and every surface was shuddering with the deep, pounding bass of the music, which, if Penny was honest with herself, she didn't like much at all. But Lisa was being so sniffy and skitty about the Goths around her that Penny felt she had to defend the whole Goth thing: the look, the lifestyle, the preference for horrible music.

Also, Lisa had got on her nerves for criticising her back-combed hair.

'God, you'll ruin the condition of it. What have you got in it?'

'You have to do it up like this at Goth weekend,' Penny told her. Lisa herself was looking straighter than straight, in her jeans and a plain white blouse.

'And what's that dye you put in it?' Lisa touched Penny's hair and made her new friend flinch. 'It'll all drop out.'

Penny bit her tongue. She was still grateful that Lisa had managed to bring Brenda and Effie out of their comas. But gratitude only went so far.

Of course, the worst thing that Lisa was doing was flirting with Michael.

The manager was swaggering up and down the long bar at Spector, keeping an eye on his staff and making the whole first night of Goth weekend go with a swing. He had come dashing in late, Penny noticed, and taken charge with a slightly manic air of forced compentency and breeziness. After her recent experience of stepping into a position of authority, she knew that wasn't the best way to get the most out of your staff. The other bar staff were glowering at his back, she noticed. Michael ignored this, and every now and then would spare a few minutes to lean across the bar and chat with his 'two best girls', as he'd taken to calling Lisa and Penny.

I like him, Penny thought, but he's a bit patronising. And a bit intense, too. He's never been the same since he started going to see that awful hotel owner on the West Cliff. Mrs Claus. There's something funny about all that. Anyway, at least tonight he's in a lighter mood.

Or so she thought. There was still a lot on Michael's mind. There was still a lot troubling him.

'Wow,' Lisa was saying, 'Maybe you're, like, psychic, Michael?'

He nodded solemnly. 'I've been wondering about that.'

I've missed something! Penny thought. She had been sucking her drink up through a curly straw and thinking about the whole Michael situation, and now she had missed what he was confiding to Lisa. 'What? Why is he psychic?'

'Well,' Michael said, frowning, 'it's just a feeling. But ever since I've been living here in Whitby, these past few weeks, I've been having . . . not exactly dreams. Or day-dreams, even. I've been having weird thoughts and sensations.'

Lisa smirked. 'Oh yes?'

'That's pretty typical of Whitby, I gather,' said Penny. 'I should tell you about some of the things Robert's told me.'

They looked at her expectantly.

'I meant, some other time. Tell us about you, Michael,' Penny urged him. 'What it is you've been experiencing . . .'

'Oh, I don't know really.' Now he was looking a bit embarrassed for having begun the conversation. 'I feel like I'm not completely here. Or I'm stretched thin, somehow. I'm living two lives, is how I feel. I'm here . . . and I'm elsewhere, somehow, living another life.'

'Really?' smiled Lisa, bugging out her eyes with interest. 'That's pretty wild.'

Penny turned to him earnestly. 'I knew there was something! I could tell you've had something on your mind. Something troubling you.'

Michael shrugged ruefully. 'I thought I was . . . I don't know . . . being abducted by aliens or something. I was losing time. I'd wake up and hours would have passed. I thought I was having past life regressions at one point.'

Lisa became animated. 'Maybe you are. That happened to my Auntie Linda. She went up on stage with a hypnotist once and he took her back to the time of Queen Victoria. She used to be in music hall back then, it turned out, and she was on the game, too. Anyway, after that she kept slipping back all the time, even when she never meant to. It became like a habit with her.'

'I don't think it's that.' Michael frowned.

Penny glared resentfully at Lisa. What was she doing, banging on about her Auntie Linda? Michael was obviously worried about something. And he had chosen this moment, in all the noise of Spector, to unburden himself to them. She suddenly wished Lisa wasn't there.

Michael sighed deeply and carried on. 'Ever since I came here . . .

Somehow the very atmosphere of this town has dredged up strange feelings I've had all my life.'

'Yes, it can do that.' Lisa nodded. 'There's magic here. Devilry, I'd say.'

'I've always felt, I suppose, that I belong elsewhere,' Michael said. 'But most kids do, don't they, when they're growing up?'

'I certainly did,' Penny said.

'But the feelings have got stronger since I've been here. And . . . these evenings I've been spending at the Christmas Hotel . . . with Angela . . . and hearing the strange stories of her past.'

'Angela?' asked Penny.

'Mrs Claus. She's been telling me about her youth and how she left Whitby and went . . . I don't know . . . into some kind of fairy tale . . .'

Penny shook her head worriedly. 'She's crackers, that one. That's what Brenda reckons.'

'No,' Michael snapped, jolting her. 'She's been very sweet to me. Telling me these tall tales. But the thing is . . . I believe them. No matter how wild her stories get . . . all this talk of walking, living dolls and the fairy court and . . . Well, whatever. I *believe* them. I believe in *her*.'

Penny opened her mouth to speak. Then she stopped. Fairy court? What was he talking about? Clearly the old bag at the Christmas Hotel had sucked him into her power. Robert had talked about such things.

But . . . *she* was believing in the things that Robert and Brenda and Effie had told her about *their* lives, wasn't she? Impossible things. Magical things. Was this any different?

'Angela's stories,' Michael said. 'They have started to ring bells with me.'

Lisa spoke up then. Penny had managed to ignore the fact that she was there for several minutes to this point. 'How do you mean?' Lisa said. Penny hated the scepticism in her voice. But Michael didn't seem to hear it.

'It is as if Angela Claus is somehow . . . awakening that separate self in me,' he said, 'She is waking the *other* me, the secret life I feel I am living . . . It's starting to feel more real than the life I thought I'd lived . . .'

Penny didn't like the sound of this at all. He was beginning to sound like a pretty complicated fella to her. And that was just what she didn't need. She consoled herself with the thought that at least they hadn't got any more involved than they already had . . . no matter what she had hoped for.

Now Michael was saying, 'Your friend Robert . . .'

Penny's heart leapt and she glanced around. 'What?' She'd stopped listening again, caught up in her own thoughts. 'What? Is he here?'

'No,' said Michael. 'But . . . you'll think I'm mad when I say this. I can hear him, Penny. I can . . . These past couple of days . . . since he's been missing. I've not wanted to say anything, in case you think I'm mad or daft. But it is as if Robert is calling out to me . . . with his mind.'

Lisa banged the bar top with her palm. 'I knew it! You've got psychic abilities. I've seen this before. Remember, I was stylist on *Manifest Yourself!* on Cable TV. When it comes to psychic phenomena, I've run the whole gamut.'

'Where *is* Robert, Michael?' Penny demanded urgently. 'Do you know? I've been worried sick. Where has he got to?'

'I . . . I'm not sure. Sometimes I can pin the voice down. Other times I think I'm just imagining it. That's why I've not said anything up to now. But . . . I think he's in danger . . . awful danger, wherever he is.'

Why would Michael be linked to Robert? Penny wondered. Why would that be? But then his words sank in fast. Awful danger. She had known it. And now it was up to her to somehow find him and get him out.

She urged Michael on, clutching his shirt sleeve. 'Think, Michael. We have to know. Where is he?'

Around them the music grew louder and the night grew more raucous, as extra visitors swarmed darkly to the trendy lights of Spector.

Frank's Dad

Robert was just a pair of eyes. He had been tied up so long and fed and watered so little that his body felt redundant to him.

He sat in the attic and he was just a pair of eyes, squinting in the half-light.

What fresh horror was this?

The elf and the postman were up to their old, terrible tricks again. Chuckling dementedly, like men possessed, they were hunched over the unprotesting Frank.

Frank had gone completely quiet and still some hours ago.

They've killed him, Robert thought. I've sat here and tried to keep out of their way . . . and I've let them kill him and hoped they wouldn't notice me.

All the fight had gone out of Frank. As they disconnected his left arm and the grinning elf-boy carried it away, it gave a token resistance. It thrashed around a bit, splashing some sluggish gore about the place. But even the massive arm didn't put up much of a fight. The elf laid it down in a dusty corner and it spasmed for a while hopelessly, but couldn't do anything more to help its master.

Off came the other arm.

How much of Frank was left?

Robert heard him muttering now. Telling the slaves of Karla

something. Perhaps warning them what he would do with them when he was free and whole once more . . . But they just laughed at him. They gave the impression of having a whale of a time. It was such a jape, this. Such a treat. Pulling the bound monster to pieces, just to pass the time.

Would they eat the pieces? Robert wondered. Were they as hungry as he was, even in their mesmerised state? But surely Frank's old parts would be tough and leathery. They were old, so old . . .

He heard the slaves' whispered deliberations about cutting open Frank's torso. What would it be like to have a poke around inside? See what made the old brute tick?

But then there was a horrible creak as the hatchway opened. Gold-white light spilled upwards into the attic gloom. They all stopped what they were doing. Even Frank stopped groaning.

Was it Karla? What would she say when she saw what her boys had accomplished? Robert's heart raced madly with anticipation. Surely she couldn't have asked them to do this thing?

But the tread on the wooden staircase was lighter and nimbler than Karla's. This was someone else. Someone who was advancing very carefully into the garret room. Perhaps someone who didn't know the territory. Didn't know who or what he was going to find at the top.

Perhaps this is rescue! Robert thought. Those gentle, cautious footsteps coming closer and closer. They were a kind of countdown to the coming of safety, freedom . . .

A very tall, thin man appeared in their attic. He dusted his hands fastidiously as his eyes accustomed themselves to the treacly dark. Robert was impressed and bewildered by his old-fashioned dress, his gaunt, ascetic face. His expression of amused relish as he took in the horrible sight of the frightened prisoners and the remains of Frank.

He smiled. He shook his head in mock sadness and actually smiled at the scene of carnage.

'Look at me, Frank,' he said. 'I know you can still see. Concentrate. Come on. Try harder. That was always your problem. Whenever you faced difficulties you'd give in to the most terrible rage and despair and you'd just stop trying. Sulking, really. And that's what you're doing now.'

It was a very cultured, clipped voice. Robert's mind reeled, trying to take in what the old man was saying.

'I tell you, Frank. Look at me. You can't ignore me.'

At last Frank spoke up. Throatily. Wheezily. 'Go away. Whoever you are. Frank is . . . Frank is not here.'

The visitor replied, 'Yes you are, Frank. Whatever these odd, feral men have been doing to you. You are still Frank. You are indestructible, Frank.'

The old man eyed the bloody elf and the postman. He lunged forward, as if to attack them, and they leapt backwards. He laughed.

'They'll do you no harm. Come on, my dear. Look at me.'

'Frank doesn't know who you are.'

'Oh, you do.' The old man rubbed his elegant hands together. They were sensitive and felt the cold up here acutely. 'You really do know me. You're worn out and in tatters. But you can still concentrate. You can still focus your attention. Look at me.'

Frank looked up and blinked. It seemed to take most of his energy just to do that small thing.

Frank said: 'It can't be you.'

'It *is*, Frank. I am as alive as you.'

'Then you won't be alive for long. Frank is . . . Frank is dying at last.'

'No, no. Merely worn out a bit. And hacked about a bit. These lads here haven't done you much good. I'll punish them later. They'll come in useful, two strapping lads like them. We always need spare parts, don't we?'

There was a prolonged pause. Robert could have sworn he heard Frank sob, 'F-Father?'

'Of course, Frank. I've come back to make things better for you.'

'Better?'

The old man made his voice gentle. Soothing. Like warm tea soaking through sugar-coated biscuits. 'I've come to help you. You are my first-born. You know that, despite everything, I am fondest of you. My greatest triumph.'

'You tried to murder Frank. Again and again.'

'Nonsense. You must let me help you.'

A new note of fear in Frank's voice now. 'What will you do to Frank?'

'I will make you young again. Set you back on your feet again. Make your life new once more.'

'I don't believe you. You hate Frank.'

'You will have to believe me. How will you resist me? You've never been more at my mercy, Frank. Not since the day you first came to life.'

Robert watched as the old man knelt to take the seeping torso and the heavy, weary head in his arms. The two figures formed a weirdly touching pietà. But the old man wasn't embracing his son. He was examining him. His pale hands moved skilfully over the unresisting and ruined body.

Then Robert couldn't watch any more.

Other People's Doings

That afternoon, Brenda took a couple of hours off work and Effie closed her shop early. For once she had a shop filled with browsers, and it was quite a job disentangling them from the junk jewellery, the antique costumery, the faded bric-a-brac.

The two ladies set out purposefully for Save the Kiddies.

There was a new sign in the window, *Save the Kiddies Welcomes the Goths*.

'They're just cashing in,' said Effie sniffily, and led the way inside.

When they saw who was coming into their shop, Teresa and Helen stiffened immediately.

'We don't want any trouble,' Teresa snapped.

Effie said pleasantly, 'And neither do we, Teresa. We're merely making enquiries.'

Teresa's lip twisted into a sneer. 'You do a lot of that, don't you? You two.'

'Making enquiries,' added Helen, mustering as much scorn as she could.

'Messing about in other people's doings,' added Teresa.

Brenda realised that the two charity volunteers were keeping their voices deliberately hushed. They were embarrassed in case other browsers overheard.

Brenda said loudly, 'We need to know about a friend of ours. A young man.'

'Young man, is it?' Teresa simpered.

'Yes, our friend Robert. He was last seen in here. He was making enquiries as well.'

'We can't keep track of everyone who comes in here.'

'We've been inundated,' added Helen. But there was something about Helen. A nervous flicker in her expression that both Brenda and Effie noted.

Effie ploughed on, 'Robert came in here to ask about those Karla Sorenson DVDs.'

Teresa laughed nastily. 'You do keep on losing men, don't you, dear?'

Brenda blinked. 'I beg your pardon?'

'We heard that your husband went west too. That big fella you're supposed to be married to.'

Effie grinned back at them, dangerously. She poked her beaky nose at them and Brenda could see that they were a whisker away from having a fight on their hands. 'That's true,' sneered Effie. 'We're always losing men, we two.'

Helen was suddenly much more nervous. 'Look, we've got nothing to tell you. You might as well clear off. That effeminate young man was in once but we never saw him again. If he's messing about with stuff to do with Ms Sorenson, though—'

'Yes?' snapped Effie.

'Then he'd better watch out,' Helen mumbled, turning back to stacking a pile of Virginia Andrewses in the correct sequence, which she knew off by heart. 'That's all I'm saying.'

Brenda tossed her head. 'Come on, Effie. These two are getting on my wick. We won't get anything more out of them.'

Just as they were leaving, Teresa found her voice again. She bellowed across the glass counter at Brenda: 'She didn't need you, you know! When you were off running about the country with that fancy man of yours. Effie was glad to see the back of you! She was one of our gang, and she was happier, she was! She was glad to be friends with the lowly likes of us back then!'

Effie hastened towards the door. 'Ooh, don't listen, Brenda. She's crackers.'

Brenda had to agree. But she knew how fierce loyalties and betrayals could seem in a little town like this. Feelings could run high, especially amongst the older crowd. But there was something else, something downright bizarre about the behaviour of these two from Save the Kiddies.

Later that afternoon, after coffee and warm macaroons in a new café they were trying out (not to their taste: it was all stainless steel, internet access, and something the waitress told them was called 'chill-out music'), they went round the shops to pick up a few bits and pieces. Woolworths first, so that Brenda could fill a pound bag with pick-n-mix, which always helped, she claimed, with her thinking when she was on a case.

She'd miss Woollies when it was gone, she thought. Strange how the shop hadn't shut down yet, even though every other Woollies in the country apparently had. A shiver went through her as she considered this, gazing at the colourful aisles and the flickering fluorescent lights. Was the Whitby Woollies one of the undead? A zombie department store? The very last of its kind, swearing eternal vengeance . . . Could such a weird thing be possible? Hmmmmm. She probably had enough on her plate to contend with as things were. Still and all, it was interesting that, as yet, the old place showed no signs of shutting up shop.

It was just as Brenda was reaching with the little trowel into the heaps of sherbet fizzers and then the chocolate limes that a very furtive Helen from Save the Kiddies sidled up to her and hissed: 'I couldn't say before. Teresa would have my guts for garters. But I like that young man. He's got some spunk.'

Effie's head shot up over the sweetie display. 'Goodness! What's she saying?'

Helen, looking haggard, whispered: 'I'm telling Brenda here—'

Effie was in no mood for further nonsense. 'Look, just you beggar off. We've had enough of you obfuscating our investigations.'

Brenda put in, 'I want to hear what she has to say.'

Helen was almost frightened. 'I haven't long. Up at the hotel. The Christmas Hotel.'

Brenda proffered a sherbet fizzer out of her pick-n-mix. 'What is? What are you so frightened of?'

A terrible look came into Helen's eyes. 'We were there. We're caught up in it. Doing her bidding. Her and the . . . Brethren. I didn't want to. I don't want . . . Oh dear. I shouldn't be telling you.'

Brenda clicked her fingers. 'Tell us. What's going on at the Christmas Hotel?'

Helen's eyes went wide. Beads of sweat stood out on her forehead. She forced her words out as though someone was trying to stop her. 'She's the very devil. I have to go.'

They watched her turn and scuttle away. Grimly, Brenda continued to fill her bag with sweets.

'What's wrong with her?' Effie tutted. 'She looked like she was doing herself a mischief.'

Brenda said, 'We have to go up there, of course.'

Effie didn't need to ask where she meant.

Brenda sighed. 'We have to check it out. It's a lead.'

'And probably a trap.' Effie suddenly cried out. 'The Bloody Banquet at the Christmas Hotel,' she squawked, as they made their way to the counter to pay for Brenda's sweets. Brenda always seemed to eat half of them before they had even been weighed.

'Hmmm?' said Brenda thoughtfully, untangling liquorice shoestrings.

'Tonight,' clipped Effie. 'It's the perfect opportunity. Mrs Claus is hostessing a huge supper to celebrate Goth weekend.'

'It's an excuse to be there, I suppose,' said Brenda, beginning a slow smile.

'And to glam up in our Gothy glad rags too,' said Effie. 'I did wonder if we were going to get the chance.'

The Bloody Banquet

'Well, she's outdone herself, hasn't she?' smiled Effie.

They were inside the Christmas Hotel again, and the place had been Gothed up a treat. Every pillar and pilaster was trimmed with black ribbon and lace; every swag of tinsel was blood red. There were skulls where usually there'd be stars, and pumpkin heads gurning and glowing atop the many Christmas trees.

Brenda was inclined to agree with Effie's observation about the decor, but she was even more impressed by Effie's get-up and the effort her friend had gone to. Effie was in full Victorian garb, complete with a little lacy brolly and some kind of feathery effort stuck to the side of her head. Effie noticed her eyeing it. 'It's called a fascinator, Brenda,' she sighed. 'It's a designer fascinator and I'm praying like mad that it doesn't drop off. Rather chic, isn't it?'

Effie had made an effort with her make-up too, Brenda noticed. She was glad, in her turn, that she'd pushed the boat out. Looking around at the other diners who were milling, cocktails aloft, in the lobby, it seemed that everyone had dressed up in something a bit ghoulishly glamorous for the evening. Ah, Frank, she thought, with a sudden stab of sadness. We were both going to glam up and swish about together, weren't we? We were going to disguise ourselves as ourselves for a change, just for a laugh. But here she was on her own.

'How on earth did you fasten that bodice up by yourself ?' Effie asked her. She glanced up and down at Brenda's rather startling ensemble.

'Oh, I had some help,' said Brenda lightly, taking a sip from her frankly not-very-nice pre-dinner drink. 'I got dressed in my attic. I, erm, got a hand with dressing, if you see what I mean.'

'Oh.' Effie looked uncomfortable as she realised what Brenda meant. But it must be pretty useful, having spare disembodied hands and things about the place. Perhaps that was how Brenda kept up with all her housework so brilliantly. That was why her guest house was so clean. She set the surplus bits of herself to work as she went out on beanos like this. But wouldn't that frighten the guests? To come in and witness, say, a severed hand flitting about the picture rails with a feather duster? Effie found that she couldn't ask Brenda any more about this. It didn't seem like polite chitchat to her. She had been brought up to believe that occasions like these demanded nothing more than the smallest of small talk. 'Well, you look marvellous, ducky,' she told Brenda.

'Cheers, lovey.' Though Brenda couldn't help wishing she'd cottoned on to this craze for fascinators herself. Quite a few women around the Christmas Hotel were sporting them that night. Ah, I'd probably be useless at getting one to stay put, she thought.

'Oh, here are the girls!' Effie said, nudging Brenda in the corset, which she couldn't feel.

'Look at you two!' gasped Penny. She had all sorts of interesting woollen attachments coming out of her hair. She was dressed mostly in PVC and she stood about a foot taller than usual on the most impractical shoes Effie had ever seen. Standing in her shadow, Lisa looked fairly conservatively dressed. Until Effie saw that she'd had some movie magic make-up applied to her, in the form of a fake gash in her throat, and the handle of a pair of scissors sticking out of her neck.

'Oooh!' gasped Brenda.

'That makes my blood run cold.' Effie shuddered.

'Great, isn't it?' Lisa grinned. 'My friend Nigel from the crew does all their gory effects. I look like a hairdresser gone crazy, don't I!'

Brenda led them to the cocktail bar, where some of the older Goths glanced at the girls with great interest.

'I do wish Robert was here,' Brenda said.

'Oh, so do I,' said Penny. 'He told me all about Goth weekend and what it was going to be like. I was looking forward to seeing what he'd come as.'

Lisa tried to cheer them. 'At least you've got us, Brenda.'

Brenda laughed. 'Yes! The young people!'

Effie said, 'And don't we all look spectacular, as a gang. But you must be warned, girls. Whenever we come here to the Christmas Hotel, it tends to end in disaster.'

Penny nodded seriously. 'I've already witnessed that once, if you remember.'

She glanced around. Brenda knew at once that she was looking for her other friend, who the two girls had arrived with. Michael, the young man Penny had been seeing something of recently, apparently. Brenda and Effie had caught no more than the merest glimpse of him as he came striding into the hotel foyer in a severe black suit, beautifully cut, and a pitch-dark silk shirt. He had waltzed off straight to the loo.

'Your friend Michael's been gone a while, lovey,' Brenda told Penny. 'Is he all right? I was rather keen on meeting him.'

Penny frowned. She didn't know what was going on with Michael. He was still in a very funny mood.

Mirror Mirror

In the gents, Michael was leaning over one of the basins. He was studying his reflection.

'Come on, come on. Get a grip . . .'

Tonight it was as if he hardly knew his own face. He was in a suit for once, looking quite different. Elegant. Everything about him felt different.

As he gazed at his own face, he had a sudden flash of Robert's face, overlaid, looking back at him. Beseeching.

'You've got to help us,' Robert was calling to him. 'They're going to cut us up! He'll cut us up into pieces!'

Michael turned the cold tap on full and splashed himself with freezing water. Trying to get some sense back. He didn't even know Robert. How could he hallucinate him like this? So perfectly? What was going on?

He wadded up paper towels and dried himself, shuddering. Struggling to regain control of himself. He had passed a hellish twenty-four hours. He had been plagued by demons. It felt like something was readying itself inside of him. Some vile thing. Preparing to break out of his body.

When he felt a bit calmer, he checked his reflection again. He looked normal. No other faces lurking there, beneath his own.

But he looked pale and blotchy. Terrible.

He returned to the hotel foyer. He caught up with the others at the bar.

Penny made hurried introductions and he tried to smile and say nice things about Brenda and Effie's outfits. But everyone could see his mind was elsewhere. Penny leaned in and hissed, 'Look, are you all right?'

Effie shoved her nose in. 'I don't think he is right at all, Penny.' Then she looked over her shoulder at Brenda, mouthing: 'Drugs – or worse!'

Brenda squinched closer (cursing her corselette as she did so). 'What is it, Michael?'

Penny said, 'He says he keeps having these odd episodes . . .'

Brenda put her hands to his face. He was burning up. His tangled black hair was wet with sweat and cold water. He looked up into her eyes, and what she saw there made Brenda gasp.

Michael looked like a lost soul. He was adrift in some kind of nightmare. He had no idea what was happening to him. Brenda recognised that expression on his face at once. It reminded her of those moments she experienced now and then, in which her elusive memories came back to her. When the pictures and voices in her head became as real as – and then more real than – her present surroundings.

To her, Michael looked beset by memories he didn't even recognise as his own.

Effie pursed her lips worriedly. Was this troubled young man going to put the kibosh on the whole evening's do? She turned to Penny and Lisa. 'Perhaps one of you girls should take him home. He shouldn't be out in a state like this.'

'I will,' Lisa offered.

There was no way Penny was letting Lisa tootle off with Michael alone. She said, 'No, it's all right. I'll—'

Then Michael spoke up for himself, in a suddenly much stronger, more determined tone. 'I'm okay here. I like it here.'

Effie pulled a face. 'You do?'

Michael smiled at her. It wasn't a very nice smile. Snide, Brenda would have called it. Like he knew something Effie didn't. He said to her, '*You* should like it here too, Effryggia.'

'I beg your pardon, young man?' Effie snapped.

'You should like it here.' He curled his lip at her.

Effie frowned heavily. '*Me* in particular? Why me, in particular? I think it's a dreadful, gaudy place.'

'But someone very close to you . . . someone . . .' He coughed, and shuddered, and seemed less certain again. Whatever had seized control of him was relenting.

'What's he talking about, Brenda?' Effie had lost all patience with the strange young man. 'Can you make sense of this?'

Brenda glugged the last of her drink. 'What is it, lovey? What are you trying to say?'

Michael stammered and shook. He was back to himself. The weird fit had passed. 'I don't know. I knew something then, but it's gone . . .'

They were interrupted then by a huge round of applause.

A crowd was gathering around two figures as they swept through reception, then the bar, and towards the main dining room.

Karla paraded graciously, resplendent in black, a black veil, a tiny, elegant hat perched on top. At her side was her new gentleman friend in a black velvet frock coat. He looked proud as a strutting peacock, Effie thought.

'The woman herself,' Brenda murmured as they watched.

Penny said, 'Well done on the hair, Lisa.'

'Thanks, Penny.'

Effie gasped. 'You did her hair? Up in her suite?'

'Yeah.' Lisa nodded, looking pretty chuffed with her own handi-work. 'She's all right, really, for a movie star. Quite down to earth, actually.'

'You're big pals with her?' asked Effie sharply. She felt like Lisa had been holding back on them a little with this information.

'I wouldn't say that, exactly.'

Effie was persistent. 'But you're well in with her? Maybe you could get us into her rooms, should we need to steal into them to investigate.'

'Well . . .' said Lisa, not at all keen.

Penny was about to comment to Brenda, sotto voce, on Lisa's obviously protecting her own professional interests, when she turned round and suddenly realised that there was something wrong with the woman. 'Brenda? What is it? Oh God, now she's gone funny as well . . .'

Effie looked up sharply and saw the same thing. Brenda's face had gone slack. She was staring straight ahead. Right across the room. She hadn't moved for ages. Ever since the arrival of the queen of Goth weekend. Effie tugged at her velvet sleeve. 'Brenda? Brenda, snap out of it, ducky!'

Brenda made a queer choking noise. Then she gasped out: 'Him! Karla's man friend.'

Effie nodded rapidly. What was the matter with her? 'Yes, yes, like in the paper we saw . . .'

A funny look came into Brenda's eyes. Something Effie had hardly seen before. Brenda was misting up. Was she about to blubber for some reason? Surely not. She said: 'But . . . but . . . seeing him in the flesh like this . . .'

Effie clutched at her friend. 'Tell me, Brenda. Tell me what's wrong!'

'It's such a shock. It can't be . . .' Brenda reeled.

What could she smell? Under the spices and booze of the Christmas Hotel. She could smell the salty winds off the coast. She could smell the past. The dark and bloody past. She could smell the charnel house. The workshop of filthy creation.

Suddenly Brenda had a whiff of her own past. Of the earliest things she could remember at all.

She could smell . . . *home*.

A Familiar Settee

In the event, the evening progressed quite smoothly. As Bloody Banquets went, it was a triumph.

Brenda's party took up their table in the far corner of the dining room, well away from the star attraction, Karla and her new man.

At one point, between courses, Effie suggested they nip out and ransack Karla's suite. It couldn't hurt, surely?

'We'd be noticed,' Brenda said tersely, her thoughts still distant. 'We can't do it.'

What was Effie hoping to find there anyway? But Brenda knew Effie. She relished a surreptitious poke about. She liked to call it investigating, but it was nine-tenths nosing around.

They were served bloody-red roast beef, bitter dyed-green Yorkshire puddings, purple gravy, black peas. Mrs Brick in the kitchen had really gone to town, but the lurid colours made her food pretty unappetising. Everybody cooed over each Gothic side dish, but mostly they got left.

Mrs Claus herself made an appearance for the main course, decked out in Gothic black. She waved cheerily at their table. Michael's spirits seemed to lighten at the sight of her, Penny noticed, and he appeared to expect her to stop by their table – but she didn't. He looked curiously deflated. He told Penny he had a rotten headache starting up. He really couldn't eat any more of the multicoloured stodge coming out of the Christmas kitchen.

Outside, between courses, Michael leaned against the cool stone at the front of the hotel and smoked a blissful cigarette. Glad to be away from all the chattering old ladies. Their intrigues and mysteries. Here he could simply watch the bay and the sea curdling and churning.

Town was busier than most Friday nights, of course. Over the harbour, the church and the abbey remains were floodlit. Goth visitors were scurrying and swooping about in full vampire drag, enjoying themselves enormously. Over that way the film crew were working hard to rig up the location, ready for Saturday night.

Michael took another deep pull on his cigarette and noticed something odd on the other side of the road. On the grass, almost hidden in the shadows, was an elegant plush settee.

Funny thing was, it was familiar to him. He blinked. It was still there.

An enormous wave of tiredness came over him. Wouldn't it be lovely to just go and sit on that settee for a moment?

So he did.

It felt like it was made for him. The springs rumbled gently as they accepted his weight. The horsehair inside bristled as if the whole thing was alive. Like a steed.

Suddenly he heard Robert again: *You must come to us . . .*

And he had this weird moment when he could remember – not imagine, actually *remember* – kissing Robert on this very settee. Bracing the slighter man's weight against him. His tongue touching Robert's teeth. But he'd never kissed him, had he? That was ridiculous . . .

Then the settee shifted slightly of its own volition. It bucked a little, as if readying itself. Despite himself, Michael gave a short yelp of shock.

A few dressed-up passers-by had stopped to watch him, assuming this was some form of typical Goth weekend street theatre. They even clapped as the settee floated upwards into the air. They applauded as if this frankly impossible thing was only to be expected in Whitby on a night like this.

Michael clung to the arm of the sofa and tried not to scream in terror. It rose as high as the second floor of the Christmas Hotel. From here he could see into all the lit windows – not that he was looking. He was concentrating harder on keeping a grip on his velveteen mount.

The settee hovered, quivered. It was looking for something. And then Michael knew. It was hunting Robert. It was taking him to find Robert. They were going to rescue him. That was what they were doing.

And in a flash it became clear to Michael.

This is who I am.

I'm the daring young man on the flying settee.

The Rescue

In the attic they were whispering again. No one held captive up there knew anything about the festivities several storeys below. This evening was progressing just as all the recent nights had.

Robert was asking Frank about the man who had visited, claiming to be Frank's long-gone father. 'Do you believe him?'

'I have to.'

'I wouldn't if I was you. Look at his past record.'

Frank didn't even want to talk about it. He grunted. 'I have no choice. He said he'll help me.'

'Do you really believe that? Look what he did to you before. And to Brenda. It was worse for Brenda.'

Frank snapped, 'What do you know about it, anyway?'

'I know plenty,' Robert shot back. 'Brenda's told me all sorts of things about her past. And your past.'

'Frank thinks she ought to keep her gob shut. We should be having secret lives, her and me.'

Robert sighed. There was no point in the two of them arguing about it. He heard the weight of sadness in Frank's voice – of decades of sadness – and let the matter drop for now. He tried a different tack.

'Anyway, what makes you so sure it's really him?'

'It is,' said Frank. He was lying in the shadows and so it was hard to see his expression. Not that Frank ever gave much away with his face. Just looking at those rough-hewn, inscrutable features made Robert's feel sore, almost. Frank's visage was waxy, stiff. As if the nerves and sensitivity had died long ago.

Robert still wasn't convinced that the man claiming to be Victor Frankenstein wasn't someone just having them on. An actor or someone. He said, 'It's Goth weekend. Everyone out there is dressed up as something or other.'

'I know it's him.'

Robert tried to inject some common sense. 'Then how is he still alive? When's he from? When did all this happen?' He could hear the exasperation in his voice: the pent-up result of days under lock and key. He took a long, deep breath, and it felt like he was drinking in those deep blue shadows. The creamy, lemony light of the moon came drumming down on his tired skull as he tried to think straight. He spoke slowly, mulling it all over. 'The turn of the eighteenth century, wasn't it? Mary Shelley published her novel in . . . when? Eighteen eighteen?'

Frank stirred with interest and irritation. 'Mary Shelley? Novel? What are you talking about, Robert?'

'Nothing. Nothing for you to fret about. Anyway, your dad shouldn't be alive. Dad. He's not your dad.'

Frank snorted. 'He's the closest Frank has. And Brenda has. And I would know him anywhere. And he will help me. Restore me. He's the only one who can . . .'

Robert urged him, 'Just be careful Frank. I don't believe him.'

'Be careful, he says!' Robert recoiled at the bitterness in the big man's voice. 'What do you care? You've always hated Frank. Ever since he came back on the scene. You'd rather Frank had never come back.'

CRAASSHH!

There was something outside. High up on the outside of the turret. It was something large and heavy, smashing itself against the slates. The narrow turret shuddered under the sudden impact.

The elf and the postman had been sleeping on the floor, closer to the sounds of impact. Now they were awake and they were whimpering like dogs. The smashing noise came again and again. Something was battering its way into the tower.

'What the . . . ?' Robert struggled to stand as the floor bucked beneath him.

CRAASSHH!

The noise came twice as loud. Something outside was redoubling its efforts.

'What?'

Frank hadn't moved. It was as if he had given himself up gladly to whatever terrible thing was going to happen next.

What did happen next was completely unexpected. Even by Robert, who had been silently praying for such an intervention.

The force from outside smashed a sizeable hole straight through the slates, bricks, lath and plaster of the turret. The air filled with noise and ancient dust, but not before Robert saw who it was behind it all.

Their attic prison was being ram-raided by a flying settee.

Soon enough, the onslaught was over and the sofa drifted into the garret quite calmly, settling carefully before them on the wooden boards. Everything went very quiet and still for a moment.

The fairy lights and moonlight, and the festive hullabaloo of Goth weekend's Friday night came swirling into the dark, musty cell.

But Robert wasn't taking any notice of outside yet. Robert was agog at the man on the settee. The man who was looking very pleased with himself.

Robert burst out laughing. 'It's you! You've come for us!' There was a tinge of hysteria in his voice.

Michael laughed back. 'It's me, all right. Hop on board.'

Robert heard a noise beside him just then, from somewhere near the floor. A frightened noise. He looked and realised that the snivelling, snarling feral elf-boy and postman were looking with great interest at the new arrival. In the light flooding through the hole in the turret, the two servants were a grisly sight, matted with blood and God knew what else.

Michael stared at them. 'Don't bring them, though. What's happened to them?'

Robert said, 'I think their minds have snapped. Because of the things Karla has made them do.'

The two savage men slunk back into the shadows. Michael watched them, both fascinated and appalled. 'What things?'

Robert coughed. 'What they've done to Frank.'

Michael turned to look where Robert was pointing.

There didn't seem to be very much of Frank left. It was hard to tell, in the distorting shadows, and with the moonlight streaming in. He could make out Frank's twisted face, his limbs – some of them, anyway – sticking up at strange angles.

Robert decided that they needed to get a move on. 'Here, help me out of these shackles. Help me lift Frank . . . and his bits.'

Michael hopped off the settee and peered down at them both. Was there much that could be done for Frank? He saw that the man monster was staring back up at him. Was that a pleading look in his black eyes?

'I'm glad you came,' Robert said.

Michael took his hands and examined the shackles. 'Me too. For a while . . . I didn't know that was what I had to do. I'd kind of forgotten who I was. I thought I was someone else. It's hard to explain. But now . . . it's all coming clearer . . .' And then, as if to prove the sudden ease of things, he yanked apart the chains like they were made of coloured paper.

Yes, things seemed so much clearer to Michael. He was coming into the full knowledge of who he was. Of who he had been the whole time along. And now he could see that Frank could be helped after all. As the two men set about carefully carrying the ruined bits of Frank to the settee, Michael was beginning to realise just where he needed to take him.

Far, far from here.

Father, Dear Father

Brenda had been shooting glances at Karla's table for two all the way through dinner. It was tucked away in the corner, presumably so that the hoi polloi couldn't rubberneck the star's tête-à-tête. But Brenda craned right round in her seat, unable to take her eyes off the pair.

Effie was losing patience with her. 'Will you sit straight and eat your sweet, Brenda?'

There came a distant booming and crashing from elsewhere in the hotel. It sounded like bombs going off, though the majority of the diners – presumably quite used to games of bingone – paid the noise very little heed.

Penny jerked up in her seat. 'What was that?'

'Ugh, there's always something going on,' Effie scowled.

'That sounded like something big,' Lisa said.

Penny started to fret. 'Where's Michael got to?'

'He's been gone smoking for ages,' said Lisa.

'He'll be with that Mrs Claus,' Penny said.

Effie wielded her pudding spoon, saying: 'No, she's over there. Oh, hello. Who's this?'

One of the elves had materialised at Brenda's side. He bent to have a discreet word in her ear. The others watched a curious smile appear on their friend's face. Brenda reached under the table for her handbag and stood.

'Karla's asked if I'll join them for coffee and after-dinner mints.'

Effie was immediately suspicious. And just a tad put out. 'What? Just you?'

'Erm,' Brenda said awkwardly. 'To be honest, he never said *just* me, but . . .'

Effie flung down her spoon and her napkin. 'Right. I'm coming with you. She might have planned anything, that one.'

'Actually, Effie, I'd . . .'

'Hmm?'

'I'd rather face her myself. And him.'

'Oh!' Effie was caught in a crouch. She felt discombobulated. So Brenda didn't want her support! She felt foolish for even offering, now. 'But why? Who is he?'

Brenda had a very funny look on her face. She looked vulnerable to Effie. Sort of soft-looking. Effie could sense that this was all about to go to the bad. Brenda said: 'I'll tell you when I get back. I'm not sure. I just have a very funny feeling in my water.'

Brenda's friends watched her amble over, squeezing between tables and chairs, easing herself towards the quiet corner: the bay window table where Karla and her elegant man friend had a view of the dark skies above the West Cliff.

Karla stood to greet her new guest. 'And so here she is. At last!'

Brenda's guard came down a little as she nodded at the film star. 'Good evening, Karla.'

She looked at the man-friend, scrutinising his face as she waited to be introduced to him.

Karla shook her silver mane in admiration. 'You, my darling Brenda, look just the same as you did forty years ago, practically.'

'And so do you,' Brenda said.

'Rubbish. But we're both pretty well preserved. And here we are again! How strange, that you should be living in the very town where we are shooting our little movie.'

Brenda raised an eyebrow. 'Not really. You were drawn here by the same forces that called out to me, several years ago.'

Karla sat down again, and urged Brenda to take her seat. 'Oh really? And what would they be, precisely?'

At last Victor spoke up. He never raised his voice. He purred at her.

'Karla dear. Let her sit. Relax. Have some coffee.'

'I will,' said Brenda, plumping herself down on the spare chair. She stared at the elderly man. She tried to look into his eyes, but they were cast down as he poured their hot, dark coffee.

Karla said, 'Brenda, this is my friend. I think you've met before?'

Brenda swallowed drily. She tried again to look into his face, but it was as if he was avoiding her eye. She asked: 'It *is* you, then?'

Then he looked up. His eyes were silver. Conflicted. She felt they were honest; that they looked straight into her. But there was summer lightning in those eyes, too. There were emotions that were twisty and complex. Things she would never understand. As he spoke, she found herself trying to hold his gaze; to fathom him out. 'I knew you'd know me,' he said. 'Even after all this time. And you hardly saw me, back then. I wasn't sure you would know my face.'

'I know it all right. Father.'

Victor chuckled. It was a chilly sound. 'You know me. I am pleased. You call yourself Brenda, I believe.' He offered her cream out of a solid silver jug.

'You never gave me a name.'

'Didn't I? I gave you so little. Sugar?'

Brenda felt herself tearing up. She wanted to grab this man. She wanted to dash his brains out. She felt like smashing his fine, thin skull against Karla's smug face and destroying them both at once. She felt her palms itch and her fingers twitch. She felt violence breaking out in her like the tide rushing in. 'I . . . I don't know what to say to you. I've imagined seeing you. Dreamed about it. How can it be true? How are you here?'

'That is something I owe to Karla, here.'

Brenda darted her a look. This could only mean bad things. What was Karla messing around with? She asked him, 'What did she do?'

Victor said, 'The necessary magic.'

Karla loaded her coffee cup with coloured cocktail sugar. Pink and purple cubes trailing bubbles as they dissolved. 'It's all down to the Brethren. They told me what to do.'

Brenda gripped the edge of the table to hold herself back. 'They always tell you what to do, don't they? You've been under their spell for years.'

Karla trilled with laughter. 'And you're so superior? What are you? Just some meddling, oafish—'

Victor looked upset. He put a delicate hand to his forehead. 'Ladies, please. I can't have my two best girls squabbling.'

'She brought you to life using magic?' demanded Brenda.

'I want you two to get on with each other,' said Victor softly. 'It's important to me. I love you both.'

'Love?' cried Brenda. 'You don't *love* me.'

'Brenda, please . . .'

Brenda felt her voice rising in pitch. The louder she got, the louder she felt she could become. Suddenly there was all this noise in her. After a lifetime of keeping schtum, of keeping mum, suddenly she felt like she wanted to yell and scream.

'How dare you talk about love to me? I never knew such a thing existed till many years after you ran out on me. Not until I'd wandered in the world alone . . . lost . . . and eventually someone showed me some simple human kindness. I wandered into the home of some poor Scottish farmers. Peasants. Theirs was the first kindness I'd ever experienced. They fed me. Gave me a bed for the night. And I was overwhelmed. I never knew people could be kind to each other.'

Victor longed to get up and hold her. Shush her. Stop her from making a spectacle of herself. 'Brenda, you must understand that back then, when I was a young man, I was crazy with my own success, my brilliance. Can't you imagine? What it was like . . . to have created *life*. The only man in history to have accomplished such a thing—'

She cut him dead. 'I remember that you tried to kill me. No sooner had I drawn my first breath, you changed your mind. You looked at me with abhorrence. With fear and distaste.'

Karla was working her way through the devilish petits fours, licking her fingers as she broke in: 'I heard that he pulled you all to pieces again and tried to chuck you in the sea.'

Victor snapped, 'Where did you hear that rubbish?'

'Can't remember.' Karla shrugged. 'But you weren't happy with the way she turned out, were you?'

Victor glared at his new lady love. 'It wasn't like that. I was mad in those days. You have to understand. Frank had chased me across the countryside, dogging my every footstep. He had blackmailed me into making you, Brenda. He had forced me into creating a mate for him.'

Karla took the last of the chocolates. The other two were too worked up to mind. 'I was sure I'd heard that right. That you chucked all her bits in the sea.'

Brenda ignored the old floozy. She said in a dangerously low tone to her father: 'You couldn't extinguish that scrap of consciousness that was me. Once you had brought it into being.'

Victor gave her a watery smile, 'I'm glad of that. Of course I am.'

'I lay there in a terrible state. You had gone. Fled.'

Victor nodded. 'It was his face. Frank's face. Taunting me at the window of the castle where I was working. His face suddenly popped into view, spying on me. Horrible, leering brute. He looked so pleased with himself. So eager and excited at the sight of you as you neared completion. That's why I took leave of my senses, Brenda. And did what I did.'

Karla piped up, in a voice rich with melted truffles: 'I never knew my father.'

'What's that got to do with anything?' Brenda snapped.

'Nothing,' said Karla. 'I'm just pointing it out. In a way, you're lucky. You can forget about the past. Let bygones be bygones. You can get to know him again. You've got that chance. Not everyone gets a chance like that.'

Victor smiled. His new love had said something sensible at last. Perhaps they could get through to Brenda. Calm her down. He told her, 'Have your coffee, dear. And a chocolate.' Then he noticed that Karla had nobbled them all.

'I don't know,' said Brenda. 'This is all a bit much.'

'I know, daughter.'

'It was only last year that Frank came back into my life.' Brenda looked down into her coffee, the confusion plain on her face.

Karla said, spitefully, 'I gather he's done a moonlight flit, though?'

Brenda stared mutely at her for a moment. Then she said, 'If I thought for even a second that you had something to do with Frank's disappearance . . .'

Karla smiled sweetly and stickily. 'Yes, dear? Are you threatening me?'

'Ladies, please!' Victor burst out. His nerves were at breaking point by now.

But Brenda hadn't finished warning Karla. 'And Robert. If you've done anything to him, either . . .'

'What would I want with those silly men of yours?' scoffed Karla. 'I think you're a little paranoid, Brenda. Really. Blaming everything on the newcomer to town. I wish you could have been more welcoming.'

'I wouldn't put anything past you,' Brenda told her.

'Charming! But what would I want with men belonging to anyone else? When I have my own wonderful fiancé right here beside me?'

Brenda – who had just taken her first mouthful of coffee – choked at this. '*What?* Fiancé?'

Victor realised that it was time for the announcement. Karla had jumped the gun. 'We are going to be married, Brenda.'

Karla could barely contain her glee. 'What do you think about that? I'm going to be your stepmother, Brenda!'

Saving the World Again

Walking back with the girls later that night, Brenda was uncharacteristically quiet.

After Lisa and Penny had peeled off, back on their way up the hill to the Miramar, Effie tackled her friend.

Brenda sighed deeply. How could she explain that whole conversation? How to describe what had gone on? It was the least expected but most ardently desired reunion of her life. And it had all gone so badly wrong, was how she felt. As they tottered up the steep hill under the horse chestnuts, she told Effie, 'I didn't want to say anything about it in front of the other two.'

'They wouldn't understand. Young people like that.'

'Come and have tea, Effie,' Brenda said.

In her attic over spicy tea, Brenda brought Effie up to date with what had been said during her talk with Victor and Karla. Effie swallowed down her surprise and listened, her eyes opening wider and wider.

'I have to admit, he was quite charming.' Brenda said. 'He was lovely to me, in fact.'

'What? Brenda . . . he's smarmed all the sense out of you! How can you believe him?' Effie watched Brenda stirring her tea round and round, looking down all the while. 'And anyway, can it really be him? Are you sure? She might have just paid some actor friend of hers . . .'

'No, that's definitely Victor Frankenstein. Even saying the name makes me shudder. I really feel that he wants to make things up to me. I felt his kindness . . . his concern for me . . .'

Brenda looked up to see Effie looking quite frosty and sceptical.

'Rubbish. He looks like a calculating old bastard to me. I was watching keenly, and I think he looked shifty.'

Brenda wondered. Maybe Effie's suspicions were right. Was she being a fool to herself?

But . . . did she also feel that curious sense of coming home? Of belonging? Maybe she was giving herself up to that feeling too easily, too readily? If she had been a different kind of person – a person more like Effie, perhaps – she would have fired off a million questions at this man who claimed to be her father. Where were you? How can you be here? She deserved answers from him. And yet, faced with Victor at last, she had demanded so little of him.

'This is all down to those Brethren people,' Effie said darkly.

Brenda thumped the arm of her chair. 'But why are the Brethren so keen on resurrecting my father? If that's what they've done. If all of this is true. What can they possibly want with bringing him to face me again?'

She stomped off to fetch the brandy. She'd had enough tea by now. Effie hoisted herself over to the record player, thinking it might be nice to have some soothing music. Suddenly she felt a little foolish in her vampire outfit. Her batty cuffs trailed over the record as she slipped it from its sleeve.

Effie thought about Victor and how she had watched him from afar. She had observed nuances in that conflab that Brenda, closer to, had completely missed. Effie could see the way he been hunched forward, avidly, in his seat. She had been able to see that pinched look on his face. An expression that was meant to be caring, but which from Effie's vantage had seemed almost cruel. It was a greedy look he had worn when he was sitting opposite his so-called daughter.

He had been studying Brenda as if she wasn't even human. To him, she was just a marvellous machine. A work of art. Something he felt proud of. But not something he *loved*. Not like a father would.

The needle hissed. Billie Holiday came on, bless her.

But what did Effie know about fathers anyway? she mused sourly. Or mothers, for that matter? She had no idea about any of that sort of business. She was the eternal orphan. And the thing was, she had always thought Brenda was the same. Except now a dad had manifested himself out of the ether for her. Was Effie envious? Was that why she ate her ginger snaps and supped her tea so crossly that night? Glaring at Brenda and wishing she could see sense and send off the old man with a flea in his ear?

Brenda was blind. Foolish. She couldn't see that whatever Victor promised, it would all be for his own benefit. He wasn't thinking of Brenda's happiness, Effie was sure of it.

But she knew that if she said any more about it this evening to Brenda, she'd cause a row between them.

'Best go,' Effie said, declining Brenda's offer of a nightcap. 'We've a busy night tomorrow night.'

'Oh. The filming.' Brenda didn't sound at all keen.

'Did you say anything to Karla about it?'

'Err, no . . .'

Effie frowned. 'You didn't warn her? Tell her to stop?'

'I was caught up thinking about my father . . .'

Effie sighed heavily. 'Well. I doubt that she would have listened anyway. So, we've got work to do tomorrow, ducky.'

Brenda lifted her solitary schooner of sweet sherry. 'Saving the world again?'

'Someone has to. Good night, lovey.'

And then Effie was off, back to her emporium.

Into the Night

Robert knew that this was his final flight with his fella.

So, he had had a new boyfriend for a little while. It hadn't really worked out. He knew that this bloke wasn't the kind to go picking out curtains with.

That night they took a little flight round the coast. They soared past the rocky cliffs and the gentle green slopes. Robert clung to the settee's arm as they scudded through the clouds and swept through the huge hollow of the Hole of Horcum.

At last they returned to town, circling high above the thronging streets and drinking in the sight of all those lights. All those sparkles. They said very little, but then they always had said very little to one another. Robert could tell his fella was different to usual. He was complete somehow, in an undefinable way. He had a purpose suddenly. He wasn't just swooping about in the night for the hell of it. He wasn't content just to diddle about with some stand-in hotel manager like Robert. Now, suddenly, Robert's fella had stuff to do. He had a mission.

The sofa drifted carefully back to earth. Michael guided it back to the erstwhile beer garden of Sheila Manchu.

He kissed Robert and said, 'I've been reminded who I am.'

'I don't know what you mean,' said Robert. 'But I believe it. You're different now. You're—'

Michael pressed his finger to Robert's lips, shushing him. He nodded at the third figure on the settee. The silent figure. The man who had been dismantled in the attic above Karla Sorenson's rooms. He told Robert: 'I'm taking away what remains of Frank here.'

'What can you do for him?' asked Robert.

'His only hope is in magic. I'm taking him away, under the hill.'

'What hill?'

'A particular hill. Far away.'

'Is that where you come from? Where you belong?'

Michael was evasive. Robert couldn't pin him down. 'I will try to save him. Whatever Brenda or Victor says, these monsters *do* have souls. I can save them.'

But why? Robert wanted to know. Who are you, saving the souls of monsters? 'Brenda will be upset,' he said.

'She'd be more upset to find that Frank has been ripped apart like this.'

'Penny will be upset too.'

'I was never the Michael Penny thought I was. That was all fake. A made-up life, with a made-up past, I'm sorry to say.'

Robert couldn't even look too closely at the ruinous form of Frank. His sluggish, tepid blood had soaked into the settee's upholstery. It would be murder to get cleaned up.

'I must go,' said Michael.

'And what about me?' asked Robert impulsively. I might as well ask. I might as well pretend that I thought I mattered to him. Then he hated himself for seeming needy. I have a right to ask, he thought. I'm losing my fella.

Michael kept his voice cool and removed. 'I never belonged to you. I am the Erl King. You belong to me. You and others, just as needy. You belong to me, for a while. And then – guess what? – I'm gone.'

He didn't kiss Robert again. He went back to the sofa and sat down. He gave a sad and playful smile as the three-seater took off.

Robert watched him set off again into the night, just as he had many other nights these past few weeks. But this time Michael – or the Erl King, or the Faerie King, whoever he was – was bearing away the mortal remains of Brenda's husband.

What the devil was Robert going to tell Brenda? How could he explain what had happened to her man?

Tempted Sorely

It was Saturday, and the ladies were poised over their tea in the front window table of the Walrus and the Carpenter.

There was increased traffic up and down Church Street this morning, as Effie observed mildly. On just a typical Goth weekend it could be a deathly crush on the cobbles. But today it was even worse. Because of the film. Because of all the various preparations for the filming of the climactic sequences that night. 'I bet it's all go up there at the abbey just now.'

Brenda wasn't saying much. She was chomping desultorily on her cinnamon toast.

Well, I can be quiet as well, thought Effie. As it happened, she had rather a lot to mull over. All about Alucard. She felt a number of sweet tingles as she thought his name aloud in her head. It felt to her like that crispiness of the caramelised sugar on her toast. Slow fumes of desire were rising up in her.

Of course he will come through again tonight. Of course he will. That is his plan. It was his plan all along to manipulate the Brethren and the servants of the Brethren. He must be behind everything. And it's all in order to get himself out of hell. To get himself back to his beloved.

Effie didn't say anything of that sort to Brenda, of course. She was scared of looking a total fool. But she found she wanted to talk about him anyway. She frowned and dithered and found she was starting to doubt herself. Just a niggle.

She said to Brenda, off-handedly, 'Maybe . . . maybe it wasn't even really Kristoff I saw that night, coming out of hell . . . Hm? What do you think, ducky?'

Brenda was brought up short by this. 'Mm?'

'Maybe I just *thought* I saw him.'

Brenda sighed, and it was as if she was dragging herself away from her own fascinating cogitations and she found Effie's rather dull. Effie flushed and glared at her friend. Brenda asked her, 'Are you starting to doubt who you saw in those final moments we were in the past? He's pretty distinctive. Those blummin' teeth of his.'

Effie shook her head decisively. 'I'm not the sort to go seeing things. It was definitely him back there in 1967, trying to get out of the underworld. And he'll do it again tonight. When they get to that bit in the film, he'll come through again.'

Brenda gasped suddenly. 'Then you don't want to stop them at all, do you? You *want* him to come back. Of course you do.'

Effie looked down at the table, mumbling something Brenda didn't hear.

But Brenda's mind wasn't really on Effie's problems, and they both knew it. Her mind was on her father. His new marriage. She found that irksome and embarrassing, more than anything.

What would people say? What would it be like, with everyone knowing her old dad was in town? And that he had this new, glamorous, apparently wonderful wife?

Brenda and Effie paid up and finished the dregs of their tea. They took a walk, still not talking very much, up Church Street, to the foot of the 199 steps. Here there were various press photographers taking pictures of the more fancily attired Goth visitors. Effie noted waspishly that only the most attractive girls were chosen to have their photos taken. The ones showing lots of goosepimpled flesh.

'I'm going up to the church,' Brenda told her friend. 'I might have a mooch about in the ruins. See what's happening up at the set.'

Effie pulled a face. 'I'm not going all the way up there. Not if we have to haul our tired old carcasses up there this evening as well. No, if you don't mind, Brenda love, I'll whiz back down the hill and get round the shops. My cupboards are looking bare at home.'

Brenda watched her friend turn and scurry away through the holidaying crowd.

Maybe Effie wasn't to be trusted. If what she really wanted was for hell to open tonight and disgorge its wickedest resident. If that was the case, perhaps the two friends were even on opposite sides?

Brenda shook her head free of nasty thoughts. She set to, marching up the shallow steps that wound an elegant loop to the church. She found them rather awkward to climb, with her slightly mismatched legs, but she was dogged.

Must be getting past it. She had to rest halfway on a bench.

Today she was really feeling her age. Her mind kept dwelling on the severity of her aches and pains. Were they worse than ever? Or was she imagining that? It had to happen, didn't it? The gradual wearing down of her body. Even though she was so much more robust than living humans, and even though she had spares galore, there was still the law of entropy to be faced up to. And there was no denying for Brenda the exhaustion that trembled even in her replacement limbs and organs. The laborious nights she sat stitching bits back on, filled with hope of refreshment and ease: now that was accompanied by an awful dread. A sense that even the freshest of her spare parts were becoming stale and overused.

This morning was when she was struck by a very startling thought.

It was the reason she was happy to see Effie go off by herself. Brenda had a very interesting epiphany to deal with. And it was best dealt with alone, tramping about in the long yellow grass of the graveyard, braving the freezing, slicing wind from the sea. She wove in and out of the gravestones, noting that their inscriptions had been almost obliterated by the sea salt in the breeze. Those stones looked almost as if they had been melted in ghastly hell-fires, it always seemed to her. But then it would, wouldn't it?

Concentrate, Brenda, she thought. Concentrate on that very tempting thought that struck you back in the café, while you were chewing on your cinnamon toast. With Victor back . . . might he be persuaded? Did he still have the requisite skill? Would he even consider helping her?

These were the tempting thoughts.

She was over two hundred years old. Bits of her were wearing so thin.

With Victor here, she stood the chance of being renewed. He could rebuild her.

Suddenly she felt greedy and excited. Buffeted by the wind at the top of the town. All of Whitby and its excited visitors swarming throught the decrepit streets. Brenda drew in a huge, cleansing breath and laughed out loud. Like a madwoman, she thought. But who cared? Who cared if anyone heard her?

I could be young again . . .

Lost Boyfriends

On Saturday morning, Penny was ecstatic to see that Robert was back home at the Hotel Miramar.

She saw him at the reception desk when she came down to work that morning. Dapper as anything in his maroon waistcoat and neatly pressed white shirt. He was businesslike and focused, behaving as if nothing had gone on at all. As if he had merely been away on leave for a couple of days. She could hardly believe he didn't try to explain himself.

'WHERE HAVE YOU BEEN? WHAT'S BEEN HAPPENING?'

He shushed her.

'WHAT? But we've all been really worried about you! Robert, tell me! Talk to me!'

But he wouldn't talk just yet. Gallingly, he said to her, 'Be more professional, Penny. You're alarming the guests.'

'WHAT?' It really stung her, this. 'Be professional?' Like that was the best thing anyone could ever be. Not kind or concerned: those things didn't matter. Her ex, Ken, had been very big on spurious professionalism too. Suddenly she felt like kicking the prodigal manager.

But he insisted that they work quietly side by side at the reception desk until the morning rush was finished with. All the while Penny gritted her teeth and burned with questions. How dare he not thank her for taking over the running of this place? How dare he just waltz back in like he'd never been away? She cast him a number of murderous glances as they went about their business. Then, after a vexed half hour, he turned to her and said:

'Erm. It turns out that . . . my fella, who I'd been seeing, he's gone now. And it turns out he was Michael. The bloke you liked.'

'Jesus,' Penny cursed. 'Typical. That's always happening to me. Where's he gone? Why's he gone?'

'Dunno,' said Robert. He seemed shifty to Penny. 'And he's taken Frank with him. Frank's not in a good way. Michael's taking him somewhere to get better.'

'Huh?' Penny didn't get this at all. What did he mean? Some kind of hospital? A resort? Rehab? What was the matter with Frank anyway? 'What are you going to say to Brenda about any of this?' she asked him.

'I don't know yet.' He was terse. He wouldn't be drawn. He tried to escape her attentions then, ducking away into his private office. But Penny wasn't to be deterred.

Wherever he went that morning, bustling about his duties all over the Miramar, Penny was at his heels. Dogging him with queries he really didn't want to answer.

'But where were you? You were days and days away.'

He grimaced. 'I know.'

Did he seem older and sadder? Like he had been away much longer than just a matter of days? Like he had seen things he had never seen before? Or was Penny just romanticising that? Maybe he just looked tired. And sad that Michael (Michael! That betrayer!) had nicked off in a flit.

At any rate, Robert kept telling Penny that he was very glad of her help. He was very pleased with the way she had kept things going. Albeit in a ramshackle manner, as he implied, with his praise. At least the Miramar was still ticking over.

'I thought you'd run away with your fella,' Penny told him. 'Michael, as it turns out.' She felt a sickly hollowness as she said his name.

This was at lunchtime. Liquid lunch. Gin in the hotel lounge bar. 'Almost. I almost went away with him.' Robert nodded. 'He asked me if I wanted to run away.' He pulled a face. He decided not to tell lies. 'Well, no, he didn't. But if he had, I'd have gone.' He stabbed his ice cubes with his straw. 'Can you believe it? Your mate Michael? From Spector.'

'All right, don't rub it in.'

'I never knew. Honest, Penny. If I'd known it was the fella you were bothered about, I'd have said something.'

'Well why didn't he say anything? Stringing me along. And . . . Jesus, he was gay? I never clocked that. God, Lisa's going to be well pissed off. She'd set her hot tongs flashing in his direction as well.'

They both had a laugh about that, once Penny had explained who Lisa was.

'Well,' Robert sighed, 'he's not here anyway. He's left us all.'

Penny suddenly made a connection. 'That's what Michael was on about, then. When he was saying that he really belonged to some other life, elsewhere . . . realising something about himself . . . He said he was linked to you. He could tell that you were in some terrible danger.'

'He rescued me. From the attic. Me and Frank.'

Heartened by the gin, Robert spent the rest of their lunch hour filling Penny in on his exploits in the attic.

'Karla kidnapped you?'

'It was terrible, Penny. I never thought I was going to get out. The woman is a monster. And I daren't tell you what happened to Frank while we were trapped up there, at the top of the Christmas Hotel. All I've eaten is dry turkey and stuffing sandwiches. For a week!'

'Frank's not dead, is he?'

'Not quite. But like I say, he's gone away. Michael took him away.'

'I don't get it,' said Penny.

'Michael reckons that Frank's only chance was to go away with him. To the place that Michael comes from, where they can maybe help him. And save his life.'

'Where's that?' Penny persisted. She thought about Michael's accent. 'Ireland?'

'I don't know. I got the impression it was somewhere . . . you know . . . like, magic. Anyway. I just know the whole life he thought he belonged to, when he was with you, it was all made up.'

'Made up?'

'But he didn't know it. You have to believe this, Penny. He was unaware of who he really was. He thought he was just the manager of a bar, but . . .' Here Robert shook his head, puzzled. 'He was yet another person in this town who was far more than the sum of his parts.'

'Ha,' said Penny. 'I never even got to *see* his parts. I bet you did, though.'

Robert winced at her abrasive tone. He told her, 'I don't fully understand all of this myself.'

Penny changed the subject, suddenly looking resolute. 'We have to tell them, Robert. Brenda and Effie. They need to know you're back.'

He nodded. 'Give me an hour or two more to get this place

shipshape. Where is everyone, anyway? There's not a guest in sight now.'

'They'll be up at the abbey. The crew and the cast and everyone else. Today's the day of the big shoot. The final Hallowe'en shoot.'

Picking Up Effie

On the way down the hill from the Miramar, they bumped into Effie. At first Robert thought he was seeing things. Effie actually looked delighted to see him.

'Robert!'

He picked her up in a clumsy hug. She was light as a bird in his arms. 'I got away, Effie! I escaped!'

'Where the devil from? What are you talking about? Calm down, young man!' She batted at his arms to put her down.

Now Penny was gabbling. 'It's true, Effie. He was being held captive up in the attic of the Christmas Hotel.'

Effie squawked. 'By Mrs Claus? I wouldn't put it past her. That old monster has kept Brenda and me under lock and key in the past.'

'No,' Robert broke in. 'Not her. Karla.'

Penny asked, 'Where's Brenda, Effie? This is serious. Frank was locked up there as well, but he's been hurt, and—'

Effie frowned, trying to take everything in. 'What are you saying? That Karla's been taking prisoners?'

'That's exactly what we're saying,' said Robert.

'We need Brenda,' Effie decided.

Quick Promenade

At Brenda's B&B, there was no sign of her.

'Perhaps she's not back yet.' Effie frowned.

But then a very alarming pair of Brenda's guests came out of the side passage. 'She's been back,' said one. 'Clive saw her in the hallway, didn't you, Clive?'

Clive – who was ingeniously dressed as a headless ghost – nodded with some difficulty.

'But then,' added the female guest in the magnificent basque, 'she went dashing out again. Looking like she had a lot on her mind.'

'Hmpf,' said Effie, and let the two guests pass by, into the main street. 'I'd hate to run a B&B, wouldn't you?' she asked Robert and Penny. 'And having all sorts of strange people traipsing in and out of your place. I mean, look at those two!'

'It's Goth weekend,' Robert reminded her. 'Everyone's a bit freakish this weekend.'

Effie tossed her head and started thinking hard. She snapped her fingers. 'You know what I think? She's gone back to the hotel alone.'

'The Christmas Hotel?' asked Penny.

Effie gave her a withering look. 'Of course the Christmas Hotel. Look, just a couple of hours ago I was having elevenses with her and she was in a funny mood. She kept talking about her . . . father. And even when she wasn't, you could tell that was who she was thinking about. She had no interest in anything I was saying.'

Led by Effie, their small party started walking at a fast trot down the hill towards the harbour and the thronging mass of Saturday afternoon in town.

Robert was perplexed, and then alarmed. 'Hang on, Effie. You're saying she's met her *father*?'

'Ooh, that's right!' Penny gasped. 'Robert's missed all that.'

Effie squinched her mouth into what Brenda would have called her sucked lemon face. 'There's some ancient old man running around claiming to be Brenda's father.'

Robert felt his blood go cold. 'I've seen him. He came into the attic. Or someone saying that that was who he was.'

'It's knocked Brenda bandy,' Effie told him. 'I mean, what does she want him for? What can he possibly do for her? Well, I tell you. My mind boggles.'

Robert felt his feet slowing with dread. Poor Brenda. What did she think Victor would do for her? Robert knew he wasn't trustworthy. He had seen the old man close at hand. He had felt his evil presence up in the attic space.

'Oh no,' he said, as they hustled past Woolworths.

Effie looked cross with herself, as if she was only just realising the danger Brenda might be in. As if the act of explaining it all to Robert had made it seem so much more alarming. 'I should have stayed with her,' she cried. 'But I was off doing my messages and groceries! Why didn't I keep an eye on her? She'll be at that hotel, putting herself in danger . . .'

Robert nodded. 'It was at the hotel that I saw the man reckoning he's her dad. He was talking to Frank.'

Effie stopped in her tracks, scraping her good court shoes. 'You've seen Frank?'

'It's a long story. Yes – we were Karla's prisoners together. Frank's gone, Effie. He's been taken away.'

Effie snorted. 'I should have known he wouldn't stick around.'

'He didn't want to go. He's been hurt pretty badly.' Now they were taking the narrower streets behind the promenade, puffing slightly at the uphill bit.

'You'd better explain it all to Brenda when we see her. I knew that Frank would let her down.'

'He's better than that. I got to know him a bit more, when we were locked up together.'

Effie wouldn't buy it. Robert and Penny both suddenly saw that she would never hear a good word said about the man. Somehow she believed that Frank was behind every one of Brenda's misfortunes. She told them so, as they came to the top of the cliff and the Christmas Hotel spread out grandly before them. 'I don't want to hear it, Robert. And frankly – no pun - we've got quite enough on our plates today.'

Still in her Headscarf

Brenda had been shown up to Karla's suite. She was surprised she hadn't had to throw her weight around in order to be allowed in.

Now here was Karla, looking rested and fresh as she sat having her hair done by Lisa Turmoil. Brenda felt a little shabby in her old winter coat and headscarf, she had to admit.

Karla was politely caustic with her future stepdaughter. 'You'll forgive me if I don't stick around for even more of your touching family reunion scenes. I've got work to do today. Oww. Watch it, girl.'

'Sorry, Karla.' Lisa gulped.

Brenda realised she was shivering. 'What's that terrible draught?'

Karla waved a dismissive hand. 'Ugh. Storms last night. Blew a hole in the turret.'

'*Were* there any storms last night?' Brenda frowned.

'Right. That's enough,' snapped Karla, and waved her stylist away.

In the corner of the room, Victor put down the gold and cream phone receiver. 'The car's waiting, Karla.'

'Okay. I think I've got everything.'

Victor came to her and studied her appraisingly. His thin lips quirked with amusement. 'You look wonderful.'

Karla nodded, as if this were only her due. 'Wish me luck, everyone. Oh, look, I'm sorry I'm such a cow. I'm nervous, that's all.'

Victor clicked his heels together. 'We understand.'

Brenda wasn't sure that she did.

Victor said, 'I'll follow you over to the abbey later, my dear.'

Karla smiled, caught out by her own pleasure. She preened herself for a moment. It had been so long since she had had anyone on her team like this. 'Why, Victor! You're coming over for the shoot?'

That wry amusement playing about his mouth again. 'Of course! I couldn't miss that, could I?'

Karla stammered, 'It's . . . very important to me, Victor, that you're there.'

'I know. I just want to stay here a little, while you are setting up and rehearsing. And you can't blame me for wanting to spend an hour or two with my beautiful daughter, can you?'

Victor turned that cool little smile on Brenda then, and she tried to smile back, or to feel flattered. But she just felt uncomfortable. Patronised.

Karla gave herself one last check in the dressing table mirror. 'Anyway, I'm off.'

Victor held up both palms in supplication as his intended made for the door. 'There she goes – the stuff of legend. Off to make cinematic history!'

'Oh, stop.' Karla smiled, basking in his attention. 'Silly old sod.'

Too Soft

When she emerged from the lift, Karla was startled to bump into Effie, Penny and Robert. They, in turn, were brought up short by the sight of her, and the two parties surveyed each other warily for a moment.

'Goodness.' Karla smiled. 'The gang's all here, isn't it?' She had a bit of a jolt, coming face to face with Robert. She narrowed her eyes and prepared herself to deny everything. Prisoners, what prisoners? she'd say. It was a pity that this smartarse little fruit hadn't fallen under her spell like all the other men in town. Gay, straight, she could usually inculcate the lot of them. This Robert, though, was strong-willed.

And so were his friends.

Effie was prepared to barge right past Karla, into the private lift. 'Out of our way.'

Robert had gone quite dumb. He muttered, 'It's Karla,' in a voice – Penny thought – somewhere between awestruck fan and freed ex-hostage.

Karla batted her fake eyelashes at the would-be intruders. 'I hope you don't think you're all trooping up to my suite.'

'We've come for Brenda,' said Effie grimly, jutting her jaw out.

Karla sighed. 'She's with her beloved father. Now, if you'll excuse me . . .'

Penny decided that if no one else was going to tackle Karla on what she'd been doing wrong, then it had better be her. She burst out: 'You kept Robert prisoner! And Frank! You're evil!'

'Who's this?' Karla frowned. 'What's she yelling about?' She really didn't have time for this. Her car was waiting; the whole crew was waiting. Standing around here where the air was sticky with fake snow spray and potpourri was giving her a headache. As were the relentless Christmas jingles.

She glared at Penny. 'It doesn't do, you know, to make rash accusations.'

Just at that point – as if alerted by fractious non-festive conversation – Mrs Claus came trundling up in her motorised chair. 'Is there a problem?' she said fiercely. She hated anyone messing up her ambience. Usually she'd send an elf to deal with it – but this gaggle were trouble, she knew, and best dealt with by her own dainty hand.

Karla drew herself up to her full height and made her bosom heave with indignation. 'These people seem to believe they can traipse up to my suite willy-nilly, just because they suspect someone they know is up there. I don't think very much of your security, Mrs Claus.'

'Don't you indeed?' said Mrs Claus hotly. 'Well, they're not going up there. Elves!' She clicked her fingers and set her tinselly jewellery tinkling. 'Please escort the young people off the premises, would you?'

Karla gave a jaded sigh. 'I suppose they are just fans. Fans are apt to get overexcited.'

'We don't want you interfered with, Ms Sorenson.' Mrs Claus

scowled. 'Especially not on the day when you're shooting your climax.'

Some of the establishment's rather burlier elves had appeared in a trice. Robert shuddered at the all-too-familiar sight of their velveteen costumes as he found himself shunted and shoved around. 'No! We won't go! Leave off!'

Penny started yelling as well, over the noise of a ska version of 'Little Drummer Boy'. 'Get your hands off me!'

Effie was helpless, jammed against the flock wallpaper by Mrs Claus's strategically parked chair. There would have been little she could do against the might of those strapping elves. She watched with a curious sense of dread as her young companions were led away to the main entrance of the Christmas Hotel.

Mrs Claus gave a very common-sounding cackle. 'Young people, eh, Effie?'

'Why haven't you chucked me out?' Effie demanded.

Karla had had enough of this lot by now. She was flustered and annoyed already, and she hadn't even left the hotel. 'Oh, look. I'm going. My car's at the front?'

'It is,' said Mrs Claus, and drew back her motorised chair enough to allow Karla to sweep past. She went without another word.

They watched her go. Effie wondered if she should be running after her. Going to the film set with her. But there was time for that later. Right now she was aware of Mrs Claus's beady eyes boring into her in a most peculiar and unsettling way.

'Just a word, Effryggia. Would you come to my inner sanctum?'

Effie's eyebrows went up. 'Not on your nelly.'

The proprietress of the Christmas Hotel was used to people doing exactly what she wanted. 'What?'

'I don't trust you,' Effie said curtly. 'Simple as that. You've tried to have us killed in the past, you have. I'm not going anywhere with you.'

Mrs Claus trilled a light, silly laugh. 'Have you killed? Don't be ridiculous!'

'Then what do you call it when—'

Mrs Claus leaned forward, hissing quietly: 'Occasionally I've had to have you and Brenda detained or constrained. Whenever you were getting in too deep. When you were being foolhardy and in danger of getting yourself hurt.'

Effie laughed out loud. She raised her voice as much as Mrs Claus had lowered her own. She wanted the passing guests to hear every word of this exchange. 'Oh, really? And why's that, then? Because you *care* so much about us, I suppose?'

Mrs Claus's reaction surprised Effie. She even looked a little hurt. She said, almost dolefully: 'Please, Effie. Come with me. We have to talk.'

Effie gave a bitter guffaw. 'Talk, she says! What about? What do we have to talk about?'

'Please, indulge me.'

Effie had a good heart really. She could hear the genuine pleading in Mrs Claus's voice. There was no deception there, surely? No hidden plan or agenda? 'Oh, all right,' she said.

You're too soft, Effie my girl, she told herself as she marched stiffly after the tinsel-trimmed scooter. You'll wind up in trouble. Well, never mind. At least if things turned nasty, she was reasonably confident of her skills in hand-to-hand combat these days.

Spare Parts

Up in the gilded suite, Brenda had started to quiz her father. 'Are you sure you really want to marry her?'

He wasn't his polite, debonair self today, she had found. He was cross and headachey. He flashed his silver eyes at Lisa Turmoil, 'Will you be long putting your . . . tools away, girl?'

Lisa pulled a face. 'Err, no.'

'Don't snap at Lisa!' Brenda said.

Victor took a deep breath and smiled uncertainly. 'My nerves are frazzled. It's all been a bit much. I've been resurrected, I've fallen in love, I've been reunited with my long-lost children . . .'

Brenda frowned darkly. '*Children?*'

'Daughter,' he quickly amended himself. 'I meant daughter.'

Brenda knew what she had heard him say. She stepped forward urgently. 'Have you seen Frank?'

'No.'

Brenda considered him. Suddenly he looked shaky and very old. What secrets was he holding in that egg-like skull of his? Could she really believe anything he ever said to her?

She said, 'Karla is well known for putting men under her spell. Getting them to do just what she wants. When I first met her, forty years ago, she had put the collywobbles on old Fox Soames, the writer of *Get Thee Inside Me, Satan*. She made him forget who his enemies were. She hasn't done the same thing to you, has she, Father?'

Victor ignored much of what she had said. He fixed only on her final word. 'You called me Father.'

Brenda shrugged. Well. What if she had? she thought.

Victor mused on the rest of what his daughter had said. 'No, Karla hasn't entranced me in any kind of sorceress's fashion.'

'Well, I suppose that's good.'

'It *is* good.' He smiled. 'This is love, not enchantment, Brenda. I haven't felt alive like this . . . well, even when I was alive. And Karla is going to be your stepmother, whether you like it or not.'

Brenda shivered. 'I'll deal with that when I have to,' she said, and realised that she was shivering with the freezing cold as much as she was with foreboding. Victor hadn't even noticed the slicing breeze that came through the luxury suite. Were the French windows standing open? Where was that chill coming from? 'That draught is terrible!' she gasped, hugging herself. 'The wind is moaning like . . .'

She listened. That moaning suddenly didn't sound at all like the wind. It was up in the rafters. At the very top of the turret. It was a whining and gnashing of teeth.

Lisa – who still hadn't left, much to Victor's chagrin – suddenly found the courage to tell Brenda: 'That's not the wind. That's their prisoners.'

Brenda blinked. 'What? Their what . . . ?'

She moved towards the source of the noise like she was wading through marmalade in a dream. 'It's coming from the attic . . .'

'Don't!' Victor called out. 'Brenda! Don't touch that—'

'Stand back, Father. Please. I'm bigger than you, and stronger. What prisoners, Lisa?'

Lisa was shamefaced and mumbling as she shouldered her professional stylist's bag of tricks. 'They've been keeping fellas in the attic.'

Brenda turned on her father with a thunderous expression and both fists clenched hard. 'This is where you had Robert?'

Lisa answered for him – and went further. 'And Frank.'

Brenda's jaw fell open. 'You *knew*, Lisa? You knew *all along* what they were doing here?'

'I . . . I wasn't sure. I thought—'

Brenda wasted no more time. She turned to the hard wooden door, around which the freezing blast of the wind was blowing. She raised both fists and pummelled it and pounded it and smashed it into firewood. The work of a minute or two.

Victor was staggered by her strength. Also by her determination and fury. He took several cautious steps backwards as he beseeched her, 'Brenda! Don't go up there!'

'Keep out of my way,' she snarled.

Through the dark doorway the wind came hurling. It brought with it something horrible: the smell of old blood. Dead blood. Dripped and dried blood. Blood that no one had bothered cleaning up. Brenda gagged.

'What is that? What have you been doing?'

Victor wailed in his own defence: 'It was all for you, Brenda. It's all for you.'

Without another word she went up into the attic. She ducked through the dark doorway and clambered awkwardly up the narrow steps. Then she was dazzled in the airy, frosty brilliance of the garret above. There, layered in crisp frozen dew, she found the postman and the elf. They were lying in hard black pools of coagulated blood.

'Who are they?' Brenda hissed, staring at the bodies.

Victor was suddenly at her elbow. When he spoke in that silvery, cultured voice, she jumped. 'They are nothing. Not people. They are spare parts. New parts for *you*, my daughter.'

In Her Sanctum

Effie settled uncomfortably in the chintzy parlour of Mrs Claus. She glared about in disapproval. It was a horrid, tacky place. Festooned and trimmed way beyond the bounds of good sense. This was the parlour of a woman who was – Effie believed – quite insane. You could barely see where you were meant to be sitting.

'What's this all about? I'm in a hurry, you know. Brenda—'

Mrs Claus guided her chair into her usual place beside the vast hearth. 'Oh, Brenda's all right. She's old enough and ugly enough to look after herself.'

Effie's mouth twitched dangerously. 'Don't you go criticising her.'

'Ssssh. Now let's not talk about her. I want to concentrate for a moment on you.' Mrs Claus was fiddling nervously with the drinks trolley.

'Me?' Effie went instantly on the alert. 'What about me?'

'We don't get on, do we?'

'What?' Effie couldn't see the relevance of anything the old witch was saying.

'We've never got on, have we, Effryggia?'

Effie burst out, 'Of course we haven't. I can't abide you and I hope the feeling is mutual. Look at the way you've treated us in recent years. The terrible scrapes you've had us embroiled in.'

Mrs Claus wafted a painted claw dismissively. 'Oh, surely not.'

'You've almost had us killed! You've kidnapped us! You brought Brenda's ex-fiancé here to mess with her mind and ruin her life . . .' Effie was in her stride now. The list came out like a torrent of grudge.

'Ah, but I was right to, wasn't I? That all worked out in the end, didn't it?'

'Murder! Cannibalism! Gangsterism! You've done it all!'

Mrs Claus was starting to look like her feelings were hurt. 'But I've never hated you, Effie. I've always been rather fond of you, as it happens.'

Effie laughed in her face. 'Codswallop.'

Mrs Claus's mighty dewlaps quivered with dismay. 'It's true. How old would you say I am, Effie?'

'I don't know. About a hundred and ten?'

'Don't be unkind, my dear. Here, what about some mint tea and Turkish delight?'

Effie didn't like any of this at all. She felt like Mrs Claus was trying to get round her somehow. She knew when she was being buttered up. There was something else going on here. Some wicked subtext. 'Look, what's all this about?'

Mrs Claus fixed her with a very serious look. 'Family. That's what it's about. Can't you feel them?'

'Can't I feel what?'

'The ties that bind. The tug of blood relations.'

Effie's face crumpled fiercely. 'What?'

'Oh, my dear. You think you're alone on this earth, don't you? All your aunties dead. No one left for you. You're so lonely. It's why you're so touchy. So defensive.'

'I don't know what you're talking about,' Effie snapped, standing up abruptly and holding her handbag in front of her like it was a protective charm.

Mrs Claus smiled at her.

She's smiling at me! thought Effie crazily. And somehow that gentle, compassionate, bizarre expression was the most terrifying thing of all.

Mrs Claus said: 'I think I had better explain myself to you. And tell you – at last – who I truly am . . .'

Taunted

It was a few moments before Victor realised that something very significant – apart from a portion of the wall – was missing from the attic.

'Oh no,' he moaned.

'What is it?' said Brenda. 'What's happened here?'

'This is why it was so chilly!' Lisa Turmoil said, following them up the attic stairs. 'Someone's blown a bloody big hole in the wall. Someone or something . . . has escaped.'

Victor looked paler than ever. 'Oh no. I have to . . . I have to find out . . .'

He turned and dashed out, pushing past Lisa rather roughly as he went.

'Father? Victor? What's wrong with him?'

Lisa shrugged. Then she nudged Brenda.

The two men on the floor had woken. Their eyes were like little pinpricks and they were coated and slathered with blood. The elf and the postman were giggling at the new arrivals.

'Who – the – hell – are – they?' cried Lisa, backing off. She fumbled in her knapsack for some suitable weapon. Hot tongs.

One of the men – the postman – was saying: 'It's Brenda . . . it's his missus . . . oh dear, too late, oh dear!'

'Get away from us,' Brenda warned. She really didn't fancy a scrap with these queer-looking specimens. Whose blood was it they were basted in? Each other's? It didn't bear thinking about. 'Where is Frank?' she yelled at them, enunciating each word carefully. The two looked like zombies to her, and in her experience, zombies could be a bit thick.

The elf boy told her, 'Frank has been taken away. There are still some bits here, if you look carefully. A scrap of his hair, a bit of his blood . . . we pulled him apart, you know. Hahaha haha!'

'Noooo.' Brenda froze to the spot. 'No, you didn't . . .'

'What are you doing hanging around with Victor, Brenda?' the postman sneered.

'He's her father,' snarled the feral elf. 'She thinks he's bothered about her. After all these years. But he's not! We've heard them talking, haven't we? We could hear it all from up here in our cosy nest. And he doesn't care about you, Brenda.'

'Yes he does,' Brenda snapped.

The postman continued: 'He's Brethren, Brenda. All he cares about is serving them. All he wants to do is return to his work for them. His experimental work. He wants your heart and lungs and liver and all your bits for scrap. The Brethren, you see, want you and Frank out of the way. You're standing in the way of the Bitch's Maw, you are.'

Lisa clutched Brenda's arms, which had gone slack, hanging by her sides. 'Come out of here, Brenda. We don't need to listen to this.'

'It's not true. My father . . .' whispered Brenda, with feeble resistance.

Lisa tugged at her and drew her away from the terrible attic, and back down the stairs.

Karla's servants giggled and chortled in Brenda's wake.

Dante's Bloody Disco Inferno

Effie wasn't prepared to listen to any more of this nonsense. Mrs Claus was acting very oddly indeed, and Effie didn't see why she should have to put up with any more of it. 'I don't care who you are. And I don't want your tea and sweets, thank you. You've probably poisoned them.'

'Oh, Effie. It hurts me that you're so suspicious of me.'

Effie was up on her feet, striding about the grotto-like parlour. 'Of course I'm suspicious of you. You and this place. It's like Dante's Bloody Disco Inferno in here!'

BANG BANG BANG.

Someone was at the sitting room door.

'Who the buggery is that?' cried Mrs Claus irritably. This was one scene she didn't want interrupting.

Victor erupted into her inner sanctum with his cravat flying loose and his hair flapping awry.

'Where is he?' he demanded, shaking a finger in Mrs Claus's face. 'Where's he gone?'

'You can't come barging in here!' Mrs Claus wailed, hoisting herself up impressively in her chair. 'I'm having a vitally important talk.'

Victor dismissed her concerns brusquely. 'You can't have failed to notice that someone has put a very large hole in the attic turret. Frank has escaped.'

Mrs Claus did a judicious double-take. 'Frank?'

Victor scoffed, 'Don't pretend you didn't know we had him.'

'I don't have to admit to anything.'

Victor reached forward to put his strong, sensitive hands round her throat. 'Where is he?'

She walloped him for coming too close. 'Clear off out of it. I don't even know where you came from, you nasty piece of work.'

Effie could stand this no longer. She broke in on their row: 'What's going on? Have you got Brenda up there?'

Victor gave her a nasty look. 'Oh, it's you. The witch. I've been hearing all about you. Yes, Brenda's told me all kinds of things about you.'

'Rubbish. She'd never discuss me behind my back.'

'You might be surprised.' Victor smirked.

'You don't care about her.' Just at that moment, Effie felt like walloping Frankenstein herself. She rounded on him dramatically. 'You've got her all gooey about Daddy coming back, but you don't care a fig for her at all.'

Mrs Claus counselled: 'Be careful, Effie. Don't get him riled. I don't trust him. We don't know how powerful he is.'

'Don't tell me what to do!' Effie shrieked at her.

Victor tossed his arrogant head. 'I'm pretty powerful. But so are you, aren't you, my dear?'

'As it happens, yes,' purred Angela Claus.

'Quite a magnificent specimen, all in all,' mused Victor. His fine nostrils flared. 'And I detect . . . some hint of faerie about you. Am I right?'

Effie said, 'Some hint of what?'

'Fey blood,' muttered Victor. 'She's been round the block. The eldritch block, that is. She's been to the wild woods and back, and under the hill. She's magical, didn't you know? A witch just like you.'

Effie licked her suddenly dry lips. She felt parched. 'So?'

'Keep away from me,' Mrs Claus warned Frankenstein.

He chuckled, patting one of her gleaming wheels. 'You can't run from me, can you, my dear?'

'I'll call in my elves. Effie . . . help me!'

Effie folded her arms. 'Why should I?'

This made Victor chortle. 'She doesn't care about you. You're at my mercy, Mrs C. And do you know what? I could cut you up, right here and now. Oh, I'll be needing all kinds of spare parts. Your heart and lights, I think. And your eyes. Maybe your whole head.'

'You ghoul,' whispered Mrs Claus. She had encountered a good deal of wickedness in her past. But there was something so calculating and calm about Victor. She felt his evil inside her like something cold ripping through her flesh. Sliding through tissues like they were silk; her seams dropping apart at his touch.

'That's right. A ghoul,' smiled Victor. 'That's precisely what I am.' He fished in his jacket pocket for what looked like a neat little spectacle case. But when he flipped it open, he produced a very fine and deadly-looking scalpel. 'Ah. Here we are,' he sang.

Mrs Claus could suddenly see the danger she was in. Yes, she was powerful. Yes, she had protection. But he was too close. He could be on her in an instant. 'Get back! Oh, help! Help!'

Effie watched him advance. She was torn. She gabbled: 'I knew you were wicked . . . I knew it . . . Brenda will hear about this.'

'Brenda won't,' sneered Victor. 'I'll be getting to Brenda sooner or later.'

Mrs Claus tried to reverse her chair. Its gears were jammed. The brake was on. The wheels were rucked on the deep pile of the shag. She was stuck. 'What are you going to do? Hack bits off me and stick them on to your precious daughter?'

'No,' he said. 'Although that is what she believes.'

Effie was gobsmacked to hear it. 'What?'

Victor said, 'Brenda thinks I am here to help her. To repair her. To resurrect her parts again and add some new ones and thus make her young once more.' He laughed at the very thought of it. 'But what scientist returns to fiddle about with some failed experiment, hm? What would be the point? However, I *am* going to start again. From scratch. Frank and Brenda were all right as far as they went. But they have outlived their usefulness. I am going to cannibalise them. And you as well, Mrs Claus.'

Mrs Claus – not given to panic in her everyday life – threw back her massive painted head and made a fairly good stab at it. 'Nooo! Effie, help me!'

Effie dithered. She hated herself for dithering in moments of crisis.

But dither she did.

'Get back, Effie,' growled Victor Frankenstein. 'What do you care about her? She's your enemy!'

'Effie, get help,' gasped Mrs Claus. 'Run away. Save yourself.'

Victor jeered at the Yuletide hag. 'And why do you care anything for her? She hates you! Do you hear me? She despises every stinking atom of you!'

Unbeknownst to the ranting Victor, Effie had stopped prevaricating. She hoisted up a very nice crystal port decanter.

She swung it around in a glittering arc, using all her strength and considerable skill.

And she brained Frankenstein right there where he stood.

He fell like a very slender, elegant silver birch. Smack dab on the shag pile. But his scalpel arm flashed out as he fell, as if by some weird surgeon's instinct. As he collapsed, he felt the satisfying thrill of connecting that blade with human skin one last time. Mrs Claus screamed as he flensed through the thick flesh of her upper arm.

'He stabbed me! He stabbed me, Effie!'

They both stood there gibbering with panic. Victor lay face down between them in the frosty glitter of smashed decanter and a monsoon of spraying blood.

White Lilies

Karla was waving at the Goths who had come to see the filming. Big ones, small ones, old and young. Every kind of Goth she could imagine, lined up in the long, waving grass at the edge of the abbey.

She had a few words with the crew. Jollied them along, though that wasn't how she felt at all. She posed for a few publicity shots against the large plastic sacrificial altar they had erected amongst the genuine gnarled stones of the abbey. She mugged and camped it up with some of the extras in their dark hooded robes. Holding up the ceremonial knives and messing about. Something about the sight of those implements, however, sent gooseflesh rippling all over her body.

They were lighting blazing torches. Putting on the arc lights. Was that dry ice? A little. But there was also real mist, curling in from the sea, as if on cue. Thick, turgid, salty mist, woolly as convent-school tights.

Seething with mixed feelings, Karla traipsed back to her trailer, to prepare herself mentally, and to warm herself through by the gas heater. She imagined crouching there, soaking in the heat, knowing she'd have to be out here soon, in the virtual nuddy. On this set she only had one trailer. No special meditation space for her these days. But never mind. This was enough. This tiny van at the top of the town. She threw open its door to the heavy, almost sickly scent of white lilies.

According to the tasteful card, they had been sent by her doting director, Alex. What disturbed her somewhat was that the card was inscribed in a tight, jagged gothic script.

Was he with the Brethren? Was he really? Was this his subtle, conniving way of letting her know? Hence his excitement. Hence his glee. Hence his delight in this whole tawdry enterprise. She remembered what he had told her, about watching a copy of the old movie. How it was brought to him especially by a man in a dark suit. At the time he'd told her this she had paused for thought.

Alex was a tool of the Brethren. They had got to him somehow. Perhaps manipulated his career. Getting him to this point, on this project, in this town, today. They had placed him here with consummate skill and irony. His old dad would be spinning in his grave, wouldn't he?

Karla found that she was a bit upset. I've never had any choice, all my life, have I? The Brethren had dogged her seven-inch heels wherever she had gone. There was never any chance of escape. There was never any choice. The Brethren were everywhere and she had to do as she was bid.

She crushed lily petals in her fists and sobbed. She was drenched in the funereal scent of the pollen.

Stomping

On the pavement outside the Christmas Hotel, with Lisa in tow, Brenda stomped straight into Robert and Penny.

'We've been chucked out!' Robert said.

Brenda cried out: 'Robert! You're alive! You're here! Where have you been, lad?'

They took a few minutes, hugging and gabbling away at each other about their respective adventures.

Penny broke into their reunion. 'And Effie's still in there. She went off with Mrs Claus.'

'What?' Brenda could hardly believe it. Effie despised the woman. What was she up to now?

'To be fair,' Robert put in, 'she was sort of dragged along by Mrs Claus. God knows what that old cow wants with her.'

'That's no good,' Brenda said. 'Time's getting on, look. I thought Effie wanted to be up at the abbey with us . . . in case . . . in case . . .'

Her words dwindled away.

Something very peculiar was happening.

Night was coming down even earlier than it should at the end of October on the north-east coast. There was a low mumble of thunder that seemed to come up from the ground and rattle the

406

teeth of all four of them standing there. The last remaining light had turned strangely flat, as in an eclipse.

'Look,' said Penny breathlessly. 'Look at the lights!'

Instinctively they all knew which way to look. Across the headland and the harbour. At the jagged ruins of the abbey.

Beneath the smouldering violet of the dark there was a dancing light. An eldritch light. Playful and rippling. It seethed and skittered all about the distant abbey stones.

Brenda said, in a very low voice, 'I don't think that's special effects.'

Robert looked grim. 'Are we going to stop them?' He gulped. The task seemed pretty major now. It was as if all the artificial lights in town were going out, draining away and turning dull, compared with the flickering halo on the far hill. 'That was always the plan, wasn't it?' he added, trying to sound braver than he was. 'We're going to, um, put a stop to them. Doing bad stuff.'

Penny squawked. 'We can't let them finish the movie. We can't let another film like that exist in the world.' She still had the DVD – which she'd picked up from Brenda's sheepskin rug – in her handbag. It was strange, but it made her bag seem heavier somehow. Almost as if it was slowing her down. It felt like Frodo's ring must have felt to that put-upon hobbit. It was weighing on her like an obligation.

Brenda was trying to think things out as they stomped away from the Christmas Hotel. She was saying, 'Effie was all for preventing the film being made, same as me. But then she seemed to change her mind . . . I think she thought we should let it happen after all. Because of something she saw when we were back in the past, behind the scenes of the original film. But I don't believe that. I think you're right, you kids. We have to get over there and put the kibosh on it.'

Robert was surveying the high horizon, which was looking rather more Sturm und Drang than it had mere seconds before. 'We might be too late. What does that look like to you?'

Brenda looked hard. To her, the swollen, heaving skies looked rather like the Bitch's Maw. The gateway into hell that she, along with Effie, was supposed to defend. It was a whispered-about thing. A secret thing. A thing of legend. But here it was. Opening up in the teatime skies above Whitby, for everyone to see.

They bustled through town. Down the West Cliff, past the tacky arcades and along the prom. Brenda could set quite a pace when she had a mind to. For the moment, she was glad of the extra reserves of energy she had managed to summon up. She even took a momentary pleasure in her renewed zest. The others were tugged along in her wake. Goths scattered as she barrelled along the harbour front, eyes gleaming.

There was a whisper of discord about the town. A shiver of apprehension. Dark was settling in like something palpable and wet, like ink streaming from the sodden skies. The heavy sea fog rolling in; curlicues and arabesques twirling round every corner and chimneypot. Clawing at ankles, nipping at throats. And really, could that be true? Was that really the baying of hounds somewhere at the edge of everyone's hearing? And the bonging of the old brass clock on the church at the top of the hill. Portents and gloom over Whitby, and the Goths were thrilled. There was a frisson of real terror in town tonight.

As they hithered and thithered through the milling crowds, waiting for the ship bridge to lower and let them across to the eastern side, Robert was biting his lip with consternation. Now that he was standing right by Brenda and breathing in her comforting scent of Parma violets, spicy tea and heavy-duty face cream, he was extremely conscious that he hadn't told her what he knew about the whereabouts of her missing hubby.

'Brenda, we have to talk about Frank. I was with him. They had us locked up together in an attic at the Christmas Hotel . . .'

'Not now, lovey.' She patted his hand and caught his eye. She smiled sadly. 'I went up to that attic. I saw that they had . . . hurt him.'

The tall ships had passed through the gloomy harbour, and now the bridge was lowering itself to the level again. The crowd massed, ready to surge.

'He's gone, Brenda.'

Brenda flinched. 'Dead?'

Robert shook his head. 'He's been taken somewhere . . . somewhere where they might be able to help him.'

Brenda grimaced and swallowed back her tears. They could really do with Frank's help right now. He was so good in a punch-up.

As the crowd started to move again, she resolved to get all the details out of Robert later, when this whole farrago was over. For now, there was work to do. She said, 'We'll just have to get on with this ourselves. That's all.'

And off they set – Brenda, Robert, Penny and Lisa – amongst the Goths, heading for the abbey.

Poked by the Companion Set

Effie was crouching awkwardly over the slumped Mrs Claus. The old woman wouldn't let her see where she was hurt.

'We should get you to hospital,' Effie said.

'Ah, I've been hurt worse than this before. It's a flesh wound.'

'Here, let me help you . . .'

Mrs Claus drew back. 'I can patch myself up. Our big problem is, what are we going to do with *him*?'

Victor was face-down on the shaggy rug. There was a spill of rather dark, thick-looking blood tufting up the wool.

Effie sighed very deeply. 'That bloody zombie. I just knew it.'

'Brenda's going to be so upset,' said Mrs Claus, unjamming the wheels of her chair.

'She was happy, you know,' Effie said. 'Deep down happy. Thinking her dad actually thought something of her.'

'And he just wanted her bits. And my bits. And the bits off the fellas in the attic. And probably even Karla's bits. He's just a nasty grave-robber.'

Effie picked up a Christmassy poker from the fire's companion set and gave him a shove. 'Where are we going to put him?' She knelt on the carpet, careful to avoid any splinters of crystal from the smashed decanter. There. His pulse was slow but persistent. 'He's alive-ish,' she said.

Mrs Claus thought for a moment. 'I think we should send him to the appropriate place.'

'Are you thinking what I'm thinking?' Effie gave a slow grin.

'It's the best place for him. Get him out of everyone's hair.'

'But how do we . . . ?'

Mrs Claus picked up a solid gold phone. Effie saw her wince with pain. She had unwittingly used the arm he'd stabbed. 'I'll get my car brought to the front,' she told Effie, and started issuing curt instructions to the elf at the other end of the line.

Effie watched her, thinking: this woman is my enemy. She has set out to foil and hinder Brenda and me in our investigations again and again in recent years. She has even threatened to have us knocked off.

But why has she got me wincing in sympathy at her injuries? Why are we working together? And what was she trying to tell me before, just before Victor Frankenstein came bounding into this room?

There was no time for speculation now.

'They're bringing my Cadillac to the front of the building,' Mrs Claus said. 'Let's go. Do you mind hefting me along, Effryggia?'

Effie grasped the handles of the wheelchair and braced herself for getting the old woman's substantial weight over the ruck in the thick carpet.

Out in the corridor, as they left the inner sanctum, they could see that it was turning dark outside. The long windows showed a fantastic view of the headland and the abbey and St Mary's church as dense purple cloud cover came rolling across. There was a band of sickly yellow sky being squashed violently under that mass of darkness. It was only mid afternoon.

Mrs Claus said, 'Something is starting . . .'

411

Karla Takes Direction

Karla was raging at Alex. 'Where is that girl? She was meant to follow me straight over here. I'm having to do my own make-up!' She turned to her director, and all at once she felt like sobbing. What was happening to her? This was the worst possible moment to break down. What was wrong with her? She flung down the false eyelash that had so far defied her. 'This is a disaster. I can't do it.'

Alex was bizarrely calm, if florid. 'You can and you will. And your hair hardly matters. Listen to the wind picking up out there. Your hairdo will be neither here nor there.' Now she knew where he got all his calm self-possession from. He was one of them, wasn't he? He was part of the fricking Brethren.

'And where's Victor?' Karla snapped, scattering the cards and trinkets on her tiny dressing table. 'He said he'd be here too.'

'Everything's fine, Karla. Everything's going to be just perfect.'

The trailer rocked then, buffeted by the wind. The lights dimmed spasmodically, as they had been doing for the past half-hour. 'Maybe the weather's too wild. It looks pretty dark out there. Maybe we should just delay . . .'

'No,' said Alex, fingering the remains of the lilies he had sent her. 'This is exactly how it should be.'

She sat back down. 'I don't want to do it.'

He came to lean over her. She could smell his clean, golden-blond hair. His expensive scent. She gasped as he took hold of her wrist. 'But you've got no choice, my darling. Just get out there. Get those shots done. You've got to do hardly anything. Just walk out there. Lie down. Scream a bit. It's me that has to concentrate. It's me that has to make it all come together.'

She looked at him. There was no reasoning with her director. Not in this mood. He was Brethren through and through.

At the back of her mind she had been thinking that if anything blew up this evening, during this shoot . . . if all hell broke loose again . . . at least she had her fella to protect her this time. At least she had Victor. But it looked like he had let her down. Just like all the others always had.

Maybe it would just be a normal shoot. This was all illusion, wasn't it? Just the magic of film?

But no.

Alex relented and drew back, allowing her to stand up and tend to her wardrobe. He stood there watching appreciatively as she donned her negligee and stared at herself in the cheval mirror. Karla could feel the tension crackling in the air, inside the trailer and out.

I look divine, she thought. Better than ever.

And I can feel real magic in the air. This is all for real. The film is reaching its climax. Just a little more to do.

But the film doesn't want to be made. She knew it. Just as it didn't forty years ago.

And yet the Brethren are determined that it will get made, this time. It will all come true, again.

'You are perfect,' Alex said, coming to stand behind her. She looked at his ice-blue eyes in the reflection. To her thinking, it was as if something had got into his heart, all those years ago in Wales, the night his mother died. Something wicked crawled into that child's soul. Even as Brenda rescued him and gunned the motor of her chip van. The devil had hidden himself away inside Alex and he was still there. Ready for this moment.

She let him kiss her a bit and she felt herself swaying and swooning under that influence. Just as she always did.

I'm bad through and through, Karla thought. I always let the bad men take me. Again and again I let them run away with me, don't I? I never ever learn.

Alex broke off from kissing her pulsing throat.

'Come. We have to see this through. Right now.'

He turned and flung open the door of her trailer.

She gasped at the livid violet sky and the wind that came in, whipping her black nightie about her and stealing her breath away.

Now there were even more Goths watching the proceedings. As she stepped through the lashing long grass and out of the shadows, on to the set, there was wild applause.

The weather was perfect. The darkness was delicious. Conditions were ideal.

I've no choice, Karla told herself. I don't even know what's going to happen to me. But I'm a pro. And I've been here before. I know all my lines. And all the moves.

It was all so familiar to her. Just the same as it had been – even better than it had been – back in her glory years of the sixties. The chanting, the extras, the sacrificial altar.

She was ready to be remade.

Penny in the Middle of it All

Penny decided that if this was what hell breaking loose looked like, well, at least it was quite pretty.

She stopped in her tracks at the top of the 199 steps.

How could Brenda go tearing past her like that? The woman was indefatigable.

The steps were busy, too, with revellers hurrying up to the top – mad keen to see what was going on. Others were actually fleeing the site. It was all too lurid, too noisy, too weird. Too real, for some of them. Word had gone round already. There was weird shit going down, up at the top of the hill. Penny caught whispers from the bodies dashing up and down the steps.

Now she could see much more clearly the green and yellow flaring lights; this nimbus of ethereal flame centred on the ancient ruins. It looked something like the Northern Lights, rippling across the jagged shell of the grand old abbey. Somewhere at the heart of it was bright light, electric light . . . casting fluttering shadows across the stone walls.

And the noise! It was as if there were hundreds, thousands of people up here. All of them chanting and moaning in terror and supplication.

Penny caught Robert's arm as he hurried past her. Her hands

slithered on the velvet of his jacket. 'It's all true,' she gasped. 'All of it's for real, isn't it?'

'What?' He laughed. There was an air of reckless excitement about him, and Penny saw at once: he *loved* all of this. He adored being in the thick of all this magic and mayhem. That must have been what had attracted Michael to him, of course. Robert's fearlessness, and his easy belief in the fantastic – they had snagged the attention of the supernatural being hiding beneath the skin of the Michael she had known.

And I didn't interest him at all, she thought. I failed to turn his gorgeous head. And it's all because . . . when it comes right down to it . . . I'm *scared*.

She was scared right now, hanging back as Brenda pushed her way through St Mary's churchyard, Lisa alongside her. They were threading their way through the wonky and weatherbeaten gravestones towards the abbey and the source of the commotion. And Penny was hanging back, clinging to Robert, holding him back with her.

He looked at her earnestly – that smile still playing about his face. But not mocking her.

'Of course it's real, Penny,' he said. 'This is what we do. All the time. These are the kinds of adventures we get ourselves into.'

She nodded. 'I'm a bit scared, actually, Robert. I always thought it was the kind of thing I would enjoy. I'm not so sure now.'

He sighed. He was keen to be off again, she could see. 'You can go back down the hill, you know. No one would think any worse of you if you just went back home right now. Back to the Miramar. I wouldn't mind. Brenda wouldn't mind.'

She looked into his face and she knew he meant it. But it wasn't true. They would mind, really. They would be disappointed in her.

'I've got to be brave,' she said.

A Nasty Fandango

'Those are screams . . . !' Lisa gasped.

'And chanting,' frowned Brenda. 'But maybe it's all part of the film?'

Lisa craned her neck, trying to see past the bodies and the crumbling walls. They still weren't close enough to know exactly what was going on. 'I've seen them rehearse this bit. I don't know. It sounds a bit extreme to me.'

'And added to that, people running away from the scene . . .'

'And the lights in the sky . . .'

Brenda looked grim. 'I think it's fair to say that things are getting out of hand up there.'

Lisa tugged at the sleeve of her good woollen coat. 'Come on! Run, Brenda!'

Brenda still lagged. 'Where are Robert and Penny?'

'They're coming – look! Behind us!'

As Brenda ran after Lisa, she was finding it harder to breathe. Her heart was playing merry hell in her echoing chest cavity. Her limbs were shaking with exhaustion and tension. That was her renewed zest gone, then.

She was suddenly vaguely glad that Effie wasn't here for this. It was all rather chaotic and messy.

Just then someone – a visiting Goth woman in heels – took a nasty tumble, right beside her. Brenda slowed to help, but Lisa urged her on. There wasn't time. There was more at stake than a stranger's twisted ankle. Brenda tried to shut out all of the noise and the horror. Why were the Goths screaming? And didn't it take quite a lot to whip them up into a frenzy? They had always struck her as rather laid-back, as a type. Were they screaming in terror, or pleasure? It was so very hard to tell. Ah – *that* was terror. Accompanying a savage crash of lightning and the awful noise of a fall of stones from the top of the abbey.

Lisa and Brenda paused at the perimeter of the ancient site. They tried to get their bearings, and a sense of what was happening on set. The lights were on. The cameras appeared to be rolling.

The extras were milling about and chanting like crazy.

There was young Alex, apparently exhorting them into fervour. His chosen method of obtaining the best from his cast and crew seemed to involve donning a horned goat's mask and his own voluminous sorcerer's cloak.

Karla was stretched out on the altar, writhing for all she was worth.

And the lights were coruscating about her. Just as Brenda had suspected, the very centre of the Bitch's Maw had opened up around her.

Brenda swore colourfully and explained to the dumbstruck hairstylist at her side, 'It's the gateway into hell.'

Lisa hissed, 'They've gone and done it then? For real?'

'Just as they did back then. Oh yes.'

Penny and Robert joined them then in the dark hollow in the ground. They were breathless and struggling to keep still. A stiff wind was pushing them all backwards. It was as if the wind was emanating from the gateway itself.

'You all right, Penny?' said Brenda.

Penny nodded queasily.

'What can we do?' Robert shouted above the din.

'It's too late,' Brenda told him.

'Was it all just a ploy then?' Robert shouted, trying to understand. 'The whole film thing . . . it was just their excuse to open up this hole into hell?'

Brenda was suddenly very upset. She was angry with herself primarily. 'This is my job. This is why I'm here. I've got to watch this thing. And make sure nothing gets out that shouldn't . . . And look at me! I'm sitting in a ditch as it all goes blummin' tits up!'

Robert had never heard Brenda swear before.

Lisa was focused on the busy starlet on the altar. She was bucking and tossing like a rodeo champion. 'What about Karla?'

Robert gasped. '*Her?* Stuff her! She can burn for all I care.'

'She's not so bad.' Lisa frowned.

Brenda looked at her thoughtfully. 'What are you saying?'

Lisa gripped her knapsack. 'We could save her.'

'WHAT?' Robert was shocked.

Lisa went on, 'Their attention is all on the gateway thing. We could nip in there . . .'

'Look, you do what you want,' Robert said. 'I reckon you're pretty fond of her. You do her hair and make-up and all that, don't you?'

Brenda thumped his arm. 'Robert! Don't be horrible! Karla's well nigh possessed! Everything she does has been controlled by those terrible men . . . the Brethren.'

'You're too forgiving, Brenda,' Robert shouted. He was out of order, he knew. 'If you only knew what they did to Frank . . .'

Brenda stared at him. He looked away, ashamed of himself.

Lisa took her chance to break away from them. With a cry of 'I'm going to save Karla!' she nipped out of their hollow in the long grass and dashed towards the satanic mêlée in the abbey grounds.

Brenda turned her attention back to the chaotic scene at hand. Her differences with Robert could be addressed at a later date. She refocused and frowned.

'What on earth is Alex doing dressed as the horned god and dancing around?'

'Alex?' Penny asked.

'The director,' Robert told her.

'Little Alex,' said Brenda mournfully, watching him caper obscenely around the supine Karla. 'Oh! So he was in on this nasty fandango the whole time! He must belong to the blummin' Brethren. Oh no. Whatever would his old dad have said about that?'

Robert urged Brenda to get out of their ditch. 'We must stop this. You have to get them to stop!'

Scissors Cut Stone

As ever, Karla was acting her socks off. Not that she was wearing any socks. Her negligee had gone west some time ago too. Now she was writhing like billy-o and overacting like she never had before.

Then, just as the pretty lights were making her feel a little bit out of control, she was aware that her hair and make-up stylist was peering over the edge of the sacrificial stone at her.

Lisa looked very worried indeed as she tried to avoid being seen by the horned Alex and his jiving lackeys.

'*What?*' shrieked Karla. 'What do you want? You weren't here before! I had to do my own make-up and styling! What the fricking hell are you doing here *now?*'

'Karla, it's me, Lisa Turmoil.'

'I can see that, you silly bint. What the frig do you think you're doing?'

Lisa was emptying out her bag of hairdressing equipment on to the Stone of Death. 'Let me help you, Karla. Look, I've got my sharpest scissors. I can set you free!'

Karla roared: 'You're ruining the scene!'

Lisa looked at her helplessly. 'It isn't a scene. It's all for real. Look at those lights. Look at that . . . maw thing.'

Karla sobbed with frustration and fear. 'I know . . . I know it's all real, but . . . it's too late for me, Lisa. It's very good of you. But this is how it's supposed to go. This is my destiny.'

But Lisa wasn't having any of that. She was sawing through the bonds that tethered Karla to her supposed destiny.

'Look! You're free! Come on, you silly mare!'

Karla had turned rigid on the slab. She lay in a very undignified position and her face had gone slack. Her voice came out in a dreadful monotone that made Lisa freeze where she stood.

'*HE* is coming!' said Karla.

Then the light from the Bitch's Maw did something very strange indeed.

Off Road

The pink Cadillac of Mrs Claus was approaching the abbey, across the flat, frozen marshland, at tremendous speed. It had taken a little while to loop around the town and to approach the hallowed site from the other direction, but it was the only way to come by four wheels.

When the abbey and all its outrageous, flaunting lights swung into view, the two women inside the car and the elf driving it could hardly believe what they were seeing.

'Faster!' urged Angela Claus as the Cadillac caromed down the rutted road.

'We're not going to make it,' said Effie from the back seat.

The elf was gripping on to the steering wheel for dear life. He told them, 'If we park at the church . . . how are you going to get across there to the abbey? You'll never get your motorised chair across the grassy tussocks and the graveyard . . .'

Mrs Claus had to agree. It was murder when she came up here for Jessie's premature funeral that time. It took ages, getting about.

Effie told the elf driver, 'You'll just have to go off-road, won't you?'

The elf baulked at this. 'What? But that's too dangerous!'

Mrs Claus was in dreadful pain. There was no time to be lost.

Every iota of her patience had fled. Through gritted teeth she told her driver: 'Danger! Ha! Come on! What do we care? We've only got a matter of seconds by the looks of that Bitch's Maw over there . . .'

The elf could see there was no arguing with her. The elves learned pretty sharpish at the Christmas Hotel that what madam wanted, madam got. He clenched his own teeth and yanked the steering wheel around.

The car lurched on to the frosty grass. It veered and wove through the swirling misty madness, sending panicking Goths streaming away, swerving to avoid gravestones. It made resolutely for the abbey up ahead and all the blinding arc lights.

'Oh no!' howled Effie.

'Effie!' screeched Mrs Claus. 'Hold my hand!'

'FUCK!!!' yelled the elf.

Apotheosis

'*He* is coming!' chanted Alex, the director. The eyes on his goat's mask flashed nastily.

Now they were all chanting the same thing: '*HE* is coming . . . !'

Brenda, Robert and Penny were shielding their eyes as hell's gate flared with even greater intensity. It was pulsating now to an unearthly rhythm. Brenda could only see black blobs where people should have been.

'What's that noise?' yelled Robert. 'It's like an engine . . .'

'Fire brigade?' asked Penny, a bit prosaically, she realised.

Robert was on his feet, squinting through the hellish radiance. 'It's a car! And it's making for the abbey, coming over the grass! It's a pink Cadillac! Brenda . . . what's a pink Cadillac doing up—'

Brenda was beside him, grabbing at him. 'Ssshh! Look ahead – at the circle!'

Alex and his demonic cronies were not to be deterred. '*He* is HERE! The Lord of the Earth!'

Some of the noise died down in an instant. The weird atmospherics calmed somewhat. Everyone stood with baited breath as they waited for what would happen next.

A dark silhouette was emerging from the Bitch's Maw.

It was a slim, dark figure in a somewhat tattered black cape. He stepped blinking into the circle of evil and smiled at them all. 'Good evening, everyone,' he said, a little uncertainly, as if he wasn't used to as much attention as this.

Brenda could have spat. 'Alucard!' she thundered.

Alex whipped off his goat's head and stared at the whey-faced figure before him. 'Master?'

Alucard ran a hand through his slick black hair. 'I'm afraid not, my son. Will I do?'

There was, however, *huge* applause from spectating Goths at this point. They at least were very impressed by this manifestation. It might not be the devil, but who cared? This was pretty good.

Lisa Turmoil turned to Karla, who was by now sitting up on her slab, rather perturbed at the lack of the actual sacrificial part of the proceedings. 'Who is it?' Lisa asked her.

'I don't know.' Karla scowled.

Lisa gasped: 'Is it the devil?'

Alucard shrugged. 'Ah, actually, no.'

Before he could explain further, there came an interruption in the form of Brenda, Robert and Penny hastening over to the centre of the circle of death.

'Brenda!' Alucard cried, seemingly delighted.

Brenda punched him in the mouth.

Robert was uncomfortably aware of the pink Cadillac, tearing madly over scrubby grass. Growling and groaning it came, louder and louder, sending the film crew and assorted Goths scattering, and then pulling up right beside the sacrificial stone and the heaving Bitch's Maw with a ghastly screech.

Brenda was oblivious to anything but the fact that no matter how often she smacked Alucard in the mouth, he wouldn't fall down. 'You! You idiot!' she sobbed. 'What are you doing here?

426

Do you realise what a fuss you've caused . . .'

Alucard merely laughed and stamped happily on the frozen ground. 'I'm out! I'm freeee! At last!'

Then the doors of the Cadillac flew open.

Mrs Claus shrilled, 'It's him!'

Effie whooped with joy and hurled herself out of the car. 'KRISTOFF!'

Alex was lost. '*Who?*'

'It's *me*!' screamed Effie as she ran towards them. Her thin body thumped into Alucard's and he smiled embarrassedly as he hugged her. She buried her sobbing face in her beloved's frilled shirt front.

Alex was studying the new arrival keenly with mounting dismay. 'Nooo! What have you done? Who is this? You aren't the master of the world!'

'Not yet,' grinned Alucard waggishly, trying to disentangle himself from Effie.

Mrs Claus was slumped painfully against the side of her beloved car. She was dripping with tinsel and her own spilled blood, but her attention was fixed on the eldritch light of the gateway before them all. 'That's the Bitch's Maw, isn't it? The doorway to hell?'

Alucard nodded at her, 'I should cocoa. Hello, Angela, dear.'

'Right! Effie!' Mrs Claus commanded. 'Elf boy, you too . . . bring him out!'

Effie reluctantly let go of her man and hurried back to the car. Mrs Claus obviously couldn't help them, so it was left to the elf and Effie to manhandle the shattered, unconscious form of Victor out of the Cadillac. He was paler than ever, coated in treacle-like blood and stuck with shards of crystal.

Karla was up on her feet. She boggled at the sight of her lover. 'No! What are you doing to him?'

Mrs Claus gazed up ironically at Karla in all her glory. 'Shoving the old sod back where he belongs! Have you got a problem with that, you mucky old tart?'

Karla tried awkwardly to get down off the slab. 'Yes! He's mine! What have you done to him?'

Mrs Claus shrugged. 'Effie brained him with a port wine decanter. She was magnificent!'

Just now Effie was puffing and panting as she struggled across the circle of death holding on to Victor's ankles. The elf was doing most of the work, looking anxiously backwards as they moved towards the scintillating gash in space.

Now it was Brenda's turn to stagger forth into the limelight. 'Noo! Father! Effie – what have you done?'

But Karla was there first, wrenching Victor out of the elf's grasp. The wretched old man slumped to the floor. The elf leapt backwards, overawed by Karla's Amazonian splendour. She gave him a nasty look and set about slapping her man friend awake. 'You've cut his fricking skull open! His beautiful skull!'

Brenda had hold of Effie, pulling her away from the old man. 'Effie, you've . . . you've . . .'

'You don't understand, Brenda,' Effie shouted at her friend. 'He was going to . . . *cannibalise* you!'

Alucard – morbid as ever – was peering over Effie's shoulder, having caught the whiff of blood. He frowned. 'He was supposed to get her and Frank out of the way. Are you saying he was going to *eat* her?'

'No,' said Effie. 'I mean, chop her up for spare parts. That was his plan. It's *always* his bally plan!'

Effie didn't notice Alucard's shifty expression. He had known full well what Frankenstein was about. Working through the Brethren, it

428

had been Alucard who had finagled Victor's return to life. But he wasn't about to go into that just now . . .

Karla was shaking her fiancé, and yelling furiously at the others, who were crowding her in. 'I don't believe you! He wouldn't have done any harm! He'd stopped with all that nonsense! Victor, Victor . . . wake up!'

Meanwhile, Robert and Penny were standing a little way back from the tight crush of yelling bodies. Penny was hypnotised by the swirling vortex in the dark air before them.

'Hell!' she gasped. 'There it is!'

Robert nodded grimly. 'I've, um, seen it before.' He didn't go into how he'd actually been down there and seen what it was like in the underworld. It turned out that hell was other people's ex-husbands. But this didn't seem like the moment to go into all the details.

Penny suddenly knew what she had to do. While all the oldies were arguing ferociously amongst themselves, she had a job to do. She had to act immediately. She gabbled, 'Robert – the film! Here, look – the DVD! Chuck it in.' She produced the gleaming disc from her handbag. 'We can be rid of it for ever!'

'Brilliant.' He grinned. 'That's a fantastic idea!'

She looked around. 'And the crew are fleeing . . . they've left all the equipment, the cameras, the shooting scripts . . . everything!'

'Are you thinking what I'm thinking?' Robert said.

Penny shouted, 'Let's chuck it all into the Bitch's Maw. The old film. And all the bits of the new one. Everything!'

They were doing just that when Alex noticed what they were about. They were carrying a relatively lightweight camera towards the gateway and were just popping it into the screaming nexus when he screeched at them: 'Stop! What are you trying to do?'

Robert faced up to him, bunching his fists. 'Putting an end to the curse of this ludicrous movie.'

Alex laughed like a mad thing. 'But we are in the movie! You can't destroy it! We're in the film for ever now!'

'Punch him, Robert!' shouted Penny.

'No,' said Robert, as Alex continued to dance and prance around the scene of destruction. 'His mind is gone. That's where devil worship and bad movies get you, Penny.'

'Shame,' she said. 'He was all-right-looking, really.'

All of this was on the periphery, however. Alex's dancing around in his sorcerer's cape went unnoticed by the others, who were gathered around Victor Frankenstein.

They all took a step back as the old man jerked into spasmodic life.

'I'M ALIVE!' he cried. Then he blinked up at the figures around him. His eyes widened at the strange light and the noise, and the fact that Karla was hovering over him in the nude. 'Karla . . . W-where are we? What are they doing to us . . . ?'

'My love!' Karla said, trying to get to him. But there was a kerfuffle, with everyone trying to grab everyone else.

Brenda heard Effie cry out, 'Don't you try to come the innocent, Frankenstein. Kristoff's here now. He'll sort you out.'

Victor flinched at the sight of the man standing by Effie. 'Alucard!' he cursed, his eyes lighting up savagely. He tried to lash out with both legs at the vampire. 'I've waited centuries to be revenged upon you!'

Some of the others backed off as they heard the sheer ferocity in the old man's voice. It was a legendary hatred, echoing through the centuries.

Effie saw her opportunity. 'Help me, Kristoff. Help me grab him, while he's still weak.'

Brenda was appalled. 'Effie, what are you doing?'

Effie wasn't about to have an argument with her best friend over this. 'I'm going to chuck him back to hell. Get out of my way, Brenda!'

Brenda screamed, grabbing hold of Effie's upper arms. 'NO! He's my father!' Effie's bones felt so brittle in her hands. She could snap them so easily. She could put an end to this right now, if she had to.

Effie leaned in as close as she could, seeing the craziness in Brenda's face. 'You don't understand, Brenda!'

'I don't understand? What?' Brenda tried to shake sense into her friend. 'What about you – allying yourself with Mrs Claus? And Alucard? I think it's you who's got it all wrong, Effie love!'

The two friends were at an impasse. 'Brenda, get out of my way!'

'No!'

Effie took a deep breath. 'All right, then . . .'

For the first time, she played dirty. For the first time, she did something to Brenda that she could hardly credit.

Effie knew far more magic than she pretended. A simple freezing spell did the trick. The work of an instant. A tiny, muttered invocation and Brenda froze solid. She'd stay that way for a whole minute – with that look of horrified dismay on her face – and that was long enough for Effie to do what she needed.

Effie pushed her backwards and Brenda toppled like a statue on to the hard-packed earth. Then she turned and placed her hands on old man Frankenstein.

'No!' he gibbered, terrified of the witch woman. 'Get off me!'

'Leave him be!' snarled Karla.

Before Karla could actually intervene, Robert was behind her, grasping her in an armlock. He looked rather awkward, seizing a naked woman old enough to be his grandmother, but he held on manfully. Lisa tried to stop him, but he wasn't listening. The hairdresser just didn't understand anything.

Alucard was beaming with joy, delighted by the proceedings. 'Oh, Effie. It's so good to see you again! I'd almost forgotten what fun we have together!'

'Shut up and help me, Kristoff,' she ground out between gritted teeth.

'If you're sure, my dear.' He frowned. 'Are you positive you want rid of old Victor?'

'Yes!' she yelled.

'Seems a shame,' he muttered. 'I had the Brethren go to such trouble to bring him back. But if it's what *you* want . . .'

Between them, Effie and Alucard scooped up the slight form of Victor Frankenstein and started to swing him back and forth to gain momentum. As the others backed away, the old zombie was shrieking the whole time. His cries cut out abruptly as his captors propelled him into the shining Bitch's Maw.

They cheered as the gap in relative space-time swallowed him up.

Karla screeched in protest, breaking free of Robert's gasp with a sudden burst of aggrieved strength.

She dashed over to Effie and stood there helplessly. All the violence drained out of her. She stared into hell and felt like she had lost everything. 'He made me happy! The only man who ever could . . .'

Effie was as sympathetic as she could be. 'He was only after your head, you daft mare! He was only after your various bits!'

Karla laughed bitterly. 'Aren't they all? But at least he cared. I'd have given them to him gladly. Whatever I had to give. What have I got now? Nothing. Nothing!'

Brenda had broken out of her freezing spell. She lumbered woozily to her feet. 'Oh, Effie. What have you done?'

As Effie slipped back to talk urgently with Brenda, Karla felt herself drifting inexorably closer to the gateway.

'That film was my last shot at stardom,' she said. Her words were like a voiceover in her mind. The chilling narration laid over the final reel of her movie. 'That man was my last shot at love . . .'

And before she even knew she had made the choice, away Karla went, into the gaping Bitch's Maw. Just as it was starting to close, she went quite calmly into hell.

Those who watched her from across the circle of death saw that she was dancing rather than shuffling off this mortal coil.

Alex came to his senses as the Maw started to fade away into the smudgy night. 'Did you get all that? Did we shoot it?' Already his brain was in overdrive, trying to make sense of it all; to make these fantastic events somehow fit the plot of his film.

One final remaining camera assistant laughed at him. 'Shoot it with what?' She nodded at Robert, Lisa and Penny. 'They ruined all the stuff.'

Robert thought that was harsh. The furious wind and panic had spoiled the filming and the equipment anyway. All he and the girls had done was tidy up a little.

Alex sank to his knees, hugging his goat mask. 'There is no film . . .' he sobbed. 'Oh, forgive me, my brothers . . .'

The weather was calming now. Everything was becoming much stiller. The abbey grounds were growing very quiet.

'Owww!' Mrs Claus broke out. 'My arm's hurting quite a bit now. I was stabbed, you know.'

Her elf came dazedly to his senses, and hastened to help his mistress back into the Cadillac.

Lisa rounded on them all, 'Why didn't anyone stop Karla? Why did we all let her go off dancing into hell?'

'I don't think we could have stopped her,' Penny said. 'Not after they'd chucked Victor in.'

'She got what she wanted,' Robert said.

Lisa Turmoil – stylist to the stars – looked at them all incredulously. 'How do you know that? How could you know she'd rather be in hell?'

There was no answer to that. Not tonight, at any rate.

Brenda was staring at Effie. 'I hope you know what you've done, lady.'

Epilogue

Before they all left the abbey grounds that evening, Effie stopped to beg a favour from the youngsters. 'Robert, Penny – PLEASE, don't let those Goths know he's here. They'll go crackers.'

Penny gave a puzzled smile. 'Who? Why will they go crackers?'

But Robert understood only too well. He gave Effie's man friend an ironic look up and down. Effie was right. The Goths would soil themselves if they knew who had appeared in their midst tonight. And who – it seemed – was here to stay. He nodded at Effie. 'Okay. Look, we're leading people back down the hill. The crew and all them lot. They're in shock. Most of them.'

Already there were ambulances and police cars arriving. They'd be taking statements, setting limbs, frowning at the damage to a world-renowned heritage spot. Robert didn't want to be anywhere nearby when they were asking their questions. Where to even start with the answers?

It was time to slink away home. And put an end to Goth night and Hallowe'en for another year.

'You can't stay here long,' he warned Effie. 'The police will be mopping people up.'

Effie nodded. 'We're just going to sit here for a bit. Look . . . look after Brenda, won't you? She's in no state . . .'

435

Robert nodded and bit his lip. He knew, deep in his heart, that Effie had done the right thing in getting rid of Brenda's dad. But he also knew that it would take a long time, and a lot of convincing, for Brenda to see it that way. He smiled sadly at Effie, ignored her creepy bloke and said, 'Come on, Penny. Let's grab Lisa. She's in a funny mood as well. We'll gather up Brenda. I can hear bacon sarnies calling . . .'

They headed across the abbey grounds, under the crazy shadows thrown by the film lights in disarray.

Effie and Alucard sat on a low wall together, somewhere close to where the Bitch's Maw had opened up. They watched the others drifting away.

Alucard turned to her with a smile. 'You *knew*, Effie. You knew that I was trying to get back to you. You had faith . . .'

She shrugged. She was spattered with blood and grimy with grave mould and grass stains, but she was vaguely happy nonetheless. 'I knew you'd come back to me. But what a long way round the houses, Kristoff. You probably caused more harm than good. Using that movie like you did. The famous curse. Setting up all of that . . . Even getting us travelling through time! And then acting through that weird cult, the Brethren. And was that really you behind Victor's resurrection? Just so you could fight him again? You've been manipulating all these people. Messing with everyone's destinies . . .'

He nodded. It was all quite true. And more! Effie didn't know the half of it really. He beamed at himself and his own success.

She was staring at him. 'It was all . . . just to get the gateway to open, wasn't it? That was the reason for everything. You put us all through this whole nightmare simply in order to bring yourself home again to me.'

Alucard winked at her, as if it was all worth it.

Effie frowned. 'People have lost a lot . . . Alex his career, look. Brenda's lost Frank. Karla has gone to hell. Brenda's lost her father once more.'

Alucard shrugged and put his cape around Effie's shoulders for warmth. 'No matter. So long as we are together again, Effie. What do the rest of them matter to us?'

Effie shook her head. 'No, Kristoff. I can't just go along with that. You mightn't care about other people, but I still do. And besides . . . since you've been away, I think my feelings may have changed. I don't know *how* I feel any more. All of this mayhem you've caused. All this upset . . .'

He was gobsmacked. 'What?'

'Things have happened. My head's all upside down. What have I done here tonight? Have I done wrong?' Her chin quivered.

'What?'

Effie pointed at a large, shambling figure across the other side of the abbey grounds. She was standing a little distance from the dazed Alex and the hairdresser Lisa. 'Look at Brenda. She's alone.'

'She doesn't look alone. She's got those young people.'

What Alucard said was right, Effie realised, as Robert and Penny came hurrying up, calling to Brenda to come away; to leave this place. To come with them, back into town.

Penny, Robert, Lisa, all clustering around Brenda. Triumphant, they were. And Effie believed they had a right to be. They had come to the end of another investigation. Everything was solved. Everything had come out right. And everybody was safe again.

But she could see, even at this distance, and in the misty gloaming of the abbey, that terrible sadness in Brenda.

She told Alucard, 'I shouldn't be sitting here. With you. I belong over there. With them.'

Alucard chuckled. A sound Effie found so very sexy. He whispered to her, 'Oh no, my dear. You are surely mine . . .'

And then he leaned in, to kiss her at last.

What a palaver.

It was all this aftermath stuff that was Brenda's least favourite part of any adventure. She felt rather distant from it all. Shock, she supposed.

She watched the police arriving. She watched the dumbstruck film crew slinking away. She watched the Goths looking startled as if they had witnessed a hellish form of firework display. Now almost everyone was streaming back down the hill. There was nothing more to see here.

She watched Mrs Claus being whisked away again in her pink Cadillac. Was she badly hurt? She had been bleeding copiously. But what did Brenda care for the old monster? Yet she found that she did. Weirdly. She wished her well, silently.

There was no sign of the gateway to hell. It was gone again. Until next time. We're not doing a very good job, Brenda mused, are we? Of keeping it a secret. Keeping its secrets safe from the world.

Robert said to her, 'What about going back to your attic, Brenda? Bacon sandwiches and spicy tea?'

Brenda smiled and nodded and let them urge her along.

Penny looked at her uneasily. 'I'm sorry, Brenda. I wasn't much use back there. I couldn't believe that it was all coming true! It was all real!'

Robert put his arm over her shoulders. 'But it was your idea to dump the film into hell, Penny! You were great!'

Penny looked abashed, but pleased.

Brenda took her hand. 'This was your first adventure, Penny.

You'll soon get used to the things we do here. You'll fit in nicely, I think. Just you wait and see.'

Then Brenda turned and took one last look at the now quiet scene of the evening's dramas.

She stood for a moment watching Effie and Alucard. They sat in their own bubble of privacy, perched on a rock under a wonky arc light.

Sadly Brenda watched them canoodling.

I'll leave them. Leave them in peace.

Effie had made her choices. Was it the end of their friendship? Brenda wondered.

She was just about to turn away, to follow the others back into the town down the 199 steps, when she saw Alucard and Effie starting to kiss in earnest. It really wasn't like Effie to make a public display. Something stayed Brenda. Some irksome, sinking, dreadful feeling. She blinked.

And she saw something awful.

Kristoff sinking his fangs into Effie's tender neck . . .